# She knew what he was thinking...

It shone in his eyes as if written there, and her heartbeat escalated. She was alone in the wilderness with Creed Bratton, alone and defenseless against her attraction to him. And he knew it...

Creed's hands found her small waist in a swift, graceful movement, and held her resisting body close.

"Let me go," she said against his chest. "I refuse to be mauled."

"Mauled? You call this mauling?" Creed's head lowered and his mouth found her half-parted lips, his tongue darting between the vulnerable velvet petals.

Hannah's thin skirts provided scant barrier for the heat of his hands. She gasped, and his tongue flicked against hers again, lightning-quick, hot and searing. Sensing response in her awkward movements, Creed murmured, "Don't look now, but you're kissing me."

Hannah gave a moan of desperation.

Hearing it, he smiled against her moist, parted lips and whispered, "Now *this* is mauling, Miss Hannah McGuire!"

Slowly, Creed brushed aside the thin fabric of her gown...

⁕⁕

W9-BFG-399

## Also by Virginia Brown

*Legacy of Shadows*
*Desert Dreams*

## Published by
## WARNER BOOKS

# Heaven Sent

## Virginia Brown

WARNER BOOKS

A Warner Communications Company

WARNER BOOKS EDITION

Cover illustration by Sharon Spiak

Warner Books, Inc.
666 Fifth Avenue
New York, N.Y. 10103

W A Warner Communications Company

Printed in the United States of America

First Printing: February, 1989

10 9 8 7 6 5 4 3 2 1

Dedicated to Chuck Bianchi, a mountain man, romantic hero, and my husband, who inspired this story and showed me the beautiful state of Idaho as it should be seen.

# PART I

*O death, where is thy sting?*
*O grave, where is thy victory?*
　　　　　　　*—I Corinthians, XV 54*

# Chapter One

Death, Hannah would later think, often came disguised as a friend. No one had dreamed that such a lovely spring day would end so disastrously.

Icy winter winds had blown up into Canada, leaving behind melting patches of snow and budding violets sprinkling the bright green grass. Only the mountain peaks wore white faces now, and the sun smiled gently down on the wind-chiseled stone crags and broad valley of Northern Idaho.

Log houses dotted the area close to the winding ribbon of the river that stretched from Canada into Idaho, then looped into Montana Territory and back up into Canada again. Gray spirals of smoke rose in lazy drifts from stone chimneys chinked with mud and straw. Men worked in the fields, chopping down trees to make room for the planting of crops, leaving only the largest stumps. It took a great deal of effort to pull the stumps, and some had been left, creating a hodgepodge effect among thick poles for beans and tender sprouts of corn.

Cattle grazed in a pasture that was partly a natural grass field, and partly laboriously cleared by hand and oxen power. Winter-thin ribs poked out their sides as the animals cropped the grass under the watchful eye of a small boy, who seemed more interested in whittling a fishing pole than watching cows.

It was a warm spring day, and Hannah Elizabeth McGuire paused in the task of carrying water in a rough wooden bucket to smile up at the sunlight slanting through the towering trees overhead. Erratic sunbeams pricked teasingly at the copper strands of hair curling around her face in tiny wisps, thrusting curious fingers through the thick lashes that fringed eyes the bright shade of bluebells. She was not deceived by the gentle spray of light that lay like a soft blanket upon her face, for she knew how quickly the brisk bite of a northern wind could sweep down through the valley and banish all warmth from the still-frozen ground. Though it was the month of May, only the topsoil had thawed; the earth beneath that delicate outer crust remained implacably hard to plow. She had heard several of the men discussing that fact regretfully the day before, as they had arrived home from the fields, muddy and tired.

"Hello, Miss Hannah!" a friendly voice called, and she turned, her generous mouth curving into a smile.

"Hello, Eric. How is your mother today?"

"Much better, thank you," the child replied, with such an impish grin that it was nearly impossible for Hannah to discipline the rising laughter that caught in her throat. The boy's mother had experienced a severe case of nerves the day before when her young son had filled the sugar bowl with a variety of ants. The memory of his patient explanation that he had only wanted to scare his sister, not his mother, still lingered in Hannah's mind.

Shifting the wooden bucket from one hand to the other, Hannah gave a stern glance to the long, slender pole the boy was carrying slung across one shoulder. "School begins in a half hour, Eric. Surely you haven't forgotten?"

"No, Miss Hannah. This is Fletcher's fishin' pole. I was just going to fix it for him. The cork needed a little weight on it, see?" He held up the cork in question, and Hannah— who had grown up on the banks of the Mississippi River— could see the lead weight now attached to the small piece of cork.

Cudgeling her mouth into a straight line, she said, "I think that seems to be an awfully *large* weight to attach to the cork, Eric. Are you certain it won't sink it?"

"Sink it like a slug!" Eric admitted cheerfully. "Won't it be a pip to see his face when it does?"

"Take it back, Eric. Without the weight," Hannah added when the boy's expression altered.

"Aw, Miss Hannah . . ."

"I'll see you in the classroom in a half hour, Eric. I hope to find that you have not been filling the inkpots with mud again."

Slanting his teacher a reproachful glance, the boy sighed and mumbled an indistinct reply as he walked away. Hannah gazed after him fondly. He was one of the reasons she found teaching geography, penmanship, and arithmetic such a nerve-frazzling task at times. But, as her father often said, patience was its own reward. That had been a hard lesson learned since arriving in northern Idaho.

Hannah shaded her eyes for a moment and took a deep breath. She had learned a great deal about this land in the three years she had lived here, but never enough. There were still so many things that she didn't know, so many mistakes that she made. But she was learning, as were her father and the others. They were all new to this land—new to the ways of survival in the high mountains and thick forests of the Northwest. It was a beautiful land, but harsh; it made few allowances for mistakes. Half their stock had been lost to deep snows the first winter, but almost all had made it through this last one.

Not far away, close to the sloping banks of the Kootenai River, a spotted pony with a fading winter coat nuzzled tender new shoots of grass at the base of a broad cedar. Hannah noted it as a tiny flicker of motion at the outer limits of her vision, and half-turned. Trickles of a breeze teased her hair into silky tangles as she stood there, listening to the familiar sounds of the tiny settlement.

An axe's solid thunk into a log reverberated through the air, joined by the metallic *cling* of a blacksmith's hammer against a horseshoe. The carefree laughter of playing children wove another happy thread through the fabric of the new day. Hannah could hear her father's baritone song of praise from the neat log church that served the sparse community, and she smiled. Life was not all hard work and no pleasure. There was often time to enjoy the simple things. Joshua McGuire loved to sing, to lift his voice in a harmony of praise for this beautiful land and the people around him.

Joshua McGuire had become both mother and father to Hannah, and always strove to impart a high degree of piety and modesty to his only child. It had been a task thrust upon him while Hannah was still an infant, and he took his duty as seriously as he took his avocation as missionary to the poor heathen savages in the Idaho Territory. Joshua was the only Protestant leader within miles.

Hannah paused to lean against a split-rail fence enclosing a neat garden plot. Vegetables had been planted a few weeks before, and soon there would be the blushing bulge of carrots and turnips, and delicate vines of beans with curling leaves and heavy pods. This was not just the idle garden plot of her childhood in St. Louis. This garden, though small, could mean survival for the family residing in the neat log house behind it. Hannah let her chin rest in the cradle of her palm as she regarded the tender green shoots thrusting up from the earth, still so tiny and fragile. The plants' existence in this territory was just as tenuous as theirs.

Even though he was full of lofty ideals and religious fervor, Joshua McGuire had not been immediately successful in carving a wilderness home and converting the various Indian tribes in the area. Nor had he been immediately successful with his only child, a rather willful girl who had been prone to escaping the white frame house where she lived with her widowed father and aunt. Time and understanding tempered both Hannah and the Indians, and Joshua now enjoyed great success. In his opinion, as Hannah had once heard him tell old Mrs. Crosswaithe, his daughter had become a modest, pious young lady—though prone to too much levity at times—and an excellent tutor in the fundamentals of education for the Indian and white children in the settlement he had named Jubile.

The tiny settlement of Jubile, nestled on the high banks overlooking the rushing Kootenai River, was slowly growing. Only the year before, another family had joined them, and Joshua envisioned a thriving town springing up from the roots he had so carefully planted and nourished with love and care. He had chosen the site himself, and in the three years they had been there, Jubile was finally beginning to resemble something more than just a cluster of rude log huts. Whitewash donated by a member of the community now cloaked the church that dominated the center of Jubile. There was a blacksmith's shop, a mill, and even a part-time schoolhouse. Hannah smiled. The school was really the main storage building for those crops which had been harvested the year before. Each family's surplus had been carefully stored in the log building, and it had been fully lined with bulging sacks of carrots, potatoes, dried berries, roots, fruit, corn, and flour. The stores were low now, and the children's desks—actually, benches and tables—squatted in more spacious comfort.

Curtains fluttered at the windows of neat log homes that had been built, and rag rugs dotted many of the hard-packed dirt floors. Yes, Jubile would be a town one day, Joshua had often declared.

He had chosen the name Jubile for his settlement because of its religious connotation. In Jewish history, every fiftieth year from the entrance of the Hebrews into Canaan was called Jubile, or Jubilee. At its recurrence, all Hebrew slaves were emancipated, and all alienated lands reverted to their former owners or their heirs. Jubile had come to mean the manifestation of exultation or delight, and he declared Idaho to be the perfect site for such a settlement.

Hannah privately thought Jubile a rather pretentious name for such an unambitious settlement, but she never mentioned that disloyal thought aloud. Joshua would be hurt if she were to tell him how she longed for St. Louis and her Aunt Ann at times; how she fretted over the unending monotony of the days. Would life always be so uneventful and boring? Then she would feel guilty for wishing for such trivial things, instead of praying for important things, like an end to the civil strife going on so many miles away. The great conflict raging between the Northern and Southern states had little effect on the mountains of northern Idaho. She heard about it, of course, from passing travelers and an occasional deserter from either side. It was said to be a terrible war, and she had written her aunt a lengthy letter praying for the state of the Union. Thus far, her prayers had gone unanswered. She must remember to pray doubly hard next Sunday.

The tiny log church in the center of Jubile boasted a full congregation every Sabbath, and Joshua could point with pride to the affability between the white settlers and the Kootenai Indians they had befriended. It was largely due to his own intervention, he felt, that no hostilities had formed between the settlers and local Indians.

Tall, blond, and quite handsome, Joshua was still a young man at thirty-nine years of age. The demanding life he had chosen had only honed him into a well-seasoned man in his prime. He had come to the wilderness with his Bible under one arm and a medical kit under the other. Having learned the rudiments of surgery and medicine, he had ranged forth to spread physical and spiritual healing among the natives. Three years had been well-spent in this wild, raw land where the trees grew so high they seemed to touch the sky, and mountain pools were crystal clear and icy year-round. Game was abundant, and sometimes when Joshua stood on a rocky peak gazing at a sun-checkered valley or the vast wilderness before him, he felt closer to God than he ever had in a man-made church, with its walls and ceiling that shut out the sky.

He stood in the doorway of the church now, a tall, golden man with a wide, easy smile, watching over his "flock," and Hannah's heart surged with sudden love for him. His joy with life was evident to all who knew him, and he was a favorite of the children, who all waved as they passed the church on their rambling way to the schoolhouse.

The early hours still retained that sharp, distinctive feel of a new day yet to be explored and enjoyed, and Hannah turned back to her task of carrying drinking water to the classroom. The wooden bucket was heavy, but she managed to carry it easily, without sloshing water over the sides and wetting her long skirts. Hannah's slender appearance was deceptive, for though she appeared to be little more than a fragile, pale doll—with delicate cheekbones high in a heart-shaped face, and thick-lashed eyes that changed from blue to green to gray, and even to a smoky black at times—she had a wiry strength that almost matched her strength of character. It had been acquired from years of lifting heavy buckets and helping plant and harvest crops, as well as guiding young minds in the scholarly pursuits of grammar and geography.

"Strength comes from within," Joshua was fond of saying, and Hannah agreed. Whenever she found herself floundering, she would only recall her father's strength, and it would help sustain her in any task, physical or spiritual.

Once more shifting the heavy bucket to her other hand, Hannah pushed impatiently at the dangling hair in her eyes. Upon arising that morning, before the sun had yet pinkened the mountain peaks that ringed their broad valley, Hannah had bound her heavy hair in a thick braid that now shone like burnished copper in the sun, but the hours had worked loose long strands that lay in silken skeins against the smooth skin on the back of her neck. Free of all vanity, Hannah never considered for a moment that the overall effect might be appealing, but only thought how she must stop and smooth back her hair from her eyes so she would appear more tidy.

For a brief moment, Hannah wondered what her father would say if she were to let her hair hang loose down her back like the Kootenai women who frequented their settlement. A slight smile pressed the corners of her mouth as she imagined his reaction should she even suggest such a thing, and Hannah pushed again at the loose tendrils curling into her eyes. Pausing, she set down her heavy bucket and tugged impatiently at the defiant strands of hair that had escaped her knot.

Dogs began to bark, baying in that way dogs have to announce strangers, and Hannah glanced up to see three horsemen riding into the settlement, rifles slung across their laps and hats pulled over their faces. They were riding their horses at a walk, almost warily, picking a careful path from the fringe of trees into the busy settlement. They paused in the center, but did not dismount. Instead, they leaned on their saddle horns and looked around them as if assessing the potential of all they surveyed.

Hannah stared at them, a frown puckering her brow, and she noticed that others did also. It began to grow quiet. The blacksmith stopped clanging his hammer against a horse-shoe to squint at them from beneath the rag he had wrapped around his forehead. Bulging muscles tensed on his thick arms as he gazed narrowly at the three men, then flicked his eyes from the weapons they carried to the tall, blond man in the center of the settlement.

Joshua McGuire emerged from the log church to stand in the doorway for a moment, then began to walk toward the men with long, confident strides.

"Good day and God bless you," he greeted the three horsemen. "How may we help you, brothers?"

A cruel grin slanted the mouth of the man in the center, and, pushing back his hat, he drawled, "You kin start by givin' us some feed for our horses, preacher-man. An' we're kinda hungry, too."

Joshua nodded. "Of course. All of God's sheep must be cared for, and though our stores are meager at this time of year, we have enough to share with those who are less fortunate than ourselves. Please," he added, indicating a log cabin at one side, "come to my home. You are welcome."

Exchanging amused glances, the strangers dismounted, but still carried their rifles in front of them. Hannah did not like the looks of them. She bit the inside of her cheek with a distracted sigh, wishing that her father would not be quite so trusting or ingenuous. She had already noted with a sense of dismay that the men wore heavy gunbelts at their sides. She could see the glint of gunmetal blue and leather holsters beneath the loose, knee-length coats they wore, and thought how the men wore the look of vipers upon their faces.

The tall leader had a sharp face, with hatchet features and close-set eyes, and his companions looked no better. One of the men had a vivid scar that ran from his right eyebrow to the lower left corner of his jaw. It puckered his lips and flattened his nose, giving him a fierce, cruel countenance. Hannah's gaze moved to the tallest of the three—a young man with lank, oily brown hair and an oddly smooth face. He was staring at her, licking his lips and smiling, and she shuddered. Compressing her mouth into a tight line, she scurried forward and took her father's arm.

"They look dangerous," she said in a low tone, but Joshua only gave her a comforting pat on the hand.

"They will not harm us," he said. "Will you please see to it that they are well fed, daughter, while I see to their horses? Oh, and ask for a small donation to our church," he added in a low tone.

Though she longed to refuse, Hannah knew from experience that it would do little good to press her argument. If her father had decided to be charitable to these men, then there was nothing she could do.

"Hey, wait a minute, preacher-man," the tall, lanky leader said before Joshua led the horses away. He grabbed his saddlebags, draped them over one shoulder, then pulled another rifle from the saddle scabbard.

Joshua regarded him with cool surprise. "You do not

need to bear arms in my settlement, sir. None here would harm you."

The man grinned. "I just like to play it safe, preacher-man, that's all. Cain't never tell what might happen."

"Trust in the Lord and you will always be safe," Joshua answered.

"Well, I trust in Nate Stillman, and I *know* I'll be safe," the man countered. He dug his thumb into his chest. "That's me—Nate Stillman. Ever heard of me?"

"No, Mr. Stillman, I have not. Have you ever become acquainted with our Lord and Savior?" Joshua asked.

Stillman snorted. "Oh, I used to talk to Him when I was just a wet-nosed little kid, but I don't figure on ever meetin' up with Him since I growed up and found out how life is. God's for kids and fools, preacher-man."

Joshua smiled. "I will belabor that point with you, Mr. Stillman, as soon as I have fed and watered your horses. Be so good as to follow my daughter, and I will join you shortly."

Hannah lifted her bucket, gripped it tightly, and, barely glancing at the men, motioned for them to follow. She walked stiffly, with her back straight and her head held high, once more wishing her father were not quite so trusting. These men were trouble; she could sense it. She hoped they would eat their meal and move on without hurting anyone. It was obvious that several other men in the settlement felt the same way, for they had ceased their work and were observing the interlopers closely. That made Hannah feel a little safer.

Pushing open the door to the cabin she shared with her father, Hannah motioned for them to be seated at the table. She could feel their eyes on her, boring into her, making her throat tighten with apprehension, but she kept her movements swift and efficient, and her tone cool and steady.

"All we have is cold venison, beans, cheese, and fresh bread," she told them without turning around from the wooden cupboard, "but it is filling."

"Sounds all right," one of the men drawled. "Got any whiskey to wash it down with, pretty lady?"

Hand-carved wooden plates clattered together as she pulled them from the pine cupboard, and Hannah tensed. "No." Her answer was curt as she wielded a sharp knife across the round of cheese. "There is cold water and a dipper in that bucket I set beside the door." Hannah set the cheese on a wooden plate in which Joshua had carved tiny, delicate flowers, arranged a loaf of bread beside it, then stirred the beans simmering in a huge pot swung over the fire. That done, she picked up the carving knife and stepped to the back door for the venison.

A burly, sweaty figure with a young face and old eyes deliberately blocked her way. "Where ya' goin', pretty lady?" he asked. His gaze made Hannah's skin crawl.

"To fetch the venison," she answered coolly. She tilted back her head to look up at him, refusing to flinch from his hot, greedy eyes. "Please be good enough to move out of my way, sir."

Something in her steady gaze must have impressed him, for the young man nodded and stepped aside, to a howl of laughter from his companions.

Outside on the little porch where the venison hung in a small lean-to, Hannah could hear their conversation and see them through the open door. She waited, uncertain if she should flee or stay, gripping her sharp carving knife as she listened.

"She gotcha cowed, Truett?" a booming voice taunted. "I think she does. Roper, what d'ya think?"

Roper grinned, and the scar that ran across his sallow face puckered his upper lip. "Yeah, Stillman, I think Truett's

kinda taken with that little gal, don't you? Look how he
stares at her, lickin' his lips an' . . ."

Truett whirled, one hand poised above the gun strapped
over his long coat, a menacing glare on his face. "Shut up!"
he snarled. His broad face was flushed and angry. "She
. . . she's a lady, that's all."

"A lady?" Stillman echoed. "She's a *woman*, Truett, an'
that's all that matters, unless you're a fool!"

"You callin' me a fool?" Truett asked in a deceptively
calm voice, and Stillman gave him a long, considering look.

"No," he finally answered after he had assessed Truett's
expectant, angry stance, "I ain't callin' you a fool, Truett.
But *she's* still just a woman."

"Yeah," the man named Truett answered softly, "but
she's a woman who's a *lady*."

Stillman grunted derisively, a cynical expression on his
pale, thin face, and said, "Whatever you say, Truett; whatever you say."

Truett relaxed and sat down at the long table. After a
moment's indecision, Hannah brought in a large hunk of
venison. She worked swiftly, filling three plates with meat,
beans, cheese, and bread, hoping the men would eat quickly
and leave. Where was her father? She would feel much safer
if he was there. Joshua always seemed to know what to say
and do in a volatile situation. His tactful intervention had
avoided many a violent confrontation between angry men
during their time in the settlement. Where was he? she
wondered with a sense of frustration, and could not help
glancing toward the open front door.

The three men—whom Hannah had decided must be
outlaws, or worse—were wolfing down their food with
noisy slurps and gulps. She stood with both arms folded
across her chest, her back to the wooden cupboard and the
carving knife within easy reach.

Hannah experienced a small twinge of guilt that she could not be as trusting as her father, and said a quick, silent prayer asking for more faith. Perhaps, as Joshua had once pointed out, she did not have enough faith in God, or she would have more in men. There were times, as now, that she felt she had failed her father, and that he must be disappointed in her. Why couldn't she be more like him? Joshua McGuire was the most admired man in the settlement— devout, strong, and brave, eager to spread joy and goodwill among all who came close. He could love men like these who sat at her clean, well-scrubbed table with muddy boots, their hats still on, eating with grubby hands that bore invisible bloodstains, while she could not.

Hannah lowered her gaze to the smooth, hard-dirt floor, knotting her fingers into the folds of her skirt. She concentrated upon the faint, sweeping tracks she had made with her straw broom early that morning, and noted that she would need to sweep the floor again after the intruders left. That was how she thought of these men who had ridden into Jubile—as intruders. Interlopers—trespassers into a serene community.

Any strangers who came to Jubile were always treated courteously—given food and shelter and companionship. Most had moved on after a day or two. Some had liked it well enough to linger, becoming productive members of the tiny settlement, but most had been Indians or fur trappers who only needed a good meal and a night's shelter. Hannah sensed that these men would not linger, and she wished them already gone.

"Hey," the man named Roper said. She lifted her head to gaze at him coolly. "My plate is empty, little filly."

A feeling of intense dislike washed through her, but Hannah moved silently to the pot hung over the fire and began to scoop out more beans for the empty wooden bowl.

"Ain't you got nothin' better than goddamn beans?" Roper asked disgustedly. "Hell, I've eaten enough beans in the last two weeks to bloat me like a two-day-dead mule!"

Hannah's fingers clenched around the handle of the wooden spoon, but she ignored him as she continued to ladle the beans into the bowl. Her back was to the table, and when she heard the scraping of chair legs against the floor, she straightened and whirled, still holding a spoonful of hot beans in one hand.

Roper was standing there and he reached for her. His fingers grazed the side of her cheek and his mouth twisted in a misshapen grin. "You, now," he said, "are soft and tender-like. Wonder how good you'd taste . . ."

Without stopping to think, Hannah hit him on the neck with the wooden spoon. Hot beans stuck to his skin. He leaped backward, howling with pain and fury.

"Don't touch me!" she snapped, brandishing the spoon at him. Her glance flicked to the knife still stuck in the round of cheese, and she inched closer as Roper began sputtering curses and clawing away the hot beans. Her heart was thudding against her rib cage with bruising force, and she wished desperately that Joshua would arrive.

Help came from an unexpected source. Truett's gun suddenly appeared in his hand, though she had not seen him draw it, and he demanded that Roper back away.

"I ain't lettin' you touch her," Truett said to his companion. "I told you—she's a lady."

There was a tense silence as Roper faced the gun and Truett, and his eyes blazed with impotent rage. Stillman watched the proceedings with mild interest, and never paused in forking food into his mouth. Finally, Roper capitulated and turned away, though he muttered that she shouldn't have burned him.

"You shouldn't have touched her," Truett countered. "An eye for an eye—that's what the Bible says. Right, miss?"

Hannah nodded silently, and felt a surge of relief when a still-cursing Roper stalked through the open door and across the porch into the yard. Her knees were the consistency of clotted cream. She looked at the boy who had come to her rescue and murmured, "Thank you, sir. I appreciate your assistance."

"Yes, ma'am. He shouldn'a tried to touch you. That was wrong, and I apologize for him, ma'am." He sounded almost shy as he holstered his gun and sat back down beside Stillman. Hannah clung to the side of the cupboard for support.

She wasn't exactly the courageous type of girl, though she liked to think she could deal with any sort of emergency, and these men were making her extremely nervous. Where was the courage of a lion her father often spoke about? The pluck and backbone that Emory Taylor had once said she had? Of course, everyone knew Emory Taylor was a bit addled, but Hannah had appreciated the old man's kind assessment of her character. Now, however, she was seriously thinking about fleeing like a hare out the open door of the cabin to safety. Hannah's fingers dug into the wooden sideboard with painful pressure.

To her immense relief, Joshua McGuire chose that moment to cross the planked porch and enter the cabin. His beatific gaze rested upon the two men at his table.

"I hope that you are enjoying your meal, my friends?" he inquired pleasantly. "My daughter is an excellent cook; she does much with the little we have."

"Yeah, it's great," Stillman mumbled around his fork.

Truett was more eloquent, saying that he had not eaten such wonderful food in a long time, and that it was even better coming from the hands of such a lovely woman.

Somewhat startled by this declaration, Joshua glanced at his daughter, noting her pallor and the strain in her eyes. He moved protectively closer, and Hannah welcomed his strength. Just being near her father gave her more confidence, and she no longer had to hold the cupboard for support.

"I am glad that you admire my daughter," Joshua said gently, and put a strong arm around her shoulders. "Hannah is more than lovely, my son. As the good book says, 'She looketh well to the ways of her household, and eateth not the bread of idleness. Favor is deceitful and beauty is vain, but a woman that feareth the Lord, she shall be praised.' I have a dutiful daughter, who follows my heart," he added. "My blessings are bountiful."

Stillman pushed back his chair and rose from the table, wiping his mouth on his sleeve and lifting the rifle he had propped against the table edge. Pursing his mouth, he leveled an amused gaze on Joshua.

"Well, preacher-man, we sure do appreciate your hospitality, but we need to be ridin' on. We got a long way to go afore we get to Fort Benton. Come on, Truett."

After hastily gulping the last bite, Truett rose and gave a last, regretful look at Hannah before following his leader from the cabin. Joshua accompanied them, leaving Hannah behind, and she peered anxiously out the open window. Her father's blond head gleamed in the bright sunlight as he stood talking to them, obviously trying to coax a charitable donation from them. This was met with expected resistance, and after a few minutes the men rode on. Hannah leaned against the wall with relief, and decided not to tell her father about the dangerous incident with Roper. It would do no good, and besides, the men were going away.

She closed her eyes and offered up a brief prayer of thanks, then opened them and began cleaning up the dirty dishes. The children would be waiting for her at the school, and she needed to hurry.

The three riders climbed the steep slope from the valley and paused for a moment to rest their winded horses. A thin trickle of smoke rose lazily in the air above the tops of the trees, and Roper's eyes narrowed on it.

"I still think you shoulda let me bring that fiery little bitch with us," he growled, gingerly touching his burned neck. "She scarred me, and I got a score to settle with her!"

"Hell, you was already scarred, Roper!" Stillman said with a careless laugh. "What difference would one more make? Anyway, we don't have time for that. Bratton is bound to be close on our tails, and we need to make time. We lost him back in the Bitterroot Mountains, but he's been close behind us since Alder Gulch. Hell, he's the only one left followin' us—you'd think this was *his* gold we stole!"

Still fingering his burned neck, Roper muttered, "Don't matter none. He's gonna collect a plenty big bounty if he catches us. Damn Plummer—I thought he was gonna fix it so Bratton couldn't follow."

Stillman slanted him an amused glance. "Creed Bratton is not an easy man to fix, Roper, even for Sheriff Plummer. I warned Henry, but he don't always listen. Gets too greedy, I guess. Hell, it's uncanny the way Bratton can follow a trail, just like a Injun, and he always seems ta know what'cher thinkin'. Mebbe that's 'cause he ain't always been so damned honest hisself."

"Yeah," Truett put in. "I heard that 'bout Bratton. He's just as likely to shoot us as he is to take us back to Alder Gulch. I don't like it," he added uneasily.

"You can count on the fact that Sheriff Plummer put that bounty on our heads *alive*, Truett," Stillman assured him.

"Henry don't wanna take no chances that he won't git part of this gold we're packin'! If Bratton does catch up to us, and the three of us can't kill him, then mebbe we don't deserve to spend all this money..."

"Shh!" Roper said suddenly, stiffening and sitting up straight in his saddle. "I smell Injun!"

The other two men immediately quieted. Lane Roper could always tell when an Indian was near. It was a sixth sense he'd acquired at the same time he'd gotten the ugly scar on his face, and he didn't question it. Nor did he take chances. Like now—he sat still and straight, staring intently down the steep, wooded slope.

"What is it, Lane?" Truett finally whispered, unable to stand the suspense a moment longer. "Injuns?"

"Quiet," Roper hissed, then pointed. Each man reached forward and pressed a hand over his horse's nostrils to keep the animals from alerting the long, thin line of Indians that moved through the trees like silent ghosts. They could see the faint glimmer of war paint on faces and copper bodies, and exchanged glances. Roper mouthed the world "Blackfoot," and Truett's head jerked in alarm.

He stared in horror as the Blackfoot rode toward the unsuspecting settlement below in the valley. Truett thought of the girl, Hannah. This was a raiding party, intent on gathering horses, plundering, and raping. Hall Truett shuddered. He'd seen what the Blackfoot could do to a victim, and his first inclination was to ride down and warn her.

Sensing Truett's reaction, Stillman put out a warning hand. "There's too many," he mouthed. "Forget it."

Truett gave an angry shake of his head and jerked at his reins, and Stillman pulled a knife with amazing speed. He held it close to Truett's throat, and his eyes said all that needed to be said.

Closing his eyes, Truett sat in numbed silence until the

Blackfoot had passed. His personal agony was etched in his formerly unlined countenance, and his eyes held the dumb suffering of a faithful dog that has been kicked when he finally looked back at Stillman.

"They'll kill her," he said quietly.

"Better her than you," was Stillman's callous reply, as he flipped his knife back into its sheath in a smooth, easy motion. "Now, come on. Let's put some distance between us and them, as well as Creed Bratton . . ."

# Chapter Two

Arriving at the open door to the log schoolhouse, Hannah set down her bucket and wiped her hands on her long cotton skirts. With the three men gone, she felt better. Perhaps they would never return, she reflected, turning to look back over the settlement. It was so peaceful here, she hated the thought of anything destroying it.

Sunlight danced over the rooftops in full force now, filtering through the trees and spattering the settlement with warmth and light. Hannah leaned against the rough-hewn doorjamb and let her gaze drift. She never tired of looking at the tall spires of the trees that crowded Jubile and even the sky, stretching up so high she had often thought if one climbed to the top of the tallest tree, it would be possible to touch Heaven.

A soft smile curved the lines of her mouth as Hannah watched a blue and yellow butterfly skim across the bare brown path in search of a blossom. Gossamer wings fluttered violently as it paused, then perched delicately upon the trembling lavender petal of a spring violet. Flowers dotted the thick grass bordering the path in erratic display, welcoming the sunshine and soft breeze with upturned faces, just like the children she taught eagerly soaked up the knowledge that she scattered upon them like sunbeams.

It was a good comparison, Hannah thought. The children did not get much opportunity for learning, as most of their time was spent helping their families with the day-to-day business of survival. When they did get the opportunity to learn, they did so joyfully. Hannah was thinking of the day's lesson—an exercise in grammar—as she finally reached for the wooden-handled school bell to summon the children to class.

The metal clapper knocked against the sides of the bell with clear, ringing tones, and the children answered the call with running feet and clamoring voices.

"Give it to me," a large, ruddy-faced boy was demanding of a smaller youngster, and gave him a rough push on the shoulder.

This action served to prompt the smaller boy to greater speed, and he arrived on the top step of the schoolhouse huddled over some object in his arms and looking to Hannah for help.

"Miss Hannah!" a pig-tailed girl was saying importantly, "Look what Eric found . . ."

"It's mine!" Eric Ransom insisted with such ferocity that it was obvious he had already been challenged several times for his prize. He gazed at Hannah with a faint trace of defiance, then opened his faded, patched jacket to show her the baby fox he cradled in his arms.

Smiling, Hannah knelt beside him and said, "You may keep the fox if you wish, Eric, but look—it's so tiny that it must be still a baby. You know, small animals often don't survive without their mothers. Think about that, and think how you'd feel if you were taken away from your mother too early.'' She stroked the quivering kit with one finger, and watched his face. "Eric—won't it miss its mother?''

Eric gazed doubtfully at the small, furry bundle squirming in his clenched fists, then gave a reluctant nod of his head. "Yeah, I guess so,'' he muttered. "Maybe I should take it back where I found it.''

"I think you should,'' Hannah agreed. Standing, she ushered the other children into the schoolhouse while Eric crossed the school yard with his prize. He disappeared into the thick fringe of trees that edged the clearing, and Hannah propped open the door for his return before she went into the schoolroom.

"Its mama won't have it back,'' Fletcher Harris muttered to no one in particular, and Hannah turned.

"Perhaps not, but it has a better chance of survival with its own kind. It wasn't nice of you to try and take it away from him, Fletcher.''

Grinning impudently, the boy nodded. "I know. But Eric can't take up for himself . . .''

"An even better reason to resist quarreling. Now go inside,'' she instructed, holding the door wider.

The children were already seated at their desks, their heads bowed and their hands clenched in attitudes of prayer as they waited for Joshua to arrive and begin their morning prayer service. It was a familiar ritual to them, and always preceded their school lessons, as he insisted that every school morning be started with prayer and verse.

"As the twig is bent, so grows the tree,'' Joshua was fond of saying.

Fresh-scrubbed faces shone when he entered the log schoolhouse and stood before them, a worn black Bible clutched in his big hands.

"Good morning, children of God," he greeted them, and they chorused a reply.

"Good morning, Brother Joshua!"

Joshua's gaze drifted over the assembled children, noting each and every face that he knew—Fletcher, Ivy, Little Bird, Sweyn, Frog, Rebecca, Jessica. "Where is Eric Ramsom?" he asked, seeing the empty desk.

Leaning forward, Hannah said quietly, "He is returning a lost fox to its mother," and Joshua grinned.

"Eric is a good shepherd!" he declared, then said to the listening children, "Who else was a good shepherd?"

Hands thrust into the air like spring cornstalks, waving wildly, each wanting to answer the question as Joshua pondered who to call upon. He hesitated, his suntanned face creased into a mask of teasing indecision, his pale blue eyes alight with mirth.

"Ah, Little Bird," he decided at last, pointing to the small girl sitting in the second row.

Standing and smoothing the fringe on her rumpled deerskin skirt with self-conscious pride, the ebony-haired child said proudly, "Jesus!" then thumped back into her seat with a flop of her long, deerskin-tied braids.

"That's right," Joshua approved. "While we are waiting on Eric to return so that we may have our morning prayer, I shall read to you from the Bible. Saint Matthew, chapter five, verses three through twelve." Joshua did not have to look at the tiny, printed pages as he lifted his Bible and quoted, "Blessed are the poor in spirit: for theirs is the kingdom of heaven. Blessed are they that mourn: they shall be comforted. Blessed are the meek . . ."

Hannah's head jerked up from her silent meditation as she heard the thump of footsteps on the wooden stairs leading to the schoolhouse, and she half-rose in alarm as young Eric Ransom burst breathlessly into the room. His eyes were wide and his cheeks so pale that his freckles stood out like inkblots on paper. The boy stood gasping for air and trying to speak.

"Eric!" Hannah said, going to him immediately. The child was quivering with fright, and his small hands grasped her by the arm with surprising strength.

"Indians!" he finally managed to blurt. "I . . . I . . . saw them when I was putting the fox back. They are *not* friendly! I saw . . ." He burst into tears. Hannah folded him into her arms and looked up at her father.

Indians. No warning had been given by the guards who usually patrolled the perimeters of Jubile. No alarm had been sounded or signal given. And from the expression on Eric's face, he had seen much more than just a few stray members of a hunting party.

"I will sound the warning," Joshua said calmly, so as not to terrify the children. "Get them to the cellar until I determine who our visitors are and the nature of their mission. *Stay* there until someone comes to get you."

His comforting smile gave Hannah the strength she needed to ignore her wildly pounding heart, and she began to herd the children into a line.

"Single file, as you have been taught," she instructed in a cool, steady voice. "We are going to stay in the root cellar for a while. There will be *no* talking. You must remain very quiet until I tell you differently. Do you understand?"

"Yes, Miss Hannah," the children replied obediently. Childish eyes were round with fear as they crossed the floor and waited until Hannah had pulled open the trapdoor behind her desk that led to the root cellar.

The cellar had been carved from the earth and covered with a wooden door. It was not a large room, but long and narrow. It was dark there, and smelled musty and stale. Hannah clawed gauzy drifts of cobwebs away from the children's faces as she helped them down the few steps and between the wooden bins that lined the dirt walls, then directed them to huddle on the floor with a partner.

"You are each responsible for the other," she said to them in a hurried whisper. "Remember—we must remain quiet and still until any danger is past. Say your prayers silently. God will hear you."

As the children paired off and huddled on the dirt floor against the walls, Hannah struggled to close the trapdoor. She skinned her fingers on the rough edges of the planks and got a splinter in one palm, but finally got the door closed, plunging the cellar into complete darkness. Hannah crouched on the top step, breathing heavily. Behind her, swallowed in the shadows, she could hear the muffled sobs and ragged breaths of the children. As her eyes slowly began to adjust to the inky blackness, Hannah could see splinters of light overhead in the cracks of the trapdoor. This served as a small reassurance until she heard the heavy pealing of the huge iron bell that stood in the settlement. It had never been used, as it was intended only for emergencies or as a warning. Hannah shuddered as she realized that an Indian attack was imminent, and she wondered what tribe had finally decided to raid Jubile.

Tamping down her own fears, she tried to make her voice calm, and whispered to the children to silently recall the Twenty-third Psalm. "It will comfort you," she added, then jerked her head around at the sound of a rifle shot.

It was immediately followed by an entire volley of shots, punctuated by wild screams and the thundering sound of hoofbeats. There were shouts and screams and the frightened neighing of horses. Dogs barked and babies cried. Hannah buried her face in her hands, and prayed that Joshua McGuire was not in mortal danger.

Hannah's knees trembled, her mouth was dry, and her

hands shook so badly she clenched them tightly together in the folds of her skirt. The screams and shouts outside seemed to go on forever, and she prayed that God's will would deliver them all to safety.

Cringing as the shouts and rifle fire seemed to grow nearer, Hannah dug her hands deeper into her skirts and waited, praying to hear her father's voice at the trapdoor. Surely he would come soon! Surely the attacking Indians would be pushed back, defeated, sent away! Her throat ached with pent-up tears, but she did not dare succumb to them. She had to be brave for the children—had to set a good example, so they would not descend into despair—but oh, God, she prayed for swift deliverance.

Hot, salty tears pricked her eyelids, but she held them back, thinking of her father, wondering if he was still alive, or perhaps wounded and needing help. She thought of their neat little cabin, with the bright, cheerful chintz curtains at the windows, the braided rugs on the wooden floor, and the sturdy pine furniture Joshua had built with his own hands. Treasured books lined the oak shelves he'd built—books Hannah had pored over on lazy summer afternoons, losing herself in tales of adventure and romance as well as the more familiar Bible stories. Now, with death and danger roaming the well-trodden paths of Jubile, Hannah wondered if she would ever see her cabin or possessions again. Slumping, she bent and put her hot, flushed cheeks against her drawn-up knees.

Then, gasping, her head jerked up and she half-rose from her crouch as she heard footsteps above her head. Papa? she thought eagerly, aching to hear the familiar sound of his voice. Tense, she waited, craning her neck to listen closely to the footsteps. The dirt floor of the storage room muffled the sound, but she could hear the children's desks overturn and harsh, guttural shouts in an unknown tongue. Indians!

Now her heart pounded so loudly she could barely hear anything else. There were marauding Indians in the schoolroom!

Hannah was positive it would not be any of the friendly Kootenai tribe, for some of their own children were here in the cellar with her. She taught them, lived with them here in the settlement, and laughed with them. But who else? The Coeur d'Alenes or Nez Percé perhaps? No, neither tribe had ever indicated any hostility toward them; they had merely ignored the presence of the settlers. Then who? she puzzled. Blackfoot? Sioux? Both tribes would have wandered from their own territory, which was not unheard of, but they never had come here before. None of that really mattered now—what mattered was the fact that her friends and loved ones were in danger, and now the Indians were directly over her head, endangering her and the eight young lives in the cellar.

Shuddering again, Hannah buried her face in her palms. The noise increased, and she recognized the sound of splintering wood. What if they found the trapdoor? She and the children would be killed—or worse!

Backing slowly down the shallow wooden steps, Hannah crawled to the terrified children and gathered them around her as if to protect them. She stroked sweat-dampened hair and clumsily patted quivering shoulders, praying all the time, hoping the children wouldn't give in to their fright and scream or sob aloud. They all waited, not knowing if each moment was to be their last, crouching like hunted animals in the darkness.

Sounds from above suddenly ceased, and the footsteps faded away. They hadn't been found! Perhaps her father and the men of the settlement had succeeded in fighting off the attack. They should be coming for the children any mo-

ment. What if they didn't? Should she leave the cellar? No,
Joshua had given orders not to until he came for them . . .

Hannah waited in an agony of indecision, chewing on her
fingernails, wondering what she should do. Time ticked past
as she intently watched the tiny slivers of light in the
wooden trapdoor. She could feel the children's stares in the
darkness and knew they were doing the same. There was no
sound now, just a heavy, ominous silence.

Was it her imagination, or did she hear drums? Hannah
wondered. Then she realized that it was the sound of her
own heart beating that she heard. She quickly covered her
mouth with her fingers to stifle the sudden, inexplicable
urge to laugh crazily. The tension was making her react
strangely, she thought. She tried to fill her mind with
Scriptures, recalling verses that should comfort her.

That helped, and Hannah began to feel a sense of peace.
She loosened her hold on the children slightly, closed her
eyes, and drew in a steadying breath. Her eyes snapped open
again immediately. She smelled smoke filtering through the
cracks of the trapdoor—they were burning down the storage
house! The implications of this act struck home, and Hannah
gave a soft cry of dismay.

One of the children finally began to sob aloud, galvaniz-
ing her into action. Leaping to her feet, Hannah hissed
softly, "There's no time for tears! Quickly now, dig up
handfuls of dirt," she ordered, and when no one moved, she
gave the nearest shoulder an impatient push. "Do it, quickly,
or we shall all perish!"

The puzzled children complied, while Hannah felt her
way along the wooden shelves lining the walls. They were
almost empty, but at last her search was rewarded with the
items she sought.

She could feel the bewildered gazes of the crouching
children when she returned and she commanded them to put

the dirt into the bowl she held. Clumsily, feeling their way
in the dark, the children slowly filled a bowl that had only a
few moments before held dried fruit. Then, Hannah emptied
the contents of a jug into the bowl, and the sweet, tangy
odor of apple cider filled the air.

"What are we makin'?" she heard little Ivy Ransom ask
curiously, but she was instantly hushed by the others.

"Mud," was Hannah's grim answer as she began to stir
the mixture with her bare hands. "We must stop the smoke
from getting in through the cracks in the wooden door. It is
smoke that kills first, and we must still be alive when they
are able to put out the fire," she told the children, privately
ignoring the fact that there might not be anyone left to
extinguish the blaze.

Hannah was hampered in her efforts at first because the
mixture was too thin, but after the addition of more dirt, she
was able to seal the cracks with the mud. It dripped on her
face and dress as she worked, but finally, there wasn't a
single crack of light left. She offered up a silent prayer that
the mud would keep out the smoke, and that the fire would
not burn through the wooden trapdoor, then prayed that the
others had somehow miraculously been able to escape.

Exhausted from her frenzy of effort, Hannah collapsed
onto the dirt floor beside the children, but could not offer
them a word of comfort. How could she give them hope
where there was none, she wondered bitterly. Shaking her
head at the thought, Hannah chastised herself for her lack of
faith, and offered up another prayer, asking God for more
strength.

Then, in the terrible silence, a thin, childish voice began
to quote, " 'The Lord is my shepherd. I shall not want . . . ' "
and the others chimed in, softly repeating the words. When
they reached the fourth verse, their young voices strengthened
as they recited, " 'Yea, though I walk through the valley of

the shadow of death I will fear no evil: for thou art with me; thy rod and thy staff they comfort me . . . ' "

Hannah's eyes filled with tears as the strong voices finished the verses on a note of triumph, and she was glad they could not see her. "That was beautiful," she said softly. "Thank you for giving me comfort. Shall we all pray now?"

Hannah tried to keep her mind on the words as she repeated prayers she'd heard her father use time and again. She was grateful for the dark, for the tears would not stay back as she reflected that she would never see him again. No one had to tell her what had happened outside, for if Joshua McGuire was alive, they would have been rescued by now. He would never allow his daughter to perish in a burning building.

Swallowing her tears, Hannah silently promised her father that she would do her best to carry on his work, that she would not let his memory die. She would strive to be like him—to love even the unlovable, and to be more trusting and devout, and . . .

Shuddering, she buried her face in her torn palms and bit her lips until she could taste blood. She was grateful for the enveloping blackness that hid her weakness from the children, and vowed to get them to safety. Perhaps she could get them to Camp Coeur d'Alene, which had grown to a few houses on the recently finished Mullan Road from Fort Walla Walla to Montana the year before. It wasn't too far away—a hundred miles, perhaps—and if they were careful . . . but how could she guide these children that distance? And what about the Kootenai Indian children with her? What would she do with them? They were probably orphans now, too, but would their tribe take them back? Could she find their tribe? Could she even find Camp Coeur d'Alene?

Hannah wiped her face on her skirt and sat up. She would find a way, just like her father would have done.

It gradually began to grow warmer in the tiny cellar as the flames soared overhead, and Hannah drew the children into a corner, as far from the trapdoor as possible. The dirt walls were cool, though damp. They sat in the shadow of death and waited.

# Chapter Three

Creed Bratton nudged his bay nearer to an outcropping of rock and studied the trail closely. Squinting slightly, he took careful note of the raw scrapes along the side of the rock, and how they had not yet weathered.

"They're only a day ahead of us, General," he said to his horse, and the bay tossed his head as if he understood what that meant. Creed patted the bay's thick neck with the palm of his hand, then readjusted one of the Henry rifles in the leather saddle scabbard and hooked one leg around his saddle horn to relax. It had been a long day—hell, a long *month*—and he'd be glad to catch up with Stillman and his gang and put an end to the chase. He'd almost gotten them a few days before—he'd sneaked up on them while they were asleep on a river bank and opened fire—but he'd been careless and they'd been lucky.

Pushing back his old, black, flat-crowned hat, Creed gazed up at the sky shining in patches through the thick tree branches overhead. He reached for the bag on his saddle and drew out a small leather pouch, took out the "makin's," and began to roll a cigarette. His dark eyes narrowed against the smoke when he lit it, cupping one hand against the breeze. He watched gray smoke curls flatten against his hat brim and drift lazily away, and it was then that he noticed the fat puffs of black smoke in the distance.

They billowed upward, over the tops of the trees, and hung against the sky like birds of prey, lingering in ominous warning. Creed remembered a tiny settlement in the broad valley ahead, and wondered if Stillman and his boys had left another one of their calling cards. It was either that or Indians, and either way, he intended to find out.

Shoving his foot back into the empty stirrup, he wheeled the bay around and headed down the rocky incline to the valley below. It was slow work winding through the trees and stretches of shale, but he finally reached level ground. The smell of smoke was sharp now, and acrid, burning his nostrils. He recognized the odor of burning pine, and the sickly sweet smell of burning flesh, and spurred General into a trot.

When Bratton reached the edge of the trees that fringed the smoky clearing he reined in the bay and proceeded more cautiously. Several yards from the outskirts of the smoking buildings he stumbled over the body of a man. He must have been a sentry, of sorts, or even a farmer coming in from the fields, perhaps. Whoever he was, he'd been scalped; his eyes stared sightlessly and his mouth was open and gaping. Dismounting, Creed closed the man's eyes and covered his face with a bloodied scarf.

Then he knelt on the path, studying the churned-up earth. The soft topsoil had been cut by many hooves, some of them shod. Obviously, this had been an Indian raid for livestock and whatever else could be taken. He pushed back his hat and gazed through the trees to the burning settlement. It had been razed and abandoned for several hours, he figured. His mouth tightened. Drawing his Colt from his holster, Creed stood and walked slowly into the ruined settlement, keeping the skittish bay between himself and the burning buildings.

The fire had almost burned out in places, but several of the log cabins were still blazing. A building in the center of the clearing collapsed in a shower of fiery sparks that flew heavenward, and blackened logs snapped in two with unearthly moans. As he paused to calm his horse, Creed's gaze drifted over the bodies of men, women, and small children, some only infants. It was obvious they had been surprised, and were ill-prepared for an attack. The sheer waste of human life angered him.

Bratton's fists clenched in impotent rage at the stupidity of people who would not recognize the dangers around them. There should have been a sturdy fence built around the settlement, and guards posted at intervals. It might not have saved them, he reflected, but it sure as hell would have given them a fighting chance. These poor people had had no chance at all.

His mouth was a harsh, straight line as he glanced down at his feet and saw a cornhusk doll with a broken clay head lying in the dust and ashes, and he suddenly remembered another massacre, another lost family . . .

Oppressed by the stifling odor of death, Creed jerked on General's reins, startling the horse and making him snort and back away. A flying ember hurtled through the air and landed between the bay's forelegs. The animal screamed in fright, half rearing and lunging violently away from the restricting reins.

"Quiet, boy," Creed soothed, putting his hand over the velvety muzzle. His fingers tightened briefly as he shortened the reins, and General stood with his head down and his legs trembling. The burnished brown hide quivered in tiny ripples as fine ash drifted down to cover the horse and the man.

Creed pulled the horse several steps away, searching the ground as he stepped around debris. It had been Blackfoot, he decided at last when he recognized the markings on a broken arrow lying atop a hump of dirt. He gave the arrow an idle kick, then wound his way through the obstacle-strewn clearing, searching for signs of life. Several times he bent to close staring, sightless eyes, or to arrange the skirts of a woman in a more decent covering. He still held his Colt .44 at ready, just in case, though it was obvious none of the settlers could do him any harm.

"An entire settlement—wiped out," he muttered angrily. His gaze drifted from what must have been the church in the center—now a blackened, smoking woodpile—to the smoldering ruins that had circled it. Creed barely recognized what must have been the blacksmith's shop, and turned away from the sight of the hairless, bloody body lying half in the charred timbers. There were a few dead horses, though most of the others were probably part of a Blackfoot herd by now. Other domestic animals had not been quick enough to escape the marauding warriors. Cats, dogs, chickens, geese—even a few pigs—lay stiffening in death.

Creed paused before a building that had caved in. The roof timbers were lying like tossed match sticks across the floor, still smoldering. Spirals of smoke curled upward, drifting on the breeze. He aimed a frustrated kick at a leaning board, and it clattered onto a dirt floor already cluttered with charred wood and the remains of what looked to be schoolbooks and slates. A school!

"The bastards," Creed said aloud. "A damn school! And now, no more books and no more kids . . ."

A faint scuffling sound caught his attention and he whirled, half-crouched, his Colt cocked and ready.

"Who's there?" he demanded harshly, peering intently at the pyramid of fallen roof timbers that lay on the dirt floor. There was no answer. Several moments ticked past as he listened, but he heard only the faint calls of birds in the trees. The entire area was as still and quiet as only death can be. His breathing sounded loud in his ears and his bay was beginning to spook. A shiver of premonition rippled down Creed's spine and he began to back away slowly, his pistol trained on the pile of timbers where he'd heard the sound. A wounded Blackfoot, maybe? Or a dazed settler who wouldn't stop to look before he aimed a gun? Why take any chances, Creed figured warily. He hadn't lived this long by being stupid.

The pyramid of timbers suddenly shifted, falling in a grinding shower of sparks and gust of smoke. Creed fell to one knee and thumbed the hammer of his Colt. His bullet ricocheted from the top timber in warning. Suddenly he heard a scream—one that sounded more terrified than pained. He leaped up and ran forward, holstering his Colt. It had been the thin scream of a child or woman . . .

Heedless of the heat, Creed began to push and kick the smoldering timbers aside, looking for the source of that sound. A survivor in all this? he wondered in amazement, then discovered the wooden trapdoor beneath the smoking logs. It took him several more minutes to clear the rest of the debris, and then he crouched and pried up the door.

The first thing he felt was a gush of stale, cool air, and the second was the slap of something large, heavy, and unyielding against the side of his head. Lights exploded in front of his eyes, but even though he was slightly dazed, he reacted with a swiftly swinging arm. It collided with a soft, limber form and sent it spinning to the hot debris littering the ground.

"What the hell?" Creed muttered as he regained his

balance again and shook his bare head. His hat had fallen off and his hair was in his eyes. He gave it an impatient shove with one hand as he glared at his sprawling attacker. It was a young boy with a shock of sandy hair, and he was doubled over clutching his stomach where Creed's arm had caught him. "What's the matter with you?" he demanded harshly of the boy. "I guess you prefer being left in that pit to cook like a slaughtered ox!"

"I . . . we . . . thought you was a murderin' Indian," was the sullen reply. "Didn't know if you was comin' to help, or comin' back to finish it."

Creed swiftly assessed the boy, who couldn't have been much over twelve or thirteen, then snapped, "Who is *we*?"

The boy's head jerked to his left, indicating the yawning opening. "Miss Hannah and the others."

Creed lifted his brows and reached for his hat. "Others?" he inquired, dusting the old hat against one leg.

"Yeah," the boy replied. He would have explained further, but it was unnecessary. Creed was already crouched beside the opening, peering into it.

"Come on out," he commanded in a rough growl, then watched in amazement as a file of badly frightened, sooty children scrambled from the cellar. He counted seven more. Creed shoved them toward the grass and out of the hot, smoldering ruins of the building, then snapped, "This all?"

"Except for Miss Hannah . . ."

A bright, tousled head appeared in the opening, followed by the slender form of a disheveled young woman. She half stumbled coming out of the cellar, and Creed put out a hand to catch her. The touch of her small, rough hand gave him a shock, and he found himself running a speculative glance over the girl's body. She was slender to the point of thinness, but with the ripe curves of womanhood straining at the bodice of her sooty dress. There was a look of the

Puritan to her, he decided when she gently disengaged her hand and ignored his narrowed gaze, and her first words confirmed that suspicion.

"Good day, sir! Oh, you are heaven sent, indeed! The blessed Lord has sent you as our savior, and we are grateful!" she exclaimed softly, stumbling over her words as she fell to her knees among the charred timbers and hot embers. Her gown was singed and torn, and he noted scrapes and burns on her slim arms and hands. Long, sooty lashes fluttered shut as her gaze swept across the carnage spreading beyond the schoolhouse, and she could not still a sudden moan of despair at the sight of the death and destruction. She pressed trembling fingers over her eyes as if to shut out the vision completely.

"Heaven sent, huh?" Creed said with a lift of one brow. "Some have said more like hell-spawned, but enough of that."

Impatient with the delay, and burning the soles of his elkhide moccasins on the hot logs and embers, Creed unceremoniously hauled her up and out of the ashes. He swung her into his arms, half-carrying the girl to the cooler shelter of grass and trees that stretched behind the schoolhouse.

The huddled group of children began to wail loudly, the younger ones sobbing and rubbing at their eyes, cringing away from the tall, buckskin-clad man who carried Hannah.

"Shut up!" Creed snarled at them as they grew even louder, and his steely glare was so fierce that the older ones grew quiet. Only the younger children continued to cry, and their sobs flayed Creed's already raw nerves. He turned on them, still holding the girl, and snapped at them to be quiet or he would throw their teacher back into the fire. This served to gain him peace, and the children subsided with round eyes and only soft whimpers. Creed nodded in grim satisfaction, feeling not the slightest twinge of guilt for yelling at them. His mouth twisted in ironic self-derision.

*That's all I need—a bunch of hysterical kids on my hands. Why did I have to stop, anyway? It's not like I can do anything . . .*

The girl was light as a feather, he noticed as he dumped her on the grass, and her color was ashen as she half-swooned. It took her several moments to gather her wits. Then, with a determined tilt of her head, she straightened and gazed up at him with such glowing eyes that Creed was taken aback. "Bless you, sir," she murmured. "We would have died in the cellar if not for you. Bless you," she added again, and he recoiled.

"I don't need blessing!" Creed growled, jamming his soot-streaked hat back on his head. "You're the one who needs the blessing, lady! Maybe you forgot—I'm the one who had to rescue *you*, remember?"

Hannah managed a wan smile and quoted, ". . . 'For they shall cry unto the Lord because of the oppressors, and He shall send them a savior, and a great one, and He shall deliver them.' "

Creed drew back. "What?"

"You are our savior, sir," she explained gently. "You were sent by God to rescue us."

"No. I saw the smoke and thought you were someone else. I wasn't sent by *any*body," he disagreed immediately, not quite sure just what he had gotten himself into. Was this lady a religious fanatic?

"God works in mysterious ways," the soot-streaked young woman responded. She stiffened, finally turning her head in a slow motion. Her eyes moved to the smoking ruins of the settlement, widened as she viewed the sprawled corpses and the buzzards already circling overhead, then glanced back at him as if for confirmation of her fears. Creed nodded slowly, and read the dismay and grief in her misty eyes before she shuttered them with a quick snap of her lashes. A light shudder rippled through her body before she stilled it, and she had to press her lips tightly together to hold back an involuntary protest.

*No, no, no, not all of them! Not my father, not the others—no, no, no!*

"Are you certain?" she asked aloud, calmly, her voice reflecting none of her inner turmoil, and Creed answered as she expected.

"All of them are dead." He was watching her closely, obviously expecting her to crack, to scream and cry and wail, but she did none of those things.

Instead, Hannah rose and brushed the soot and ashes from her charred skirts. Her hands trembled only slightly, and she refused to look in the direction of the bodies that fanned out across what had once been Jubile. Even livestock lay slaughtered in the fields, and the newly planted corn had been reduced to blackened stubble. But she could not think about that now—could not let herself think about anything but survival and the welfare of the children.

Hannah's voice was composed as she collected the children in a group and took them away from the gutted schoolhouse toward the snaking line of the river. "Gather close, children, so that we might pray," she said.

Creed stared after her in some amazement as she firmly kept the children in line, guiding them away from the scattered bodies as best she could. The girl was young, maybe eighteen or nineteen, he figured, and the prettiest he'd ever seen. She had clean lines, and a face that looked like a painting he'd once seen. Even dirty, with mud and ashes covering her hair and clothes, she was beautiful.

Beautiful but fanatical, Creed decided moments later as the young woman called Hannah led the children in prayer.

She prayed aloud, thanking God for the good, kind man who had rescued them from the smoky prison of the root cellar.

Enough of *that* nonsense, Creed thought grimly when she went on for several minutes. He stalked over to the half-circle of kneeling figures.

"Excuse me, lady, but unless you want to get caught in the open again, you'd better gather up your pupils and get outa here pretty quick," he said bluntly. "That smoke is liable to draw the curious, and I ain't too sure as to the curious *what*. If I was you, I'd hightail it to the next settlement right now. I'll point you in the right direction."

"Yes, we should," Hannah agreed immediately, and got to her feet. "You are quite right, of course. We just wanted to offer a prayer for . . . for the others." She paused and gazed around the ruined settlement for a moment. "As soon as we have given our . . . our loved ones a Christian burial, we will go," she said. Her voice faltered before she gathered her composure and continued with a potent, ethereal smile, "What is your name, sir? I should like to place a name to the man who has saved our lives."

For some reason this girl made him uncomfortable, and he took his time answering. He pulled out his tobacco pouch, rolled and lit a cigarette, then blew the smoke into the air as he considered how to answer. He didn't want this girl thinking they were going to become best friends just because he'd happened to stumble across them and help out a little, but then again, he *had* saved their lives. And dammit, she was looking up at him so trustingly that his slow answer was rougher than necessary. "If you just *have* to know, it's Bratton. Now if you would just . . ."

"But what is your Christian name, Mr. Bratton?" she interrupted.

"I don't have a Christian name!" he snapped. "My *first* name is Creed..."

"Creed Bratton," she said quietly. "That is a fine name, sir. I am Hannah McGuire, and these children are my students. This," she said, pointing to the boy who had hit him with the wooden bowl, "is Fletcher Harris. The little girl with blond hair is Ivy Ransom, and her brother is Eric. Lift your hand when I say your name, children," she instructed, ignoring Creed's harsh comment that he didn't need or want to know their names as she continued. "This is Little Bird, who is a member of the Kootenai tribe, and her cousin Frog. Sweyn Johanssen, Rebecca Hillenbrand, and Jessica Gray," she finished as each child obediently lifted his hand in response to his name. "Children, this is Mr. Creed Bratton, who will be escorting us to safety."

He reeled at her announcement. "What?" Creed demanded in amazement. "The hell you say! Now, just *when* did I ever say I would do that?"

Hannah's gaze was slightly disapproving as she looked at him and said, "You did not say you would, Mr. Bratton, but I know you are not the kind of man who would abandon a woman and eight helpless children."

Bridling, he retorted, "How do you know I didn't just massacre an entire orphanage somewhere, lady?"

"My name is Hannah Elizabeth McGuire, not lady, Mr. Bratton, and I do not have to be told you did not do such a reprehensible thing in order to know it for myself."

His mouth quirked into a mocking line. "You don't, huh? Lady, you've still got a lot to learn," he muttered, and thought briefly about the three outlaws only a day's ride ahead of him. There was a hefty bounty on their heads, and he didn't have time to help these people—not if he intended to find Stillman and his men and collect that bounty.

Anyway, why should he be saddled with a preachy girl and eight snotty-nosed kids?

Rocking back on his heels, Creed leveled a cold gaze at the slim, red-haired girl who was watching him with such a trusting expression on her lovely face. Then, sighing, he knew she was right. As irritating as it was, he couldn't leave them to die.

"I shall look for shovels to bury our dead before we leave," Hannah said then, reading the capitulation in his face even before he said anything.

Creed shook his head. "Ma'am, if you don't mind me sayin' so, it would take a lot of time to bury all these folks. It might . . . Why don't you step over here with me?" he added, seeing the wide eyes of the listening children fixed on his face. "Listen," he began in a low tone when they had stepped several feet away, "seein' as how there's already a fire, and the ground ain't quite as thawed as it could be, maybe you should consider cremation."

The girl's finely arched brows rose in revulsion, and he could see by the expression on her face that she was having difficulty retaining her self-control.

"Cremation?" she whispered, and briefly closed her eyes against a sudden spasm of pain. "I . . . I don't know! It seems so . . . so *final*, somehow!"

"Death usually is," Creed said, and in spite of himself, he felt a pang of pity for this girl. She was bearing up pretty well under the burden placed on her slender shoulders, and he stifled any urge he might have to comfort her. It was the way of the world—some lived, some died. There hadn't been anyone around to give him any sympathetic words when he had needed them, and he'd survived, hadn't he? He'd even grown stronger for it. She would, too.

"Make up your mind," he said in a rough, indifferent way, and pushed his dusty hat back on his head to stare at her through narrowed eyes. "I ain't got all day, and neither do you, whether you realize it or not."

Hannah's eyes widened slightly at his harsh tone, and she gazed up at him with a considering stare. What choices did she have? This man had at least stopped to help, and though grudgingly, he was attempting to give her what he considered sound advice. His appearance was not very comforting, but then, most men in the wilderness looked rough and unkempt. She remembered the three outlaws who had ridden into Jubile that morning.

Within the space of a few seconds, Hannah took note of Bratton's tall, muscular build, evident even in the shirt and pants of fringed buckskin. He wore knee-high moccasins of elkhide, and he stood with legs astride, his gun belt slung low on one hip and his gun within obviously quick reach. His dark felt hat looked incongruous somehow, as if it should be on a man in a dark suit with an embroidered vest, instead of a man who looked as if he would be more comfortable crouched beside a campfire. Bratton wore his thick black hair long, sweeping over his neck and onto his broad shoulders, framing a face that could best be described as ruggedly handsome. His jaw was square and strong, bristling with a half-grown beard, and his eyes were so brown as to be almost black, wide apart and full of expression as now, when he was gazing at her with an assessing stare. High cheekbones slashed downward, complementing a straight nose, and his lips were curved into a half-mocking smile.

He looked hard and cynical, but he was also smeared with soot and ashes from the hot timbers he had shoved aside in order to rescue them. Dare she trust her life and those of the children to this man? But what other choice did she have, Hannah thought, gazing sadly around. Everyone was gone now—her father, the parents of these children, everyone . . .

"Perhaps cremation would be best, Mr. Bratton," she agreed quietly. "But I insist that we say prayers over each of them first."

"Lady!"

"I insist," she repeated firmly, and turned back to the waiting children as if the matter was already settled. Then she turned back to him. "Thank you, Mr. Bratton," she added in a soft voice.

"I haven't agreed to anything yet," he shot back with a scowl.

Hannah smiled. "I know."

Creed slanted a sour glance at the sky. It would be dark soon, and he wanted to be well away from this spot before night fell. Maybe he was superstitious, but he didn't relish spending the night with ghosts, whether real or only memories, and he certainly didn't look forward to spending any time with a Bible-spouting female and eight bawling brats!

But when he would have opened his mouth to refuse to take them, to say that they could fend for themselves, some small vestige of humanity prevailed. Instead, he heard himself telling the girl to hurry or he'd leave them all behind. It was as near as he would come to compromise.

# Chapter Four

"No, you can't!" the child sobbed wildly, resisting Hannah's efforts to calm her. Young Ivy Ransom clung to her dead

mother frantically, tangling her hands in the long skirts and
holding on. The grieving child ignored Hannah and even her
brother Eric as she fought their attempts to place Lavinia
Ransom and the infant daughter in her arms with the other
bodies.

"Ivy," Hannah said gently, fighting back her own tears,
"you must let us give your mother and sister a proper
farewell. Do you want to leave them like this . . . ?"

"I don't care!" Ivy cried. She wound her hands more
tightly in her mother's skirts. The child resembled a small,
determined terrier as she clung tenaciously to the body, but
when Creed would have attempted to remove her, she flung
herself at him in a fury. Her small feet flailed wildly,
bruising his shins and making him swear.

Ivy's breath came in small, hurting gasps as she ranted at
him to leave her alone, that he only wanted to put her
mother in the same fire he'd threatened her teacher with,
and that she hated him. Taken aback in the face of the girl's
fury, Creed released her immediately and snapped an order
at Hannah to do something or he'd leave without them.

Hannah glanced helplessly at Creed, who now stood
several feet away. He said nothing else, but shrugged his
broad shoulders and indicated with a nod of his head the
location of the sun, as if to say she'd best hurry.

Kneeling beside the distraught child, Hannah did her best
to soothe her, but it was Little Bird, the stoic, dark-haired
Kootenai girl, who was able to comfort Ivy. The ten-year-
old was already wise beyond her years, and she simply held
Ivy's hand, somehow imparting a sense of strength and
compassion that finally stilled the girl's violent protests.

The earthly remains of Lavinia Ransom were reluctantly
yielded up, and the funeral services hastily performed.
Hannah read from the Bible and led the children in a short
prayer consigning the souls of their loved ones to eternity in

Heaven, then gathered the weeping orphans in a loose embrace before leading them away from the ruins of the church. Its still-smoking timbers were to be the funeral pyre, but she could not bring herself to rekindle the blaze. That was left to Creed Bratton.

Her throat ached with unshed tears, and though she knew it was useless to weep for those who had already passed into Heaven, she longed to weep for herself. Joshua McGuire, the guiding force in her life, her beloved father, was dead. She had lovingly folded his arms across his chest and looked a last time upon his face, which had been strangely peaceful in spite of his violent death. Even though Creed Bratton had merely looked on, obviously restless and remote, she sensed he was somehow moved by the children's grief.

The funeral pyre blazed brightly, smoke billowing into the air in great, black clouds like giant vultures blotting out the sun. Hannah once more led them all in prayer—briefly, as Creed Bratton impatiently reminded her more than once to hurry—and then they left the ruins of Jubile behind.

Hannah did not look back as they rode away. Instead, she kept her gaze ahead, trained on the thick-wooded slopes and mountain peaks not far away. The broad valley ran in a wide cut between towering peaks that still bore caps of snow on them. Mountains rose sharply on each side, though miles away. In the valley the sun lingered longer, the air was warmer, and the ground more fertile. The spring runoff from the melting snow ran in swift-moving creeks and formed icy lakes.

There was no talk and little noise as they traversed the loose rocks and springy turf of the marsh that bordered the Kootenai River. She looked at its familiar curves, remembering the many times she had splashed in it or walked along its banks. Now, she was leaving it behind. It glittered serene and uncaring in the late afternoon sunshine, a fluidly winding ribbon that flowed through the verdant, lush valley she had called home for the past three years.

They were all earthly orphans now, Hannah thought, as they rode through the tree-choked valley. Her gaze drifted over the heads of the quiet children as they marched along, most of them walking so that the youngest could ride on the two horses they had been able to find. With an aching heart, she wondered what would happen to the children. Who would care for them now? Some could probably be sent back East to relatives, but most of the children did not have any family left. Except for the Indian children, they were all immigrants to this wild, sprawling Northwest Territory.

Hannah's gaze flicked thoughtfully to Creed Bratton. He rode ahead of them on his big bay, having obdurately refused to allow any of the children to ride beside him.

"I ain't a damn nursemaid!" he'd growled, wheeling his bay around and moving several yards ahead of the others. Now he rode in stiff silence while they followed.

Hannah wondered briefly why the man had such a thick armor around him. He *seemed* nice enough, in a gruff sort of way, though rough and abrasive in his talk. Having been brought up to say "please" and "thank you," and "may I," it was difficult for her to understand why Creed Bratton felt it necessary to be so rude. Being polite took so little effort, and had such a pleasant effect on others most of the time. A slight frown tucked her delicate brows into a knot as she remembered Mrs. Crosswaithe and how crabby and ill-tempered she could be. Poor old Mrs. Crosswaithe. She had been bent and old and in pain a great deal of the time, so rudeness was expected from her. It had been the only outlet she had. Perhaps this Mr. Bratton was in some sort of pain, and his rudeness was his only outlet, too. Hannah made a mental note to be patient. Men could be so touchy and sensitive about infirmity. She had often wondered in amazement how such strong creatures could bear heavy loads, endure suffering and wounds and all manner of aches and pains, yet go to pieces over such a minor thing as a cold. She'd observed it time and again while helping Joshua on his medical visits.

Sighing, she supposed that Mr. Bratton must be suffering from some unknown ailment and was simply too proud to explain. Time would ease matters.

"Stop it!" came a high-pitched voice, snaring Hannah's wandering attention and causing her to look up.

Fletcher Harris, big and brawny for his age, had grown tired of walking and had jerked impatiently at the lead lines of the poor, weary animal carrying the younger children. "I don't see why I've got to walk while they ride," he'd muttered, softly at first, then more loudly when he got no reaction. His eyes narrowed on Ivy and Little Bird, who were astride the broad back of the mare.

Little Bird gave no sign she'd heard him at first, but as Fletcher's voice grew louder and more impatient, Ivy protested, then began to cry. Huge tears welled in her eyes, and her narrow shoulders began to shake helplessly as Fletcher gave her dark, angry glances. Little Bird put one arm around her, then glared at the sandy-haired boy leading them.

"Be silent!" the Kootenai girl hissed furiously. Her brown arm flashed out to tug sharply at a lock of his hair. "You are making her cry."

Fletcher stopped and belligerently thrust out his lower lip. "So what? She's a crybaby anyway . . ."

At that, Ivy began to cry more loudly, and Eric came to the aid of his sister. He ran up beside the much larger boy and demanded that he leave Ivy alone. Fletcher responded with a rough shove that sent Eric sprawling into the dust of the narrow path, and the younger, smaller boy leaped to his feet with a furious howl to fling himself at his antagonist.

They grappled, rolling on the ground in a tangle of arms and legs.

Hannah rushed forward and attempted to separate them, her voice rising as the boys refused to heed her commands.

"Fletcher! Eric! Stop—stop it at once, I say!"

Ignoring her as they thrashed about on the ground, the boys tumbled over the path and dead limbs, grunting with each furious flash of their fists. Hannah turned helplessly to Creed when she saw her efforts were futile, and glared at him. He sat on his horse watching, an amused smile curling his lips. Putting her hands on her hips, Hannah snapped, "Well, can't you do anything about this?"

Shrugging, Creed drawled, "Sure, I can. But why should I? They're kinda funny..."

"*Funny*! You call fighting among children *funny*?"

"Yeah. What do you call it?"

"I call it distressing, Mr. Bratton, and most dismaying that you would consider violence amusing!"

Creed let his cool gaze drift slowly over Hannah's flushed face and irate eyes as he considered her comment. He pushed back his hat and pursed his lips, rubbing his chin thoughtfully as he regarded her. "I disagree," he said finally, flatly.

Almost beside herself with anger at both the fighting boys and Creed Bratton, Hannah struggled to control her temper. It was simmering like a hot stew, dangerously close to boiling over. Her father had often cautioned her against letting her ever-ready temper spew out of control, and now she tried in vain to recall the scripture he had urged her to recite in place of angry words. It was no use. The Scriptures eluded her; all she could think about was Creed Bratton's mocking face and refusal to help.

"You, sir, are the most despicable, contemptible, loathsome, odious creature I have ever had the misfortune of encountering,'' she began breathlessly, ''and I truly regret having made your acquaintance!''

''Do you, now?'' Creed leaned forward to say, his arm resting across his broad saddle horn. ''Does this mean you're no longer grateful that I rescued you and these children from a slow death in the root cellar? You would have been baked like turnips if I hadn't come along and gotten you out of that damned oven . . .''

''It's unfair of you to remind me!'' Hannah stormed bitterly. ''But you did so unwillingly, I might add!''

''Ah, but I *did* rescue you, you must admit. You could not have removed those burned roof timbers by yourself.''

The solemn reminder halted another spurt of anger from Hannah, and she struggled for control. Gathering the shreds of her dignity with a supreme effort, Hannah managed to nod calmly. ''Yes, Mr. Bratton, you did save us, and I apologize for losing control just now.'' She took a deep breath. ''Would you please be so kind as to help me separate these boys before one of them does great damage to the other?''

''I seriously doubt either one of them could inflict much of a wound, but I'll see what I can do,'' Creed said as he dismounted. He crossed the path to the tangled boys, reached down and grasped each of them by his shirt collar, and hauled them easily to their feet. Their arms and legs churned like windmills, as they snorted and panted and glared at one another. Creed gave them a halfhearted shake that was meant to warn them, but they made the mistake of resisting. Creed flexed his arms and banged their heads together with a loud crack that made Hannah gasp and the boys moan. Then he released their shirts and they dropped to the ground like stones. ''I think that ought to curb their tempers for the moment, Miss McGuire,'' Creed said. ''Anything else you want me to do?''

Swallowing a hasty reply that would only have made matters worse, Hannah shook her head. Creed nodded with satisfaction, asked in a pleasant tone that they please follow him more quietly, and remounted his horse. He turned the bay back up the climbing slope of the path and nudged him into a walk while Hannah gathered up the prone combatants and the other—much quieter—children.

"He's got a nasty way of settlin' things," was all Fletcher Harris could say in a dazed mumble as he nursed his aching head, and Hannah had to agree.

"But it was effective," she added as she took young Eric's chin in her hand and examined his bruised face. "I suggest you gentlemen refrain from such activities in the future."

"Yeah," Eric said, "but I still coulda whupped ole Fletcher!"

"I'll hear no more of that!" Hannah put in before Fletcher could retort in kind. "As a lesson in humility and harmony, I think you two boys should walk side by side for the rest of the day. Where I see one of you, I want to see both of you. And I want you to work *together*. Is that clearly understood?"

Both crestfallen boys nodded silently, casting wary glances toward the bay and Creed Bratton. It was obvious that they did not wish to invite any more action from the rough-tongued, strong-armed mountain man.

They covered the next few miles in silence. Very little sunlight filtered through the towering trees, and the only sounds were an occasional call from a wild animal, or the syrupy chirp of nest-building birds. Just off the narrow path the trees grew so closely together it would have been impossible to ride or even walk between them. Spruce, fir, birch, cedar, hemlock, and pine seemed intertwined at times, vying for the life-giving rays of the sun, crowding

out the smaller growth beneath. Greenish-brown moss cloaked
thick tree limbs in lacy shawls, dripping down in graceful
curves. A primeval forest, Hannah thought suddenly—that
was what it was like. Untouched, unseen by any but the
eyes of the wild creatures who lived there, the forest waited
in serene solitude.

Nothing disturbed it, or left its mark for long. Only an
occasional summer fire begun by a bolt of lightning cleared
the taller trees and allowed new growth. Hannah recalled the
few fires she had seen, and how terrified she had been
knowing the flames could decimate miles of thick forest.
Fortunately, none had ever come close enough to Jubile to
destroy homes or crops.

Here and there she could still see an ancient, charred tree
that bore mute testimony to a long-forgotten blaze. Hannah
wondered if the trees made any sounds when they died, then
scolded herself for having such fanciful thoughts. Of course
they didn't. Plants had no souls, and therefore, felt no
suffering. Yet animals had no souls, and they were capable
of suffering, she silently argued. How many winter evenings
had she and her father sat before a fire and discussed this?
Joshua was of the firm opinion that animals had no soul and
were put on earth for man's use, yet she had often put forth
the argument that surely God must love them, for hadn't He
favored the animals with a sense of love and loyalty to their
masters? Joshua's answer had always been that certainly
God loved all His creatures, but He'd given only man the
gift of reason and compassion. A surge of bitterness swelled
in Hannah as she remembered her father's reply. Compassion?
*If that was so, were the Blackfoot men or animals?*

Hannah tried to wipe away the clinging cobwebs of such
doubts from her mind. She must remember that all men
were created in God's image—that she must love them
equally. She sighed. It could become such a thorny prob-

lem, and she was beginning to realize her deficiencies. Compassion for someone who had murdered her father was very difficult. She felt only fear and hate.

Almost stumbling, Hannah jerked her thoughts away from the Blackfoot. Instead, she recalled her father again—the wonderful qualities that had made him unique, so perfect in her eyes. She could not recall any faults—would not recall any faults. Joshua McGuire had been a good man—a man with dedication and a purpose, and she would not allow his memory to be tarnished in any way.

Hannah's head lifted briefly, and she vowed with renewed determination to be the kind of daughter that her father had wanted.

Walking beside her, Sweyn Johanssen faltered as he tripped over the knobby root of a tree, and she put out a hand to catch him. In places the path was almost impassable because of a fallen tree or broken limb, but the children would surmount the obstacle without speaking as they followed Creed Bratton. He rode with his back straight, never looking back at them, almost as if he wished they would disappear.

Hannah kept her gaze trained on their guide, wondering if he was as cold and emotionless as he tried to seem. Bratton obviously kept a close watch on his emotions, yet Hannah couldn't help noticing that he paced his horse so as not to tire them too greatly.

A half smile curved her generous mouth as Hannah reflected that Creed Bratton was not nearly as wicked as he pretended to be, either. There must be some good in him, she thought, or he would not have agreed to escort them to the next settlement, twenty miles away. Wetting her dry lips with the tip of her tongue, Hannah wondered how he would react when she informed him that she wished to go to the burgeoning settlement of Camp Coeur d'Alene.

She knew someone there—or rather, Joshua had known

someone there. She knew Joel Allen only slightly. He had come to Jubile once, two years ago, and she remembered him as a tall, fair, rather spiritual man. His pale eyes had burned with fervent conviction. Though Hannah had thought him rather *too* fervent, she had liked him, and Joshua had made no secret of the fact that he promoted a possible marriage between his daughter and Joel one day. Yes, Joel would see that the children were cared for much better than she could do.

Hannah sighed again. She knew Bratton would balk at the suggestion that he take them. The rough mountain man would bluster and swear, of that she was certain, but could he be persuaded to agree?

God would provide all the answers, Hannah told herself in the next instant. She would just put the proposal to Mr. Bratton and wait.

She didn't have to wait long. When they were camped for the evening and the children had fallen asleep in the few blankets salvaged from Jubile, Hannah quietly informed Creed of her decision. She steeled herself for his reaction, watching his rugged face in the silver glitter of moonlight that flirted with the flicker of night shadows.

Stiffening, he just stared at her for a moment, his face mirroring astonishment, then disbelief, then annoyance, and finally anger.

"What?" he finally shouted, and Hannah quickly shushed him.

"Please! You'll wake the children, Mr. Bratton—"

Loudly, he began, "*I don't*—I don't care," he finished more quietly, snarling the words and glaring at her through narrowed eyes. "Looka here, lady, I don't care what crazy notion you've gotten in your head, I ain't takin' you and a passel of brats all the way to Coeur d'Alene! Hell, it's over a hundred miles from here!''

"I find your language offensive," Hannah commented, "but I am certain you will temper it in my presence. As for the children, merely leaving us at some remote homestead will hardly eliminate our problem. There are people in Camp Coeur d'Alene who can help the children. The settlement is on the new road just built from Fort Walla Walla to Fort Benton in Montana, and will have more traffic. It is important that the children find passage to any relatives who may be left. They *are* just children, Mr. Bratton, and they deserve a good start in life, with people who care about them..."

"Yeah?" he cut in with a growl. "Well, not all kids get that kinda chance, lady!"

Hannah stared at him for a moment. There was so much bitterness in his tone and face—a rough edge that was obviously still raw. She suddenly understood more than he intended. She paused, then continued gently, "No, not all children get that chance. But you are probably more aware of that than most and the only guide we seem to have at the moment, so I will be pleased to accept your kind offer of assistance, Mr. Bratton."

Slumping back against an outcropping of rock, Creed gazed at Hannah's earnest face in utter astonishment. He was momentarily speechless, a condition that could not last long, and when he regained his power of speech, she flinched from his verbal blast.

Surging to his feet, Creed snarled, "Look, lady! I ain't got no reason to take you to Coeur d'Alene, and I'm doin' pretty damn good just letting you tag along until we get to the nearest homestead! If I did like I wanted to do, you'da been left back there by that river to find your own way." He towered over her, glaring down into her pale, moon-drenched face, his hat brim shadowing his features as he added, "I've already lost the trail of the men I was followin'. There's no telling when I'll be able to pick up on it again, and that's gonna cost me some money, lady. Now, take my advice and settle for what you've gotten out of me, or you might just find yourself and your little band of ragamuffins out here on your own . . ."

Tucking his thumbs into his gun belt, he stared down at her belligerently, obviously expecting her to argue. When Hannah merely nodded her head in silent acceptance, Creed's eyes narrowed with suspicion. Then, squaring his shoulders, he pivoted and stalked away into the deeper indigo shadows that hid the trees and sky from view.

A small sigh pursed her lips as Hannah watched Creed's angry retreat. He would change his mind—she was certain of it. In spite of his angry resistance and harsh words, he must have a good heart, or he would not have displayed any sympathy for their plight. Perhaps his gruffness only masked embarrassment at having softer feelings, she mused, and wondered what had happened to make him that way. She'd altered her earlier opinion of Creed Bratton, in that she no longer thought some strange and personal illness made him so surly. No, there was definitely a deep bitterness in the man—a festering that needed release.

Sitting back against a fallen log, Hannah began to unbraid her long hair, a nightly ritual that was familiar and somehow comforting in this alien, frightening situation. They had camped in a small clearing that was ringed by a half-circle of towering firs, pines, and tamaracks, with the other curve of the circle formed by a high wall of ridged shale. Jack pines studded the steep slopes in a haphazard pattern, and it was apparent that large rocks occasionally slid down the sides. A rock shower was better than an enemy attack, Creed had informed Hannah when she questioned the safety of camping there, so the weary children were nestled safely in their blankets against that impenetrable fortress wall. They cuddled together under a rocky overhang, sidling next to one another for warmth like puppies. It was cold, but Creed had not allowed a fire.

"It ain't that cold yet," he said. "No point in tellin' every Blackfoot within a hundred miles just where we are by our smoke." Shuddering, Hannah had agreed, relying on Creed's superior knowledge of the Blackfoot.

Now she was alone, with only the sleeping children for company. Tugging at her loosened braids, Hannah tried not to recall the day's events. She finger-combed her hair, listening to the sounds around her, waiting for Creed's return. He would come back, wouldn't he? But as time passed, it began to look doubtful. Biting her lower lip, she glanced over her shoulder and pulled the edges of a frayed blanket together around her.

Unfamiliar night sounds surrounded her—vague rustlings and murmurings that were exaggerated in her mind. She rested her chin on her drawn-up knees and sat huddled in the ragged folds of her blanket, shifting uneasily at the sound of a muffled whicker from one of the horses. She sat for what seemed like hours, peering into the deepening shadows that grew darker and darker, until she could not distinguish one from another. If not for the wavering patches of moonlight, she would have been terrified. The memories of those long, dark hours in the root cellar were still too vivid, too real. She could almost hear the echoes of the shouts and screams...

Rising abruptly to her feet, Hannah twisted her long hair into a thick rope and pulled the blanket more snugly around her shoulders. She had to keep busy—had to keep the memories at bay. How else could she remain strong for the children?

She stood uncertainly, shivering in the chilled night air,

searching the darkness for Creed Bratton. The checkered squares of moonlight did not reveal any sign of him. A hundred different thoughts plagued her, rising like demons in the night, and Hannah thrust them firmly from her mind. She would not be foolish enough to panic. As irritated as Creed Bratton might be at having to take care of them, he would not abandon her and the children.

She stiffened, and the hair on the back of her neck curled as she heard faint, rustling steps in the thick undergrowth of leaves and fallen branches. Were they human or animal? she wondered.

"Mr. Bratton?" she called nervously. Her voice trembled as she called again, but there was no reply.

It was the time of year when mother grizzlies closely guarded their cubs. She recalled an unfortunate encounter one of the men in Jubile had once had with a huge, muscled mountain of fur and razor-sharp teeth. The mother bear had not left enough of him to bury. But grizzlies did not hunt at night—did they?

Hannah whirled, searching blindly for something to use in case of an attack, and seized a fallen limb from the ground. Damp, rotting leaves clung to it; she brushed them away with a shaking hand. The blanket dropped, forgotten, as she listened with widening eyes. She clenched the limb tightly, holding it in front of her and across her body as she backed slowly away from the approaching footfalls. They drew closer and closer—firm, stealthy steps on the crackle of dried leaves and snap of twigs—and she took a deep, steadying breath.

A large shadow loomed suddenly ahead of her, stepping from behind a tree. Swallowing a scream, Hannah took just enough time to ask "Who's there?" before she began to swing with all her strength.

"Whoa!" an angry male voice shouted. Hannah's arm

was grabbed by steely fingers and she was shoved roughly backward. She lost her balance and fell, with Creed Bratton atop her sprawling form.

His face was only inches from hers as he wrenched the tree limb from her listless fingers and flung it away, but he made no attempt to get up. His lean body was pressed close, his hands digging into her wrists as he stared down into her eyes. There was a subtle pressure of his fingers, then he released her wrists, but only pushed slightly away.

"Mr. Bratton?" Hannah inquired breathlessly when it seemed as if he did not intend to move. "Would you mind? You are crushing me."

"You almost bashed my head in again," he growled in reply. His tone reminded her of an angry mountain cat.

"Again? When was the first time?" she gasped, then added, when it seemed as if her ribs would snap at any moment, "Please get up!"

Creed didn't move, but shifted slightly. Hannah could feel the length of his body pressing against her—the cold prod of his gun belt digging into her soft stomach, and his lean thighs covering her trembling legs. There was something intriguing about the way he held her—the way his eyes locked with hers. She could almost feel the thud of his heart against her breasts. She should be frightened, or at least angry, but she was not. Instead, she found herself gazing at his mouth curiously, wondering why his lips looked so soft when the man was so harsh and unyielding.

As if he knew what she was thinking, Creed smiled—a slow, knowing smile that made her flush and look away. "The first time was when that kid banged me with a wooden bowl," he reminded her, dragging Hannah's attention back to the question she had asked.

"Please get up," she said then. He grinned and released her abruptly, rolling away and sitting with his arms across

his knees, staring at her. "Why didn't you answer my call?"
Hannah ventured to ask when she had caught her breath.
"Did you not hear me?"

His grin faded. "Hell, yes, I heard you!"

"Then . . ."

"What were you tryin' to do—alert every Indian in the
area?" Creed shook his head, raking his spread fingers
through his hair like a comb, then fumbled for his lost hat in
the dead leaves on the dew-wet ground. He muttered a
comment about damaging his hat before adding, "Don't you
know how far sound travels in the woods at night? I thought
I'd give you a lesson on bein' quiet. I didn't know you
intended to bash my head in with a damned tree."

Hannah gazed at him in the hazy moonlight, her eyes
skimming from his dark, hot eyes to the tightened slash of
his mouth, and she felt the beginnings of anger stir in her.

"Am I to understand that you *intended* to frighten me,
Mr. Bratton?"

"Yeah, I sure as hell did!" he shot back. "You obviously
need a lesson on the importance of silence in the woods,
lady. What I didn't know was that you were armed . . ."

Fury battled with common sense as Hannah struggled to
see his side of the issue. Perhaps he had only intended to
teach her the value of silence, but he could have chosen
another method to do it. Folding her arms across her chest,
she said icily, "I think you could have shown a little bit
more common sense in your educational lesson, Mr. Bratton."

His long legs straightened as his body uncurled, and he
stood over her, brushing away clinging leaves as he shot
back, "Think again! I'm willing to bet you're gonna remember not to shout in the woods anymore."

Hannah deftly countered his sarcasm with a potent smile
and soft voice. "Yes," she agreed, "I am certain that I will

not do *that* again. I beg your forgiveness, Mr. Bratton. Will you help me up, please?'' Extending one hand, she waited.

After a brief hesitation, Creed reluctantly reached down to pull Hannah to her feet. She stood beside him, a fragile creature with clouds of copper hair and mysterious eyes that were sometimes the color of the sky, sometimes the color of grass, or even smoke, and he felt an odd lurch in the pit of his stomach. Women were deceptive creatures; he couldn't forget that. She must have carefully calculated the effect of her smile and soft voice on him, as well as the touch of her small fingers in his roughened palm.

''Thank you,'' she was saying softly, and Creed stilled the inexplicable impulse to jerk her even closer to him. Why did she look so different with her hair hanging loose and free? It swung with her every movement, and the moonlight silvered wayward tips that curled toward her face in a caress.

Creed dropped her hand and took a step back. A vague memory of Samson and Delilah surged through his mind, and he wondered why he'd remembered that particular Bible story. What was he thinking? he wondered in a flash of self-mockery. This Bible-quoting, pious girl with the huge eyes and the wealth of burnished hair could probably think of very little other than her precious Bible verses and scruffy orphans. She would certainly not appreciate the kind of ideas he was having right now!

His mouth quirked in sardonic amusement as he drawled, ''You're welcome, missionary lady. Now how about doin' us both a favor by stayin' outa my way? There are some things a man has little control over. It's a dark night, and you're lookin' at me with those big eyes all soft and pretty like a doe's, and I'm havin' thoughts I shouldn't. Do you understand what I'm trying to tell you?'' he finished, and she nodded.

"I believe I do, Mr. Bratton," Hannah whispered through suddenly quivering lips. Her heart was hammering against her rib cage as she recognized the flare in his eyes—a light that was oddly like the one she had seen in the outlaw's eyes that morning, yet somehow different. "Good night," she said then.

Creed watched her as she joined the sleeping children, curling up in a blanket among them, looking like a child herself. More disturbed than he wanted to admit, he rolled a cigarette and leaned one shoulder against a broad tree trunk. He stood that way for a long time, staring into the darkness and thinking of things that could never be.

# Chapter Five

The horse clattered noisily into the wide, arched mouth of the shale cave cut into the hillside, and a man slid down to face the two awaiting him. He was frowning and shaking his head, and his first words caught Nate Stillman by surprise.

"You sure about this?" Stillman demanded, fixing Truett with a narrowed gaze.

"Sure as I can be."

Stillman swore softly. "What in the hell is Bratton up to now, traveling with a woman and a bunch of kids?"

"I swear to you I saw him. I fell back on the trail, jus' like you told me to, and waited for him. I was gonna bushwhack him, until I saw ..."

"Saw some gawddamned woman and bunch of kids!"

Roper sneered. "You're too soft-hearted, Truett! Too womanish!"

Truett rounded on the scarred man, standing with legs spread and hands hovering above the pistols he wore on each side, and still managed to draw before Roper could do more than graze the butts of his own pistols with his fingers.

"Care to change that, Roper?" he drawled. His pale eyes burned deep in the sockets, and his lank hair shifted slightly in the breeze that wafted over the river and into the cave. No point in telling Roper who the woman was. The scar-faced outlaw never forgot an insult, and he had taken a great dislike to the pretty lady from Jubile...

"Naw, I won't change it, but I won't say it again right now," Roper finally conceded while Truett waited.

"Hell, you two are just like a pair of wildcats fightin' over the same kill," Stillman commented in disgust. "Now, let's get on to business. We got Bratton on our tails no matter who he's travelin' with for the time bein', and we got this contact we're s'posed to make. Only I don't know exackly when..."

"Plummer said..."

"Plummer's an idiot! He sits fat and soft in his desk chair while we do all the work and take all the risks," Stillman spat over one shoulder. "I don't intend to spend too long in this cave waitin'. It's dark and damp, and I don't like it. I ain't got no intention of waiting for that damned bounty hunter to give up. We'll jus' take our chances on gettin' seen makin' the contact."

"D'ya think Bratton's wise to what's goin' on?" Roper asked, hunkering down on his heels beside Stillman and keeping a wary eye on Truett.

"Naw! He's still followin' three guys who jumped a gold shipment. He ain't got no idea what he's liable to get into if he catches up with us..."

*  *  *

Creed rode without looking behind him, ignoring the
children and their teacher as best he could. They were damn
nuisances, as far as he was concerned, and he regretted the
weak moment in which he had agreed to get them to
Carlisle's in the next valley. Thank God it was just ahead,
he reflected glumly, then swore softly under his breath.
*God*—hadn't he already heard enough about Him from that
Bible-thumping wench? Where had her God been when he'd
needed Him so long ago? Creed's lips thinned to a harsh
slash, and his dark eyes clouded with the memories that
always lurked at the fringes of his mind. Damn—would he
never forget? No, how could he? It was always fresh in his
mind, always there—that sense of utter loss and despair that
had haunted the child he had once been and never quite
escaped.

Glancing down, he saw that his knuckles had whitened
where he tightly grasped the reins, and he forced himself to
relax. That line of thought always led him into dangerous
territory. Creed shrugged it away and turned his attention
back to those struggling behind him.

Creed jerked on General's reins and pulled him aside on
the steep path overlooking the wooded valley. He had
decided to halt and wait for Hannah and the children to
catch up with him. Might as well not get too far ahead of
them; then, he'd just have to wait longer, he mused. A
caustic smile slanted his mouth as he recalled Hannah's
flashing eyes earlier that morning, when he had bluntly
informed her that he had no intention of taking them any
farther than the next settlement, whether she liked it or not.
He had to kinda admire her pluck and self-control, he
reflected, thinking about how her eyes had gone from blue
to green to smoky gray as she stared at him. But she'd not

argued—only tightened her mouth briefly, then nodded and told him that God would provide.

"Well," Creed had drawled, "if you're talkin' about the same God who provided the Blackfoot for that massacre, you might be in trouble, Miss McGuire. What if He ain't watching anymore?"

Hannah's back had straightened and fire had flashed from her eyes as she replied softly, "There is only one God, Mr. Bratton, and He also provided you to lead us away from the smoking ruins of our homes, so I think He is still watching over us."

There had been no ready answer for that last, because he certainly didn't intend to listen to her platitudes all the way to the Carlisles'. No, he'd been smart enough to keep his mouth shut. With any luck at all, he could get shed of them within the next few hours before nightfall.

Pushing back his battered felt hat, Creed squinted at the straggling line of children and the two weary horses they shared. They were sorry specimens, but better than nothing, he supposed. At least no Indian would be raiding this pitiful group for their horseflesh. He grinned at that thought, and reached back into his saddlebag for the bottle he always kept handy. He pulled the cork, then held it up. The bottle was half full—or half empty, depending on your point of view. He tilted it up and drank deeply. It burned all the way down, hot and fiery and good and numbing, just the way he liked his rotgut.

Wiping his mouth on his sleeve, Creed turned his attention back in the direction of the hill they had just climbed. Hannah and the children were still struggling up the steep incline, avoiding the large rocks and water-scoured ruts that marred the wooded path. He watched as the slender girl shepherded the children along with gentle hands. Her hair had come loose from its severe braid again and hung loose in her face. Creed spared a flash of reluctant admiration for Hannah's loveliness, in spite of the dust creasing her face and the hair in her eyes, then turned up his bottle once more. *In that direction lay madness*, he phrased silently.

"Mr. Bratton!"

Hannah's scandalized tone elicted small interest, and when Creed lowered the bottle, he was surprised by her fury.

"Yeah?" he asked warily, not quite certain what had set her off. She stood only a few feet away, her hands resting on her hips as she glared up at him disapprovingly. He hated the way she made him feel the need to defend himself. "What is it now, Miss McGuire? The woods not to your liking?"

"The woods are fine, Mr. Bratton. It's that bottle of spirits that is not to my liking," she answered promptly. "I find it distressing that you would imbibe in front of the children."

"Oh, you do, do you?" Creed snapped. "Well, I find it distressing that you would saddle a man with yourself and this passel of brats! How does that strike you, Miss McGuire?"

"That is not the issue, Mr. Bratton."

"Oh, yeah? What do you think is the issue?" he shot back with a sneer. "I know all about you missionary ladies, and how you take all the pleasure out of everything, so let me warn you now—don't try it. I'm not real understanding when it comes to that."

"There can be no real pleasure in putting a thief into your mouth to steal your wits, Mr. Bratton," Hannah returned stiffly. "Strong spirits are not meant for a man to . . ."

"Now, look here," Creed growled, leaning forward with one arm on his saddle horn and the bottle clutched tightly in his fist, "I ain't gonna say this again—I don't want to hear a word from you about what I do. Understand that? We've only got another hour or two before we reach the Carlisle spread, and I don't intend to spend it listening to you preach! If that's what you want, you can go the rest of the way by yourself..."

"Mr. Bratton," a small voice called insistently, and Creed gave the boy standing by the bay's head an impatient glance.

"Not now, boy—can't you see I'm talking?" he snapped, and turned his attenton back to Hannah's tight-lipped face. "In fact, Miss McGuire, I just might..."

"But Mr. Bratton," the boy insisted again, stepping forward to pull at Creed's trouser leg. He stared up at the mountain man with big, urgent eyes, and tugged at the fringe of buckskin again. "Mr. Bratton, I just wanna..."

Creed swore softly and straightened in the saddle as Hannah reached forward and put an arm around the boy's shoulders. She struggled for control of her temper, and managed a smile and soft voice for the boy.

"Eric, Mr. Bratton and I are having a discussion right now. Why don't you step over there with the other children? I will talk with you in a moment."

"No!" the boy disagreed, and there was a tinge of desperation in his voice that made Hannah pause and look at him more closely before her attention was once again distracted by Bratton.

"Oh, for Gawd's sake!" Creed exploded, and wheeled his bay around in disgust. "I musta been crazy to agree to take you anywhere—can't you control these kids, lady?"

Ignoring him with an effort, Hannah turned back to Eric and asked, "What is it?" at the same time she heard Creed's sharp exclamation.

"Dammit!" Creed swore, and Hannah looked up at him with a frown.

"That's what I was tryin' to tell you, Mr. Bratton!" Eric

was saying excitedly, and he pointed to the blue sky in the distance. Hannah turned to look, too.

Where the valley dipped below them, ominous black smoke clouds boiled above the tops of the trees. Creed reacted swiftly.

"Well, you shoulda spoke up, boy," he said as he jammed the whiskey bottle back into his saddlebag and grabbed his rifle. He tugged at the brim of his flat-crowned black hat and snapped out an order for Hannah and the children to hide in the bushes while he investigated. Then he nudged his horse into a trot.

Hannah did as he commanded. She had Fletcher Harris take one of the horses and three of the children with him, while she took the other horse and children with her. They hid as best as possible in the thick bushes and towering trees, crouching or standing with dry throats and hammering hearts. She glanced over at Fletcher once, and saw the youth standing with one hand over the horse's nostrils to keep it from making any noise. She motioned for Frog to do the same. The Kootenai boy nodded silently, and placed his hand over the quivering gray mare's flaring nostrils. Frog's liquid brown eyes were wide, and mirrored the fright that all of them must be feeling. Hannah forced a reassuring smile to her lips.

Sliding down with her back against the rough bark of a towering pine, Hannah knelt on the ground beside the smaller children—seven-year-old Ivy and nine-year-old Jessica. Ivy stared up at her trustingly, and Jessica's wide, direct gaze pleaded for comfort.

"It will be all right," Hannah murmured softly. "Mr. Bratton is quite skilled in these matters, and he will not allow anything to happen to us."

"But how can he stop them if there are too many?"

Jessica returned. Her blue eyes bored into Hannah. "There were too many for the others to stop."

Hannah gazed at Jessica helplessly for a moment. What could she say? It was the truth, and there was little point in lying to the children—especially Jessica, who had no patience for sugar-coated answers.

"We will just have to trust in God and Mr. Bratton," she answered wearily. "That is all we can do."

Jessican nodded, and Ivy whimpered softly. Poor, timid Ivy. She was so frail and weak. Hannah pulled her closer under her arm. It seemed so quiet in the forest. The thick underbrush and fallen leaves cushioned even the fall of a pine cone, so that it made only a muffled plop when it landed almost at Hannah's feet. She jumped slightly, startled by the prickly cone's descent, and Ivy made a slight murmur of protest. Hannah was reminded of the cellar again, when they had all crouched in fear for their lives and waited, and she closed her eyes. All these years without having to face such dangers, and now she was being gravely tested.

Lowering her head, Hannah rested her chin on hands folded across her drawn-up knees. Ivy nestled close, and Jessica—whose hair and coloring made her look almost like Hannah's younger sister—sat in a stiff knot of anxiety at her feet. Frog still stood beside the mare, and Little Bird clung close to her brother's side.

Left to her own silent thoughts, Hannah contemplated the events that had led her to this point—the outlaws, who were somehow connected with Creed Bratton; then, the marauding Blackfoot who had massacred every living thing in Jubile—and she wondered wearily if some divine judgment had not decreed such things to happen. Why else had a good man such as her father been allowed to die? Oh, if only she had more of her father's supreme faith, then she would not ask these questions like she did, would not doubt the divine

order of things. It was so hard, but she must strive to do as
Joshua McGuire would have done.

Ducking her head so that none of the children would see
the hot wash of tears stinging her eyes, Hannah buried her
face in her soiled cotton skirts. She smelled strongly of pine
tar and good earth, and she thought longingly of a tub and
large bar of soap.

"Miss Hannah!" Sweyn Johanssen whispered from his
hiding place beside Fletcher, Rebecca, and Eric. "Miss
Hannah, I t'ink I hear somet'ing . . ." Sweyn, a lanky youth
of twelve, lifted one arm and pointed down the trail.

Biting her lower lip, Hannah glanced from Sweyn's pale
face to the spot where Creed had disappeared. They had
been waiting for what seemed like an hour—could it be
Creed? Or perhaps . . . The other possibility was too horrible
to consider; her mind swerved from it.

So they waited, finally hearing the faint clop of hooves
against soft dirt. Hannah's fingers tightened on Ivy's shoulder, and the child murmured a soft protest that Hannah
never heard. She was craning her neck and gazing intently
through the thick foliage, praying silently that it would be
Creed Bratton, and not an apparition from her worst
nightmares.

Hannah's prayers were answered, for Creed rode over the
crest of the slope on his bay. Relief flooded her, leaving her
too weak to move for a moment. Creed—he looked so safe
and comforting, with his broad shoulders and air of confidence. But Hannah's relief turned to dismay as a large rock
flew through the air and struck the side of Creed's hat,
knocking it from his head and sending it spinning in the
dust.

Ducking and swinging down from his skittish bay at the
same time, Creed launched a volley of swear words that had
Fletcher and Eric exchanging glances of admiration.

"Sorry," Eric began, standing from his hiding place in the bushes. "We didn't know it was . . . hey!"

Creed's well-muscled arm shot through the bushes to jerk Eric from his hiding place in a lithe, easy motion. He hauled the struggling boy close by his shirtfront, and his face was creased in anger. He shook him, rattling Eric's teeth and making his head snap back and forth.

"Mr. Bratton!" Hannah cried in horror, rushing from the bushes to the boy's rescue. Fletcher remained cowering in the bushes, crouched down to avoid Creed's notice.

Swinging Eric across his knee, Creed's broad hand slammed down against the boy's buttocks in a stinging slap. Eric howled, his thin arms and legs flailing as Creed lifted his arm again.

"No!" Hannah cried out, grabbing at Creed's arm. He shook her loose with an impatient motion, and his hand smacked across the seat of Eric's trousers again. Hannah lunged forward and snatched at his arm, this time succeeding in slowing his blow. "Wait! He didn't know it was you!"

Pausing, Creed took a deep breath and stood Eric on his feet. The boy's face was red, and his mouth was thinned in a straight line as he promptly flung himself at Creed. His arms waved like windmills, and he was howling with humiliation and fury.

"Whoa!" Grabbing the boy again, Creed lifted him from his feet and slanted Hannah an irate glance. "Can't you do something with these brats, lady?"

Crossing her arms on her chest, she glared at him. "If you would stop and ask questions before you attack an innocent child, perhaps action would not be necessary!"

"If I always stopped to ask questions before I acted, I wouldn't have lived past twelve!" Creed snapped back. "There's not always time to be polite and congenial."

"Put me down!" Eric shouted, twisting futilely in Creed's

steely grip. Creed promptly released him, and the boy dropped to the ground with a groan.

"Brute," Hannah muttered as she bent to help him.

"Teach these brats better manners, or I'll do it for you," Creed growled, bending to lift his hat from the path.

Still kneeling beside Eric, Hannah looked up at him. His eyes were cold and dark, unreadable, and she felt a sudden qualm. "Is something the matter?" she asked after a moment of strained silence.

"Yeah, I guess you could say something is the matter," he replied. His attention was concentrated on his hat as he dusted it off with flicks of his hand; then, his gaze shifted to Hannah. It was direct, penetrating, and for a moment, his eyes held a flicker of emotion before becoming once more cold. Creed's tone was flat when he said, "They're all dead. Massacred."

"They . . . ?"

"The Carlisles. Mother, father, children, livestock—all of them dead and the house on fire." Creed's black eyes narrowed on Hannah, searching her suddenly pale face. "Are you all right?" he asked then, and she managed a nod.

"Yes . . . yes. I was just thinking of those poor people," she choked out. Her hands knotted, and she shook her head. "Did you bury them and say a prayer for their souls?"

Creed stared at her in disbelief. "Bury . . . pray . . . say, are you crazy? I got out of there as fast as I could, lady! There's time later for that sort of thing. It looked like I just missed the Blackfoot as it was, and I wasn't hankerin' to stick around!"

Hannah's knees gave way, and she plummeted abruptly to the soft dirt of the path, where she buried her face in her palms. Just the thought of the massacre, the marauding Blackfoot, and the deaths of the innocent made her weak. Where was her inner strength? she despaired silently. And the children were watching, so she had to be strong. Lifting her head, she looked up at Creed's watchful expression. He hovered over her, looking askance, as if he expected her to descend into hysterics. She smiled faintly.

"I'm all right, Mr. Bratton. It was only a moment of grief for what those poor souls must have suffered. Of course, you did the right thing in not lingering. It was very wise of you."

"I'm happy you approve," Creed said with a lift of his dark brows. A hint of sarcasm tinged his voice and the twist of his lips, but he said nothing else about it as he turned to the listening children.

Sweyn Johanssen stood with a protective arm around Ivy Ransom's shoulders, and Rebecca, Jessica, Frog, and Little Bird gazed at their elders with anxious eyes. Fletcher and Eric stood warily to one side, poised as if for immediate flight.

Noting the latter, Creed gave a nod of satisfaction. It would suit him if they all avoided him. "Look," he suggested, "why don't we make camp for the night? The Blackfoot were headed in the other direction, so we don't have to worry about anything but filling our empty bellies right now."

The children flicked a glance from Creed to Hannah, who nodded her head. "Yes, that seems to be an excellent idea, children."

Again Creed's brows lifted as he noted how the children looked to Hannah for guidance. But he shrugged indifferently and turned away, leading General through the brush at a rapid pace. The others followed him as best they could; he could hear their efforts to keep up with him as they crashed through the bushes and stepped over fallen logs. There was an occasional soft cry as if one of them had stumbled, but other than that, they tried to be as quiet as possible, and Creed smiled mirthlessly.

Maybe he'd scared them into silence. He didn't care one way or the other, just so they left him alone. It was a vague triumph of sorts, he thought, remembering how noisy and quarrelsome they had been upon first beginning this tiresome trek. Of course, Hannah's stoic quiet and uncomplaining nature might have something to do with it, but he was inclined to think his demands for silence had been more effective—that, and the way he had banged the boys' heads together.

Moving restlessly through the woods, Creed squinted up at the sky visible through the thick branches of the trees. It would soon be dark, and he had to find a safe place to camp for the night, so he turned his attention back to the surrounding area. They were well off the main path, with a steep mountain slope angling off to one side. He could smell the fresh scent of water, and feel a cool rush of air that could only mean a stream or lake nearby.

Creed searched his memory, trying to recall the terrain, but it was hard after so many years. He seemed to remember a wide lake not far ahead, which was not surprising, considering the many mountain pools that dotted the land. Creed glanced once more at the sky to study the angle of the sun. Then he changed his direction slightly, and several minutes later, stood in a small clearing overlooking a broad lake. It glittered in the late afternoon sunlight, with the reflection of the sky and surrounding trees shimmering on the surface. Twin mountain peaks with snow-capped cones rose in the distance, and the shimmering waters faithfully reflected their image in the turquoise depths. Creed gave a nod of satisfaction, and turned back to beckon to Hannah and the children.

When they emerged from the thick fringe of trees to stand

on the banks, Hannah gave Creed a sweeping glance. "This is beautiful," she said with a sigh.

"Yeah, I guess it is," he agreed shortly.

"Is this where we're camping tonight?"

"I think it's a good spot—pretty well hidden and near water. We could do worse, you know."

"Isn't there another settlement nearby?" Hannah asked.

"Not really. A man by the name of Bonner recently settled in somewhere close by, but I don't know where, and I think we're just as safe here." Dark eyes narrowed thoughtfully, and he squinted at her in the deepening gloom. "What'sa matter? Don't you trust my judgment?"

"No, no," she hurried to assure him. "That's not it at all! It's just that . . . I suppose I would feel safer in a house of some sort—that's all."

"A house? Like the one you were in when I found you? Like the house the Carlisles had?" Creed asked, then added, "It didn't seem to do any of you much good."

Hannah nodded and stared down at the ground. "You're right, of course, Mr. Bratton. I suppose I am just frightened."

Creed's mouth tightened into a grim line, but he said more softly, "You have a right to be. But don't worry—I think we've got less chance of being seen here than in a house that would be noticed by anyone passing."

Letting her gaze drift along the line of trees fringing the ice-blue waters of the lake, Hannah thought how lonely and isolated it looked. With the shadows of night slowly falling in soft drifts over the land, she was once again aware of how frail and vulnerable they really were. Her father had told her she should not be afraid of death, yet she was. She was afraid of death for herself and for the children, and she was ashamed of herself for being so cowardly.

"We will stay here, of course," she said aloud, making

her voice as strong and firm as she could. "This is a fine spot to camp for the night, Mr. Bratton."

His glance was faintly amused as he said, "I'm glad you think so."

A faint flush stained her cheeks at his dry tone, and she turned away to settle the children. Hannah was surprised at how much better she felt once Creed had started a fire. He fed it with the dry brown moss from the trees, then sent the boys to gather fallen limbs from a tamarack, so there would be no smoke to give them away.

At first Hannah felt numb. She plopped down on a fallen log, and pulled Ivy close to her. Perhaps with a cheery blaze and something to eat, she could face the world in a better frame of mind. When Creed wordlessly handed her several strips of a half-cooked grouse he had killed with a rock, she sat with a forked stick held over the flames, the meat sizzling and popping as it roasted. Occasionally, Hannah assisted the smaller children with their sticks, holding them out over the fire until the bird was scorched. Though the grouse had been fairly large, their meal had to be supplemented by lean strips of jerky from Creed's pack. Few berries were ripe enough to eat yet, but some of the boys had found some bushes heavy with chokecherries. Those were saved for last, as a treat, and Hannah doled them out sparingly.

Watching her from the shadows beyond the fire, Creed reflected on the miles ahead of them. It wasn't that he doubted his ability to get them to safety—what he doubted was that he could keep far enough away from Hannah. She was too lovely, and it had been far too long since he'd been with a fair-skinned young woman. She was tempting, with her mist of copper hair and her pale skin, her sculpted features and promising curves. Creed's eyes narrowed. Her lips were smeared red with berry juice, and they looked moist and inviting in the firelight. He wondered briefly if she knew how tempted he was, then decided she must. Women always seemed to know those things.

Creed's fingers tightened around the bottle of whiskey he held, and his brows drew down into a scowl. Dammit, he was having thoughts he shouldn't again, wondering what the lovely Hannah would look like without her high-necked gray dress and multitude of petticoats . . .

Flexing his arm, Creed drank deeply, then recorked the bottle and shoved it back into his pack. Even rye whiskey couldn't wash away that particular image. Hannah was laughing at something one of the children had said, and the firelight caught in her loose hair, glinting like red gold. Creed shoved his flat-crowned black hat to the back of his head and stared at her. His hands knotted into fists as he let his warm gaze drift over the pure lines of her face and throat, to the opened buttons of her dress, where a creamy expanse of skin gleamed. Deep shadows flirted with the light, and his imagination drew him further into the magic that was Hannah.

She looked up then to see his brooding gaze fixed on her, and the smile that haunted her lips grew still. A deep breath caught in her throat, hanging there for what seemed like hours before she expelled it in a long, sighing rush of air.

Though she wanted to lower her gaze, she couldn't. Her eyes remained on his face as if trying to commit it to memory, taking in the firm, sensual molding of his lips, the high cheekbones and thick-lashed dark eyes that seemed to hold all the mysteries of sensuality in their warm depths. Perhaps it was just the reflection of the fire that glowed in his eyes—flaring lights that caught her imagination and made her think of things she'd never dwelled upon before.

There was something so magnetic about Creed Bratton—a rough, compelling aura that drew her to him in spite of herself. She'd tried to ignore it—tried instead to concentrate upon the welfare of the children, or even the dangers that faced them—but she'd been unsuccessful. She could not forget the previous night, when his lean body had lain across hers on the dew-wet ground, pressing so closely, his iron grip on her wrists hard yet gentle at the same time. Hannah had sensed his desire then—sensed it the way an animal could sense a human presence nearby—and she'd known. She'd known in every fiber of her body that Creed wanted her, and her own traitorous pulses had responded with fiery surges that had shamed her. It had shocked her, too. Never before had she experienced such a swelling tide of reaction to a man. But there was something about this man that attracted her, and she didn't know why. What was it that was so different?

Hannah swallowed the lump in her throat and lowered her gaze back to the fire. She didn't want him to know how he affected her.

But she was too late. Creed had recognized that curious expression in her eyes, the quick dilation of her pupils, and the almost imperceptible widening of her eyes. He'd seen it before in young, inexperienced girls who were fascinated with a man. It was an easily recognizable look—haunted, sort of—with that trick of light that seemed to imbue innocent faces with an inner glow. It was a glow too easily banished with knowledge.

He stood up abruptly, and left the intimacy of the fire behind him. *Danger* shrieked at him from those heavy-lidded eyes, moist lips, and gentle curves. He'd been a man who always knew what kind of danger to court and what kind to avoid.

Hannah watched him go, disappointed, yet relieved. Her shoulders sagged and her facial muscles tightened. It was best this way. She was poised on the fringe of unexplored territory—dangerous territory—and she knew it.

Beside her, little Ivy Ransom tugged at her sleeve and whispered an urgent plea to step into the bushes, and Hannah rose. Her mind still remained on Bratton as she escorted the girls into the privacy of the thick juniper bushes. Nighttime hours brought with them all the thoughts that she managed to hold at bay during the lucid hours of daylight, and she shook her head. Satan must have first approached Eve during the twilight hours, knowing her vulnerability.

*In the clear, bright light of day, phantoms were ofttimes chased away*, she quoted to herself. Author: Joshua McGuire, who used it as a frequent reminder to his small daughter. It had been so easy to believe then, and she found it so hard now. With maturity came new fears, new devils to be fought and conquered in the nighttime shadows.

"Miss Hannah?" Jessica was saying, and Hannah looked down at her. "Miss Hannah, where will we go now?"

Hannah paused to part the thick bushes with one hand before she answered. When the girls had stepped through and they were near the fire again, Hannah replied, "I hope that we may go to Camp Coeur d'Alene, where I have a friend who will help us."

"Who?" Jessica asked, direct as always.

A faint smile touched Hannah's lips as she sat down on the fallen log again and pulled Jessica beside her. "A kind, godly man by the name of Joel Allen. I don't suppose you remember him, because it has been some time since he came to Jubile, but my father knew him well. Pastor Allen will be delighted to help us."

"Why?" Jessica asked, again abruptly direct.

Hannah touched her fingertips to Jessica's upturned face in a gentle caress. "Because he cares about us all."

"Are you going to marry him?" Jessica shot back, startling Hannah.

"*Marry* him . . . ?"

"I heard my father say once that you were s'posed to marry some preacher over to Coeur d'Alene. I remember it, 'cause I didn't want you to go, and I cried," the child said in that same disconcerting matter-of-fact tone.

"Why, Jessica, what a thing to say!"

"But are you?"

"Yeah, missionary lady," a familiar voice drawled from behind the pool of firelight, "are you?" Creed stepped from the shadows into the light. "Is that why you're so determined to go to Coeur d'Alene, maybe?"

"Don't be ridiculous!" Hannah snapped. Her fingers twisted together, and she wondered why he should make her feel so uncomfortable—almost as if she had purposely lied. "I stated my reasons for going to Coeur d'Alene, Mr. Bratton. The children must be properly cared for, and . . ."

"And this Joel Allen can do that better than anyone else in Idaho Territory, right?"

"No, I never said that. I only said that there were people in Camp Coeur d'Alene who could help them get situated in proper homes, or even with relatives."

"Oh, and this Pastor Allen never entered your mind, I suppose?" Creed jeered, not even certain why it should matter if she *was* supposed to marry some preacher.

The same thought had occurred to Hannah, and she looked up at Creed. He was silhouetted against the firelight, his back to the flames and his face in shadow.

"Why does it matter to you, Mr. Bratton?" she inquired gently.

Creed just looked at her. "It doesn't," he said in a flat tone. "But I do expect the truth."

"I told you the truth. When I said there were people there who would help the children, I was referring to Pastor

Allen. I didn't realize you would expect names and occupations, Mr. Bratton.''

"And I didn't realize you'd be a hypocrite, Miss McGuire!" he shot back.

Hannah gasped. "Hypocrite? Why, how dare you . . .''

"How do you define hypocrite, then?''

Slowly rising to her feet, Hannah met Creed's dark gaze with burning eyes. "And how do you define *Philistine*, Mr. Creed Bratton?''

He made a disgusted sound. "I shoulda known you'd come back with something biblical . . .''

"I'm amazed that you even recognize it as such!''

Creed stared at her for a long moment, and his lips quirked in an odd smile, half-mocking, partly self-mocking. "Oh, I've heard the Scriptures, Miss McGuire . . .''

Incensed that he had labeled her a hypocrite, Hannah could not stop the angry words that tumbled from her mouth. "I find it impossible to consider that you paid any attention to what you heard, then! Are you certain you heard Scriptures from the *Bible*, Mr. Bratton?''

His mouth was still slanted in that odd smile as he said softly, "Oh, I think so. You see, my father was a preacher, too . . .''

# Chapter Six

For a long moment Hannah could not speak. She only gazed at Creed with a faintly puzzled expression. The impact of his words had not yet penetrated her sluggish brain. When

she finally understood what he had said—that his father had
been a *preacher*—she shook her head in slow disbelief.

"No . . ."

"What?" he mocked, tucking his thumbs into his belt as
he cocked his head to one side and returned her stunned
gaze. "Can't you believe that such an obvious degenerate
and sinner as myself might have had better beginnings?
Have you never heard the tale of the prodigal son, or . . ."

"Cain and Abel?" Hannah finished for him. "Please,
Mr. Bratton, you must understand that I find your total
disregard for spirituality to be completely at odds with a
childhood in the church."

"Do you? Maybe I just grew up and found out that all
those nice fairy tales were just that, Miss McGuire—fairy
tales. Maybe I found out that there really is no God—not the
way you missionaries like to paint Him, or the way my
father liked to paint Him. Maybe I found out that all the
faith in the world won't do any good against murder,
neglect, and cruelty. *Faith without works is dead*, my father
used to say. Well, he didn't know how close to the truth he
was—faith *is* dead. It's all dead—cold and buried and
moldering in the grave."

Creed paused to suck in a deep, steadying breath, cursing
himself for bringing back all the old hurts, breaking open all
the unhealed wounds.

"*My* faith isn't dead, Mr. Bratton," Hannah said into the
silence. She could feel the gazes of the children, their intent
faces and the aching strain in their bodies.

"Yeah, well, see if it's still alive when I remind you of
Jubile, Miss McGuire! Are you going to try and tell me you
haven't had your doubts since yesterday? Because if you
do," he said softly, "I'll call you a liar."

Hannah's throat convulsed, and her fingers tightened into
the folds of her skirt like the claws of a drowning victim.

How had he known? How had he known how bitterly she'd questioned her God and her faith? Then it came to her in a flash of understanding—his tone when he'd talked about his father, the hard glitter in his eyes when he sneered about his father's faith, and she knew. He'd felt what she'd recently experienced, only Creed Bratton had not recovered from his disillusionment. It was still with him, still shadowing his life. Somehow, the anger and fear she'd been feeling eased. She even managed a tender smile.

"You lost them, didn't you? You lost your father and your God, and now you have no faith in anything or anyone."

Startled by her words, Creed took a step away from Hannah, realizing he'd revealed far too much of himself. "I didn't lose anything, Miss McGuire. I just discovered who I could really depend on, that's all," he said before pivoting on his heel and stalking back into the shadows.

Her voice floated behind him. *I don't think you waited long enough for help to arrive, Mr. Bratton,* Hannah called.

But as she gathered up the quiet children and began the task of getting them settled for the night, she faced her own naked doubts, stripped and left bare by Creed's harsh words. He'd come very close to the truth—very close to knowing what was in her heart and mind—and it was frightening. He must have faced those same agonies alone and they had left him bitter and disillusioned. Would it do the same to her? *Only if I let it*, Hannah told herself.

And later, clad only in her petticoat and chemise, lying curled in her blanket on the ground not far from the fire, she found she could not sleep. For a brief instant she had caught a glimpse of Creed Bratton's soul, and it had left her caught between pity and fear. She had glimpsed her own loneliness and felt her own fear when faced with his, and it was too

close for comfort. But where Creed denied his, she was
only too ready to admit hers.

Hannah rolled from her side to her back, and stared up at
the patches of indigo sky that glittered through the thick
leaves overhead. Only vague, shifting splinters of light
pierced the leafy canopy. Somewhere beyond the stars the
moon glowed silvery and bright, but here, on the ground
beneath these ancient sentinels, little light shone. The fire
had burned low, with sullen eyes winking red and gray in
the banked embers. Dim shapes fanned out from the fire—
feet placed closest to the rock-rimmed coals, heads tucked
beneath blankets as everyone slept. Everyone but Hannah.

Tucking her hand beneath her cheek, Hannah let a long
sigh escape, stirring a tendril of hair that had fallen over her
eyes. Blurry images danced before her eyes—shapes and
shadows, ghosts of the light that had long-since fled the
forest. It was quiet, with only the slight scuffling sounds of
the night creatures to add to the mysterious silence. She
could almost hear the faint slap of the water against the
grainy shoreline of the lake, and felt that if she tried hard
enough, she would hear the mist settle in cat's paws across
the water's mirror surface. Vague rustlings, the murmurs of
falling limbs, the whisper of wind through pine branches,
and the faraway cry of an owl spiraled through the night.
Hannah closed her eyes.

When she opened them again, she thought she must have
turned to face the fire by mistake. Two huge spots of light
burned not far away. But then she realized that she was still
facing in the same direction—away from the fire. A cold chill
scampered up her spine with icy fingers, and she froze in
place. She was paralyzed with fright. It was a wild animal—
it must be. And it was crouched not far away on a tree limb
that would be eye level with Creed Bratton.

It was only when she let her breath out in a small, rasping

cry that she realized she must have been holding it for several seconds. Maybe even a minute, for her cry was a weak, wheezing gasp of air that would not have frightened away a titmouse. Hannah closed her eyes again, willing the creature to go away. But when she opened them it was still there, a malevolent, steady gaze that never blinked but only remained staring, until she could feel the scream well in her throat again, this time full-bodied. It burst forth in a loud gush of air, and the creature blinked. There was a whoosh, a heavy, muffled thud that sounded like a great, rhythmic heartbeat on the wind, oddly familiar yet eerie, then Creed was at her side.

"What the hell?" he was demanding, his hand heavy against her shoulder. "Are you all right?"

She nodded, one arm lifting to point, and he turned. It was gone. She heard his impatient query, wanting to know what he was supposed to see, and she turned her head back to gaze up at him. A shaft of moonlight chose that moment to stream through the canopy overhead, striking Creed's face, and Hannah could see the genuine concern in his eyes.

"It was a wild animal," she said. "I saw it. It was over there—two huge eyes just staring at me like beacons of fire . . ." Creed interrupted her with a quick question.

"It never blinked?" And when Hannah nodded, Creed said, "I bet it was a great horned owl. Haven't you ever seen one?"

She nodded. "Yes, but always in the daylight, and it didn't seem that . . . that *malevolent*."

Creed chuckled, a warm comforting sound. "Don't worry. You're much too big to be carried off by an owl. Besides, you'd bore it to death, quoting proper verse and platitude."

"Thank you for your comfort," was Hannah's icy reply, and Creed grinned. The moonlight striking his face was

silvery, highlighting the faint sunbursts of lines at the
corners of his eyes, the shadow of his half-grown beard, and
the groove on his left cheek where he had been cut a long
time before. She wondered then what kind of life this man
had led, what had brought him to the precipice of lost faith
and then sent him careening over the edge into the abyss.
Had he suffered greatly? Had he lost his home, his family, a
wife and children, perhaps? Had he ever loved and lost, as
she had—as had most human beings at one time or another?

Hannah curled her fingers into her palm, letting her nails
dig half-moons into the flesh so that she would not yield to
temptation and reach out to stroke his face. She steadied her
voice and said, "I'm fine now, Mr. Bratton, really I am."

His hand remained on her shoulder, shifting only slightly
to move down her arm, and Hannah recalled she wore just
her petticoat and chemise beneath the rough blanket. She
swallowed hard. There was a different look to his face now,
a subtle altering of muscular structure that lent a sharper
look to his features. His ebony hair was tousled, falling over
his brow, as if he had just been awakened. Now she became
aware that he wore no shirt. His chest was bare, the smooth
muscles and pelt of hair catching her attention. Her gaze
dropped involuntarily, but he was wearing his buckskin
trousers. Her eyes flicked back up and she was mortified to
find that he had seen her quick glance, knew that she was
aware of his partial nudity. It must have amused him, for his
smile deepened, and the tiny groove on the side of his face
shifted. Hannah wished fervently that the earth would swallow her up, and somehow he seemed to know that, too.

Creed's hand on her shoulder did not move, but lay on
her silken skin like a badge of determination. He'd been
lying in his blankets thinking about her, seeing her in his
mind's eye—the tilt of her head and the bright flash of her
hair beneath the sun. Then she'd cried out, and it had

seemed as if it was preordained that he should go to her. But now that he was here, with his hand on her soft skin and the warm woman-smell of her wafting up to his nostrils, he hesitated. Too many other voices were crowding him, prodding at his brain with warnings that he could not ignore.

"What are you doing?" she whispered, her voice thick with tension.

"Nothing."

"Yes, you are! I feel it . . . some sort of trick with your eyes, or something."

He grinned. "Magic. Sleight of hand. Now-you-see-it-now-you-don't kind of thing. The pea in a nutshell."

Hannah throbbed with uncertainty, with the knowledge that his touch had somehow affected her, turning her bones to jelly and her flesh to steam.

They stared at one another in the dark quiet, both aware of age-old yearnings—the mutual attraction they shared, and the obstacles that stood between them. One of the obstacles stirred now, a sleepy voice that drifted across the space between the blankets to ask for a drink of water.

Hannah was the first to break the spell that seemed to hold them suspended in some magical world made of ice crystals and moonlight. Her voice splintered the dream into hundreds of slivers, and she felt as if she were a sleepwalker just awakening as she turned to Ivy and said, "I will get it for you, Ivy. Just a moment."

Creed watched quietly. Had she felt the same tremor when he'd touched her? The same sweeping rush that made his blood feel like liquid fire in his veins? It would be the best joke played on him in some time, he thought, and there had been far too many of fate's little jests at his expense. Creed's hand fell away from Hannah's shoulder and he sat back on his heels, his face once more cold and remote, watchful, with that familiar expression of disdain and amusement.

When Hannah turned back, she saw the change in him—saw it and recognized it and was glad. Not now. Not him. He was too strong-willed, too full of dissension. He would only confuse her with powerful emotions, leave her feeling weak. Suddenly she felt lost again—lost and alone in this grim wildwood of her worst nightmares and fairest dreams.

Something in Hannah's lost, woebegone face must have touched a reponsive chord in Creed, for he reached out to her with a smile and a soft gesture.

"It will be all right, Hannah. No harm will come to you while you're with me."

She believed him, and she returned his smile, oddly soothed. "I know. Thank you."

Hannah took Ivy her water, then returned to her blankets. She was sleepy now, and there were no more sounds or creatures in the night to keep her awake. She fell asleep almost instantly, and did not waken until dawn.

Creed was already awake and had a fire going. Coffee bubbled in a blackened pot atop a makeshift rack of wet, green wood, and he slanted Hannah a curious glance when she sat up.

"Do you like coffee?"

She nodded almost shyly, remembering the exchange between them the night before. "Yes, I do."

"There's plenty." He poured a dark curve of steaming brew into a battered tin cup and handed it to her, letting his fingers brush against her hand as he drew back. Just touching her made him catch his breath, and he scowled. He was letting the situation get to him. So he'd allowed her to see past his defense to the bitterness beneath—so what? That was no reason to go getting soft in the head over this woman, who was probably much more fervent in her duty than she would be in bed anyway.

"I buried them," he said abruptly, startling her into jerking her head up to gaze at him with wide eyes.

"What?"

"The Carlisles. I went back and buried them while it was still dark."

"Oh. Oh, I . . . I'm glad."

"Thought you might be."

Creed rose in a swift, lithe motion, standing flat-hipped and graceful, one hand coming to a restless halt on the wide leather gun belt slung low from his waist. He raked a hand through his hair and muttered something about checking on the horses as he left. Hannah stared after him, sensing his frowning embarrassment. Half-shrugging in acceptance, she glanced at the still-sleeping children curled into vulnerable knots beneath their blankets. They were so tired; she would let them sleep as long as possible. With waking came awareness, and sleep was the best cure for sorrow at times.

She sipped at the scalding, bitter coffee carefully. It warmed her in the cool morning air. A fine mist lay on the forest, shrouding the low-lying bushes, lingering in wisps as sheer as a bridal veil over lacy fingers that seemed to hold it up in delicate delight. She now heard clearly the slap of water that had seemed only an echo in the dark. She recalled that they were not that far from the banks of the lake. Hannah hummed softly to herself as she rose and pushed through the bushes to step down to the curving slope.

Perhaps after washing the sleep from her eyes, she could bring the children down to do the same. They would wake soon. Clinging fingers of bushes and vines clutched at her feet and skirts as she forced a path toward the banks. She could hear the faint rush of water, the cry of a water bird as it skimmed the surface in search of an unwary morsel for its breakfast. A branch swung forward and slapped against her cheek, stinging, and Hannah pushed at it impatiently.

She felt a certain vindication when she stepped from the thick foliage into a clearing on the edge of the lake. She had made it after all, in spite of the forest's seeming determination to keep her within its shade. But here the sun shone brightly, limning the shale peaks on the far side with gold light. Snow still frosted the highest peaks, glittering in the morning light with pink, rose, and shades of mauve. Hannah caught her breath. It was lovely.

Hannah thought suddenly of the lights that occasionally glittered in the sky on clear nights—startling lights like tiny, colorful explosions. Sometimes they would hang in draped folds, but most often they would form streamers like the spokes of a wheel, shimmering in vibrant colors of pale green, white, pink, red, purple, blue, and gray. Once the lights had lasted for several hours, weaving and shifting almost throughout the night. It had been an awe-inspiring sight—a sign from God, Joshua had said. But young Hannah had thought that the entire world was a sign from God, for wasn't his creation lovely in every aspect? There was as much beauty in the delicate budding of a spring flower as there was in the more spectacular lights, she had said to her father, and he had smiled gently.

Now Hannah smiled. She was still moved more by simple beauty than the spectacular. The determined flowering of violets in a late-winter snowbank had often inspired her.

Still smiling, she bent to remove her shoes and peel down her stockings. She would wade into the shallows to wash her face. Hannah wiggled her toes, relishing the temporary freedom from her confining shoes. A moment later found her gingerly balanced on a large rock that jutted into the bubbling surface. She sat down and stuck her feet into the water, then shivered with pleasure at the icy lap around her ankles. It was deliciously cold against feet tired of walking.

A snap of brush behind her gained Hannah's instant attention, and her head swiveled around to see Creed approaching. Relief flooded through her, and she realized that she should have thought to tell him where she was going—a fact he began to point out to her in an irate tone.

"You know, it wouldn't have taken too much time or thought to let me know you intended to explore on your own, lady..."

"Hannah," she corrected flatly.

"...and if anything had happened to you," he continued with an angry glare, "what would those kids have done?"

Hannah pushed her skirts down to cover her bare legs before she answered, an act that drew Creed's notice. His dark eyes narrowed, and she flushed. She didn't know whether to be more embarrassed because he'd seen so much of her bare legs, or because she had not thought to inform him of her destination. The latter won out, and her chin lifted slightly as she met his gaze.

"I only came to wash my face and feet," she began in defense—a defense he immediately slashed to ribbons.

"Well, you might have ended up on some Indian buck's pony, Miss McGuire! Or maybe even with those guys I've been trailing—or was trailing, until I got impressed into your service, that is. Did you ever stop to think about that?"

"No," she said honestly, defusing some of his anger. "I am sorry, but that did not occur to me. It should have, I know, but it didn't."

Creed took a deep breath, still staring at Hannah. He could admit to himself that he was more distracted by the sight of her bare legs than he'd been angry at her wandering off by herself. "That was a damn fool thing to do," he ended in a low growl.

"You're right. I apologize."

Creed stood awkwardly now, his hands resting on his hips, his dark felt hat pushed to the back of his head. For some reason Hannah recalled his bare chest from the night before, and the dark mat of curls that furred his muscles. Now his chest was decently covered, with his buckskin shirt partly unlaced, but still covering him. He was staring at her with a fathomless gaze, eyes black as night and just as concealing, and she looked away.

"Are the children still asleep?" she asked as she reached to retrieve her shoes and stockings.

"No. The tall, skinny kid . . ."

"Sweyn?"

"Yeah, I think so—the Swedish kid. Anyway, he's got the kids up and dressed, and they're rolling up their blankets. I left him in charge."

"Sweyn's a good manager," Hannah observed. She wondered if she should attempt to put on her stockings with him standing there, then decided against it. She would just put her feet in her shoes instead of risking another unseemly display of leg.

Rising, Hannah smoothed down her skirts and smiled at Creed, completely disarming him. He made an impatient gesture with his hands. "Well—do you think you can follow me back now?" he asked, then turned to stomp back to the bushes on the shoreline.

Left to follow, Hannah began to wish she had put her stockings on as the abrasive leather shoes rubbed against her wet feet, but she dared not ask Bratton to pause so that she might. His mood wasn't conducive to patience.

Ducking the tree limb that Creed did not bother to hold for her, Hannah wondered why he had been pursuing a band of outlaws. He'd only mentioned it once, and had not elaborated, so she decided to ask.

"Why are you pursuing those men, Mr. Bratton?" She let the tree limb swing past in a rustling whoosh, then bumped to a halt against Creed's solid frame.

He had stopped and turned to look at her. "What?"

"The men," she began hesitantly, taken aback by his fierce scowl. "The men you said you were following—why are you pursuing them?"

"For money. What business is it of yours?" he wanted to know.

"Why, be . . . because just a moment ago you said they might have captured me," she blurted, hating the way he made her stammer, "and I imagine that they must be dangerous men for you to worry about such a thing happening."

Creed stared at her narrowly. "They are dangerous. Those men would just as soon slit your throat and all the kids' throats, too."

Nodding, Hannah cudgeled her rebellious tongue into submission and said without a single stammer, "I thought they must be rather like the men who stopped in Jubile."

"What men?"

"Why, the three outlaws who came for food . . ."

Crossing the narrow space between them, Creed snapped, "Who were they? What'd they look like? Did they say where they were headed?"

He looked suddenly as dangerous as those outlaws had been, and just as remorseless as he towered over her, glaring down at her and repeating his questions when she remained frozen in awful silence. Why must he feel it necessary to loom over her so nastily? she wondered with a vague tremor.

Hannah gathered the chilling morsels of fear that were

settling into her lungs and injected them into her voice as
best she could, saying icily, "The leader was a tall, bony
man, with very sharp features, and another man had a scar
across his face like this . . ." She drew one finger from her
right eyebrow to the lower left corner of her jaw, and saw
Creed's expression tighten. "And the third man was young,
almost innocent in appearance, though he was with those
men. Is that what you wanted to know, Mr. Bratton?"

Instead of answering, Creed asked, "Did they mention
their names or where they were going?"

Hannah cast wildly about her fogged brain for a reason
not to tell him what he wanted to know, but she could not
come up with one. They were innocent enough questions, if
a bit short and demanding. But why would he want to know
the identities of such dangerous men if he was not acquainted
with them? And how acquainted was he?

It didn't seem unreasonable to ask him the motive for his
avid interest, so she did. Unfortunately, Creed did not share
her viewpoint.

"Just answer the questions, Miss McGuire! You don't
need to know why I want answers." When she paused,
gazing up at him with a furrowed brow and doubt clouding
her eyes, he pressed his point. "I'll be shed of you soon,
anyway. It can't make the least bit of difference to you
where I'm going or what my business is. But it can matter if
I become a bit put out with you and refuse to take you any
farther, now, can't it?"

"In that case, I think I can remember. Let's see—there
was Stillman, Roper, and, mmm . . ."

"Truett?" Creed finished, and Hannah nodded.

"Yes, that was it. Truett. He was the young one."

"Where were they headed, Hannah?"

Startled by his use of her given name, Hannah's eyes flew
to Creed's face, but he was obviously intent on her reply,

instead of his own words. She floundered in a sea of uncertainty, trying to recall their destination, knowing he would not believe her if she said she didn't know. But it eluded her efforts and she sighed. "Why, I'm not sure. I heard them s-s-say, but I can't recall . . ."

His hands flashed out to grasp her shoulders, and he gave her such a rough shake that she dropped her stockings to the ground. "Remember, dammit!" he grated between clenched teeth. "It's important!"

An angry gasp hissed into the air as she knocked his hands away, forgetting her vow to control her temper as she flared, "Do not *dare* touch me in anger!"

After his initial surprise at first his own actions, then Hannah's reaction, Creed grinned. "You yowl just like a mountain cat, Miss McGuire!"

"Do I? Then perhaps it's best that you remember all cats have claws, Mr. Bratton." Her heart was pounding and her teeth were chattering like the lid on a boiling pot, but she refused to back down—especially in light of his amused smile.

"Yeah, maybe I better." There was a brief pause while Creed debated whether he should attempt to force an answer; then he thought better of it and tried another tack. "It might be a good idea if you could remember where they were headed, you know. Nate Stillman is not a good man to stumble across in the dark. And he knows I'm after him, so he might just be very nasty about it."

"I'll do my best to remember, but all your threats won't coax an answer if I just can't recall it," Hannah said. Ignoring the thumping of her heart and the erratic pop of air that left her lungs starved, she bent to pick her stockings up from the ground. They were damp and coated with leaves. "Oh, dear," she murmured in dismay, "my only pair."

"A band of marauding Blackfoot and three dangerous

outlaws on the loose, and you're worried about a pair of stockings?'' Creed inquired with politely lifted eyebrows.

"Well, *this* is something I can handle. The outlaws and Blackfoot are not," Hannah pointed out.

"True." Hooking his thumbs in his belt. Creed looked down at her for a long moment. He still regretted the necessity of taking them to safety instead of pursuing Nate Stillman, but somehow he knew he could have done no less. A man had to recognize what was decent in life, had to know when to choose between what he wanted to do and what was right. Maybe that was what being a man meant. And sometimes—maybe—there were compensations for doing the right thing. Compensations like Hannah. She was pretty, spirited, and totally innocent of her own desirability and sensuality. It lay just beneath the surface, waiting to be awakened by the right touch, the right man. He wasn't that man. Hannah was trusting, filled to overflowing with fervent dedication to the more spiritual nature of man, and he was too cynical, too world-wise to believe in miracles. There were no miracles, and, he suspected, no God. How could there be? No merciful God would allow the things he had seen . . .

So Creed just shrugged and pivoted on his heel to lead the way back to camp, saying none of the words that burned on his tongue to be spoken. He would trust only in himself, and at least then he would know where he stood.

The sun shone brightly that day as they followed the ancient trail, and the thick forest thinned to rocky ground. It was almost pleasant, and if not for the still stark memories of what had happened in Jubile, it might have been any leisurely outing. The children were more rested now, and they chattered quietly among themselves as they walked.

Hannah, with Ivy on one side and Rebecca on the other, did her best to assure them about the future.

"Camp Coeur d'Alene is a thriving little town," she said. "It boasts a chapel and several stores, and there is a real schoolhouse there, too. It's at the junction where the lake flows into the Spokane River, and they've just completed the Mullan Road that goes all the way to—to Fort Benton in Montana." Fort Benton! That was it—that was the destination she had not been able to remember. Hannah glanced quickly toward Creed. He was riding several yards ahead of them, refusing to acknowledge their existence most of the time, and absolutely refusing to be civil.

"Will you still be our teacher, Miss Hannah?" Rebecca was asking. Liquid hazel eyes quivered with shadows of doubt and hope as she gazed at Hannah.

"No, they already have a teacher," Hannah replied in a gentle tone. "But she is very nice, I am sure."

"But I want you," Ivy said in a small voice. "I won't like any other teacher."

"Neither will I!" Fletcher Harris said.

"Or me," Eric added.

Hannah looked at the rebellious faces and smiled. "You will change your minds once we get there."

Tree branches snapped back, swishing across the path as Creed's horse brushed past, and she felt a flash of irritation. How could he be so callous? Did the man have no sympathy for children, or her? She knew what it was. He was still unreconciled to the hard fact that he must escort them to Camp Coeur d'Alene, though Hannah knew of no other place for them to go. The small settlement may not have been the closest, but it was the most feasible location. She shrugged helplessly. She would just have to take each moment as it came, and accept what she could not change.

Sucking in a deep breath, Hannah tilted her face up to the

sky. After the chilly night, it seemed impossible that it could be this fair. Warm sunlight caressed her cheeks, and she smiled. After the darkest of nights came daylight, renewing one's faith in God and nature.

"Daydreaming, Miss McGuire?" came a softly mocking voice, interrupting Hannah's reverie and making her stumble over a rut in the trail. Creed had reined his bay back to talk to her, and was regarding her with that familiar and infuriating smile. It reeked of arrogance.

"Yes," she answered when she had recovered her balance, "I was. Don't you ever daydream, Mr. Bratton?"

"Dreams are for the dead, Miss McGuire."

"Do you really think so? Perhaps you're right, or perhaps dreams are only for those whose faith is still alive."

"You have an answer for everything, haven't you?" Creed shot back.

"As a matter of fact—yes. Did I tell you that the men you were following said they were going to Fort Benton?" Hannah added innocently.

"Fort Benton? In Montana?"

"Is there another?"

"Probably, but I've got a hunch that's where they're going. Dammit!" Creed smacked a fist into his open palm and swore again, this time under his breath. "I never shoulda stopped trackin'... Look, do you think you could follow this path on to Coeur d'Alene without me?"

Hannah shook her head. "No, I don't. I mean, I could follow the path, such as it is, but what about our safety? Would you leave us your weapons?"

He gazed at her for a long minute. "Yeah, that's what I thought. How about seeing if you could hurry it up a bit? I've got a long way to go, and a hard way to get there. I don't have time to be a wet nurse."

Hannah bit back the hasty words on the tip of her tongue.

Instead, she smiled sweetly and said, "We'll try, Mr. Bratton. That's all I can promise."

"It figures," he muttered.

The big bay pranced across the trail just ahead of them, his hide gleaming in the sunlight, and Hannah admired both horse and rider. Creed sat his horse easily, with that natural grace and balance that is given to only a few. His buckskin-clad thighs were lean and taut as he gripped General's sides. Hannah's gaze slid to the decorated knife sheath strapped to Creed's thigh. She wanted to say something—anything—that would drag the conversation away from a possible argument, so she said the first thing that came to mind.

"Is that Indian?" she asked in the sudden silence after his last rejoinder, and Creed followed her gaze to his leather knife sheath. Beads and quills formed a rough picture of what looked to be a tiny sun and a buffalo. The wicked blade of the long steel knife shot back splinters of light in tiny star bursts.

"Very observant of you to notice, Miss McGuire," he said sardonically. "What gave it away—the quills and beads? The buffalo-sinew threading?"

"No, anyone can use those. It's the design. Isn't that Shoshoni?"

This time Creed was faintly impressed by her recognition, and he nodded. "Yeah. How'd you know that?"

"My father converted a Shoshoni warrior once, and he came to stay with us for a short time several winters ago. He told me a lot about Shoshoni customs and traditions—among them, the use of designs to tell a story."

"Really?" Creed let his amusement tinge his voice as he said, "Do go on, Miss McGuire."

Irritated by his condescension, Hannah managed to keep her tone neutral as she said, "The design on your knife sheath depicts an Indian sunflower. Only people who have good hearts and a clean spirit can see those special Indian plants. The buffalo denotes plenty. Therefore, the pictures mean that you are a good man who shall always have food.''

"Hogwash," Creed observed.

"Perhaps, but I think . . ."

"Maybe the trouble with you, Miss Holier-than-thou-Hannah, is that you *think* too damned much!"

"Which is infinitely better than not thinking at all, Mr. Bratton!"

They glared at one another, oblivious of the stares of the children and the bright sun beating down on their heads; oblivious to the brisk wind that scoured the ridges and steep slopes—oblivious to everyhing but the burn of one another's eyes. There was more than animosity between them, Hannah realized—much more—and it made her heart lurch and her tongue cleave to the roof of her mouth. If only they could reach Camp Coeur d'Alene before too much was said or done . . .

"He's not very nice, is he?" Eric remarked as Creed jerked his bay's head around and nudged him into a brisk trot.

"I think he's mean," Rebecca said darkly, and Ivy tucked her hand into the curve of Hannah's arm and elbow as if Creed would turn on them at any moment.

"Will he leave us, Miss Hannah?" Ivy wanted to know.

Hannah did not answer for a moment, then she said, "Well, if he does, we can go on, children. Trust in God to provide for us."

"What if God doesn't want to provide?" Little Bird put in. Her normally stoic features were strained, and even Frog seemed ill at ease. He stood awkwardly beside the horse, his deep, dark eyes fixed on Hannah as he waited for her answer.

Glancing from the Indian children to Fletcher, then Sweyn

and Jessica, Hannah took a deep breath. Reality was too close to attempt an easy answer, and they deserved the truth, she decided.

"Children, we must accept whatever is in store for us. It may not be what we would wish, but we must be brave and constant. I do not think Mr. Bratton will abandon us, but even if he does, we shall persevere."

"What does that mean?" Eric Ransom asked, his clear brow furrowed in confusion.

"Persevere? It means that it spite of the odds and trials we face, we do not falter. We go on. Now do you understand?"

Eric nodded. "Yes. But does that mean that Mr. Bratton won't help us anymore?"

Sighing, Hannah repeated. "I do not think he will abandon us," even though she held little faith in her own words. Creed had made no secret of the fact that he disliked escorting them. He only did it because of some long-buried sense of duty, and he resented every moment of his time. It was obvious he was impatient to be in pursuit of the three outlaws he had come to Idaho Territory to find, and Hannah still did not know why he was chasing them, or even if he was one of them. He'd said he was following them for money—his share of stolen loot, perhaps?

Maybe he *was* one of them. Maybe he was supposed to meet Nate Stillman and the others, but had lost their trail. It was entirely possible, wasn't it? And that could explain his irritation at having missed them. This thought struck Hannah with all the force of a hammer forged from ice, leaving her to shiver in the sunlight.

# Chapter Seven

The little caravan wound up the wooded path, climbing steep grades and descending into shallow valleys. Towering jack pines and moss-draped cedar limbs shaded the path with dark shadows, and the wind was brisk. Sunlight filtered through in wavering patches, marking the passage of the hours.

Dust rose around them as the larger children plodded wearily beside the horses, while the smaller ones rode. Walking beside the dun mare, Hannah considered asking Creed to pause and rest for a time. Her calves and thighs ached, and she thought she felt blisters rising on the soles of her feet. Though it was cool from the winds blowing into the valley, the brisk pace he insisted upon kept her warm, and she drew in another long breath of air as they began climbing another steep slope. She thanked God they were still in the valley, for she didn't think she or the children could manage climbing a mountain path.

When they stopped for a rest beside the clear, chattering waters of a mountain creek gushing down through the rocks and pines, Creed rode ahead. Too tired to even wonder where he was going, Hannah concentrated on refreshing her blistered feet in the icy creek. She sat on the damp ground with her legs dangling over the banks, her shoes and stockings next to her. He'd been acting strange all day, she mused as she paddled in the water. She'd seen him staring at the ground as they rode along, pausing to dismount and look at broken tree limbs and overturned rocks. What did he think he was going to find? Not more Indians, she hoped.

Pressing her hands to the small of her back, Hannah stretched to loosen her tightened muscles. Sunlight glittered in shards of broken prisms that swirled along with the current, and she watched idly as a leaf spun in the tiny eddies.

Then Creed was kneeling beside her, his voice low and tight, and his face shadowed by the low brim of his hat. Startled by his sudden appearance out of nowhere, Hannah drew back with a gasp and he smiled.

"Jumpy, aren't ya? Well, you should be." He nodded his head in the direction of the trail they were following. "You know, that's an old Indian trail. It's been here for years, with a few changes here and there, improvements and shortcuts, changes made by man or nature . . ."

"What is your point, Mr. Bratton?" Hannah interrupted as she pushed her skirts down to cover her bare legs.

"My point is, lots of folks travel this trail, Miss McGuire. Some of 'em are nice—some ain't." He squinted at her, plucking a stem of grass and sticking it between his teeth. "I've been trailing some guys who fall into the last category, and if I'm not mistaken, they're not far ahead of us. Now, that leaves me with a couple of choices: I can forget about you and these kids and go after 'em—maybe get them before they get me—or I can forget about them and keep playin' nursemaid."

"So, what do you intend to do?" Hannah asked bluntly. Her gaze fastened on his face, on the tanned features and black, velvety eyes that were regarding her shrewdly. "I take it you have already made up your mind, and I am only being consulted for the sake of courtesy?"

He grinned. "You're not nearly as dumb as you look, Miss McGuire . . ."

"Am I supposed to say thank you?" she snapped back.

"Naw, that's not necessary." Creed spit out the grass stem and gazed at the frayed end thoughtfully. "Just stay on the main trail. I'll circle back and check on you when I can . . ."

"Don't do us any favors!"

"Don't get touchy."

"You're abandoning a woman and eight helpless children, and you tell me not to get touchy?" Hannah burst out. Her fingers wadded in the folds of her skirt as she glared at him.

"Helpless?" Creed sliced a glance toward the boys on the banks, his brows lifting dubiously. Fletcher, Eric, and Frog were balanced on a fallen log, spearing passing fish with sharpened sticks. "I would hardly call a single one of these kids *helpless*. Dangerous, maybe, but not helpless."

"They are just children, Mr. Bratton."

"And you're getting away from the subject, Miss McGuire. I'll only be gone a day or two if I'm unlucky, and if I do catch them . . ."

"We're on our own?" she finished for him, unable to keep the tremor from her voice.

"I'll send somebody back for you."

"How generous!"

Creed straightened, his lean frame casting a long shadow over her as she sat on the banks. Feeling at a disadvantage with him looming over her like the wrath of God, Hannah stumbled to her feet and stood with mud squishing between her bare toes, meeting Creed's sharp gaze.

"Don't try and make me feel guilty," he warned in a tight voice. "You knew I didn't want to guide you to the next tree stump, much less ninety miles away!"

Hannah gazed at him, struggling with the sudden terror that washed through her at the thought of being alone on the trail. "Why do you do what you do?" she asked softly, her eyes fixed on his face as she tried to understand. "Why must you hunt men like they were animals?"

"Because I'm good at it," he answered. "It's what I do best."

"But why can't you do something decent—something less dangerous?"

"Oh, for the love of—Look, it's what I *do*, all right? And it's profitable. I make no excuses for it."

"I see."

"No, you don't see, but that doesn't matter. I'm going to ride ahead. I'll circle back and check on you, leave you a rifle and supplies—it's not like you'll be alone. I didn't want to take you this far," he repeated again, a trace of impatience in his voice when she just gazed at him with wide, scared eyes.

"Yes, I know," Hannah admitted quietly. "And I am grateful you have been kind enough to escort us this far." She gave a soft sigh, fighting back the single tear in the corner of one eye.

Creed's eyes narrowed in sudden suspicion. "Oh no, you don't. Go ahead and get mad. Yell and shout and accuse me of being whatever you want, but don't start that damned silent crying . . ."

Hannah hiccoughed. "I'm not," she defended herself.

"Good, because it won't work."

"Oh, I never thought it would!" she flared, suddenly angry in spite of her better judgment—in spite of her efforts to recall suitable Scripture that would suffice on such an occasion. But what could one quote to a man who was blithely riding away and leaving her alone on a trail rife with dangerous animals and men? Nothing came to mind—no words of acceptance, or an inclination to turn the other cheek. All Hannah felt was a surge of anger that made her hands curl into fists and her body vibrate. "I never thought you would be susceptible to feminine frailty or fears, Mr. Bratton, I assure you!" she grated.

Shrugging, Creed swept her with a narrowed gaze, then pivoted on his heel and strode to his horse. "You can manage," he said over his shoulder. "I've left you with enough fresh game for a few days. And those boys can fish if they put their minds to it. Here." He flung her a rifle. "Shoot whoever you have to."

Catching the rifle in a reflex motion, Hannah gazed down at the gleaming metal and wood, feeling the weight of it in her hands. Could she actually shoot someone? It was doubtful. Not Hannah Elizabeth McGuire, whose worst moment until lately had been when the Simpson baby had had a chest cold and she'd helped nurse the poor little thing until it died. But even that had been remote, without personal danger or responsibility. Actually shooting another human being was not in her realm of experience.

Hannah looked up at Creed's dark, mocking face. "How do you know I won't shoot *you*?" she asked boldly.

He grinned. "Instinct. Your style leans more toward tree limbs and wooden bowls."

"Traitor. Deserter. Renegade. You *should* be shot."

"Probably. And I probably will be, too. But you won't do it." He swung onto his horse and brushed his fingertips against the brim of his hat in a mocking salute. "Until later, sweetheart."

Hannah watched him ride away, dull misery seeping into her bones, making her feel sick. She was aware of the silent, intent stares of the children, and knew she could not give in to the wash of nausea that made her stomach churn and her knees weak. Sucking in a deep, steadying breath of air, she turned to them and said firmly, "Well, we shall go on now, single file, Sweyn at the head and me at the rear. Step quickly now, and Fletcher, you and Eric each take up a pack. Pull your blankets around you so they won't snag on the bushes, children."

They marched quietly, and the path, which had been, if not friendly, at least not hostile, now seemed darker, more sinister, with the sun unable to penetrate the thick leaves overhead. Bushes rustled ominously, and there were strange coughs and moans, distant howls that suddenly sounded too close.

Dragging her blanket more snugly around her shoulders for warmth and as a flimsy barrier against danger, Hannah tried not to let the children see her fear. Time limped slowly past, the hours filled with long-submerged memories that now surfaced like dragons waiting to be fed. They gnawed at her soul, biting off chunks at will, it seemed, curdling her blood and chilling her even more than the whip of the wind coiling around her legs.

What would she do if they were suddenly confronted with danger? With a bear, or worse? Could she shoot the rifle Creed had left? It was doubtful. The only targets in her experience were wooden fence posts or broken bottles. Joshua had not worried overmuch about her ability to fire ordnance. He had taught her only the simplest rules of a rifle—how to load and aim, taking into account the wind and elevation. It was common sense to learn to shoot, but not necessary, he'd said. Hannah's throat tightened. How wrong Joshua McGuire had been . . .

Dark shadows drifted over the land in shades of purple and mauve, lovely to look at but darkly frightening. Hannah chose a camp site just off the trail—a wooded glen with an outcropping of rocks. Afraid to start a fire for fear of attracting dangerous beasts—human or animal—she fed the children dried fruit and jerky Creed had left. They drank water from leather pouches, grimacing at the flat, stale taste, then curled up to sleep in the blankets they wore as coats during the daylight hours. Hannah lay with the rifle clutched grimly across her chest, one finger curled into the trigger guard, just in case . . .

*In case of what—bears, wolves, or outlaws? What would I do? What could I do?*

Finally, just hours before daylight, when the forest lay still and quiet at last, with no alien sounds to startle her into sitting up and looking around, Hannah fell into a deep, dreamless sleep.

Dreamless, that is, except for the wavering image of Creed Bratton behind her closed lids. He lingered, dark and mocking and deceitfully handsome. He seemed so real that when she awoke, she thought he was nearby.

"Creed?" she called softly, her voice still sounding much too loud in the dark, smothering silence. "Mr. Bratton?"

But there was no answer, unless one counted the muffled call of an early morning bird in search of breakfast. Her heart pounded, and Hannah swallowed the surge of fear that rose in her throat. Nothing. Only the slight crack of twigs and murmur of wind through the tree branches broke the air. She shivered. It had been a dream, a shifting kaleidoscope of vague images—Creed, lying in a ditch with his handgun leveled at a dark, burly shape, his hat pulled low over his eyes as he took careful aim. The scene had wheeled in slow motion, showing Creed ducking as a shower of bullets rained down on him. Hannah sat up and peered through the inky shadows as she pulled her blanket around her shoulders and held the old rifle more tightly. Where was he?

At that particular moment, Creed was very much as Hannah had seen him in her dream—a trick of time and space that doesn't often occur. He lay belly-down on a rocky crag, waiting for it to grow light enough to throw a hail of lead down on Nate Stillman and his companions. It was too dark to see, too risky to chance missing them. The outlaws lay next to a dying campfire, heads tucked into their chests and hats pulled low over their eyes, seemingly unaware of any interlopers. Creed waited.

When the first pale fingers of dawn finally broke the horizon and lightened the sky, Creed took careful aim and shattered the silence and their sleep with a fusillade of bullets. This was the second time luck was against him. One bullet caught Stillman in the leg, another passed harmlessly through Roper's coat and lodged in the saddle he was using as a pillow. Truett was winged in his right arm. The coffeepot atop the fire pinged loudly and sprouted streams of cold brew onto still-hot ashes, smoke hissing in curling streams. Frightened horses screamed shrilly and lunged against the ropes tying them to trees, nostrils flaring, eyes gleaming white and wide in the dark. The men scrambled for safety behind a pile of rocks, cursing and tugging pistols from holsters as they ducked and ran.

"Goddammit!" Stillman swore, clutching his leg and wincing at the fiery pain. "Who in the hell . . . ?"

"Bratton!" Roper snapped, rolling to a scrunching halt behind the same rock. "Only one it could be."

A hot shower of rock splinters grazed his cheek as a whining bullet smacked against the surface and ricocheted, and Roper added his curses to Stillman's. They lay against the rough scrape of the rock, straining to see through the murky gloom.

"Bushwhacker!" Truett moaned from a short distance away, nursing his injured arm. His pale, boyish face was creased into a grimace of pain, and the blood dripped steadily from the small, puckered hole in his flesh. His shirt sleeve was rapidly soaked in spreading stains, and he cradled his arm gently, glancing across the small area separating him from Stillman and Roper. "I'm hit," he said through the spatter of bullets.

"So am I!" Stillman shot back.

"So, what do we do now?" Roper put in, squinting through the acrid smoke and watching for the telltale spurt of orange flame that would give away Bratton's position. "We can stop and worry about scratches later. Right now, I'm more worried about Creed Bratton. The man's too good a shot, and I ain't got no hankerin' to be plugged through the gullet while I sit here frettin' about minor wounds."

"You call my gun arm minor?" Hall Truett demanded. "It ain't—but I kin still shoot better'n you, Roper!"

"Then, why don't you just put one through Bratton's head?" the outlaw asked with a sneer.

"Why don't we quit arguin' amongst ourselves and see to Bratton?" Stillman rasped.

Creed was echoing their curses, slamming more bullets into the chamber of his Colt .44 and hoping the damn thing didn't misfire. Unless carefully loaded, it was likely to set off the other cartridges in the chamber, and he didn't have time to check. He slid his Henry .44 up, laying the rifle atop the rock and pumping the lever. Only in an emergency would he use his revolver. The rifle was far more accurate at long range, and he had his shotgun for close range. But the element of surprise was gone now, and Creed's chances for success were narrowing with every shot he threw at them. He was stalemated, lying in a narrow depression atop a rocky crest and firing off an occasional shot—just enough to pin them down, but not enough to outmaneuver them.

Frustrated, but recognizing the futility of remaining until his ammunition ran out or one of them succeeded in circling behind him, Creed decided to retreat. There would be another time, another place. He hadn't done too badly. At least this time he'd managed to wound one of them, possibly two, judging from the hoarse cries of pain he'd heard. And he'd been wondering all night how Hannah was doing—if she was all right, and if she had managed to get herself lost, or worse.

He squeezed off another shot to keep curious heads down and give them something to think about, then sprinkled a thin trail of gunpowder atop the rock. At three intervals he piled a few percussion caps that would explode when the fire reached them. That should keep them busy and thinking he was still up there for a few more minutes, he reasoned. Backing down from his vantage point, Creed struck a match and lit the gunpowder, then slid the rest of the way to the gully where he'd hidden his horse.

The full flush of daylight brightened the trail and banished the fears the dark had provoked. After a sparse breakfast of cold corn cakes and tough jerky, Hannah led the sleepy-eyed children up the narrow, winding trail again. It was warmer this morning, and the day promised to be fair. She began to sing, partly to ease the children and partly to ease her own strain, her clear, melodic voice lifting in a song that had been her father's favorite. It was a song he had composed— one of promise and faith and love.

The words rang in the air, clear and sweet, hanging as gently as a summer breeze. Hannah glanced down at the path to avoid the network of tree roots that snaked across, still singing, and when she glanced back up the words froze in her throat.

A horseman blocked the trail, his shape vague at first. She automatically swung the rifle up. The horseman's amused, "Don't shoot, Hannah," made her knees weak with relief.

He was sitting easily, one arm resting across his saddle horn and the other pushing back his hat.

"And don't stop singin' on my account," Creed drawled when she jerked to a stop and stared at him. "I kinda liked it."

"Did you?" she managed to say, the words choking past the lump in her throat. "I'm glad. It was a favorite of my father's."

His brows lifted. "It figures."

"You must have been unlucky," she said then, ignoring his mocking words and grin. "You left intent upon murder and mayhem. Couldn't you find your victims?"

"I found 'em." There was a creak of saddle leather as his gaze flicked over the group, then he added curtly, "You can lower the rifle now. I said I would take you to Camp Coeur d'Alene, and I will. Only this time, try to keep up."

Creed swung his horse's head around, and nudged him into a brisk trot up the trail. Hannah sagged with relief and lowered the rifle, gazing after him with a smile curving her mouth. It didn't really matter why he had come back to guide them—the main thing was that he had. Even his abrupt mood changes and rudeness didn't matter, at the moment.

They trudged along for several miles, with the wind whipping at their clothes and the sun making the weather bearable. Dust lay in a thick haze over the trail until a light rain began to sprinkle, spattering through the thick leaves of the trees overhead. The sun still shone behind them, gilding the treetops with a gauzy yellow light.

"It will probably snow soon," Hannah muttered, tugging her blanket shawl more tightly around her shoulders. "This weather is so erratic . . ."

"I like it," Eric Ransom piped, steeping up beside her

and tucking his hand into Hannah's. "Where else does it rain and have sunshine at the same time?"

She ruffled his hair affectionately. "You're just easy to please," she teased him.

Casting a dark look ahead of them, Eric said, "Yeah, but *he* ain't!"

"Isn't," Hannah corrected with a sigh. "At least he came back to help us, Eric. You must remember that Mr. Bratton has other things he must do."

"Like kill outlaws!" Fletcher Harris said, bending in a half-crouch and spraying imaginary outlaws with fantasy bullets. "Kapow, kapow, kapow!"

"Maybe he's an outlaw, too," Jessica Gray said. "I think he is. He looks like one, with that long hair and those old buckskins he wears. And he has all those guns!"

"I'm glad he has guns," Ivy defended him, her small, heart-shaped face lifting anxiously. "If he didn't, who would protect us?"

"I could!" Sweyn put in. "If I had a gun," he added when they all looked at him. His pale, thin face sharpened into a sheepish grin, and he shrugged.

Frog, normally quiet and reserved, said softly, "He is a dangerous man. I have seen his kind before, and it is good that he is our friend."

"Yes," Hannah murmured, watching as Creed circled back to see what was keeping them. "I agree, Frog."

"Miss Hannah," Rebecca said softly, and she turned to look at the girl's flushed face. "Miss Hannah, how long before we get to the Camp Coeur d'Alene settlement?"

Overhearing Rebecca's question as he reined his mount close, Creed gave a harsh snort. "Another two, three days at this pace! If you'd walk instead of talk, we'd get there a lot quicker."

Hannah put an arm around Rebecca's shoulders and gave

her a brief squeeze before slanting a dark glance at Creed. "It's hardly necessary to rebuke the child for asking the question that is on all our minds, Mr. Bratton. For children who are unaccustomed to so much walking they are doing quite well."

Creed glared at her from beneath the felt brim of his hat, and she could feel his dark eyes burning into her. She kept her eyes on his shadowed face, refusing to look away, until finally he shrugged and left them behind.

"He hates us," Rebecca said dully, pushing at the reddish strand of hair that hung in her eyes. It curled damply in spite of the cool wind, and her face was flushed a rosy color. Hannah reached out, and was startled at the heat beneath her hand.

"No, I don't think he hates us," Hannah replied, frowning as she tested the girl's forehead for fever. Rebecca was hot, and her eyes looked feverish. "Do you feel unwell, Rebecca?"

The girl shook her head. "No, only tired. I'm all right, really I am."

Reluctantly, Hannah took her palm away. "If you begin to feel ill, you must tell me at once, Rebecca."

"I will," the girl promised, then sliced a glance at Creed's retreating back. "Why is he guiding us if he hates it so, Miss Hannah? Why doesn't he just go ahead and abandon us and get it over with?" she burst out. "I keep thinking that we'll wake up one morning and he'll be gone for good."

"Rebecca, even if he did—which I don't think he would now—we will go on," Hannah soothed her. "And lower your voice so you don't distress the younger ones."

The other children were looking from Hannah to Creed and back uneasily, sensing a discussion that was important to their futures. Nothing was said, and only the plodding of hooves on the hard-packed path sounded in the soft afternoon air. Flies buzzed close to the horses, and there was the piercing cry of a wide-winged eagle soaring overhead.

Not far from the winding path that curved and slashed through the trees, an icy creek gurgled through the tall grasses, splashing over rocks in geysers of white foam and curling against the muddy banks. The creek followed the twists of the path, offering cool drinks for children and horses. They paused more than once as the afternoon progressed, much to Creed's disgust, and he growled at them to hurry.

Another day passed—another long day of walking through thick woods and up steep slopes. As afternoon shadows lengthened into dusk, the path ended at the shores of a lake. It stretched in a wide, mirrored curve that reflected the late afternoon sunlight in glittering shards of light. Cranes skimmed the surface in graceful dips, scooping up their evening meals. Blurred images of trees and sky swayed on the watery surface of the lake the French had named Pend Oreille. The lake had been named after the Indians in the area, who wore pendant ornaments in their earlobes. Laughing, Hannah corrected Eric's pronunciation of the name.

"No, that is Pond-Or-ray, Eric," she said. "And the settlement of Camp Coeur d'Alene is just on the other side . . ."

"Yeah, thirty miles on the other side," Creed put in, "and we have to ford a river to get there!"

Hannah ignored him. "We should reach it in only another day or two. You will like it there," she told the children. "There is much more to see in the settlement of Coeur d'Alene than there was in Jubile."

"How do you know so much, if you've never been there before?" Creed grumbled as he dismounted and gathered General's reins in one hand. Sweeping off his hat, he raked a hand through his hair.

Hannah slanted him a glance. "We came through the settlement when we first arrived in this territory three years ago. And besides, my father went to Coeur d'Alene several times, to visit the priest at the nearby Sacred Heart Mission. And Pastor Allen from the new church in the settlement came a few times to visit us. I know it mainly through their eyes. But you must recall that I am a teacher, Mr. Bratton. I listen and I learn. I am quite capable of instructing the children on Coeur d'Alene."

"That so?" Creed nodded thoughtfully, tapping his reins against his thigh in an absent motion. "It might be different from what you're expectin', Miss McGuire."

"I am well aware of that, Mr. Bratton. But if Pastor Allen is there, it will not matter."

Creed gave a sour grunt, and his eyes narrowed. "You might be expectin' too much of this Pastor Allen you talk about like he was Moses."

Smiling, Hannah shook her head. "I don't think so. I recall him as a gentle man, filled with dedication and love for his fellow human beings. He will not disappoint us."

"Maybe not, but he might put a price on his help," Creed said shortly.

"As you have done?"

"What price! Have I asked you for one damned thing, Miss McGuire?"

"No," she said softly, "but you have subjected us to your anger and resentment, and instilled in the children a fear that you will abandon us again. That is a large price for them to bear, Mr. Bratton."

"Don't worry about it. They're getting even," Creed shot back at her. "I have to shake my boots out in the mornings to remove the little creatures that just happened to find their way in there, and instead of good rye whiskey in my bottle, I found a large amount of lake water!"

"I . . . I had no idea," Hannah said faintly, trying unsuccessfully to hide the smile that sprang unbidden to her lips. "I'm sorry . . ."

"I'll bet you are!"

"No . . . really! I'll speak to them," she said with a small gasp of strangled laughter.

Creed's eyes narrowed. "Don't bother. I've learned to shake out my boots, and I have more whiskey. But you might warn them—one more trick, and they'll regret it!"

"Oh, I'll tell them," Hannah promised. "You . . . you won't do anything rash?"

"I make no promises," he retorted. Turning away, Creed pulled General along with him to a nearby bush and tethered the animal. Flipping back the leather stirrup, he began to unsaddle the horse with quick, efficient movements, ignoring the eyes he felt boring into his back. So what if he was irritable? At least he'd brought them this far, hadn't he? That was more than a lot of men would have done—more than *most* of them would have done. And he'd had to listen to a Bible-thumping schoolmarm most of the way, to boot!

Creed heaved his saddle to the ground, dumping it with the cantle upended so that it could dry. Then, slinging his damp saddle blanket over the bushes to dry, he began to rub General down with a fistful of grass. The bay's sides were wet, and as they cooled in the slowly dropping temperatures, small swirls of steam rose into the air. It was a familiar smell, pungent and lingering. Creed wrinkled his nose.

"I think horses smell good," a childish voice said at his elbow. Creed barely glanced down at the boy.

"Yeah? Better than some things, I guess."

"My pa used to say they smelled as good as a woman's perfume to him," Eric continued. His gaze was reflective and sad as he watched Creed.

"Well, I don't know that I quite agree with *that*, but horses do have a certain kinda smell that isn't too bad." Creed stroked the bay's thick neck with the grass for a moment, watching the curls of steam rise, thinking of how many times he'd done this very thing in hundreds of different places. How many towns? How many desolate ridges and wooded clearings had he stood in and curried General while in pursuit of some outlaw? A lot—too many, maybe. But it was what he had chosen to do. He was a loner, had been a loner since he was twelve years old, and he liked it that way. He didn't need extra baggage along. Creed nodded his head in the direction of the two bony mounts the children had been riding. "Why don't you tend to those horses, boy?"

"My name's Eric. Fletcher and Sweyn tend to them," was his calm unhurried reply. There was a brief pause, then Eric offered the information, "My pa was the blacksmith."

Creed remembered the body in the charred ruins of the farrier's shop, the staring eyes and bloody scalp, and said nothing.

"He was a good blacksmith," Eric continued doggedly. "I heard some say as how he was the best they'd ever seen."

"Then you must have been proud of him," Creed said at last, unwillingly, reluctant to talk about the dead man. It was a memory he'd just as soon forget. But the boy wasn't as willing to let go of the subject. He pursued it with a grim determination, as if recalling his father would bring him to life again.

"Yeah, I was real proud of him. Why, my pa could hold any horse, and he could fix their shoes so they would walk straight. He even healed a crippled horse one time."

"Did he?"

"Yeah, he sure did. I watched. I sat there in his shop

while he heated up the forge, and he let me work the bellows a little while. Then he took his long iron tongs and stuck the shoe into the fire until it glowed as bright and hot as . . . as the sun. Then he had to shape it just right, see, so it would change the horse's walk. It was a young bay mare, kinda like your horse.''

''General's no mare,'' Creed observed with amusement.

''Oh, I know, but he's the same color. Mr. Bratton?'' the boy added, and when Creed glanced down at him, he saw the hunger in Eric's eyes. He knew that hunger, recognized it for what it was, for he had once felt the same, aching pain that never seemed to lessen, never really went away.

''What?'' he asked, though he already knew the question.

''Is my pa really dead?''

For some reason, there was a hard knot in Creed's throat, so that he was obliged to wait for a moment before answering. What was the matter with the boy? Didn't he remember seeing his father's body? Didn't he remember the funeral pyre, with the thick clouds boiling up to smear the blue sky with gray? Creed leveled a thoughtful glance at the waiting child. ''Yes, Eric. Your pa is really dead.''

''Yeah, I knew that,'' the boy said, ducking his head so that Creed wouldn't see the sudden spurt of tears in his blue eyes. ''I just thought that . . . maybe . . . he'd gotten away or something. You know. But it don't matter none.''

''Yes, it does. It matters. It's all right to miss him,'' Creed said quietly. ''And it's all right to mourn the dead. It's only right that someone should mourn their passing.''

Eric's big blue eyes bored into him, and he had a little catch in his voice. ''Is it true what Miss Hannah said—that you lost your pa, too?''

Creed's hands tightened on the fistful of frayed grass he was using, and his throat closed. No, he didn't want to remember that—didn't want it brought back so vividly, like it had happened just the day before. He could still see it if he closed his eyes—still see the black smoke and licking tongues of fire consuming the log cabin and the brush roof, still hear the screams . . .

Creed threw the grass to the ground and wiped his palms on his buckskin pants. He stared past the waiting boy. A cool wind blew across the land, bringing the promise of summer on the swirling air currents that flirted with the budding leaves on the bushes and trees. Soon it would be summer, and the grass would grow thick and green on the mountainsides. Deer would grow fat and fawns would frolic in the safety of the high grass. The snow would melt and swell the icy mountain streams, deepening the lakes and rivers. Flowers would spread in a rainbow of colors over the valley, and lazy butterflies would dip and sway above the nodding blossoms. Life renewed. What was death but passage into another life—a door opening to another world?

*There the wicked cease from troubling; and there the weary be at rest.*

Creed hands clenched. Now *he* was remembering verses from the Bible!

"Yeah," Creed said to the child, "my father's dead, the same as yours. They won't be back. Death is forever."

"Not always, Mr. Bratton," Hannah said as she approached. "Ofttimes, it is simply the passage into a better life. Heaven awaits . . ."

"Yeah? Who do you know who has come back to tell us about it?" Creed demanded with a curl of his lip. "And don't say what I know you're about to say—I've read the Bible!"

"Yet you would try to tarnish the faith of a child with your heresy?" Hannah returned.

"Not heresy, Miss McGuire—common sense. Life is for the living, and dwelling in the past won't change that. You don't need to perpetuate fairy tales for these kids. Harsh realities will shatter 'em soon enough.''

"I'm not perpetuating fairy tales, Mr. Bratton! I'm simply trying to get these children through a difficult time without destroying their faith!" Hannah paused and turned to Eric. "Go help the other boys gather firewood, please. I will be with you in a moment."

"Aw, you just don't want me to hear you and Mr. Bratton argue again," Eric mumbled, but he slowly turned and walked to join the others.

Rounding on Creed before he could say anything else, Hannah said in a low, tight voice, "If you have lost your faith in God and man, I am sorry, Mr. Bratton, but I will not allow you to destroy the faith of innocent children!"

"No, you'd just as soon they believed in things that will never happen," Creed returned cruelly. "Can't you see the the truth? Or are you so far immersed in the fantasy of make-believe that you can't see reality, even when it sweeps down on your home and turns it into an inferno?"

"I can see reality, Mr. Bratton, and I can also see that you are a man with a lost soul." She paused to take a deep breath, then continued, "It has been said that God works miracles, Mr. Bratton. I choose to believe that he will do so with you."

"I doubt it!" Creed shot back.

Hannah smiled. "I don't. God is after your heart, Mr. Bratton."

"Yeah? Well, the devil is after my ass, lady! Care to make a wager on who gets me first?"

Nonplussed, Hannah watched wordlessly as Creed pivoted on his heel and stalked away. He was so bitter, so closed up, there seemed no hope of reaching him. How could she ever make a difference in his life if he would allow no one to get close to him?

At the same time, she wondered if there was more to her feelings for him than her desire to convert him. Oh, he was a challenge for any woman, with his dark good looks and rather swaggering air of masculinity, but it ran deeper than that. There was an indefinable thread between them that she could not deny—an attraction that sparked tiny fires in her nerve endings and sent flames shooting through her blood if he accidentally touched her or caught her eye. At first she had been confused by it, but now she recognized it for what it was.

Sighing, Hannah absently stroked the bay's thick neck as he cropped the new shoots of grass beneath the bushes. As if she didn't have enough worry with the children and the future, she must now worry about succumbing to the temptation of her attraction to Creed Bratton.

# Chapter Eight

It was dark again, and with night the aches and pains of the long day's walk became more noticeable. The younger children complained heartily. Now that danger from the Blackfoot was no longer imminent, they found other concerns to consume their time. Eric and Fletcher gave one another dagger looks across the fire, and Sweyn and Rebecca got into a squabble over who was to watch which younger child. Jessica and Ivy quarreled over who was to sit beside Hannah. Only the Kootenai children, Frog and Little Bird, were quiet.

Creed, listening to the dissension, gave a shake of his

head. He was thinking that he much preferred the terrified silence to constant bickering.

He stalked away to the edge of the clearing and let the night swallow the sounds of their squabbling. He needed time to think—time to plan what he would do once he got rid of his human burdens. Fort Benton was over five hundred miles away. If that was where Stillman and his men were headed, they would probably go to Coeur d'Alene first, then take the Mullan Road east. But why Fort Benton? It was three hundred miles past Alder Gulch—three hundred miles past Henry Plummer's jurisdiction. And there was no doubt that Sheriff Plummer had his hand in this pie, Creed reflected. It smacked of his plotting—the aimless pursuit and long chase, with the pursuers eventually giving up and forgetting about the outlaws and the gold. Then the outlaws simply rode back into Alder Gulch and divided up the spoils with the sheriff. At least this time, he had managed to slow them down. *Blind justice.* But wasn't justice always blind?

Creed stared into the thick, leafy shades of night and built a cigarette. He stuck it between his lips without lighting it, eyes narrowed in thought. Then he stiffened, hearing slight scuffling sounds in the bushes behind him. His keen senses were sharpened even more since the recent bout with the outlaws, and his hand dropped to hover just above the pistol in his gun belt. His nerve endings were attuned to the unfamiliar sounds behind him, and his muscles tensed. When the branches rustled again he swirled, dropping to one knee and pulling his pistol at the same time. Thumbing back the hammer on his Colt, he barked, "Who's there?" at the slightly swaying leaves.

There was a faint shimmer, a nervous cough, then two boys emerged from the bushes—Fletcher and Eric. Straightening, Creed drew his brows into a thunderous scowl.

"You stupid idiots! I almost shot you!"

"Yeah, we . . . we didn't th-think about that," Fletcher stammered finally, his eyes huge in the murky gloom. Sweat popped out in small beads on his forehead in spite of the chill night air, and he swallowed convulsively.

"Don't you know better than to sneak up on a man like that?" Creed demanded, reholstering his pistol. The gun slid in with a leathery smack, and the boys relaxed slightly.

"We just didn't think about that," Eric repeated with a sigh of relief.

"What do you want out here?" Creed shot at them. When they shrugged, his gaze narrowed suspiciously. "I don't trust you," he said bluntly. "What are you up to now?"

"Nothing!" they chorused innocently, which only served to make Creed more suspicious.

"I'll bet—tell you what, let's walk back to camp, with you two ahead of me," he suggested, and his suspicions were confirmed when the boys exchanged uneasy glances.

"No—no, we came out here to . . . to relieve ourselves," Eric said with a faint flush of embarrassment that Creed could detect even in the dark.

"Fine. I'll wait on you."

Eric and Fletcher exchanged glances again, then shrugged their shoulders. On the walk back, Creed herded them just ahead of him, prodding them when they slowed and wondering just what mischief they had planned. It was when they were just outside the camp, on the narrow path he had taken earlier, that Creed found his suspicions had been justified.

Though Fletcher gamely tried to sidestep in time, he was yanked into the air by a length of coiled rope attached to a bent tree limb. Eric leaped sideways in time to avoid the trap, and fell neatly into Creed's grasp.

"This what you boys had planned for me?" Creed asked, eying the swinging, howling Fletcher. The stocky youth hung by one foot, and he was swaying in the night air. "Looks like a turkey trussed for market," Creed observed when Eric remained silent. He gave the boy a rough shake, then slid his knife from the sheath on his belt and held it out. "Cut a switch from that tree," he instructed, indicating the same tree that now held Fletcher several feet off the ground.

"C-c-cut a switch?"

"Cut a switch. A good stout one, or I'll have you cut another one when that one's worn out," Creed said.

"B-b-but . . ."

"Now!" The sharp command sliced through the air and galvanized Eric into action. The boy jumped, and took the knife Creed held out to him. Reluctantly, he selected and hacked a stout limb from the tree and gave it to Creed. After testing it—swishing it through the air and bending it to test its flexibility—Creed pronounced himself satisfied.

"Now, what do you think I want with this switch?" he asked both boys. Fletcher, still hanging upside down and filled with misery, muttered an incomprehensible answer that Creed had him repeat.

"You're gonna whup us!" the youth shouted.

"You bet," was the immediate answer.


Back in camp, Hannah barely glanced up when Creed returned with Eric and Fletcher in tow. Then her head jerked up again and her eyes narrowed. Both boys were red-eyed and snuffling, and Eric was rubbing surreptitiously at his backside.

"What happened?" she demanded.

Shrugging, Creed replied, "Just ran into some tree limbs out there, that's all. Right, boys?"

"Right!" they chorused.

Though not entirely satisfied with their reply, Hannah had

no choice but to accept it. She watched silently as Creed sat near the fire. Fletcher gave him a wide berth, and sat as far as he could from him. He wasn't really sitting, actually—he was leaning against a fallen log. Eric solved the problem by just crouching down close to Creed, his wary gaze flicking from the fire to the man and back.

Creed leaned back against a fallen log and stretched his arms out to the side, relaxing. He sat that way for a while, staring into the flickering flames and remaining silent. Finally, Hannah turned her attention back to the girls.

Idly reaching out with his right leg, Creed shoved one of the logs back into the roaring fire, almost burning the toe of his knee-high moccasin in the process. There was the sharp, acrid odor of burning elk hide, and he cursed softly as he dug his toe into the dirt to snuff out the smoldering leather.

His actions caught Hannah's attention, and she looked up at him. Not that Creed had been far from her thoughts, for he hadn't. He lingered, always on the fringe of her mind, where she kept him at bay, hoping he would not intrude any more than he already had. Why must she think of him so often—so longingly, and always with that pull of attraction? There was little peace at night, when she was alone with her thoughts, staring up at the sky with Creed not far away. The daylight hours provided her with the only respite from him, for Creed Bratton also inhabited her dreams.

And now, looking at him in the hazy glow of flickering light and shadows, she knew he would soon invade every moment of her thoughts. Even though his hat was tilted forward so that the wide brim shadowed his face, she could feel his eyes resting on her.

Turning away, Hannah resisted the temptation to talk to him. Let him speak first, make the first move. Since his return from wherever he'd gone—and that was another thing that bothered her—they had exchanged only wary words.

What had happened out there in the forest? He had refused to talk about it, and she couldn't help but wonder if he had killed the outlaws he'd sought. Maybe that was easier than taking them back alive.

"Miss Hannah?" Ivy lisped, tugging at her sleeve. She glanced down at the child. "Miss Hannah, I have to go," she whispered urgently. There was a slightly desperate tone to her plea, and Hannah rose immediately.

"Of course, Ivy."

The boys snickered, and Eric remarked, "She's *always* gotta go."

Hurt by her brother's unwarranted assault, Ivy defended herself. "At least *I* didn't wet my pants in the cellar!"

Eric surged to his feet, his face growing flushed and red with embarrassment. "You said you wouldn't tell!"

"Well, I did. You hurt my feelings," Ivy returned.

"Children," Hannah intervened before it could get out of hand, "anything that happened in the cellar is excusable, as far as I am concerned. We were all frightened. But still, Eric, harsh words only prick the soul and satisfy nothing. Do you understand?"

The boy nodded, and crouched back down not far from Creed. He twisted his hands together, occasionally slanting a glance at the mountain man to see if he was laughing. Creed was not. He stared into the fire and did his best to ignore them. After several moments of silence, Eric could stand it no more. He edged closer to Creed and nudged him with his elbow, earning a dark glance.

"Mr. Bratton—could I sleep close to you tonight?" he asked, swallowing his fear. "I'd feel safer."

"Safer from what?"

"From what . . . whatever's out there." Eric shivered and gazed beyond the comforting glow of the fire to the shadows wavering at the fringe of the circle of light, then inched closer to Creed, until he was against him.

Creed's hand fell on his shoulder. "There's nothing out there, boy—nothing but the wind and the stars."

"And God," Hannah added softly, earning a stare from Creed. She did not flinch from his dark, burning gaze but returned it boldly, daring him to disagree. He did not. He gave a careless shrug of his broad shoulders and reached for his tobacco pouch and papers.

Eric watched with fascination as Creed curled a thin sheaf of paper and poured tobacco in the center, then sealed it with a flick of his tongue along the edge. After Creed stuck the cigarette between his lips, he leaned forward and lifted a burning twig from the fire to light it. Then, leaning back against the tree trunk behind him, Creed sucked in a deep drag of his cigarette and watched the thin gray curls of smoke drift upward. The smoke made a swirling pattern in the air, hanging like low-lying clouds, and the boy couldn't resist putting out a finger to disturb it.

"Look at it now," Creed said to Eric. "Look at the smoke. What's it doing?"

"It's all broken—scattered, and moving away from my finger," Eric replied with a puzzled expression. "Why?"

"Because that's what happens to your fear when you face it," Creed said. "It's just like that smoke. It shifts and moves away, doesn't sting as much. See what I mean?"

Nodding, Eric said slowly, "Yeah, I think I do. If I stand fast and don't give in—if I just face what's botherin' me—it'll go away."

"Well, maybe not go away, but it'll lessen, anyway." Creed took a last drag from his cigarette, then flipped it into the fire. Sliding to the ground, he crossed his legs at the ankles and pulled the brim of his hat over his eyes, signaling that he was through talking.

Eric took the hint and lapsed into silence. He stared at the smoke from their fire and thought about the past few days. He'd been listening to Miss Hannah and Mr. Bratton talk about what was going to happen to them, but somehow he wasn't so worried anymore. Somehow he knew that Miss Hannah would take care of them, and that Mr. Bratton—in spite of his rough denials—would, too. It didn't even matter that Creed had switched him and that his backside was still stinging and smarting from the sharp cuts of the tree limb. He'd deserved it, hadn't he? After all, he'd known the risks when he'd agreed to Fletcher's plan. It was Fletcher who was angry—Fletcher who had planned revenge—and Eric suddenly didn't want any part of it. Mr. Bratton wasn't so bad. He'd even tried to explain things to him, hadn't he? Yeah, and he hadn't really gotten mad about the stupid rope trap they'd tried to spring on him. Why, he hadn't even said anything about the lizards and tree frogs they'd put in his boots, or the lake water in his whiskey bottle, or the burrs they'd stuck to his saddle blanket so that his horse bucked early in the morning and almost threw him off. No, he'd just waited, then done what any man would do.

Eric slanted another glance at Creed's shuttered face. Blinking, the boy suddenly realized that he was sleepy. He smothered a yawn with one hand.

Hannah realized it, too, and began to shepherd the children to their blankets, supervising the spreading out of the pallets on the ground and deciding who would sleep close to whom. When they were all settled, she returned to the log close to the fire. It was cool at night, and she pulled her blanket around her shoulders to ward off the chill. She should sleep, but her thoughts were too jumbled now, too confusing. The source of her confusion lay drowsing across from her, his arms folded across his stomach and his chin on his chest. She couldn't even see his face, and was suddenly glad.

Instead, she stared into the fire, watching the flames burn lower and lower. White, orange, red, yellow, and blue, they danced in eerie patterns, and the tamarack branches hissed and popped as they were consumed. Cupping her elbows in her palms, Hannah rocked forward.

The night sounds slowly penetrated her thoughts, and she heard the deep-throated query of an owl trill through the tree branches, reminding her of a few nights before. The round, burning eyes of the great horned owl had frightened her until she'd discovered the source, and she wondered if the same would apply to Creed Bratton. Perhaps if she discovered the source of her attraction to him, she could put it aside as she had her fear of the owl.

Lifting her gaze from the fire, Hannah glanced at Creed. He was still lying with his chin on his chest, and he seemed to be oblivious to the world around him. Sighing, Hannah rose and left the circle of light formed by the fire. She followed a faint path cut through the woods, then paused on the muddy banks of the lake. Leaning against the trunk of a huge cedar, she pulled her blanket more closely around her shoulders.

The sharp smell of cedar filled the air, and as she stared across the lake, she was struck by the beauty of the moon's reflection on the surface. It was a full moon, and it threw a shimmering ribbon of light across the dark water of Lake Pend Oreille. Humps of land like the scales of a dragon broke the far horizon in a faint silhouette cast by the moon behind the peaks. It was quiet, and a breeze stirred the branches of the trees and ruffled the lake.

Hannah closed her eyes for a moment and pretended she was home in Jubile. It was night. Joshua was working late on one of his sermons, and she had taken a walk to the banks of the Kootenai River. All was peaceful and quiet. No Blackfoot had stormed down into their quiet valley to lay waste to them . . . there had been no massacre, no deaths . . . all was as it had been as long as she could remember.

The ache that formed in her throat spread to her chest, and she shuddered. Hot tears stung her eyes, then spilled onto her cheeks, weaving a wet pattern down her face. Hannah put her hands over her face to muffle her racking sobs. Though bewildered by her reaction, by this yielding to weakness now when she had not before, she could not stop. Where was her strength now? Where was her faith and determination? She felt lost and alone, as small as one of the children asleep in their blankets.

She fell to her knees, crying softly, her shoulders shaking with her grief. She sobbed for her father, for the others in the settlement, and for herself. They were beyond hurting, beyond caring, but she had been left behind to grieve, and it hurt. It hurt to think she would never see them again—never see her father's smile, or hear his careless laugh, or even listen to his solemn lectures. What would she do? Where would she go? How could she carry on without him? It shouldn't have been Joshua. It should have been her, for she was so weak and so insignificant, while her father had been a powerful man of God. Why had she lived and he died?

Anger surged through her, and Hannah lifted her face to gaze up at the cold, silver-dollar moon. Her fists clenched and she struggled against her rage. *Why had Joshua McGuire died? Why hadn't God spared him? Why did He allow those heathen Blackfoot to kill so many good people—women, babies, old men, children. They were all children of God, yet He did not spare them. Why, why, why?*

An inarticulate cry of rage escaped her, and she fell forward to beat at the soft, yielding earth with her bunched fists. The grass was dew-wet, streaking her face as she pressed against the ground. Hannah could taste the rich loam, feel its grit against her mouth and cheeks, and welcomed it. She welcomed the sharp pain caused by the scattering of rocks beneath her, the scrapes on her knees and hands. She felt like doing as the women of old Israel, and even the Indian women—beating her breast and tearing her hair, sitting in sackcloth and ashes . . . anything to take her mind from the prod of pain that tore at her heart and soul.

As a harsh sob racked her, she felt hands upon her shoulders and jerked away. "Leave me alone!" she rasped in hurting gasps.

"No. Hannah . . . Miss McGuire . . . let me help you. I know what you must be feeling . . ."

Hannah surged upward, knocking Creed's hands away. "You know nothing of what I feel! He was all I had, and now he's gone!"

Creed crouched beside her, his dark eyes unreadable in the shadows, but his tone soft. "Yes, I do know what you are feeling, remember? I know, and I know the pain will lessen some, even if it never really goes away."

Shaking her head until her heavy hair tumbled free of the pins holding it and whipped about her face in stinging tendrils, Hannah muttered disagreement. "No, it won't."

"Yes, it will, Hannah. Trust me."

That made her laugh—a harsh, guttural sound that was alien to her soft nature. "Trust *you*, Mr. Bratton? What an odd thing for you to say! Do you really think I would trust a man who has shown only impatience and dislike to me and eight innocent children? Why in God's name should I trust *you*?"

Creed exhibited no reaction to her words. He shrugged and said, "Because you have very little choice, at this point, and because you know I'm right."

"Do I? Do I know you're right, Mr. Creed Bratton?"

Hannah edged closer on her knees, gazing at him in the fitful light cast by moon and shadows. "I wonder—I wonder if I even know what's right and what isn't anymore."

Creed reached out and let his hand trail along the soft curve of her cheek. "You know what's right, Hannah. You know."

She gave a violent shake of her head, and the curling whips of auburn hair flicked across his face. "No, I don't think I do. I try—I really do try—but I have these doubts that haunt me, that make me wonder if I *ever* knew right from wrong. I mean, you'd have had to know Joshua McGuire. He was so devout, so strong, and I've always been weak. I can't count the times he had to support me, to show me the right path . . ."

"Look," Creed cut in impatiently, "will you stop flogging yourself? If you want to wear a hair shirt and sackcloth and ashes, fine, but at least do it for the right reasons."

"And I suppose you know the right reasons?" Hannah flared. "I suppose you are on familiar terms with repentance in some form?"

"Don't be a hypocrite," he said shortly, adding over her gasp of rage, "Man has never been perfect, Hannah. Why do you chastise yourself for being human?"

"Why do I . . . ohhh! You have no conception of what the Bible is all about, Mr. Bratton!"

"Maybe not, but I do know what life is all about, Hannah McGuire, and I know that if you don't get off this self-pity trail you seem so fond of riding, you won't survive." He reached out to grab her by the shoulders when she began to rise, and gave her a rough shake. Her blanket fell in a dark huddle to the ground as he shook her. "Look, stop for a minute and think about what you're doing to yourself with all this. Can you honestly say your father would want you to be so unhappy?"

"That has nothing to do with my grief at his death, Mr. Bratton!"

"Yes, it does. You're blaming yourself for not being the one to die, am I right?"

Startled, Hannah gaped at him with wide eyes. "Why, I . . . yes, I guess I am. How did you know?"

"Then, stop it. Your father wouldn't want that," Creed answered, ignoring her question. His fingers loosened their grip and slid down her arms to cup her elbows. "Cry if you want to, Hannah, but for the right reason," he murmured then, pulling her close to him. "It's all right to cry, as long as you cry for the right reason."

As Hannah's tears began anew and she lay her head on his chest, Creed had the thought that he should take his own advice. He knew how she felt, because he had felt the same way—first grief, then anger. Only he had grown bitter, and he knew it. The bitterness had consumed his soul, leaving the man he was now—the man without purpose except to exist. This tender woman-child would not grow stronger with bitterness; she would be consumed by it. And for some reason, he didn't want that to happen. She appealed to his protective instincts—instincts he'd thought long dead. And some of them weren't just protective . . .

Creed's hands shifted from Hannah's elbows to her back, and he caressed her gently. He rubbed the hard knot between her shoulder blades, easing it, smoothing out the tension. The luxurious feel of her beneath his fingers was oddly disturbing, and Creed caught his breath.

Hannah felt his sudden stillness, and she grew quiet. She drew in a deep, shuddering breath, inhaling the scent of tobacco and leather, her nose pressed against his chest. She could feel his heart beat beneath her cheek, could feel the steady, strong rhythm, and was comforted. All of a sudden it felt right to be here with Creed, to be held in the safe circle of his arms. She lifted her head to gaze up at him.

Drawing slightly away, Creed looked down into her face. There was a shimmering beauty in the wet pools of her eyes that drew him in, made him feel as if he were drowning. He briefly wondered if she knew how lovely she was—if she realized how much he wanted her . . .

That thought startled Creed, and his mouth tightened. *He wanted her.* Yes, he did want her. He wanted to hold her close to him and caress her soft skin, cradle her sad face in his hands and kiss her lips, her nose, her eyelids . . . but how could he tell her what he wanted? And should he?

Then Hannah was leaning closer, her arms moving to circle his body, her face curious and afraid at the same time. She lifted it to him, and it was the most natural thing in the world to kiss her.

When Creed's lips brushed against hers in a soft caress Hannah closed her eyes. She needed him to hold her, to kiss her sweetly and gently. Her arms tightened around his neck. He seemed to understand that she needed him, and his hands moved across her back to press her against his hard body. They were on their knees holding one another, and Hannah forgot the time, the wet grass, and the children asleep not far away. She let everything spin into oblivion as Creed held her.

At first his kisses were gentle, almost brotherly, then they subtly altered. The soft pressure of his lips deepened, became fiery and insistent, and Hannah made a moaning sound deep in her throat.

How had she never dreamed a man might kiss this way? It had always seemed as if it would be loving and safe, not this wild, turbulent emotion that began to pound through her now. It was almost frightening in its intensity, and she was not prepared for it.

She pulled slightly away, her mouth trembling and her eyes searching. "Creed," she began, using his given name for the first time aloud, "Creed, I don't think . . . I mean . . ."

"This is not the time for thinking, Hannah," he muttered thickly, and his mouth seared a path from her lips to her ear, making her shiver. "This isn't the time for rational thought or reaction," he whispered into her ear. "It's a time for feeling."

The waters of the lake slapped against the rocks and banks, and Hannah shivered again. She was cool, yet burning with an inner fire that threatened to blaze out of control. Common sense urged her to break away now, but the attraction that had been there since the beginning was smothering that faint voice. Perhaps it wasn't so wrong. Perhaps this was the great love her father had once said she would have one day—this consuming emotion that swept from her toes upward, a burning, coiling fire deep in the pit of her stomach. She needed Creed—needed him with her, holding her, kissing away her fears and doubts. And how could she resist when he was holding her like this? The blood was pounding in her throat at his gentle explorations with lips and hands. The pads of his fingers grazed across her face to her throat, then moved down to caress the tiny hollow of her collarbone.

Lowering his head, Creed kissed that wildly fluttering pulse that betrayed her emotion, and she could feel his mouth curve in a smile.

"There, that isn't so bad, is it?" he was murmuring against her skin, and she shook her head mutely. "Is this your first kiss, Hannah?" he asked then, his mouth still teasing the warm skin of her throat and shoulder. Then he added, "Never mind."

Hannah turned her face away, unwilling for him to see the confusion and doubt that must be etched upon her features, or to watch as she ran the tip of her tongue over her throbbing lips to soothe them. They tingled with unfamiliar sensations that were making her senses riot.

She kept her face averted, pressing the palms of her hands against his broad chest in silent resistance, but Creed grasped her chin with warm fingers. He turned her back to face him, his eyes hot and dark, melting her fears with silent promises. He slanted his mouth across hers, and the combined weight of his hand and the exploration of his lips removed the last vestige of her resistance to his kisses. It was too much for Hannah.

Her mouth throbbed and ached, needing relief from the torment, and only Creed's lips could supply it. He obliged immediately.

Creed, who had always been able to control not only the pace of his breathing but his response to the female sex, was finding it difficult to decelerate the intake of air in his lungs. It came rapidly and shallow, and he began to feel like a callow youth just out of short pants. And then it happened— the tiny voice of a conscience he thought long dead and buried voiced disapproval.

*You savage—would you really take her like this? Would you really destroy her when she trusts you?*

Startled by the reappearance of that voice, Creed paused. This was ridiculous. She was just a woman, and he was a man, with a man's needs. What did it matter? There would be a first time for her someday—why not him?

*Because you know it's not right,* came the persistent voice again.

Frustration coiled in his brain, and Creed rejected that voice he'd forgotten existed. Hadn't he gone out of his way to rescue her and escort all those troublesome children? Hadn't he temporarily given up his chase of the outlaws—

come back when he could have ridden on? There should be some reward for doing such a magnanimous thing . . .

*Not the ruin of another human being . . .*

And—astonishingly—he felt his passion ebb. This had never happened to him before. Creed stifled a groan. He had always thought of women as warm, yielding creatures who served his needs—whether physical or in some other capacity—and then could be forgotten. And now this slip of a girl was sending all his long-held theories rocketing out of sight. It was a disturbing moment for a man who preferred having no emotions at all.

Yet this moment had been postponed since the first time he'd seen her rising up out of the soot and ashes of the ruined building. He had thought her the most beautiful woman he'd ever seen. It wasn't just her physical beauty, but the light that shone from within Hannah—a light that imbued ordinary features with extraordinary beauty. And now, with her in his arms, trusting him, he found it impossible to do what his every sense urged—to take advantage of an inexperienced girl who clung to him in the faith he would be a righteous man.

Creed sat up, gently pushing Hannah away from him with a light kiss upon her brow. She seemed confused and disoriented as she struggled for breath and understanding, and he smiled as he cupped her chin in his palm. Creed could hardly believe it himself as he heard his own words.

"It's late, sweet Hannah, and we have to get up early. I'll walk you back to the fire."

It took a moment for his words to register, but she accepted them with mixed relief and disappointment. If only the raging blood in her veins would cool, she could answer him without her voice quivering.

"Yes," she finally replied without betraying too much emotion, "we should go back to the fire." Hannah managed a smile as she smoothed her skirts and the bodice of her old gown. "It's grown much cooler," she offered in an attempt at light conversation, feeling awkward. What did one do in such circumstances? What was she supposed to say? And how could Creed look so unruffled and composed when she felt so flustered and embarrassed?

When she stood, Creed gently draped the blanket around her shoulders. "This should keep you warm," he said. Hannah's head jerked up and her eyes widened.

*But I feel as if I have been bathed in fire, as if it is not yet out, but only slumbering . . .*

# Chapter Nine

Morning brought disaster. Rebecca's fever had worsened in the night; the child was nearly delirious. And Fletcher Harris had the same symptoms.

"What shall I do?" Hannah fretted aloud, pushing at a tumble of hair obscuring her vision. She stood uncertainly in the middle of the camp, having bathed their faces with cold wet rags and tucked more blankets securely around them. Both children shivered with chill, yet their flesh scorched her hand. "What shall I do?" she worried again, and slanted a despairing glance at Creed.

Shoving his hand through his hair in a now familiar gesture, Creed shook his head. "I'm no doctor, but won't some kind of plant help bring down that fever?"

Hannah nodded miserably. "Yes, monkshood. But I'm not sure if I could find any this early in the year, or even where I'd begin to look. I've only been in this territory for three years, and I'm afraid I'm not very confident when it comes to..."

"Look. Are you going to stand there and make excuses, or go to look for that plant?" Creed cut in. He put his hands on his hips and narrowed his eyes at her. "I can help you look, you know. I've been out here longer than three years."

Hannah's first flush of anger changed to hope, and she asked, "Do you really think you can find some?"

In the end it was Creed who searched for it, and he came back into camp bearing a leggy plant with bell-shaped blossoms. He also concocted the foul-smelling brew for the children, and gave it to Hannah.

"Try this," he said, and she took it gratefully.

She'd already bathed Rebecca and Fletcher in icy lake water, and their fever had abated only slightly. The other children grouped near, watching. There was an air of ominous regard about their solemn figures as they sat stiffly and watchfully.

Rebecca moaned softly, and her eyelids fluttered as she tried to protest the noxious liquid being poured down her throat, but Hannah persisted. Fletcher, the blond, stocky youth who was so often the most obnoxious of the children, was sunk so deeply into a coma that he never knew when Hannah gave him the medicine. It flowed freely down his throat and from the sides of his slack, open mouth. Hannah stroked his throat in order to coax him into swallowing, and when she decided at least some of the medicine had been ingested, she put down the tin cup.

"Fletcher seems much worse than Rebecca," she murmured to Creed, who was crouched not far away. "I'm worried about him."

Creed didn't want to say what was on his mind—that he'd

seen the same gray look on a human face before. The pinched nostrils and blue-tinged shadows beneath the eyes were the shroud of death.

But when he lifted his gaze to Hannah, she saw the look in his eyes and knew. "No!" she whispered, anguished, and Creed's mouth grew taut.

"We'll do what we can for him."

"He needs a doctor! We need to get him to a doctor as soon as possible. Then he will get better . . ."

"Hannah, there's nothing a doctor can do. This may be cholera, for all I know. It's happened before . . ."

"No!" Her voice rose on the word, and she struggled for control, adding more calmly, "No, I disagree, Mr. Bratton. I think that a doctor could give him the proper medication and save him. Do you think we could get to Coeur d'Alene in time?"

"No, I don't." Creed's brittle tone snapped Hannah's head around, and she glared at him.

" 'Oh, ye of little faith . . . ' "

"Don't start that again!" Creed shot back. "I'm in no mood for it, and it sure as hell won't help him!"

"Your language is unseemly, Mr. Bratton."

"And your obstinance is unseemly, Miss McGuire," he growled roughly.

"Nonetheless, I do think if we could just get both the children to Coeur d'Alene . . ."

"Dammit! Do you intend to move kids as sick as these? It would kill them for sure!" Glaring at her, Creed tucked his thumbs into his gun belt and squared his shoulders as he recognized the militant light in Hannah's lovely, stubborn eyes. She would go to Coeur d'Alene, and kill them all trying. How could such a soft package contain such a strong, determined will? But it did, and he was beginning to realize that nothing would dissuade her once her mind was set on a course of action. Creed cleared his throat. "Maybe I should ride on to Coeur d'Alene and see if they have a doctor . . ."

Her head snapped up eagerly. "How long will that take?"

"There and back? A day, maybe more."

"Do we have that much time?"

Creed slowly shook his head. "No, not really. But I already told you that." There was a brief, pregnant pause, then he added in a resigned tone, "Burn all the cloths you use, and don't let anyone else near these two. You'll have to do all the nursing, to cut down on the chance of infecting the others. And, Hannah," he said, turning back to look at her, "don't get your hopes up."

After he'd gone, Hannah remained at Fletcher's side, constantly bathing his face and dosing him with herbs. The children did their best to help, but Hannah would not allow them near to those stricken.

"Keep your distance," she commanded sternly. "There is no point in risking the same illness for yourselves. I can manage."

Jessica and Ivy took over the chores of providing clean cloths and food for Hannah, while the boys quietly gathered firewood and hauled water. Frog and Little Bird suggested the use of a sweat lodge to bring out the evil spirits, and Hannah was so frantic she almost agreed.

She tended the patients as best she could, burning the used cloths and using her petticoat for more, sitting by their sides and constantly mopping their fevered faces with cool water. And she prayed.

*Please, God—they've been through so much. Don't let them die. Show me the way to care for them . . .*

At the back of her mind was the nagging guilt that she had somehow caused this sickness with her fall from grace the night before. She shouldn't have yielded to her emotions, shouldn't have let—no, *invited*—Creed Bratton's caresses, but she had. Was this her punishment, perhaps? Was this the sacrifice demanded for her sins? No, no. God would not be so unjust.

"Miss Hannah?" Eric said, coming as close to her as he dared.

Her head snapped up and she gazed at him through bleary eyes. "Yes, Eric?"

"Miss Hannah, I know me and Fletcher . . . well, we don't get along so good, but I don't want anything to happen to him. I didn't mean all those things I said to him. It . . . it isn't my fault he's sick, is it?" he ended in a rush, huge tears welling in his bright blue eyes.

Hannah went to him immediately, kneeling in front of the distraught boy and smoothing back the rumpled hair from his forehead. Her own feelings of guilt ebbed, and she was able to say with conviction, "No, no, Eric! Oh, it isn't your fault at all, truly it isn't. This is just one of those things that happens sometimes. We must accept it . . ."

"Accept it?" Jessica put in sharply. She stepped close. "Like we've accepted everything else? What good does it do us to keep accepting things if God just does more to us?"

"Oh, Jessica, *God* isn't doing this to us," Hannah said, reaching out to catch the girl's hand and hold her when she would have turned away in scornful disbelief. "Sometimes— sometimes there's just a greater plan than we can see. I'm sure there's a reason for all this, whether we know it or not."

Eric and Jessica's gazes moved to their friends. Hannah could read the stark disbelief in their eyes, and she sighed. How could she explain it when she didn't understand it herself? None of this made any sense to her, none of it! Why had the burden been placed upon her shoulders when she

wasn't ready? She needed more time to prepare for such
things—more patience, more knowledge—and now she felt
so helpless. Her head ached, and she wished Creed was
there. Even with his cynicism and barbed tongue, she could
draw comfort from his strength. What would happen to
them if they were faced with intruders or wild animals?

As if reading her thoughts, Sweyn came close and knelt
on the fallen leaves nearby. His angular face was earnest,
his eyes steady and calm. "Mr. Bratton left me a gun to
use, Miss Hannah," he said quietly. "I can shoot, yah, and
we are safe. You must save your strength for tending the
others. I will keep us safe until his return."

"Thank you, Sweyn," she said softly, and a slight smile
touched her lips. "You are all so good. You must be brave.
We shall do our best for Rebecca and Fletcher."

But her best wasn't enough. During the long night, filled
with mysterious forest noises and the soft sobs from the
children, Fletcher Harris died. The stocky blond boy first
regained consciousness, opening his eyes to look up at
Hannah and smile.

"Miss Hannah," he whispered hoarsely.

She jerked her head up to stare at him and paled, seeing
death in his eyes—a bright shimmer that already seemed to
be otherworldly.

"Yes . . . yes, Fletcher, I'm here," she managed to say.
Her hands covered his hot, dry ones and held them
comfortingly.

The boy's gaze shifted to Eric Ransom, curled up in sleep
as close as he could get to Fletcher's pallet without being
sent away. "Eric's not a bad fighter," he said with the
condescension of a thirteen-year-old for a ten-year-old.

Hannah's throat closed. "No, no, he's not."

Fletcher's lips quirked in a slight smile. "But I'm better," he said. There was a long pause in which he struggled

to breathe, and the bright light in his eyes began to dim. "Miss Hannah!" he cried out suddenly, his body stiffening and his gaze darting to her face. "Miss Hannah, I'm scared!"

Fighting back the tears, Hannah soothed, "Don't be frightened, Fletcher. I'm here with you. God is with you, and Jesus is watching over his frightened lamb..."

"But I can't see him! I...I can't see you either, Miss Hannah," the boy said, and his hands began to flail the air. Hannah grabbed them again, curling her fingers around his and holding tightly.

"I won't leave you," she promised, "and you can hear me. You know I'm here, just as...just as God is near us, too. He's with us always, Fletcher..."

The other children had awakened at Fletcher's cry, and were sitting up, coming as close to their playmate as they dared.

"I'm here, Fletch," Eric Ransom choked out, "and...and I just want you to know that you're the best...best all 'round guy I know."

"I t'ink so, too," Sweyn offered quietly, and the others chimed in with similar assurances. This seemed to comfort Fletcher, and his eyelids drifted closed.

Hannah drew him into her lap and held him in her arms while the children began to weep. Fletcher made only one other sound, a faint rattle in the back of his throat, then his muscles relaxed. Holding him against her, Hannah let her tears drop onto the boy's blond hair. She rocked him back and forth, too distraught to care if the children saw her lose control.

It was Sweyn Johanssen who gently disentangled Hannah's arms from around the boy, who lay Fletcher back on his pallet and pulled the blanket over his peaceful face. And it was Sweyn who quoted, " 'And we know that all things work together for good, to them that love God . . . ' "

"Do they, Miss Hannah?" Eric cut in hoarsely, his face crumpled in grief as he waited for her answer. "Do they?"

She managed to nod, to wipe away her tears and assure Eric and the other children that there must be a reason for Fletcher's untimely death.

"But what?" Little Bird asked, her dark eyes swimming with unshed tears. Her self-control was strong, though gravely tested, and her small mouth was held in a taut line. "Why did he have to die? Why do we have to be so sad? Why?"

Helplessly shaking her head, Hannah thrust her doubts as far as she could, searching her memory for a verse that would answer their questions. Oh, if only she were as wise as her father. Joshua McGuire would have known. Joshua could have comforted the children . . .

Help came from a surprising source. Jessica Gray, the sharp-tongued, cynical child who always insisted upon solid proof, quoted softly, " 'Woe is me for my hurt! my wound is grievous: but I said, Truly this is a grief and I must bear it.' "

Surprised, Hannah gave her a nod of approval and appreciation. "Thank you, Jessica . . ."

On the pallet not far away, Rebecca began to thrash, her arms and legs waving like thin windmills, knocking the blankets away. Hannah rushed to her, grateful for the distraction, for anything that would push the reality of Fletcher's death to the back of her mind.

As the hours passed, night drifting into morning and then afternoon, it became obvious that Rebecca would live. A prayer had been answered. Hannah sank down on her own pallet in weak relief. Deep circles curved under her eyes, and her mouth sagged in weary lines. Her gown clung to her sides in damp wrinkles, and burnished waves of hair hung over her forehead in untidy disarray.

"Shall we bury Fletcher now?" Sweyn came to ask her, and Hannah gave a start.

"Bury him? Yes, yes, we should. We have no shovel, no digging utensils at all. We'll have to place him under stones," Hannah decided after a few moments. "And we shall have a service for him, of course."

Everyone gathered stones, which, fortunately, were plentiful. The smaller stones were placed over Fletcher's blanket-wrapped body first, and then larger gray stones were placed atop, piled high so that it would be difficult for animals to uncover him. Frog fashioned a cross from two hickory limbs, tying the limbs at the juncture with a thick vine. It was wedged at the head of the small grave as a reminder.

Hannah conducted the service, quoting passages from the Bible and offering up a prayer for Fletcher's peaceful repose. She had just finished when the sound of hoofbeats echoed through the thick woods.

"Miss Hannah!" Eric said nervously, and edged closer to her.

"It's all right, children. Sweyn, do you still have the rifle?" she asked calmly, and when the boy nodded, she told him to bring it to her. "We shall be cautious, but not foolish," she told the children.

Creed Bratton was more than a little startled to ride into the clearing and come face to face wih a cocked rifle—his own, at that.

"Hey! Don't shoot. I came back, didn't I?" he threw at them as he dismounted, and Hannah lowered the rifle.

"I was only being careful."

"Glad to hear it. Glad you waited to see who it was before you took a potshot at my hat, too," he muttered. "I sure would hate for anything to happen to it."

"Why?" Eric asked. "You're always worrying about it. It's just an old hat..."

"No, this isn't just *any* old hat, boy," Creed shot back. "But, never mind that." He pointed to the grave. "I see the herbs didn't help."

Swallowing the lump in her throat, Hannah shook her head. "No, they didn't—not Fletcher, anyway. Rebecca seems to be improving, however. Did you find a doctor?"

Pushing back his hat, Creed gazed at her for a long moment. "No, I sure didn't. I'll explain later."

"Later? But..."

Tossing his reins to Sweyn, Creed gave a careless order for the boy to care for his horse while he talked to Hannah. A firm hand cupped her elbow and steered her to a remote spot on the sloping banks of the lake.

"Look," he began in a familiar harsh tone that made Hannah's eyes narrow with irritation and exasperation, "I left camp just to make everybody feel a little better—not because I had any intention of bringing back a doctor..."

"You what?" Hannah gasped out. "Do you mean you did not even *try* to secure a physician in Coeur d'Alene?"

Creed grabbed her wrists to hold her still when it looked as if she might stalk away; his voice was hard and curt. "Hannah, listen to me. There was nothing a doctor could have done for these kids. The girl is just lucky to be alive, and the boy... well, he wasn't so lucky. For me to push a good horse for a futile cause just didn't make sense. I only thought it might avoid some argument if I pretended to..."

"*Pretended*! Why... why you coward! You deceiver! You let me think that you had gone for help. I waited and waited, and you didn't come back, and Fletcher died..."

Creed jerked her toward him, stopping her tumble of words. "Listen to me! Fletcher still would have died. Do you understand that, Hannah? If I had ridden all the way to

Coeur d'Alene, found a doctor, been able to persuade him to come with me, then ridden as fast as I could to get here, I still wouldn't have been in time. Do you understand that?''

Jerking away from him, Hannah leaned against the rough bark of a pine and gazed out over the crystal blue waters of the lake, watching the reflection of snow-capped mountains and blue, blue sky in the shimmering depths. She could feel Creed behind her, could feel the weight of his brooding gaze on her. How was it that he could be so right, even when his motives were so wrong? Or were they? Couldn't he at least have tried?

"Hannah . . . Miss McGuire . . ." Creed's hands were on her shoulders, turning her around to face him, his rough fingers cupping her chin and tilting her face to his. His dark, liquid eyes were boring into her, and faint lines fanned from the corners in tiny sunbursts as he squinted down at her. His mouth—the same mouth that had awakened such tumultous emotions inside her—was set in a straight, taut line, and his voice was even rougher than usual. "I shouldn't have deceived you," he said abruptly, startling her with his concession.

"No, you shouldn't," she agreed after a moment. Then, in all fairness, she had to add, "But I left you with little choice."

"No, you didn't."

Resisting the impulse to lean into him, to beg him to hold her in a secure embrace, Hannah said briskly, "Well, let us put all that behind us now. We cannot go back, but only forward."

"Right. And we've still got thirty miles to go before we get to Coeur d'Alene. Do you think we can manage to do the distance without another argument, Miss McGuire?"

She smiled. "No, I don't, but let's try, Mr. Bratton."

Smiling, Creed shrugged his shoulders. "I'm game if you are."

"Truce?"

"Truce . . ."

The truce lasted the rest of the day. It was only later, after the children had curled up in their blankets and gone to sleep, and the fire was burning down to glowing embers, that they quarreled again.

Creed was slumped against a log, using it as a headrest while he gazed into the fire. A cigarette dangled from his mouth, and he held his whiskey bottle in one hand.

"Must you drink those strong spirits?" Hannah asked in a stiff, disapproving tone. "I find them offensive."

"Then, don't drink any," Creed muttered without looking at her.

"I have no intention of drinking such filth!" she shot back. Her fingers curled into the material of her skirts as she bit her bottom lip to keep from saying more. She should not have said anything, she knew, but she had not been able to keep the words from being spoken when she had seen him tilt back his head and swallow half the bottle. "It's not right to court drunkenness, Mr. Bratton," she added when the bottle lifted again.

Creed sat up abruptly. "And it's stupid to court disaster with a wagging tongue, Miss McGuire!"

"I am only trying to point out the pitfalls of strong drink . . ."

"No, you're trying to nag me into fitting some kind of goddamned picture you've got in your mind of how a man should be! Well, it won't work, Miss Holier-than-thou! You won't fit me into any mold, so stop trying!"

"That is *not* what I am attempting to do," she began indignantly, but Creed surged to his feet, uncoiling like a snake. He towered over her, making her quail with sudden fright as he glared down at her.

Hannah's heart began to pound loudly, thudding against her rib cage with bruising force. Her mouth was suddenly dry and her throat tight, and she gazed up at him with wide eyes. How could she have forgotten for a single instant that this man was as rough and brutal as the land he lived in? How could she have goaded him into a reaction, when she knew that he had so few principles? He would not hesitate to leave them if it suited him, and she wondered why he had not already done so. Perhaps she had misjudged him—perhaps she had lent him more character than he possessed. Hannah briefly considered flight from the dark reactions evident in his face.

But then he was telling her that she could just go the rest of the way by herself, that he was damn sick and tired of putting up with a shrewish woman and whining children. "And you've cost me some good money to boot!" he added in a harsh growl.

"Good money?" Hannah asked, rising to her feet so that she would not feel so intimidated by six foot two inches of angry man towering over her. "And just how have I cost you good money, Mr. Bratton?"

"I'm a bounty hunter, Miss McGuire, and instead of catching up with the men I was chasing, I ended up playing guide to you!" he snapped, and Hannah's eyes widened.

*Bounty hunter, not an outlaw...thank God...*

"Oh, yes, those men. I remember you telling me about it. These are the same men who were in Jubile, is that right?"

"I'm sure of it."

"Did I tell you that I remembered where they said they were going?" Hannah asked, smoothing her skirts and avoiding Creed's suddenly narrowed gaze.

Curtly, "Yes."

"How far is Fort Benton?"

"Why? You're not going along..."

"I know that, but you should be glad we're so near. Don't they have to travel the Mullan Road? And we are going to be in Coeur d'Alene in two days," Hannah pointed out.

"Oh, yeah, that'll be real convenient," Creed snarled. "And it only means that I'm a week behind and they'll be in Fort Benton with the gold a long time before I get there!"

"But why should that matter, as long as you catch up with them?"

Tilting up the bottle he held, Creed slanted her a grim glance. He took a long swig, then lowered the bottle and wiped his mouth on his sleeve. "Because once they pass the gold on to their connection, I can forget about getting any of it."

"Getting any of... do you mean that you were going to confiscate the stolen gold and keep it?"

Creed's mouth tightened, and his tone was faintly ironic. "You catch on pretty quick."

"But that... that's dishonest!" Hannah gasped. "That's stealing, and one of the commandments warns..."

"Oh, for the love of... Look—do you have to spout off every time I say something you don't like? I've heard it all, Miss Missionary Lady, and I don't want to hear it again. Go preach to somebody who does! I've got places to go and things to do."

Hannah gazed at him steadily, disappointment almost choking her. Clearing her throat, she said softly, " 'The wicked flee when no man pursueth; but the righteous are bold as a lion.' "

"One more quotation, Miss McGuire, and I will make sure that you regret it," Creed warned.

" 'There is no peace, saith the Lord, unto the wicked.' "

When he took a menacing step forward she lost her courage and bolted, picking up her skirts and fleeing over the rocks and fallen limbs that littered the ground. She heard him swear loudly, then call for her to come back before she got hurt or lost, but she ignored him. Disillusioned and hurt, she ran away from Creed as fast as she could, heedless of direction or the fact that the night was dark.

The bitter thought came to her that she was contradicting the quotation she had just used, that she was fleeing as if she were the wicked one. Where was the boldness she had just boasted of? Perhaps she wasn't as righteous as she thought . . .

*How could he? How could he be so faithless when I wanted him to be . . . to be good and righteous?*

A harsh sob clawed at her throat, threatening to erupt into the still night air, and Hannah finally paused. She was at the edge of the lake, with the dark forest stretching endlessly behind her and the waves lapping at the muddy banks in front of her. Her breath came in short, panting gasps, and her side ached from running so hard. There was no sign of their campfire, no sign of Creed Bratton. She sank to her knees on the soft ground and buried her face in her hands.

The breeze blowing across the lake was cool, making her shiver as she felt it cut through her thin skirts. She had ripped up her petticoats to make cloths, and now she felt the loss of their warmth in the night air. Huddled on a cushion of fallen pine needles beneath the spreading branches, Hannah tried to make some sense of her muddled thoughts.

Branches swayed above her in the breeze, and the long, sharp-scented pine needles occasionally brushed against her shoulders. Somewhere in the distance a mountain cat coughed loudly, menacingly, and she heard the sharp cry of a night bird. Muffled plops rippled in the lake waters, and Hannah stirred restlessly. Perhaps she should go back. It was late, and she wasn't certain how far she had come in her headlong flight from Creed.

Rising, Hannah turned, but a dark shadow blocked her path. She swallowed a scream when she recognized Creed, but her chin thrust out belligerently. He was leaning against a tree trunk, his moon-shadowed face set in harsh lines.

"Where do you think you're going?" he demanded.

"Anywhere away from you!"

"Yeah, well, think again. You're not sticking me with those damned kids if you happen to fall down a hill and break your neck, Miss Missionary Lady . . ."

"I refuse to stand here and talk to you," she began, and attempted to push past him. His arm caught her around the waist and slung her back against the tree trunk. It knocked the breath from her lungs and she gasped, gazing up at him with wide, fearful eyes.

"I'm gettin' tired of this," Creed warned. His forearm pressed against her rib cage, and he could feel the erratic thud of her heart hammering against his tensed muscles. She was staring up at him with those wide doe eyes, and her mouth was half open as she sucked in quick, panting breaths of air. Creed's gaze dropped slightly, narrowing on the soft expanse of skin gleaming through her partly unbuttoned dress. Vague shadows flirted with him—promising shadows that sent a lightning jolt of desire to his nerve ends. He felt a familiar tightening in his groin, and his mouth thinned to a straight line.

"Getting tired of what, Mr. Bratton?" she was snapping at him. "Getting tired of doing what you know you should do, instead of what you want to do? I think you are more selfish than I had ever dreamed a person could be. I think that . . ."

"You think and talk too goddamned much," Creed muttered,

leaning his body against hers, pressing her against the rough bark of the towering pine.

Hannah could feel the bark scratch against her back, could feel the hot press of his body against hers through the thin material of her skirts. When she looked up at Creed's shadowed face she read the desire in his eyes. There was the briefest moment in which she wanted to lean closer to him, to put her arms around his neck and yield to the raging desire that surged through her veins, but she resisted. She couldn't. Her beliefs in how it should be would not allow her to surrender to that aching need inside her, that sweeping attraction that she had felt for Creed Bratton from the moment she had first seen him.

Summoning all her strength, she pushed him away, taking advantage of his surprise to wrench from his grasp and run blindly, stumbling over fallen logs and crashing through thick bushes. She was running from her own longings as much as she was running from Creed. She could hear his pursuit, his angry curses and demands for her to stop, but she couldn't.

Thorny limbs tore at her skirts, dragged through her hair and loosened it from its bun on the nape of her neck, but she forced her way through the dark shadows as if all the hounds of hell were behind her. Trailing vines lashed her face in stinging whips, and knobby roots clawed at her feet as if trying to slow her flight.

A huge rock loomed just ahead, and when Hannah would have stopped she found her feet sliding from under her, sending her crashing down a steep gully. She tumbled head over heels, her skirts flying over her head and limbs snagging her plummeting body. There was no time to scream, no time to put out her hands to slow her descent. When she reached the bottom, she was only dimly aware that she had somehow stopped rolling. A loud buzzing roared in her ears, and her head began to thud painfully.

She lay limply, spitting out leaves and dirt, too scared to look around her. The roaring in her ears came and went, loud then fading, so that she was startled when she felt something warm curl around her arm. A shrill scream ripped from her throat then, and she stumbled to her feet, thrashing wildly with her arms.

"Dammit!" a rough voice growled, and she was jerked back down. "You're crazy, you know that?"

"Creed?"

"Well, it ain't George Washington, sweetheart!"

Hannah shuddered. "Good," she said weakly. "He's dead."

"You will be, too, if you keep up this stupid game!" He gave her a rough shake that rattled her teeth and made her head snap back, then growled, "You could have killed yourself!"

"So?" she shot back at him. "What difference would that make to you?"

"Not a damn bit," he said promptly. "But then I'd be stuck with all those squalling brats . . ."

"They don't squall . . ."

"And might end up having to kill 'em. That might not make me as happy as it sounds." He gave her another shake, then thought to ask, "You all right?"

"Not that you care, but I was doing a lot better before you began shaking me like a rag doll," she sniffed.

Creed released her immediately, then sat back on his haunches to gaze at her with a critical eye. She looked a mess. Leaves and sticks were tangled in her long, loose hair, and her skirts were torn and bedraggled, with long smears of mud and dirt on them. Her stockings were torn and she'd lost a shoe. One leg was half bare.

Noting his gaze, Hannah shoved her skirt down over her leg and gave him an indignant glare. She surged to her feet and stood indecisively, and Creed reached out to grab her arm. A flood of moonlight glittered over the gully, and overhead loomed the dark bank down which she'd slid only moments before. Her head tilted back and she met his gaze with deliberate disdain.

Any words she might have uttered remained unsaid, for when she met Creed's intent stare she knew what he was thinking. It shone in his eyes as if written there, and her slow heartbeat escalated into a rapid tattoo. She was alone in the wilderness with Creed Bratton—alone and defenseless against her attraction to him—and he knew it . . .

# Chapter Ten

Creed's hands found her small waist in a swift, graceful movement, and Hannah was pulled into a harsh grasp before she had time to swallow the hard knot lodging in the middle of her throat. He held her resisting body close, his arms folding around her and pressing her trembling legs tightly against him.

"Let me go," she said against his chest, her squeaky voice vibrating between loathing and longing. "I refuse to be mauled!"

"Mauled? You call this mauling?" Creed's head lowered and his mouth found her half-parted lips, crushing against them, his tongue darting between the vulnerable velvet petals in a lightning flicker of fire. There was no gentleness in this kiss, no tenderness. Strong arms held her pinned against the hard length of his body. He was smothering her, drawing her breath from her lungs with his intensity. His hands shifted from her arms to her back, splaying against the curve of her spine to pull her even closer to him.

Hannah's thin skirts provided scant barrier for the heat of his hands, and she could almost feel the roughened callouses on his palms and fingers. She gasped, and his tongue flicked against hers again, lightning quick, hot and searing, an intrusion. Hannah knew little about intimacies between a man and a woman, but she was getting brisk clues from her body's unexplainable reactions. Her head was light, and all the blood in her body seemed to have congealed in one shocking area.

Hannah strained away from him, but it only seemed to invite his caress, for Creed's hands slid lower to cup her and lift her against him, so close that she could feel the sharp press of his metal belt buckle against her stomach. A hot flush stained her cheeks, and she writhed in his arms—another invitation to bold caresses. Creed's grip tightened. She felt faint, and the muscles in her legs—which before this had given her very little problem—no longer cooperated with her brain's sluggish order to remain taut and hold her upright. Instead, her knees quivered weakly, turning to the consistency of jelly and threatening to deposit her on the ground in an untidy heap. What was he doing to her? And what was this strange, fevered pounding in her ears?

Sensing a trace of response in her awkward movements, Creed murmured, "Don't look now, but you're kissing me back."

A gasp of outrage shuddered into the air, and he laughed softly, drawing back to look down at her face. Long lashes were shuttering her eyes, lying in graceful swoops like moth wings against her flushed cheeks, and her soft, bruised mouth was quivering. Silvery moonlight graced her pale skin with ethereal beauty, and the satiny texture was as soft to the touch as a baby's. For once she was silent, a fact for which he was infinitely grateful, and he could have sworn she was leaning into him.

Did she realize how lovely she was—how innocent and appealing and appallingly childlike? It was a heaven-sent gift most women would use without a qualm, but he had yet to see her take advantage of it. She didn't seem to consider outer beauty important, and maybe that was what he found so endearing. Or maybe this was just a brief resurgence of the desire that had been pricking him since he'd first felt her in his arms that day in Jubile—felt the heavy weight of her breasts pressing against his chest and the delicate curve of her thighs against his arms. Or it could be just the whiskey he'd swallowed that made him think of these things—the sharp bite of the numbing alcohol that left him deliciously attuned to the needs of his body.

Whatever it was, he saw no need to deny himself any longer. No need to deny her either, for he could tell by her heightened breathing and the warm flush spreading from her cheeks to her breasts that she was as aroused as he was. Creed's hands moved to circle her waist, then rose to brush lightly against the hard rosettes tipping her breasts. Hannah gave a moan of desperation.

Hearing it, he smiled against her moist, parted lips and murmured, "Now, *this* is mauling, Miss Hannah McGuire!"

Slowly and unhurriedly, Creed brushed aside the thin fabric of her gown. The buttons seemed to pop open of their own accord, freeing the alabaster globes to the chill night air. Apprehension shivered through her as Hannah tried to back away, to keep Creed at arm's length. But he yanked her back, his fingers digging into her soft skin as his mouth found the fluttering hollow at the base of her throat. Hannah

moaned again, despairing and helpless. She felt her bodice
gape wider, felt his fingers brush inquisitively against her
shrinking flesh. But, instead of being repulsed, Hannah felt
a strange fire igniting inside, coiling deep within the pit of
her stomach and curling upward, threatening to consume her
with an intensity she had never dreamed existed. Her bared
breasts grated against his shirt in a tantalizing caress that
made her gasp, and Creed's exploring mouth took quick
advantage of her open lips. He kissed her deeply, hungrily,
as if trying to absorb her into his own body.

It was like sipping molten lead, drinking liquid fire,
swallowing heated air. Reeling as if drunk, Hannah curled
her fingers desperately into his deerskin shirt to keep from
falling off the edge of the world into infinity.

Minutes slid past before Creed could think about anything
other than the pressing need to bury himself within this
curving, delicate woman in his arms. Dimly, at first, then
with a sharper realization, he became aware of her faint,
futile struggles against him, the thrust of her legs and
fluttering beat of her bare foot against his shin. His spread
hand slid lower to still her frantic churning in his arms,
and his mouth released her bruised lips.

"That won't work," he muttered thickly, his voice sounding too slow and lazy even to his own ears. "You're only
bruising your toes..."

Light-headed from his intimate caresses and suffocating
kisses, Hannah somehow found the strength to say, "I don't
care." It was a childish response, at best, and she knew it.
"Let me go!" she tried again, more forcefully, but with the
same disappointing results.

"No, no, sweet Hannah. Not this time. Not now. It's too
late to let you go, too late to stop this..." His fingers slid
into the gaping edges of her dress and drew it from her
shoulders to her waist in a swift, expert motion that brought

a gasp from Hannah's tight throat. It also had the result of effectively binding her arms so that she was helpless to do more than protest verbally when he lifted her from her feet into his arms. "Am I too slow for you?" he murmured against her ear when she arched away from him. "Sorry, I'll try to be quicker, love."

Half sobbing, she felt the rustling press of leaves against her bare back as he placed her gently on the ground, felt Creed bend over her, blocking out the moonlight washing over the ravine. Under the heavy weight of his body Hannah burned in vivid colors like the rainbow: the glowing red of a campfire, the misty rose of a sunset, the lemon haze that had furred the horizon, the hot blue of daylight, and the deep purple of the night. Pinpoint pricks of white light wheeled in graceful, dusty patterns across the sky, vying with the silver moon for dominance.

Playful moonbeams danced across the grass, leaves, and rocks, spotlighting objects at random. It glittered over Creed's hair, the rich, dark sweep of it falling over his forehead and almost into his eyes—those deep, fathomless eyes that could be as warm and rich as coffee, or as black and stormy as the darkest night. There was a subtle magic in his sleepy eyes—a sorcery of sorts that lured the unwary into his trap, like a spider spinning a web.

*Come into my parlor*, was the treacherous invitation, delivered in a sensual package of smooth, tanned muscles and features expertly woven into a handsome tapestry. *Don't look behind the mask*, the whispery voice cautioned.

Warning bells rang in her head like all the chimes of St. Louis's cathedral, and Hannah tried to concentrate on anything but Creed Bratton. She focused on the brisk night air whisking through the thick tree branches overhead, occasionally loosing a long-dead leaf and sending it spiraling down to join the others already blanketing the bottom of the ravine. There was a singing rhythm to the wind, a sighing song that made her think of unseen sirens. It was seductive, luring, soothing, like a mother's lullaby at bedtime. But it wasn't proof against Creed's magic.

Hannah's concentration was shattered when Creed rolled away, leaving her lying still and quiet as he shoved to his knees and stared down at her. Her throat tightened with anticipation. She couldn't acknowledge him—she just couldn't! It would be deadly. Turning her head away, she tried to pull her dress up, but he stopped her, his hands gentle but firm as he parted the dress from her shrinking flesh. She shivered, hot and cold at the same time, humiliation rising in a white heat to stain her cheeks and darken her eyes. Ignoring his smooth, graceful movements as he unbuckled and drew off his gun belt, slicing it through the air in a coiled arc to land not far away, Hannah desperately recalled instead the stubborn antics of their old milch cow, Tabitha. She searched frantically for a topic to distract her reeling brain from what was happening to her body—something that would put it all into proper perspective. Even that failed her when Creed began to shrug out of his clothes, and she gave a long, sighing shudder.

He was absorbed in what he was doing—dragging off his buckskin shirt and unbuttoning his pants. His hawk-sharp features were knotted into a frown as he tugged at the laces of his shirt. The absurdity of the situation struck her then—that she was lying in wait like a chicken ripe for the plucking—and Hannah fought against the sudden swell of laughter that threatened to burst from her throat and into the air. She was hysterical, no doubt about it, she thought. Her mind had snapped.

She might have taken advantage of his distraction to flee, but her muscles were suddenly paralyzed. Nothing worked right. No part of her body responded to her brain's commands. The machine had gone awry, run amok in a normally orderly and sane world. Her only defense was mental detachment—a refusal to yield him all that he seemed so determined to wrest from her. He might plunder her body, coax it into fevered responses in spite of her resistance, but he would never have that essential part of her that was uniquely Hannah. That was hers alone to give—hers alone to bestow upon whom she wished to share such a gift.

Creed stared down at the girl lying on the bed of leaves, admiring her distant beauty. Even naked, she still seemed untouchable, her wide eyes gazing back at him, limpid pools that mirrored his own uncertainty. Or was it fright he saw in those smoky depths?

Blinking, Hannah dragged in a slow, heated breath, unable to look at Creed but unable not to. He looked *different* from the way she'd thought he would, somehow more powerful, with harsher lines. Why had she never noticed the smooth bulge of muscles under his shirt, the flowing weave of skin and tissue and muscle that blended so perfectly—a marvelous creation that proved God's existence? Or maybe she had, but hadn't wanted to admit it—hadn't wanted to acknowledge his physical perfection. It was evident now, even in the unfamiliar angles and planes of his masculine form—the rich, dark pelt of hair furring his broad chest and dipping down to form a vee; the knotted ridge of muscles and the flat, washboard surface of his belly; and the lean thighs that had held her pressed against the cushion of leaves and moss. Hannah drew in a ragged breath and turned her face away from him.

Sensing her detachment, her mental withdrawal, Creed honed his considerable skills on her resistance. It was a test, a battle of wills. Slowly, delicatedly, he drew the pads of his fingers over her skin, tracing the curving line of her jaw, skimming over the elegant thrust of her high cheekbones, dipping into the tiny whorls of her ear to make her shiver. His hand moved downward, palming the lush weight of a breast, his lips tasting the ripe, blushing peak that curled into a tight knot at the flick of his tongue.

One hand curved over the tight, narrow band of her waist, then slid up the gentle swell of her voluptuous hips and paused. He kneaded the supple flesh with slow, languorous motions, reveling in the feel of skin as soft as a rose petal. Then his hand drifted across her in a light caress, dipping into silken hollows, exploring the subtle mysteries of her body.

A gush of lubricous sensation shot through her in a burst of light and color, spangling the world with shades of rose and purple as Creed touched her . . . there . . . in that shadowy cleft between her thighs, the velvety folds that quivered beneath his hand. An inarticulate cry rose from her then, spiraling up to hang in the night air. Creed ignored it, and she surged desperately against that knowing hand.

"No! Oh, please don't!"

"Why not? Don't you like it?" His voice was thick, as slow and warm as the summer sun, lazily drifting over her in a rush of heated air. "Doesn't it feel good?" Lifting his head, Creed gazed at her through eyes heavy with desire.

Shimmering light fell in gauzy veils over Hannah's body—a brushing of stardust over skin so pale that the delicate tracery of veins could be seen beneath the velvet texture. A faint, hammering pulse fluttered like the wings of a trapped butterfly beneath her rib cage, that fragile arch of bones curving over her heart. Drenched eyes gazed up at Creed, liquid pearls crystallizing on the long sweep of thick lashes fringing them, and he paused.

A remote sting of his conscience that was not too fogged by the potent brew he'd imbibed earlier briefly emerged before being firmly dragged back down, and he curled her

pliant body beneath him. In the warm, steamy space that
barely separated their bodies he could feel the insistent
contact of her bared breasts against him, the abrasive rub of
his chest hair against the taut peaks. It was tantalizing,
tormenting, taunting, and he felt the pulsing surge of his
desire strengthen.

*Sweet Jesus, does she know what she's doing to me?*

In the next instant he knew that she did not, for he could
feel the rounded prod of her hands caught between them as
she attempted to push him from his position atop her. The
firm detail of Creed's hard male body was indented into the
swell of her stomach, and he felt her shift in alarm at the
touch.

"There's some things a man has no control over," he
said against her ear, "but, even if I did . . ."

Hannah let the unfinished sentence die. It didn't matter.
She knew what he meant. She could fell the tightly curved
muscles of his chest slide beneath her frantically pushing
palms, could feel the determined thrust of him digging into
her. Why was his breathing so steady while her lungs ached
and rattled with each tortured breath? And her traitorous
heart popped convulsively in an oddly escalating tempo.

If only she wasn't so naive! If only she knew more
about . . . about the things that happened between a man and
a woman, perhaps then she could combat this confusing
surge of emotional and physical response that threatened to
overwhelm her. It rolled over her in ever-increasing waves,
higher and higher, like the breakers of the sea. Hannah felt
lost and adrift, buffeted by the whim of the wind. She ached
with unexplained need, throbbed in the very core of her
being for . . . something. Creed seemed to know the answer—
seemed to know what would cure her of this sweeping ache,
but he was the enemy.

Outmaneuvered, Hannah closed her eyes against him.

She was lost. Her blood rioted in her veins, and her brain
was drugged by her exploding senses. Nothing was safe—no
last bastion could be held against his inevitable victory, the
slow, rolling tide that would ultimately drag her beneath the
waves.

"Only this once, love," he was whispering in her ear,
and Hannah winced at his use of the endearment he did not
mean, before the import of what he was saying struck her as
forcibly as a fist.

"Only this once . . . *what*?" she whispered back in an
agony of apprehension.

A soft laugh tangled in her hair, stirring the coppery curls
that drifted in abandon across her face and over her shoulder. "It'll only hurt once," he promised, touched by her
vulnerability in spite of himself.

Appalled by the thought that not only was she to be taken
in grudging submission, but that it would actually *hurt*,
Hannah made a pitiful sound in the back of her throat.
"That's not fair," she said after a moment when Creed did
not move, except to stroke back the sweat-tipped tendrils of
hair from her eyes.

"No," he agreed, "it's not."

"But you still intend to . . . to do it."

"Yes," he said, nuzzling her hair. "Afterward, you'll
know why."

"I doubt it," she mumbled against his shoulder as he
shifted to lie atop her, his movements gentle and soft on her,
once more coaxing an unwilling response from the body she
had begun to think of as treacherous.

And when it came, that sudden, knifelike thrust that felt
as if it was hewing her body in two, Hannah stiffened
against him, arching her back and digging her bare heels
into the cushion of leaves beneath them. Her breath came in

short, panting gasps, and her eyes were wide and accusing as she stared up at Creed's moon-shadowed face.

"Don't move," he said, his breath suspiciously short, his fingers curled around her wrists to hold her arms out to her sides when she pushed against him.

As if she would—as if she *could* move! His entire weight rested on her, the heavy length of his lean legs and his broad chest pinning her effectively down on the moss and leaves. And he was buried deep inside her, a painful melding that abruptly ended her innocence. Sorrowful tears stung her eyes, and she had to clear her throat of the pooling moisture before she could speak.

"Is it over?"

A light shudder passed through his body at her disgruntled question, and he shook his head. "Not yet, love. The best part is yet to come."

*I hope so*, she thought. It would be a shame if this was all there was, especially after the buildup of her expectations. Had she lost her maidenhood, her innocence and dignity, for *this*? It seemed incredible that men and women would want to finalize such an act when the climax was so...so disappointing.

But then Hannah discovered that there really was more, that Creed had not lied to her. When he began to move again there was no more pain, only the fierce urgency of his hard male body as he moved within her melting warmth. Then his body rocked against her in a rhythmic motion, and she was stunned to feel the same breathless expectation that had filled her earlier. It built up slowly—a tight knot of anticipation that burst into flower in rippling explosions that should have been heard from Idaho to Canada and back. Hannah felt as if she were in the midst of the northern lights that she'd seen hanging in the summer sky—the cascading shower of blues, greens and yellows that slowly melted from the heavens to earth. Why had she never known that a person could *feel* in color before?

Her hands slid over the smooth muscles of his back, bumping over the ridges of his spine, the pads of her fingers digging into the sweat-slick flesh and holding him.

*So this is what it's like . . . this expectation . . . this soaring above the stars . . .*

A roaring filled her ears, reminding Hannah of the sea waves crashing against the coast—foamy geysers spewing up, only to crash back over the rocks. Her entire body shuddered with the force of the wild, sweet release, and she felt Creed's arms tighten around her. He was holding her gently, almost tenderly, and she wondered if this could be the same man who had not listened to her pleas—the same, rough man who had swept away her objections with a careless shrug. But it was. And he was kissing her closed eyelids, the tip of her nose, and her quivering mouth—tiny, gentle kisses that were meant to be soothing.

Buffeted by emotion and shivering reaction, she felt as if she'd been caught up in a storm and barely escaped with her life. She was trembling all over, her arms and legs shaking uncontrollably, and Creed drew her gown over her.

"Cold?" he murmured softly, and she shook her head.

"No. It . . . it's not that."

He didn't ask what it was, but just held her. She felt good in his arms, soft and yielding. He'd almost forgotten how sweet a woman could be—women like Hannah, anyway. The other kind of woman didn't count—the one who gazed at him with hot, greedy eyes when he rode into a town, wanting to part him from his money more than they wanted to linger. Oh, there had been a few who'd wept when he left, who'd pleaded with him to stay, but he'd never felt the slightest inclination to do so. Not that he did now either, but at least with Hannah, he felt a surge of tenderness. She was complex and fascinating—one moment a pious, preachy female spouting Bible verses and gazing at him with disapproval, the next a sultry woman with steamy kisses and reluctant surrender. A chameleon, he thought then—she was an unpredictable chameleon who could change colors at will. That was Hannah. Like now. Who would have dreamed that she would respond like she had—would put her arms around him and meet his body with such sweet, driving urgency? But she had. And now she was sorry.

Creed bit back a smile at her expression of dismay and anger, at the damning realization of her body's betrayal. He sighed. The passion that had just misted her eyes was burned away with the fires of wrath. She intended to make him regret what had just happened—maybe not his forceful taking of her, but the fact that he had coaxed a response from her body.

"Get up," she said through teeth clenched to halt their skeletal chattering.

"Already?" Creed mocked. "What if I'm not ready to get up?"

She pushed at him with the heels of her hands, prodding him. He was laughing at her! And after what had just happened between them! It was inexcusable, unforgivable! She lashed out with a fusillade of angry words meant to hurt.

"Rapist! Degenerate! Despoiler of women!"

Curling his fingers around her wrists and pulling her arms out to her sides, Creed sighed. "Hannah, it's normal for a woman to enjoy sex," he began reasonably, but she cut across his attempt at reasoning.

"Enjoy it! I *loathed* every minute of it!" she lied with only the slightest qualm. "It was disgusting, degrading, detestable . . ."

"No more 'de' words, please. I get the picture!" Creed snapped, beginning to lose his patience.

"Disgusting begins with a *d-i*," Hannah shot back. "And if you were as smart as you think you are, you'd know that."

Releasing her wrists, Creed surged to his feet. "I can't say I think much of your love talk," he commented as he bent to scoop up his clothes.

"And I can't say I think much of you," Hannah returned, fighting back the distressing glut of tears that stung her eyes. She sniffed, dragging her dress more tightly around her bare body, wishing Creed would just go away—melt into the ground, or fade in a puff of smoke. Everything was made much worse by the knowledge that she had responded to him, that she had ached for the sweeping release. Hadn't she always hated injustice? So why couldn't she admit that she had ached for him? Granted, he had known just where to touch, just which caress would provoke a response, but if she had been strong, she could have turned his victory to a defeat.

But Hannah said none of those things as she slithered her dress over her head, loudly complaining when Creed refused to turn his head. Buckling his gun belt over his buckskin trousers, he lifted a dark brow and said, "Why bother now? Isn't that rather like shutting the barn door after the cows have gotten out?"

And she'd had no good reason, of course, other than her belated sense of modesty, so she had dressed in the silver press of moonlight and hated him for his insensitivity. It was only when they returned to camp and she stood at the fringe of the small clearing where the children lay asleep, that a provocative comment came to mind.

Turning to face him, gazing at his carefully blank expression and the wary set of his shoulders, Hannah said, "I hope that God forgives you for this evening, Mr. Bratton, for I am certain that I never shall."

Not replying, Creed had just watched as she crossed the clearing to her blankets. He was likely to lose out on both counts, he reflected.

# Chapter Eleven

Hannah woke before the others. She lay there in her warm blankets, listening to the familiar sounds around her—the liquid warble of early-morning birds, and the faint, husky whisk of wind through the trees. It was still dark. The soft blush that would signal the rising of the sun had barely lightened the eastern sky, pushing back the cold black velvet of the night to a pearly gray.

She snuggled deeper, blinking sleepy eyes at the shadows swaying above her. A pine cone loosened its tenuous hold on the curve of a branch overhead and plummeted to earth in a haphazard fashion, bouncing erratically, then rolling to the edge of her blanket and snaring her attention. Snaking one arm from beneath the warm haven of the blanket, Hannah reached out an idle fingertip to touch the barbed spear of the cone. It lay like a tiny hedgehog, the curving spines of the individual seeds jutting outward to prick her skin, and she drew back sharply from the quick sting. She put her finger to her mouth in an absent motion, and winced at the soft tenderness of her still-bruised lips. How easily she bruised, like ripe fruit that protested too-rough handling.

She should be more thick-skinned, less vulnerable to the hazards around her.

Closing her eyes in a sudden spasm of pain and shame, Hannah struggled against the whimper that rose in her throat. The memories of the night before lurked at the fringes of her mind, haunting her. In some remote, empty area of her bruised spirit there had been a burgeoning hope that Creed would care for her, that his desire for her would suddenly sprout wings of love. But daybreak brought the harsher light of reality with it, dashing all her fairy tale hopes into dust. There had been nothing so honorable as love in Creed's mind. The simple truth was that he had wanted her, and he had taken her.

Hannah's body sagged with weariness. Her dress was torn and ragged and her hair in wild tangles. She looked, Hannah thought sadly, like a used woman. And wasn't that what she was now? Her thighs still ached, and there was a vague soreness between them. But her physical discomfort could not compare to the sharp, biting edge of pain that gnawed her whenever she thought about what had transpired between them. How could she honestly deny that she had wanted him, too? She couldn't. Honesty came hard and swift now, shaming her into the admission. Hannah Elizabeth McGuire, who prided herself on being truthful, had lied not only to Creed Bratton—who, after all, probably deserved being lied to—but to herself. Where had all her childhood teachings gone? Flown away like a bird since meeting that harsh, handsome man who tormented her thoughts and dreams.

There had been no love words exchanged between them the night before. Creed's skillful fingers and mouth had wrested the reaction he wanted from her, had seduced her with fevered caresses and age-old yearnings, and she had been a willing accomplice. Oh, perhaps she had resisted just enough to satisfy her conscience, but not enough to satisfy that coldly logical part of her brain that now scolded her.

And, after all, what had she expected from him—a declaration of undying love, perhaps? Nice, but hardly realistic. Creed had never hinted at such emotions, had never suggested by word or manner that he might want to give up his solitary life and take up farming in a cozy white frame house filled with children and the aroma of freshly baked pies. Oh, he was well aware of his sensual attraction to her, of how she could not resist the hesitant, shy glances at him when she could. He'd made *that* plain enough! And she hadn't been able to deny that, either. During the past days she'd watched him when he'd made an occasional stab at shaving, filling a tin bowl with water and scraping the rough stubble of whiskers from his jaw and cheeks. Indeed, she could not have looked away from the lean perfection of his well-honed body as he'd stood without a shirt, squinting into a small piece of polished mirror as he shaved. Admiration had swelled when his tanned muscles flexed in the early morning sunlight, luring her gaze again and again. And he had known it, though she'd rather die of a snake bite than admit it to him. Fortunately—or unfortunately, as the case may be—there were no poisonous snakes in Northern Idaho.

But last night had been different. Last night she had given in to her physical needs, had yielded to the temptation that she had successfully avoided for a week. Her token struggle had been duly noted, and her surrender sweetly met. And when she had chastised him afterward, she had really been chastising herself. And he'd known that, too.

Creed had walked beside her in stony silence on their return to the camp, his face set and harsh. Though several questions had trembled on the tip of her tongue, Hannah had not dared utter a word for fear of unleashing a torrent of accusations against him, and that would not have been wise.

He knew too much—knew too well how she had felt, how even over her verbal protests and token struggles she had wanted him. No, it would not have been at all wise to provoke the truth from Creed Bratton, for she had yet to come to grips with it herself.

There had been nothing she could say, no offer of explanation she could make. Away from the dark shadows of the forest and in the bright light of the campfire still burning, she had faced reality. She had gone about the business of checking on the children and tucking blankets more closely about them, feeling the brunt of his gaze on her the entire time.

Creed had once more erected the familiar barrier between them, not because she had demanded it, but because it was necessary. Perhaps the right word, the right look from those shaded black eyes would have sent her scurrying into his arms, but it didn't happen. He remained determinedly silent. Sitting with his back against a tree trunk and a full whiskey bottle in one hand, Creed had not offered a single word— friendly or hostile—while Hannah tended her duties. He'd not even taken a drink from his bottle, but sat in brooding silence until she rolled up in her blankets close to the fire and turned her back to him.

Sighing, Hannah wondered why she couldn't see things in shades of gray at times, instead of always in stark black or blinding white. There was right and wrong, no in between. Right? No, wrong. There were subtle gray areas that fringed what was right, skirted what was wrong. Creed seemed familiar with them, was definitely on friendly terms with those mysterious gray areas. *He* wasn't having any trouble sleeping, while she—she had lain awake for what seemed like hours, agonizing over the night's events and trying to alter them in her mind. If she had said this or done that, then this would have—or not have—happened.

But she couldn't change it. And now she lay awake while he slept blissfully on, uncaring, his world as intact as it had been the day before. Hannah felt a burning surge of resentment. How could he sleep so soundly when her entire world had been shattered?

She sat up, glaring in his direction, spurred into making a noise, doing anything to disrupt his untroubled sleep. But when her fingers curled around a tree branch and she would have yielded to the inclination, she paused. *Shades of gray, Hannah Elizabeth, shades of gray*, she scolded silently. The limber tree branch fell from her fingers, back to the ground, and she crawled under her blankets again, pulling them over her head.

Burrowing her face into the crook of her arms, Hannah tried not to think of Creed, tried not to envision the way his eyes crinkled when he laughed, or how the sun shone in the ebony wealth of his thick hair, but it was no use. Try as she might to recall other things, the memories haunted her. She recalled how he had held her gently, his soft words whispering against her ear, and the sweat-slick feel of his taut muscles beneath her fingers. That was even worse, for then she would recall the tiniest details of the intimacy and flush. What had happened was bad enough, but the knowledge of her willing participation pricked her soul.

Lifting her tousled head, Hannah peered from under the tent of the blanket draped over her. Her narrowed gaze shifted to Creed. He lay as innocent and guileless as one of the children, his hat pulled low over his eyes, his long form wrapped in his blankets.

Hannah sighed, blinking away a sudden, unexplainable tear. She couldn't allow herself to think of it anymore. It was over and done with, and now she must go on.

*No rest for the wicked*, echoed in her head, and she shook it resolutely away. She wasn't wicked—just weak.

Hannah dragged herself up from her blankets and pulled the rough wool material around her for warmth, arranging the hanging folds like a shawl as she went to stir the fire. It was cold in the brisk mist of early morning, and she shivered. Crouching beside the rock-ringed pile of charred wood, she poked at the glowing embers buried deep in gray ashes in an effort to rekindle the blaze. It caught finally, and she held her hands out to the warmth.

Idaho Territory—warm one day and cold the next, with icy northern winds sweeping down from Canada and bringing a flurry of snow that would dust the ground and melt within a matter of minutes. Then the sun would shine again, warming the air and ground. Whatever had possessed Joshua McGuire to come out to the wilderness and try to carve a niche for them? It had been doomed to failure from the start, Hannah reflected gloomily. This pitiful group was all that was left... She glanced at the blanketed cocoons wheeling out from the fire.

It would soon be light, and the children would be waking. Rebecca had slept easily at last, her fever broken and her color normal. Perhaps they would break camp and travel the final miles to Coeur d'Alene today. Then it would be over. Hannah and the children would find new homes, new lives. Creed Bratton would move on, would ride away after the outlaws he was chasing and forget about her—forget about the days they had spent together. Maybe at some point in the distant future he would remember her, would think of the girl who had quoted Scripture to him and lain naked in his arms on a moon-drenched night beside Pend Oreille Lake.

Hannah's throat closed, and her fingers tightened convulsively around the handle of the blackened coffeepot. Too late to think of that now—too late to go back and change it. She had to move forward. Straightening, she stood up and moved to fetch a tin cup from one of the packs.

"Going somewhere?" a soft voice drawled, startling her into almost dropping the coffeepot.

"Creed! I mean, Mr. Bratton. What are you doing awake? I th-thought you were asleep," she stammered, feeling foolish and young and vulnerable. Coaxing the breath back into her lungs and straining to slow the sudden, rapid beat of her heart, Hannah gazed down at Creed. He had pushed his hat back from his face and was gazing at her with a dark, critical stare. *Danger* shrieked at her, and she stiffened her resolve against him. His mouth—that mouth she remembered too well trailing fiery kisses over her body—was crooked in a slight smile, and she managed a shaky smile in return. "Do you want some coffee?" she offered in an attempt at normalcy.

"Coffee? Maybe, maybe not." There was a brittle-edged friendliness about him this morning that had not been there the night before. The unexpectedness of it lulled Hannah into a sense of false security, so that when his hand shot out to curl around her wrist, she was startled. "Is that a new fashion, or do you find the weather too tropical for your comfort?" he asked.

Bewildered by his question, Hannah let her eyes follow his deliberate gaze. She gasped, staring in horror at her skirt. It was ripped on one side from waist to ankle, and a long expanse of bare leg gleamed through. It must have happened in her mad flight the night before. Desperately clutching at the jagged edges with the fingers of one hand, and juggling the coffeepot with the other, she did her best to ignore Creed's interested gaze.

"My . . . my skirt is torn beyond redemption," she mourned.

"Yes," he agreed, "it is."

There was a brief silence, then he offered helpfully, "You could take it off."

Blue sparks flashed from her eyes. "No, thank you!"

Creed gave a long sigh and suggested that she wear a pair of his trousers. "Not that I have many to spare, but it's better than nothing—which is basically what you're wearing now."

Hannah stiffened, her voice icy as she said, "Through no fault of my own!"

"Did I tell you to go running through the woods at night? Any idiot knows better than that!"

"Meaning that I am an idiot."

"Not just any idiot," he said graciously.

Hannah's fingers tightened on the handle of the coffeepot as she resisted the urge to pour it over his head. "I don't intend to stand here trading insults with you," she began, ending in a gasp when he gave her skirt a sharp tug that deposited her on the blanket next to him.

A dark, potent gaze rested on her flushed face, and he gave a shake of his head when she glared at him furiously. "*I* don't intend to argue, Hannah. I have something I want to say. About last night . . ."

"No!" Hannah pushed at him in her haste to rise from the blankets—a mistake, because she dropped the coffeepot and spilled grounds and water all over both of them. Creed grabbed her wrist when she would have fled, his face tightening as she flared, "No, I don't want to talk about last night! I don't want to remember everything . . ."

"Are you actually hiding from the truth?" Creed chided rudely, refusing to release her wrist from his iron grip. He slanted a disgusted glance at his ruined blankets, but said nothing about the mess as he pulled her closer to him. She was trembling from reaction and from being so near to him, and he almost smiled as he held her more gently. "About last night—Hannah, it doesn't mean things have changed."

"Oh, no," she said brightly, desperately, struggling against the curdling in her stomach. "I never expected things would. After all, it was only an interlude for you. I understand that, and I don't expect you to give me roses and champagne, or sing paeans of praise . . ."

"Hannah . . ." Creed said irritably.

"Never fear, Mr. Creed Bratton!" she rushed on, the words tumbling unbidden from her lips, "I will not expect a single thing from you! I know that must be your greatest fear—that someone will expect you to behave decently and with responsibility . . ."

"Hannah!" he ground out roughly. "I don't mean that. I only meant . . . oh, hell! I'd rather be blunt now than risk hurting you."

"Oh, and your declaration that I was only a mild, passing fancy won't hurt me?" she demanded shakily. "Thank you!"

"No, it's not that," he said with a trace of impatience. "You know what I mean."

"Oh, yes, I certainly do! I was nothing more than a mild case of fever, or a prickly heat rash. Now that you're cured, life can go on as normal, is that it?"

"No, it isn't that at all! I just don't want you expecting white picket fences and neat red barns from me, that's all!"

"Oh, please! Credit me with a modicum of intelligence, Mr. Bratton!" Half sobbing, half laughing, she succeeded in pulling away from him. Smoky blue eyes shimmered with unshed tears, but her face was composed, her voice steady. "Please! Do I look that shallow, that inexpensive? Oh, no, I want ropes of pearls and diamond tiaras, caskets of jewels and fine raiment . . . I detest white picket fences, and I've never longed for a neat red barn. It should be evident how materialistic I am, Mr. Bratton!" Her voice broke now. Salty tears filled her eyes and dripped so that she was forced to use her skirt hem to stem the flow. Her shoulders shook, and she sobbed, "You made it quite evident a short time ago that you've no intention of changing your style of life. I never expected you to . . . to change. It's just that . . . that I've failed. I've failed myself, my father, and . . . and God.''

"Oh, for Chrissake!" Creed exploded irritably. "You didn't fail anybody, Hannah! I'll take the blame for it all if you won't degenerate into spasms of guilt over the whole silly mess. For the love of God! It's human instinct to want . . ."

"Silly mess! *Silly*—you are a sick individual," Hannah said flatly, gazing at him with the wadded hem of her skirt pressed to her nose. Slender thighs peeked from beneath the trailing material, distracting Creed's attention so that she was forced to cover them. Her hands clenched in the cotton folds as she held the skirt down over her legs. "How can you treat what happened so lightly? Do you go about the countryside deflowering virgins at will and riding happily on?"

"*Deflowering?* You make me sound like a gardener," he said, flashing her a sour glance.

"Forgive me. Nothing so mundane and trite should apply to a man such as yourself, I assure you!"

Creed's mouth tightened. "Look, all I wanted to say was that things don't have to change between us. I won't touch you again unless you want me to."

"Thank God for small favors," Hannah said bitterly. "I am grateful for your delicacy and discipline. Where was it last night?"

Creed didn't answer. He just looked at her, and somewhere in Hannah's bruised and tormented spirit she felt a small surge of shame. She was punishing him for her own lack of control, her own lack of discipline. Injustice again—shades of black and white, instead of gray. For the first time, she understood the scourgings of old—how people tormented with the knowledge of their sins had fashioned hair shirts to remind them every waking moment. It was a penance of sorts, but more than that, it was a justice. Even if those around them didn't know what the sins were, they could not be hidden from God.

It occurred to her then that Creed Bratton was very familiar with hair shirts and penance; he carried with him the markings of contrition. But none of that was evident in his hard gaze, or the harsh lines of his face.

Surging to his feet, sending Hannah sprawling backward on the blankets, he towered over her, glaring down at her and saying softly, "Damn you! Must everything be so clearly defined? Don't you ever deal in moderation, Miss McGuire?" He scooped up his gun belt, buckled it around his lean waist, and stalked away, leaving Hannah staring after him.

What he hadn't said pricked her far more harshly than those few words, and Hannah had the grace to feel ashamed. She should have explained, should have confessed that she knew she was wrong, but she hadn't.

Sitting back on her heels, Hannah glanced up to find Jessica's gaze resting on her. The child was sitting up in a tumble of blankets, regarding Hannah with a grave expression that she found most unsettling.

"Why were you arguing?" Jessica asked in her usual blunt way.

After a brief hesitation, Hannah replied. "Mr. Bratton and I frequently have disagreements, Jessica. This is nothing unusual. Why don't you help me clean up this mess, and then we shall wake the others."

Rebecca's convalescence took two more days—two more days of sullen silence and occasional barbed comments flung between Creed and Hannah. She ungraciously accepted his loan of a pair of trousers, feeling conspicuous and uncom-

fortable. She was also forced to wear moccasins on her feet
instead of shoes, because one leather pump had been
irretrievably lost on what she had come to think of as *that
night*.

"I look like a drudge," she muttered, and—overhearing
her remark—Creed offered the differing opinion that she
looked more like a sullen little boy.

Stung by this observation, Hannah had ignored him for
the remainder of the day. He certainly hadn't seemed to
think she looked like a boy on *that night*! No—then, he had
been exceedingly aware of her femininity!

Creed watched her annoyance with a slight smile, keenly
aware of Hannah in the snug trousers that skimmed her hips
and long legs in a most becoming fashion. Trousers looked
good on her—much better than those concealing skirts that
were so much more modest and proper. All she needed now
was a large felt hat and bandoliers crossed over her front
and back, and she would look like a bedraggled bandit. Poor
Hannah. She didn't know that he could read the expressions
that flitted across her face, and see that she was struggling
with an overload of guilt. It was the sad result of a
too-active conscience, Creed reflected, and he was doubly
glad he had clubbed his own back into submission.

Time dragged slowly, and on the night of the second day,
Creed bluntly informed Hannah that he was leaving the next
morning.

"With or without you," he added.

She stared at him, then nodded. "Very well. We shall be
ready, Mr. Bratton."

Creed's brows lifted. He had expected some sort of
argument—an accusation, or anger. But Hannah merely
looked up at him with wide eyes of a bright, stabbing blue,
and he shrugged. "First light," he warned.

She nodded again, curling a blanket around her shoulders

to ward off the chill as she met his wary gaze. "I said we'd be ready." There was a brief pause, and then she asked, "Was there anything else?"

"Yeah. Try keeping up with me this time."

Hannah stared at his back as he pivoted and strode away, his shoulders squared. She wanted to shout at him, to throw something at his head and stamp her feet in frustration, but she didn't. There was a certain satisfaction in remaining calm, though it eluded her at the moment. Perhaps it would be better later—later, when she had learned to live with the constant, dull ache in the region of her heart...

Late afternoon shadows purpled the sky and clung to the tips of towering firs, cedars, and pines. Coeur d'Alene lay before them, a tiny collection of wood cabins and scattered buildings on the scalloped shores of Coeur d'Alene lake.

"I remembered it as much larger," Hannah said in a small voice, staring down the last descent at their final goal. "I can't think why..."

"It's hardly bigger than Jubile, Miss Hannah!" Eric Ransom said in disappointment. "I thought it would be a lot bigger."

"So did I, Eric. I guess I was wrong." Hannah pushed back trailing strands of hair from her eyes. Doubt clouded her eyes as she stared down at the straggling line of buildings. "Maybe I just thought it was larger because my father and I had been traveling for so long, and any sort of town was more than I was accustomed to seeing," she mused aloud.

Creed Bratton reined his bay in beside her, leaning one arm on his saddle horn and staring down at her from beneath the shadow of his hat. "Do you think you could walk and talk at the same time, Miss McGuire? I'd be much obliged if we could get there before dark."

Smarting from his sarcasm, Hannah said curtly, "Of course, Mr. Bratton! But feel free to ride on if we are delaying you too greatly. After all, the town is in sight now and we *can* find it!"

Glancing from Creed to Hannah with a troubled expression, Eric put in, "Please don't leave us now, Mr. Bratton! I'd rather you stayed, and so would the rest of us, I know."

"Would they?" Creed drawled, his gaze resting on Hannah's averted face. "Somehow, I doubt that, boy, but I won't leave you behind," he added when Eric bit his lower lip and sighed. "Come on—" Bending from his saddle, he swung the boy up and behind him, much to Eric's delight. It was the first time Creed had allowed any of them to ride with him. Circling Creed's waist with his arms, Eric allowed himself a triumphant glance at the other children as the bay was nudged into a trot.

Tired, dusty, and heartsick, Hannah dreaded these final steps of the journey. It had been a long walk around the shores of Lake Pend Oreille, and splashing through the shallow ford of Priest River had left her cold and wet. Then there had been the final trek to Camp Coeur d'Alene on the shores of yet another lake. But with each step had been the knowledge that they were not yet there, that there was still time before—before parting. Now that time was up. The sands had run through the hourglass and the hour was almost at hand. A plethora of similes and metaphors raced through Hannah's mind, none of them seeming to fit her mood.

"Come along, children," she said wearily, gesturing for them to follow. "Our destination is almost achieved. There is hope and hospitality awaiting us."

Creed reined his mount to a halt, half turning to glance back at Hannah. "You better pray those folks have the same idea," he said. "I've got a feeling you may be in for a disappointment—you may have to look elsewhere for hope and hospitality.''

"If that's what it takes, Mr. Bratton,'' Hannah said to his back, ''that is what we'll do. You'll find that adversity only makes my determination stronger.''

"That right?'' Creed whirled his mount around. His cold gaze raked her stiff figure. ''You're a real martyr, aren't you?''

"No, just confident that God will provide for our needs.''

"Yeah, well, you better hope Coeur d'Alene is the answer, 'cause this is as far as I'm taking you,'' he shot back.

Hannah flinched from the hardness of his tone. It was obvious he was anxious to be rid of her as quickly as possible. ''I'm certain it will be the answer to our prayers. The new road leading east should provide the children with the opportunity to find family or new homes. That was my main concern, you know.''

"Was it?'' Creed drawled. ''I had the impression that you were more worried about your preacher-man who lived here.''

"Ah, another misguided conception, Mr. Bratton! How unfortunate for you that you have so many!''

Creed jerked on General's reins and nudged him into a trot, away from where Hannah stood, gazing at him steadily. She stared after him, then sighed and herded the silent children ahead of her.

"I still say he hates us all,'' Rebecca muttered from atop the spindly shanked mare she rode. Perched behind her, Ivy Ransom nodded vigorously.

"He does, Miss Hannah!'' Ivy confirmed. ''Only, sometimes, I think maybe he likes us a little...''

"No,'' Frog chimed in solemnly, ''he only pretends he don't like us!''

"Doesn't like us," Hannah corrected gently, staring after Creed and wishing it were true.

"Doesn't like us," Frog amended. "But he does, truly he does, else he wouldn't have watched over us so good, or have went hunting so we could eat something besides beef jerky and dried berries."

"Gone hunting, Frog," Hannah corrected again. "Maybe you're right, but it doesn't matter now. We're almost there, and we shall not see Mr. Bratton again."

"That makes you sad, doesn't it, Miss Hannah?" Jessica asked, earning a sharp glance from her teacher.

How much had the too-perceptive Jessica overheard? Hannah wondered. She managed a smile and replied, "Well, yes, Jessica, of course it makes me sad that a man who has been such a great help to us will be riding on. I doubt we will ever see him again, but we can recall him fondly."

Jessica's level gaze burned into her, and Hannah looked away. "Let's keep moving, children," she said briskly. "We have only a little bit farther to go before we reach our destination and can rest."

The last mile into Camp Coeur d'Alene was the hardest. Creed still rode ahead of them, Eric Ransom clinging to his saddle and occasionally looking back to see that they were following. The youngest children rode the two swaybacked mares, while the others plodded wearily alongside. It was a shabby group that finally strode through the muddy main street of Camp Coeur d'Alene.

Horsemen rode leisurely down the wide street, and wagons rumbled through the ruts between the buildings. A cold wind whipped through the small settlement in chilling gusts that made men hold tightly to their hats.

Feeling rather shabby and conspicuous, Hannah clutched the tattered folds of a blanket around her for warmth. Creed's trousers sheathed her legs, but her thin blouse offered no protection from the bite of the wind. All the children wore their blankets like shawls, and it was a strange caravan indeed that trod the street.

She made an effort to stand tall, ignoring the curious stares slanted in their direction. It had been a long, hard trek, sparked by the loss of everything she knew, but she had made it. Perseverance has its own rewards, but at this moment, the sight of the town she had struggled to reach was reward enough. Her goal had been attained.

Fatigue curved her mouth in a thin line, and the week spent walking from Jubile to Coeur d'Alene had given her a long, loose stride, so that she was much different from the girl Creed had first found in the blackened ruins of the log cabin. The blanket snapped against her knees in the wind. She held her shoulders stiffly, her spine straight and unyielding. Long copper braids fell down her back, tied with strips of her ill-fated skirt, and her face was a golden peach color from the sun.

This was the girl that Joel Allen first saw and didn't recognize. He heard the dogs barking, heard the soft curse of a male voice, and left his cozy log house to stand upon his porch and see the travelers. Newcomers to Coeur d'Alene were becoming more frequent since the opening of the road to Fort Benton, but this was by far the strangest group yet to arrive. Men had ridden through, pausing for only an hour or maybe a night—men who looked dangerous, bristling with rifles and pistols and knives—but those were few and far between. Outlaws had not yet discovered the thriving metropolis of eighty-seven residents. There had been mountain men with their pack-laden mules, swathed in cured and uncured animal skins and stinking to high heaven, but that was normal in Idaho. A slender, copper-haired woman surrounded by children and clad in a man's trousers was not normal.

Joel Allen halted on his shallow porch, squinting at the group. His Bible was tucked under one arm, his constant and often only companion. Not many people sought his company these days. They were too busy, with warm weather—or what passed for warm weather in Idaho—gracing the days and encouraging crops to grow. So Pastor Allen had hours to himself—hours he spent perfecting his Sunday sermons and praising God.

Now he stared hard at the small caravan winding through the street, a dim memory stirring him as they drew closer. Then he was smiling, his eyes lighting as he stepped down from the porch into the street and half ran toward them.

"Miss McGuire! Hannah McGuire! What are you doing here in Coeur d'Alene?" he was asking, rushing forward and taking her by both hands. His bright blue gaze skimmed her slender figure in a slightly shocked gaze, then rose to her face. "It's so very good to see you," he said, his gaze dropping again to her muddy trousers as he still held tightly to her hands.

Confused by this sudden recognition, Hannah hesitated. She knew him, of course—recognized his tall, spare frame and the thatch of unruly blond hair that defied the best efforts of a boar-bristle hairbrush—but he looked much different from what she recalled. Then, realizing that she must also look quite different, Hannah smiled.

"Pastor Allen! I am glad to see you, too. We have come a long way . . ."

"Of course, of course! I see that you must have endured much to get here." His gaze slid past her to the children standing in a quiet circle. His brows dipped in a frown when he did not see Joshua McGuire with the company, but when he opened his mouth to ask after his old friend, a dark shadow fell across them, and he paused.

From one corner of her vision, Hannah saw Creed rein his

bay to an abrupt halt and swing back around. Sunlight glittered on General's burnished hide as the horse wheeled and trotted back to where she stood with her fingers imprisoned in Joel Allen's hands. She gulped in a deep draught of air, and would have spoken, but could think of nothing to say. So she stood awkwardly, shifting in place, her toes digging into the soft, thick dirt of the street as she cast about for a casual comment.

As it turned out, it wasn't necessary. Creed's dark, narrowed gaze rested on them from his vantage point above their heads, and Hannah could feel his eyes boring into her head like . . . a worm in an apple, or a termite into wood—or any number of various and unflattering comparisons that cluttered her mind at the moment, effectively pushing out a rational approach to the touchy situation.

"Ah," Creed was saying in a silky tone, "I see you have found your friend, Miss McGuire. That relieves me of any further responsibility toward you, I trust?"

There was the leathery creak of his saddle, and Hannah felt rather than saw Creed lean forward to rake Joel Allen with a critical, faintly amused stare. Eric Ransom's arms were curled around Creed's waist as he held on, and the boy uttered only a faint protest as he was swung from the horse to the ground.

"Aww!" Eric said, and Creed flicked him a glance.

"This is where we part," was his short announcement, earning a quick gasp and start from Hannah. Creed met her wide gaze steadily. "I won't say it's been enjoyable, but it's certainly been . . . educational," he drawled then.

Hannah could feel Joel Allen's quizzical eyes on her face, and she could not halt the flush that rose from her neck to her cheeks, staining them a bright rose. Her flush deepened as she gently withdrew her hands from his grasp.

Resentment flashed through her at Creed's amused stare—

at the cynical curl of his mouth as he gazed pointedly at her—and she bit back a sharp retort that it certainly had not been that enjoyable for her, either. Did he think it had?

Throwing off the murky weight of gloom that inexplicably filled her spirit, winging it to earth with a crashing thud, Hannah managed a civil nod and bright, uncaring smile. Let Creed Bratton take *that* with him, instead of absolving words of anger or repudiation. Why make it easy for him to forget her? And she certainly would not yield to the biting pressure of the tears behind her heavy lids. That would come later, in private.

And so when he rode away, nudging his bay into a brisk trot up the wide, rutted street, Hannah waved gaily, gazing after him with dry eyes and a wide smile that revealed none of her inner torment.

"My dear Miss McGuire," Joel Allen was saying, gently reminding her of his presence, "have you made arrangements? Is your father close behind, or..." He paused delicately.

Turning back to face the astringent blue of Pastor Allen's steady gaze, Hannah said, "I had hoped to find shelter with you, sir. My father is ... is dead. We are all orphans, and I did not know where else to go."

"And the man who just rode away?"

"Is a passing stranger who was good enough to guide us here."

"I see." Joel Allen curled an arm around Hannah's shoulders and propelled her toward his log house. "Come in out of the wind and chill, and you can tell me what happened to your father. We can make plans," he said to her softly.

Plans. Yes, that was what she needed, a definite plan for the future—for her future, and the futures of the children with her.

# Chapter Twelve

Hannah stared listlessly out the cabin window at the rain slashing against the thick glass panes. Joel Allen's voice droned on and on, washing over her in wave after wave of gentle rebuke.

"I've inquired about this Creed Bratton who brought you here, you know. He's said to be a rough, uncouth man with no moral character. How is it that you traveled all this way with him unharmed? You *were* unharmed, weren't you, Miss McGuire? I mean no offense, of course. It's just that it might not be an easy task to avoid the unwelcome attentions of such a man. But the children were with you at all times, of course, weren't they, Miss McGuire? Of course they were. A tragedy about your father. He was a good man—a pious man who had every reason to be proud of his daughter. And now that the children have all been temporarily placed in decent homes, we can think what to do with you, Miss McGuire."

Hannah turned at that last, fixing Pastor Joel Allen with a quizzical gaze. "Must something be *done* with me, Pastor Allen? I had rather thought I might be given a day or two to consider my options."

"Options?" Pastor Allen gave a bewildered shrug of his shoulders and a light laugh. "How many options do you think are available in this small settlement, Miss McGuire?"

Hugging her arms to her chest, Hannah said more sharply

than she intended, "I was under the impression that America was a vast land, full of opportunities and options!"

"For men, yes, but not for unmarried females alone in the world." Joel Allen rose from his chair and crossed the floor to stand close to Hannah. "Through marriage to a good man, a woman can fulfill her promise—the promise that God gave every female."

"And that promise is . . ."

"To honor and obey her husband, to bring children into the world and clothe herself with righteousness," Joel finished for her.

Hannah stiffened. Her fingers knotted in the skirts of the blue dress donated to her by a friendly townswoman, and she lifted her brows. "No, Pastor Allen, that promise is to fulfill herself as a woman in whatever fashion her talents deem proper."

"My dear Miss McGuire, that is not based on the Scriptures," Joel said, obviously aghast. "What a novel, scandalous notion!"

Hannah struggled for her temper, thinking how greatly matters had changed since her arrival. Joel had been so helpful at first, so anxious to please, and then they had happened to quarrel over—of all things, she thought with a despairing shrug—Creed Bratton. It was ridiculous, really, to exchange differences of opinion over such a subject, but they had. And that she had found herself in the unenviable position of *defending* Bratton had rankled her for several hours afterward. Joel's tone had been as close to sharp as she had ever heard it, and he had offered what he assured her was popularly held opinion about the man who had accompanied her to Camp Coeur d'Alene. Hannah had wondered only briefly what he had heard, then decided it didn't really matter. There was no future for her here, with Joel Allen or without—not after what had happened with Creed. It could never be explained.

"A scandalous notion? Yes, I suppose it is," she agreed.

A thick silence fell. Rain pattered against the windows and the fire popped and crackled as they eyed one another. "I suppose you have some sort of plan in mind?" Allen asked, after several moments of strained silence.

"Yes, I do," Hannah replied. She regarded Joel for a moment, then said more gently, "Please, let us sit down at your table and drink our tea while I explain. I was awake most of the night thinking, and I am sure that when you hear my idea you may feel more comfortable."

But when Hannah outlined her plan—her decision to travel home to St. Louis and prepare herself for a lifetime of teaching—she was met with stubborn resistance.

"I'm afraid that is impossible," Joel Allen said. His sketchy brows rose high over his pale eyes, and his thin lips twitched in dismay, reminding Hannah of a rabbit as he gazed at her.

"Impossible? May I ask why?" Hannah inquired politely. Her hands clenched around the thin china teacup she held in her palms, and she made an effort to speak calmly and quietly, in spite of the sparks of rebellion Allen had managed to ignite with his attitude.

"It is quite simple. There are no funds available for your travel to St. Louis, nor would it be advisable for you to go on such a journey alone."

"I see." She stared into the teacup, counting the floating specks of tea that bobbed in the pale brew. "I can work," she said at last, "and earn the money for my journey home."

"Work where?" Joel's arms waved expansively. "My pay for providing the word of God comes in dribbles—mostly chickens or flour or cast-off clothing. I have no coin or legal tender with which to purchase goods. Those who work here are those who have a trade and can exchange their skills for goods, Miss McGuire. What can you do besides teach?''

Crestfallen, Hannah bent her head. She saw the futility of the situation, but what could she do?

Joel had an answer for that unspoken question, though it was not the one she wanted. Sliding from his chair to kneel before her, he took her suddenly icy hands between his own palms and began earnestly, ''I would deem it an honor to have you as my wife, Miss McGuire. If you . . .''

Shaking her head, Hannah reached out to place her fingers against his lips. Her throat was full, and she felt the familiar, annoying press of tears in her eyes. ''I am the one who's honored, Pastor Allen, but I must refuse such a noble and flattering offer.''

''Why?'' he asked, his sad gaze seeming to pierce her soul. ''Is it because of Creed Bratton?''

Startled, Hannah withdrew her hands from him. ''What do you mean by that?''

He shrugged, and the corners of his mouth turned down in a sad smile. ''Just that it is fairly obvious how you feel about him, and I had hoped that it was only because of the fact that he had rescued you from the ruins of Jubile. I was fooling myself, for I've noted how your voice changes when you speak of him, and how your entire face alters . . .''

''But it is as you said, Pastor Allen,'' Hannah croaked, ''he saved my life and the lives of eight children!''

''It's more than that.''

There was a long, appalling silence that seemed to fill every corner of the cabin, drifting through in a great, dark cloud and squatting in the corners to brood. Hannah could not speak, could not offer another word in her defense. She was distressingly aware that there was more than a grain or two of truth in what he said. It *was* more than the fact that Creed had scooped her from burnt ruins, more than the fact that he had agreed to lead them a hundred miles. But she had not thought it would be so apparent to virtual strangers.

"Well," Hannah said at last, breaking the heavy silence and shrugging helplessly, "I am not at all certain that I agree with you, but I don't disagree, either. I can't explain to you exactly how I feel about Mr. Bratton, because I don't know myself."

Bowing his head, Joel stared down at his hands for a moment, then rose to his feet. "I shall endeavor to help you in any way I can, Miss McGuire," he said softly. "It won't be easy for me in some ways, for I have cared about you since first seeing you, but I shall do my best."

"Thank you," Hannah whispered. "That's more than I could ask."

The small brass clock on the mantel struck eleven, and Hannah gave a long sigh. It was still raining, sheets battering against the thick glass windows with a steady rattle that was both soothing and irritating. The fire had burned low, and still she sat in a chair in front of the hearth, wrapped in a soft woolen cloak, gazing at the dying flames. Her hands absently shredded a lace handkerchief lying in her lap as she watched the fire. She couldn't sleep, had not been able to for the past three nights. Only fitful snatches of slumber would come to her. Maybe a glass of warm milk would help, or a long, boring book. Or surgery to remove all memories from her fevered brain . . .

Hannah sighed. A glance at the hapless handkerchief made her put it on the table before it was nothing but a collection of frayed threads. It had also been donated—a fragile linen and lace dainty with the letter "W" embroidered on one edge. Mrs. Wentwhistle—who had kindly donated her eldest daughter's old clothing—had cheerfully said as how Hannah could turn the handkerchief upside down and the "W" would be the initial "M" for McGuire. She had seemed so pleased by this happy coincidence that Hannah had not had the heart to tell her the W was too elaborate to ever be mistaken as an M. None of which mattered in the least, Hannah decided as she tossed the handkerchief atop the smooth pine table.

Now she was left with nothing in her lap but her fingers, and they clasped and unclasped at least ten times as she fretted. It was bedtime already—past bedtime. However, tonight she had not yet bothered to don the clean linen bed gown—why put on a bed gown, when she would only spend the night pacing the floor?—donated by the same kind woman who had given her the pretty blue dress and all the accoutrements a lady needed to be decently garbed.

Accustomed as she was to constant activity—either the lessons she taught or household chores or, like the past few weeks, survival—Hannah found it difficult to be idle. Her hands itched for useful work—something that would take her mind off things—things like the fact that Creed Bratton was known to still be in Coeur d'Alene, yet had not bothered to visit her. Or like the glimpse of him she had caught the day before when she was standing with Mrs. Wentwhistle in front of the log house that served as church, jail, and meeting hall. He had to have seen her, yet he had not turned to acknowledge it.

Smoothing the folds of the blue cotton dress over her knees, Hannah wondered why he was still in Coeur d'Alene at all. Hadn't he been in a big hurry to run after those desperate criminals he'd been following—the same outlaws he would have caught by now if not for the fact that he had been drafted into the service of a "Bible-thumping school-marm and her brats?" Her shoulders sagged, and Hannah slumped down in her chair, eyes staring blankly at the smoldering logs in the stone fireplace.

The tiny one-room cabin seemed to close in on her like a fruit press, pinning her against the walls so that she could not breathe. Poor Joel. He spent his nights on a hard cot in the church house so that she could stay in comfort, and she didn't have the heart to tell him that she detested this little house. Even in Jubile she had enjoyed more room and a greater feeling of space, but since the past weeks spent in the open—with only the sky for a roof and towering jack pines, cedars, and firs for walls—she found it almost impossible to stay inside.

Rising from the chair with a restless surge of impatience, Hannah began to pace the planked floor. Perhaps it was just the effect of the dreary weather on her—the constant rain for the past several days, and the cool temperatures. Soon it would be warm, with lovely soft days and brisk nights—the perfect summer weather she had come to love.

Sadness enveloped her then, as she thought of leaving Idaho Territory. It represented three years of struggle—years she had spent with her father carving out a home from the harsh wilderness. She'd made—and lost—friends here. She still felt protective of the seven survivors from Jubile—the children for whose futures she felt responsible. They trusted her. How could she let them down? And she still had three of them to place.

Sighing, Hannah raked a hand through her heavy tumble of hair, lifting it from the nape of her neck, where it clung in waving strands. The clock ticked on, sounding louder and louder in the whispering silence, the unfamiliar creaks and moans of the settling house, and the patter of rain. The rain rattled a window, and wind pounded against the door so forcefully that Hannah was startled.

She turned, pulling the crocheted wool shawl more tightly

around her, frowning at the closed wooden door. How had the weather suddenly become so fierce, when . . . ? It came again—a pounding rattle that made the door vibrate. It wasn't Joel, for he always knocked politely and waited for her to answer. No one else would be out on such a rainy, windy night. As Hannah stared in horror, she saw the latch slowly lift.

She immediately thought of outlaws, marauding Blackfoot, and a hundred other dire and dreadful fates. They came to her in a dark rush that drove out any rational thought, and Hannah seized the first weapon she could find.

It was an impulsive choice, and being one of the shoes given to her by Mrs. Wentwhistle the day before, it ranked among her worst in terms of logic. Gathering her courage, she brandished the high-top leather shoe like a club and reached for the door handle. She pulled the door open with a jerk, and swung the shoe at the same time.

She heard a muffled curse, but all she could see was a huge, vague form looming out of the dark. She flailed again and again with the leather shoe, hearing it smack against the intruder with a peculiar rustling sound. Finally, a voice penetrated her fright-fogged brain.

"Hannah? Dammit, it's wet out here!" the voice snapped in irritation, and she paused in mid-swing. An unwilling smile curved her mouth, traveling up over sculpted cheekbones and satin skin to light up her eyes. It was Creed.

She dropped the shoe, paused in indecision, then held the door wider, silently cursing herself for being so weak. This was the final proof—evidence that the events of the past weeks had driven her completely insane. She was mad, utterly mad, but deliriously happy at the same time. He had come to find her, come to talk to her, and she was blithely letting the wolf into the sheepfold. It must be love—blind, foolish love . . .

"What the hell were you hitting me with this time?" he was demanding as he pushed into the room in a shower of silvery raindrops. Hannah closed the door behind him and leaned back against it. Rivulets of rain poured from the curled spout of his black felt hat, draining onto the braided rag rug in pools. Creed looked at the limp leather shoe lying innocently on the floor. "Do you know, I am beginning to envy men whose terrified women merely scream. And I could never fault your imagination when it comes to innovative weaponry," he muttered as he swept off his hat and banged it against the heel of his palm.

His tone, overall, was friendlier than she had expected, considering she had attacked him.

"Sorry," she said with a helpless shrug.

"Sorry? Well, that cures everything, of course—even the bruises on my head."

Splattered with secondhand rain, Hannah only half heard what he was saying as she drank in the sight of him. Even wet, with his thick black hair plastered close to his skull and his ridiculously long eyelashes clustered with crystal drops of rain, he looked magnificent. His damp clothes clung snugly to his lean-muscled body, outlining details she had tried not to remember, and Hannah jerked her attention back to the angles and planes of his face. Had it really only been a few days since she had last seen him so close? Why did it seem like longer, much longer? And why was her heart beating so hard and fast, the blood pulsing through her veins at an alarming rate of speed and congealing in that one area? Her confusion at his unexpected arrival and the odd behavior of her body were swiftly and firmly marshaled into obedience, and Hannah schooled her ridiculously fawning features into a sterner expression.

"Why have you come?" she asked when she was reasonably certain her voice would not quiver in betrayal.

Creed slanted her an inquiring glance, pausing in the act of removing the wet slicker he wore over his buckskins. "I haven't been abused lately. I was beginning to feel neglected." His glance shifted around the room. "Ah, I didn't think to ask, but—were you expecting someone else?"

"You don't have to be sarcastic," she snapped with the rising irritation she usually felt when conversing with him. "It's a normal enough question. I mean, I've been here for four days now, and you have not bothered to visit me before. Why *are* you still here?"

"Certainly not to visit the good and wholesome Pastor Allen." The oilskin slithered to the floor with a wet crackle, and Creed kicked it aside. "Why do you think I came?" he asked bluntly.

"I don't know . . ."

The soft, breathy answer hung in the air for a moment—air that was crackling with a static that had nothing to do with the weather. Creed's beautifully shaped eyes were glittering with amusement, irony, and could it be—affection that she glimpsed in the velvety black depths? No, that would be entirely too much to expect from a man whose range of emotions seemed limited to irritation, cynical amusement, and lust. She would not even dignify that last with the softer definition of desire. Desire was a more tender, less harmful emotion than lust. Lust was brutal, animalistic—an emotion that peeled one to the gristle and left him stripped of humanity. Lust smacked of furtive rustlings in the dark, where desire implied moonlight and magic. Maybe that was the difference, the distortion between the two—like shadows on the wall. One was romance. One was just a vague shadow of romance.

Romance. Did that word belong in the same sentence with Creed Bratton? Doubtful. He was shed of any pretense at sentimentality. It was cut and dried with him, no shades of rosy idealism. Where she had grown up with a starry-eyed notion of what love could be, Creed had never considered love as a valid word in the English language. Love was as substantial as sand castles, as solid as a cloud, as far as he was concerned. And how had she ever been so foolish as to fall in love with a man like that?

She'd forgotten in these past few days how handsome Creed was. He was deceptive, she couldn't forget that—couldn't forget the sultry magic of his hands, which worked miracles on her too-willing flesh, while his lips promised nothing. There had not even been any soothing lies to salvage her pride. Now he was here again, and she could feel the betraying response of her heart to his proximity.

A smile flickered on his erotic mouth. "You're usually much more vocal, Hannah. Have I been gone too long?"

*Yes, too many days, hours, minutes, seconds . . .*

"No," she lied. "I simply have very little to say to you."

"How fortunate. Then you can listen for a change, while I talk," he said, guiding her unresisting body toward the chair she had recently vacated. She sank into it gratefully so that her quivering knees would not embarrass her by refusing to keep her upright any longer. Creed remained standing—obviously a ploy to intimidate her—and she waited quietly.

Her aqua eyes altered to pure green in the candle- and firelight as Hannah regarded him warily. He was too casual, too congenial. *No, no—I won't be deceived this time, Creed Bratton!* she thought.

Correctly reading the challenging light in her eyes, Creed allowed himself a moment of detached admiration. She was lovelier than he'd ever seen her. Her gentle, ethereal beauty seemed so much more in place in a civilized setting than out on the wooded trails. This was a woman who needed silks and satins, not buckskins and cottons. The past few days seemed to have done her good, for in spite of all the privations she had suffered, Hannah glowed with youthful health.

Reaching out, his movement slow and unhurried, he cupped her jaw in the palm of his hand, holding gently. "Did you miss me, sweet Hannah?"

"Is that what you came to talk about?"

A low chuckle vibrated into the air, and he released her chin. "No, it's not. I came to tell you goodbye."

"I thought you'd already done that. And why haven't you chased after those men you kept grumbling about the entire time we traveled?" she demanded crossly, unable to meet the steady, amused gaze of his eyes. It was too dangerous right now, when she was still quivering with reaction over seeing him again.

"I didn't tell *you* goodbye. And I couldn't go anywhere until General healed..."

"He was hurt?"

"No, just a split hoof that took a few days of hot tar treatment to heal. I'm leaving before dawn tomorrow, and I heard how you were staying here alone..."

"Who told you that?" she interrupted again, feeling his intent stare burning into the top of her head.

"Eric. He's not a bad kid when you get used to him, even if he does get a bit rowdy at times. Hannah, look at me. No, I mean look at *me*," he insisted in that silky, soft voice he was using, his fingers coaxing her head up when she would have kept it down.

Obeying the commanding urgency in his tone, she looked up, then cursed herself for being so foolish. There was something hypnotic in his gaze. Hannah shivered, tremors running all the way to her toes. Her reflexes were slow, her brain drugged with the hot, fluid magic he was spreading through her body with just his touch. Where was her detachment, her resistance? The answer came to her immediately: Nonexistent. Vanished. Disintegrated.

She said miserably, "I can't look at you for long—I'll go blind. It's like staring into the sun, or keeping your eyes open when there are ashes in them. It hurts. I don't want to look at you. I want you to go away and leave me alone."

"No, you don't," he disagreed softly, his hands tunneling beneath the heavy weight of her hair and beginning to rub the vulnerable nape of her neck with his fingertips. "You want me to do this . . . and this . . ."

She shook her head slowly, as if it was too much effort. "No, not really. I may not *sound* like it, but I really do want you to go away. It's only my . . . my voice that is contradictory. The rest of me longs *desperately* for you to leave."

"Is that any way to treat a guest after he has come through wind and rain to see you? And after being met at the door with—" He glanced at the offending shoe on the floor. "—a dangerous weapon?"

Her voice was slow, lugubrious, and her eyes grew heavy-lidded as his fingers worked through her hair to cradle her head in his palms. "Only if the guest is you," she said.

And Creed—who was busy cudgeling a sympathetic smile into submission—gazed at Hannah's lovely heart-shaped face and understood. He hadn't wanted to come here any more than she had wanted him to come. It was something far stronger than any willpower he possessed that had brought him here, an irresistible lure that he'd fought for the past three—no, closer to four days. She'd inhabited his dreams at night if he didn't drink, and if he did drink, it was even worse. He'd remember her when he'd first seen her, rising from the charred ruins of the schoolhouse with a sooty face and huge, stricken eyes. Then he'd recall her angry eyes at times, and how condemningly they could blaze at him. And even worse, he'd remember that night in the forest, when she had fled from his embrace and he had caught her and taken her on a bed of moss and leaves. She had looked up at him with a special glow in the luminous depths of her eyes that had caught him unawares. He'd had to come—he had to end this nagging feeling of unfinished business.

So he laughed against her ear, dragging her up from the chair and into his arms.

"I thought you had something to say to me?" she said breathlessly, desperately casting about for a distraction.

"I do . . ." His hands moved from her neck over the sharp curve of her shoulder blades, tracing the gentle sway of her spine with exploring fingers. "Sometimes I talk better with my hands."

"I can't listen that way . . ."

"Try it. You'll be surprised how easy it is to pick up. Did you know you have the smallest waist I've ever seen? Almost like a child's—only you're definitely not a child. I remember how soft your skin is . . ."

"No!"

". . . and how sweet you taste, Hannah, love."

"Don't call me love. It's not right." Her knees were failing her again, melting to the consistency of hot wax, and her ears were beginning to ring as if the bells of a hundred churches were all chiming at once. How did he do this so easily? And had he guessed how often she'd dreamed of him—dreamed that he'd come to her just like this and hold her in his arms, pressing her close to his hard, lean body and breathing against her ear until she shivered like she was doing now? She could feel his smile against her cheek, feel the swift certainty of his hands as they moved from her waist to the tiny row of buttons on the bodice of her dress.

Hannah's slow-acting brain, lulled to sleep by the lazy

motions of Creed's lips and hands, recovered enough to
prod her mouth into making a faint, incoherent protest, then
subsided into lethargy once more. The man should be a
doctor, she thought hazily—a famous physician who could
advertise insanity for sale. *One treatment—insanity guaranteed*,
the signs could read.

Then all thought, all time, was suspended as Creed swept
her from her feet and into his arms, striding across the tiny
cabin to the bed against one wall. It had a feather mattress,
with goose feathers instead of ticking, and it sank beneath
them when he laid her down. She could feel it dip as he
stretched beside her, and felt as if she were drowning in a
dreamy haze. She'd wake up soon and it would be daylight,
and she would be vaguely disappointed that he had been
only a dream and not real.

Rain pattered against the windowpanes and the wind blew
outside. The dying fire burned lower and lower, while the
candles flickered and guttered. The clock on the mantel
ticked steadily. A low, rumbling growl of thunder briefly
rattled the cabin, and Hannah wondered distractedly why
she suddenly felt so safe wrapped in Creed Bratton's arms—
safe from the elements, from intruders, from everything but
her own tempestuous heart.

Heated lips found the sensitive cord along her neck, and
teased the golden hollow where a rapid pulse fluttered in
wild abandon. The confining strictures of her dress were
somehow loose, then gone, and she felt the cool whisper of
air across her flushed skin. Her head was spinning dizzily in
the swift current of churning desires being awakened in her
body. This wanton abandonment was still new to her, still
strange and frightening, and she moaned beneath his lips. It
was true. One could lose oneself in a heated rush of
passion, could swirl helplessly in a torrent that swept
inexorably toward release.

The sensations were heightened when Creed's mouth left hers and nibbled in tiny kisses down her neck to her bared breast. The light flick of his tongue against the hardened peak drew an unwilling moan of pleasure from her, and Hannah arched against him, realizing then that somehow he had shed his clothes and was as bare as she.

There was no urgency in the slow passion of his mouth and hands, but the languid, coiling fire deep within her burned hotter and hotter. Creed's exploring hands strayed over her flat belly, dipping between her thighs, and the world exploded into rainbow colors that hung suspended on the shadowed ceiling. He probed her intimate secrets, and she twisted and turned, straining against him. All her fears and inhibitions slowly faded away until she was boldly running her hands over Creed's furred chest.

She explored him greedily, caressing the smooth muscles and hard ridges, listening to his harsh breathing with a sense of satisfaction. She could feel the naked, rippling muscles of his shoulders beneath her hands, the hard thrust of his shoulder blades, and the ridged curve of his ribs. When her hands moved across his flat belly and lower, she heard the sharp intake of his breath and felt his lungs expand with it.

Overpowering her with an impatient growl, Creed levered his body across hers, parting her thighs with the thrust of one knee and wedging between them. His breath fanned her silken cheek a moment before his mouth swooped down over her parted lips hungrily. It was torment—sweet, savage torment—to be imprisoned in his embrace.

Hannah's body ached for him; her raw nerves screamed for release. Trembling uncontrollably, her hands moved across his back and shoulders. Her pale body heaved upward, writhing and twisting in an agony of unfulfilled need.

But Creed waited, toying with her, kissing her eyes, her nose, lingering over her full, ripe breasts. He waited until he could wait no longer, until he was almost bursting from holding back, and then thrust forward in a surge to fuse their bodies together.

A purr of satisfaction sounded low in Hannah's throat as she was enveloped in a misty cloud of sensation. Arching toward him, her heels digging mounds into the scratchy wool blankets beneath them, she clutched him even closer. Prisms of firelight spangled the air, sparkling like tiny stars on the ceiling, glittering in a diffused light over Creed's body so that he looked made of stardust and air instead of flesh and muscle.

It was magic—sweet, hot magic. She was caught up in swirling clouds of it and transported beyond the stars. The end waited, just out of reach, a prize they both strained toward with heated breath. When it came, Hannah was consumed by a velvety mist of swirling sensation. It caught her up, swept her along on a rolling tide that lifted her to the heights and left her for a long, rapturous moment before letting her drift gently back to reality.

Buffeted by the response of her body and the delayed prick of her conscience, Hannah sagged in Creed's embrace, barely hearing his murmured love words—words he did not mean, of course. They were only something to say—something to ease the awkward moment after passion ebbed and reality surfaced.

As the whirlwind of strange new emotions gradually receded, Hannah lay stunned by the aftermath, depleted of strength. Nestled into the tangled wool blankets beneath her and curled into Creed's embrace, she contemplated what she had just done.

A hot press of tears stung her nose and eyes, and she blinked rapidly. Tears again—her usual reaction to any kind of shock or distress. When would she learn to be brave and unemotional—or would she ever? As a defense, tears did not rank very high on the list of effectual bulwarks against rampant dangers, nor had they ever solved any crisis at any time in her life. In fact, tears had never impressed anyone she knew, including Creed Bratton.

Slanting her head sideways, she dared a glance at him. He was lying with his face turned toward her, his ridiculously long lashes shadowing his tanned cheeks and his mouth still curled in the faint remnant of a smile. How dare he sleep so peacefully when she was racked with guilt and remorse?

One slender finger nudged him. "Creed."

He grunted in response, and opened one eye. "Wha'?"

"Wake up."

"Why?" The lid drifted down again, shuttering the dark eye against her. His arm tightened in reflex action, bringing her up under the tight curve of his chest and the thrust of a lean thigh across her body.

"You have to go," Hannah whispered, her throat aching at just the thought. "It's not right that you're here with me like . . . like this."

Both eyes opened, and the palm of his hand drifted lazily across the satin swell of her stomach to cup her tingling breast. "No? Why not?"

"You know why!"

"I know why some folks might think so, but not you. Why would you want me to leave, sweet Hannah?"

*Oh, I don't want you to go! I want to hear the right words from you, the words that would bind us together for all time . . .*

Banishing any such hopes from her mind with a firm thrust, Hannah said hoarsely, "It's against God's commandments, Creed."

"Not according to Genesis," he said after a moment. "God made man and woman—'Male and female created he them; and blessed them . . . '"

"It's wrong according to Deuteronomy," she returned miserably. " 'Thou shalt not . . . ' "

"Dammit! Don't dare quote any of those 'shalt nots' to me, Hannah McGuire!" he flashed, jerking upright and glaring down at her. "I've lived a life of 'em, and I don't intend to go on living like that."

Flinching from his anger, Hannah fought against the desire to throw herself at him—to cling to him and ask only to be allowed to love him. She couldn't. It was not right, and could only end badly. There had to be more between them—more than just the sweet intercourse of their bodies to hold them together.

"All right," she agreed softly, fresh tears thickening her voice and curdling in her throat. "I won't quote any platitudes to you, Creed, but neither will I go on like this. I require more than just sensual attraction in order to be happy. There should be something else . . ."

"This isn't enough for you?" he asked after a moment, his voice flat, emotionless, as if he were discussing the price of bread instead of their future.

She shook her head, coppery curls shimmering in the rosy light thrown by the dying fire and melting candles. "No. It isn't."

"Fine. If that's what you want—" He left the rest unsaid as he rose from the sagging mattress and began to pull on his clothes.

Hannah watched silently, her heart sinking like a stone in water. Fiercely, firmly, she schooled her crumpling face into obedience, keeping her eyes as dry as possible and her mouth from forming the words she shouldn't say. It had to be like this—had to end this way. Without commitment or promises, she could see no other way.

"What are you going to do?" he flung at her when he

was dressed and buckling on his gun belt. "Stay here in this burg and marry your preacher?"

Amazed at how calm and emotionless she sounded—*See, Hannah, it is possible to lose one's ability to feel, if buffeted often and harshly enough*—she said, "No, I think that I shall go on to St. Louis after all."

"Somebody die and leave you a fortune? Or are you expecting your preacher to pay for it?"

Anger flashed briefly, her eyes a hot, stabbing blue as she looked at him. "No, and he is *not* my preacher. There was money left from the sale of the horses, after we placed the children. Pastor Allen brought it to me this evening."

"How tidy." Creed stalked across the floor and scooped up the oilskin. "Eric Ransom isn't placed. I talked to him today outside the general store."

"No, because we did not feel it right to separate him from Ivy—she is so frail and timid. But Pastor Allen knows a family in Fort Walla Walla, and the next time a coach passes through on its way . . ."

"You get shed of the kids. Right. All loose ends wrapped up nice and tight. You've got everything figured out, haven't you, Hannah? Everything except where what you really want fits in. Have you thought about what you're going to do twenty years from now? Will you still be an old maid schoolteacher, quoting Bible verses and watching others live?" His eyes clashed with hers, dark and stormy and clouded with an expression she couldn't recognize. If it wasn't for the fact that it was Creed, and that she knew he was incapable of caring about another human being, she would have thought it was regret. But his next words erased any such notions from her mind. "Do like I do, Hannah—take what you can when you can and don't worry about anyone else, 'cause they sure won't worry about you."

"An excellent philosophy to live by if you're a dog or a

scavenger, Mr. Bratton, but unfortunately, it doesn't work so well for people.''

"It has for me," he shot back.

"Has it?" Hannah smiled past the pain in her throat. "Not so you can tell . . ."

Stiffening, Creed jammed his wet hat on his head and yanked open the door. The echo of its slamming remained in Hannah's ears and heart for a long time afterward . . .

# PART II

*"The heaven for height, and the earth for depth..."*
*Proverbs 25:3*

# Chapter Thirteen

Three men crouched in the curling shadows of a barn and discussed their plans, voices lowered as if the weathered boards had ears. It was dark, with only the light from a sputtering lamp to illuminate the dusty, straw-strewn interior.

"Here's the way I see it," one of them said, sketching in the straw dust with the point of a stick. "The coach'll head this way outa Coeur d'Alene after pickin' up a few travelers. We hit it 'bout here—" The stick made an X in the dirt. "—just past that old mission."

"Are you sure it's carryin' gold?"

"As sure as I'm here in this damned dusty barn, it's got our man on it!" came the confident answer.

Nate Stillman pushed his hat back from his head, his lips pursed thoughtfully. His creased, leathery face held the slightest trace of doubt, and his eyes narrowed. "What about Bratton?"

"He rode out two days ago. I saw him leaving early in th' mornin', headed down th' Mullan Road."

Stillman nodded. "Good thing we doubled back on him. He gets too damned close sometimes."

"Too close? Hell, it was over a week before I could use my gunhand again," Truett complained, flexing his fingers, "an' it still ain't quite right!"

"It won't matter once we make this one, Truett. Nothin' will matter anymore. We'll be too rich to care. Hell, I've waited a long time for this, and there's been times lately I thought things had gone too wrong, but now . . . now we're here, and it's time."

Rising to his feet, Stillman limped over to the half-open barn door and peered out. His leg hurt. The bullet was lodged next to his spine, in a spot the doctor claimed he couldn't get to without a great deal of risk. Damn Bratton, he thought with mounting hate. The man would get his— and soon. One hand caressed the butt of his pistol, and his fingers curled into a fist.

"Let's ride, boys," Stillman said.


Hannah sat stiffly, like an ancient Chinese statue, gazing out the window of the rocking stagecoach as the small square of countryside passed by. Her world had been reduced to that one square slice of scenery, the dusty clouds obscuring trees, bushes, and anything remotely interesting. The leather flaps had been lifted when she could no longer bear staring only at the rather grim interior, and now dust coated the inside with a brown film. The stagecoach would lurch occasionally, tossing her sideways onto the portly man seated beside her.

How had she come to this? She, Hannah Elizabeth McGuire, whose biggest concern until a short month ago had been the whims of the weather, was now rocking along in a primitive coach designed for the grueling torture of its passengers. Her fingers curled into the leather strap hanging from one side for the convenience of those unfortunate souls being churned like butter inside the vehicle.

High-button shoes pinched her feet, and her neck was encased in a tight collar that rose to just beneath her jaw. The bodice of the donated blue gown was too tight, stretching across her more generous curves to a point just short of indecent. In one hand she clutched a rather worn velvet reticule with braided cord drawstrings. Nestled inside—between two clean linen handkerchiefs that had been a gift from Mrs. Wentwhistle—was the last bit of money from the sale of the two weary horses that had brought them from Jubile to Coeur d'Alene. Pastor Allen had insisted that she take it.

"You will surely need it on your long journey," he had said, staring sadly at Hannah. "I would not have you do without."

Why couldn't she have fallen in love with Joel Allen, instead of Creed Bratton? It would have made life so much simpler, so much more orderly. Joel Allen would have taken care of her, seen to her needs and provided for her, yet she had not been able to muster the necessary emotions that were required to marry him. Respect was not enough. Perhaps she would have married him, if not for Creed—if not for that moonlit night near the shores of the lake when she had discovered the heights and depths of love. Now, she could not settle for less. She had tasted the sweetness of love, but had Creed—the kind of love that transcended physicality and touched the purity of mind and heart? And just because he had wanted her enough to seek her out in Coeur d'Alene did not mean he wanted her enough to make a commitment. One fact should follow the other. Hannah sighed.

In retrospect, the act had meant no more to Creed than

would washing his hands. It had been a basic urge, a need fulfilled, and that was all.

*Shades of gray, Hannah Elizabeth, shades of gray*, she cautioned silently. Perhaps it had meant a little more to him than that. And at any rate, it did no good to chastise herself for what was already done, to berate herself for yielding to what was, after all, an instinctive human need: love.

Shifting on the seat, Hannah glanced crossly at the portly man at her side. The last bump had made him shift so that he was pressing against her, his shoulder nudging hers. His head was tilted back now, and he was snoring loudly, his mouth gaping open wide enough to provide cozy refuge for a thousand large flies. Hannah gave him a brief shove with both hands, and glanced away in annoyance when he slumped against the wall without waking.

Her gaze strayed to the other passenger, a rather distinguished-looking gentleman with flecks of gray at his temples and a hard, chiseled face. He had been on the coach when it had briefly paused in Coeur d'Alene—had, in fact, refused to step down even for a moment to stretch his legs. That had seemed peculiar to Hannah, who knew that he had ridden all the way from Fort Walla Walla—though not without stopping, of course—and seemed to be guarding some sort of heavy metal box tucked under his seat. The contents of the box were a mystery, but as far as she was concerned, not a particularly interesting one. His destination was no secret—Fort Benton, Montana. It was the end of the line for this coach, though she would connect with another one at a stop just past the Clark Fork River.

Imagine, she mused silently, in just a few short years, the Butterfield Overland Mail stages had accomplished miracles, traveling west from St. Louis to California twice a week. Twice a week! Twenty-eight hundred miles in twenty-five days. But she had to travel a more circuitous route to get there. She had a long trip ahead of her. Fort Hall still lay a week's travel ahead, and from there on to Wyoming, Nebraska, Kansas, and finally Missouri. Back home to Aunt Ann and city life—home to pursue her studies, become a teacher and lead a productive life. A life without . . .

Hannah's drifting thoughts were diverted by the sudden bump and lurch of the coach, and she was thrown from the uncomfortable seat into the even more uncomfortable floor. Her out-of-style bonnet tipped rakishly over one eye, the feather curling down to tickle her nose and make her sneeze, and her thick skirts and yards and yards of muslin petticoats tangled in her arms so that she was quite effectively caught, like a heifer in thorn bushes.

"Ohh!" she muttered between clenched teeth, feeling ridiculous and embarrassed at the same time. One leg was twisted beneath her, and she could hear from the rasping pants and wheezes above her that the portly gentleman had been tossed about the coach also.

It was left up to the distinguished-looking gentleman to offer assistance, which he did with a gracious smile. "Allow me," he said, reaching down to put a hand beneath Hannah's elbow and gently disentangle her from her skirts and petticoats. He lifted her from the floor and returned her to her more dignified position on the hard seat.

"Thank you," she said rather breathlessly. "I'm afraid I wasn't paying close attention, and lost my balance." She gave him a faint smile, which he returned with a gallant nod of his head.

"You're quite welcome, Miss . . . ?"

"McGuire—Hannah McGuire. And whom am I thanking, sir?"

"Edward Mullen, at your service, ma'am."

"Mullan? As in the Captain Mullan who is responsible

for the building of this road?'' Hannah asked in some surprise.

"Oh, no, no relation at all. With an *e* instead of an *a*, and *Edward*, not *John*,'' he explained.

"I see.'' Hannah rearranged her skirts in decent folds and tilted the dipping brim of her hat out of her eyes. The feather wobbled dangerously, and she adjusted it.

"Do you go all the way on to Fort Benton?'' Mullen asked politely, apparently deciding to attempt conversation after almost twenty miles of silence.

"No, I will change to a more southerly route just past Clark Fork in Montana,'' she answered, giving the rebellious feather a last firm pat of her hand.

"Hey, I'm going that way also,'' the portly man offered with a too-bright smile. He drew in a deep, nasal wheeze that reminded Hannah of a stuck pig, and wiggled his plump body closer on the seat. She drew back slightly when he thrust his face close to hers and asked, "Are you meeting your husband there?''

Pressing back against the hard sides of the coach, Hannah shook her head and managed a polite, "No, I am not.'' She put a palm against his chest and added, "Please move away, sir.''

"Hey. Sorry. My name is Chessman,'' he said with another nasal gasp. "I'm not married either, hey.''

Sensing the direction of the man's pointed questions and suggestions, Hannah immediately said, "I never said I was not married, Mr. Chessman.''

Disappointment etched his face, and Chessman sighed. "Hey, sorry.''

Edward Mullen added no comment, but gave Hannah a long, assessing gaze. His eyes glinted briefly, and a faint smile touched the corners of his mouth.

There was a brief lull in the conversation, during which

Hannah decided silence was the best course at this point, and she turned her face to the open window again.

They passed an old mission nestled in the curve of the Coeur d'Alene River, perched upon a high, grassy knoll easily seen from the road. The road was little more than a wide track through thick forest and up steep hills, passing the occasional avalanche chute carved out by tumbling tons of rock and decorated by nature. Fuchsia blossoms waved in a snaking pattern, closely following the winding path of a small spring that oozed from the ground and trickled down the steep slopes. Tall stalks of Indian paintbrush and yarrow, with their small, flat-topped clusters, ranged across hillsides in bright shades of vermilion and white. Nearer the ground bunched Saint-John's-wort, pussy willows, yellow pentemons, and cinquefoils—tiny, delicate flowers in a rich carpet. The swaying coach crossed an occasional meadow. Early that morning she had seen deer, elk, and moose grazing in the tall grasses, but as the sun rose higher, they had retreated to dim forest glades.

"Hey, they say gold's been found in Idaho and Montana," Chessman offered after a few minutes of rocking silence. "Steamers are bringing in prospectors by the thousands, I hear, hey."

"The steamers disembark passengers at Fort Benton, Mr. Chessman," Mullen said. "The majority have not yet made it this far—only a few of the more intrepid."

"Hey, they will. Just like the rush of '49 in California. This time, I mean to be in on the profits, hey."

"Are you by any chance from Canada, Mr. Chessman?" Mullen asked politely, his dark brows lifted.

"Hey, yes I am! How did you know, hey!"

A faint smile tugged at the corners of Mullen's mouth. "Just a hunch."

Hiding a smile behind her fingers, Hannah tossed Mullen

a gleeful glance. The portly Canadian had the habit of preceding his every comment with "hey"—a habit she had found peculiar to those from British Columbia. It was a habit like that of her aunt's, who was from the South, and insisted upon referring to everyone as "y'all," even when she was only speaking to one person. Such habits were hard to break, Hannah reflected, as were some others . . .

As dust clouds roiled into the open windows and the stifling interior began to grow a shade too warm, Hannah drew off her gloves and began to fan herself with them in a slow, lethargic motion. It only stirred the hot air in gentle gusts, sweeping dust clouds through the coach and making her cough.

"It's either too warm or too cold in Idaho," Mullen complained after a few moments. "I've never seen the weather just right."

"Oh, I have," Hannah returned softly, her eyes straying back to the trees and sky and jagged mountain peaks rising so high they seemed to spear the very heavens. "I think it is beautiful country."

"I've no quarrel with the terrain," Mullen said. "It is the weather that distresses me—either cold, raining, or snowing, with very little sunshine."

"Have you ever been here in July and August?" Hannah asked then, wondering why she felt moved to defend Idaho. After all, she was from Missouri, and had only spent three years in the territory. She hadn't even known she felt this way until now—until a stranger made caustic comments about the countryside that held such fond memories for her. If Joshua had loved it so, how could she do less?

"I have to admit that I love the deep, powdery snow that carpets the ground in the winter," Hannah said. "It lies so white and pure—a fairy tale sprinkling of magic dust that glitters in different colors of rose and blue when the sun shines down. And when it rains, the air smells so fresh and clean, it's like God's own perfume, Mr. Mullen. It's lovely in July and August, with warm sunshine and soft, balmy days, when one can lie in the shade of a tree and listen to the grass grow. The wind blows soft then, humming down from the mountain peaks and across meadows filled with flowers, and the rain keeps it all green." Pausing, she flashed him an embarrassed smile and added, "It's not very dusty then."

Mullen smiled back at her. "I apologize for casting aspersions upon a land that obviously means so much to you, Miss McGuire. Please forgive me."

"You're forgiven, of course."

"I had no idea we shared a coach with a poet, did you, Mr. Chessman?" Mullen asked. His tone was warm, and when Hannah quickly searched his face for signs of ridicule, she found none.

"A poet?" she inquired carefully.

"Yes, you praised this land so eloquently and lyrically that I find myself quite impressed."

"Hey, that's right, that's right," Chessman piped.

A faint blush stained her cheeks, and Hannah looked away from Edward Mullen's hooded gaze. She felt suddenly uncomfortable, as if she had somehow trespassed into forbidden territory. The admiration she saw in Mullen's eyes was different from that she'd seen in Creed Bratton's. Creed's had been more honest . . . more forthright. He had said what he thought, not made flowery compliments that were insincere.

Glumly, Hannah reflected on the fact that she seemed to have elevated Creed Bratton—whom she knew to be a merciless bounty hunter and general ne'er-do-well—to the ranks of the exalted in her faulty memory. The truth had been exhibited to her time and again—why was she so foolish as to remember him as something he was not? The man had probably not given *her* a second thought since he'd ridden out of Coeur d'Alene three days before.

But Hannah was wrong. She had been very much on Creed's mind the past three days. He could still remember the wounded expression in her eyes, the hopeful smile that had wavered and faded away when he had not reacted as she had obviously wanted him to do. But, dammit! A man had to finish one job before he took on another, and he wasn't too sure he was ready for what Hannah required. She was too fine to be treated as a light-o'-love—he had realized that mistake as soon as it had occurred to him. Yet he had not wanted to give her up entirely. Couldn't she have waited? Did it have to be all or nothing? he wondered bitterly as he reined his bay to a halt beneath the spreading branches of an oak.

Cupping his hands around a match to ward off the wind, Creed lit the cigarette that had been dangling from between his lips for the past ten minutes. Somehow, he wasn't the same as he used to be. His reactions were off, his reflexes too slow. Maybe he'd gotten soft while leading Hannah and those noisy brats. And that was another thing: he'd even grown rather *fond* of that boy with the big blue eyes—eyes so large they were almost like caricatures in his elfin face. Creed gave the match an impatient snap to extinguish the flame, then tossed it to the dust in the road. Had he completely lost the keen, sharp edge he'd always held? Now he was vulnerable, where before he'd always been detached and ready. Too many worries sapped a man's alertness, and that could be fatal.

Nudging General's sides with his heels, Creed wound up through the trees alongside the road. No point in traveling the same path traversed by others—not when the element of surprise was still the best advantage he had. Stillman and his men had eluded him for two months now—two months of constant tracking, except for one notable interlude, and frustrating failure. Tenacious—that's what Henry Plummer had called him one time. Stubborn as a hound and twice as mean, Plummer had said—and it had not been a compliment. Instead, it had been a grudging observation after Creed had brought in a man he'd followed for almost six months of grueling cat-and-mouse. That had been through the Black Hills—rugged country with little water and harsh rocks that hid thousands of caves and cubbyholes. A man could hide there for days without being seen—months, if he had to—but without a good supply of water, it would be impossible. This country, now, was a lot easier. It had trees and shade and plenty of water—places a man could hide in comfort. No wonder Stillman had chosen this area, following the Wild Horse Trail up almost to Canada. But why so far? And why double back to Fort Benton in Montana? Unanswered questions circled like vultures in his head as Creed leaned forward, urging the bay up a steep slope.

Pausing on the crest of a rocky ridge at last, Creed shaded his eyes with one hand and looked down at the trail winding below like a snake slithering through the woods. It ran beside the faint, glittering ribbon of Coeur d'Alene River before switching to run alongside the St. Joe. Nothing moved below, no sign of life along the meandering trail headed east.

Creed tilted his hat back over his eyes and reined the bay around. Might as well rest for a while. The past three days had been hard riding, searching and backtracking and circling again, looking for sign of Stillman and his two companions. Northern Idaho seemed to have swallowed them up, leaving only enough traces to reassure him they were still in the area. He was close—he could feel it, like he could often feel an approaching storm. A sixth sense, maybe, that made the hair on the back of his neck rise and all his senses sharpen, warned him that Nate Stillman was not that far out of his range...

"There it is," Roper said in a tight voice, and lifted one arm to indicate the swaying, lumbering coach rounding a bend in the road. "And right on time."

"Yeah, only a day late," Truett added. He slanted a thoughtful glance at the scarred gunman beside him. "No killing, okay, Roper? I don't like it when you do..."

A harsh laugh erupted from Nate Stillman, and he fixed the much younger Truett with a narrow gaze. "Gettin' soft on us, boy?"

Truett didn't flinch. "No, I just don't like killing that ain't necessary."

"All our killing is necessary," Roper shot at him. "Ain't you figured it out yet? It's either them or us. Ain't no other way."

Stubbornly, flatly, the lank-haired youth returned the older gunman's obsidian stare as he said, "Yeah, there is."

Roper turned to Stillman. "Where'd you find this puppy? He needs to grow some hair on his ba—"

His words ended abruptly as he found himself gazing down the barrel of Truett's pistol. "I got all the hair I need, where I need it," Truett said softly. "But if you think you're qualified to look for it...?"

He let the sentence go unfinished, and Roper swore loudly. Stillman cut him off.

"Hell, Roper, leave him be! You know how damn fast he is with that gun, and how touchy he can be! We don't need no fightin' a'twixt us now. We got a job to do here." Turning to Truett, Stillman snapped, "Save your fancy gun play for Creed Bratton! You may need it!"

"I didn't do bad, did I?" Truett remarked with some

satisfaction. "Even with that bullet wound still hurtin' me, I managed to outdraw Roper . . ."

"Well, so could my horse!" Stillman growled irritably. "Now, you two settle down and listen up . . ."

A loud shot split the air, screaming past the open coach window and making Hannah gasp. It was closely followed by another and another—a volley of wild shots that made the coach driver increase his speed. The guard began firing back, while Hannah clung to the leather strap and flashed a stunned glance at the other passengers.

Mr. Chessman was almost hysterical, and had begun babbling about murderers, cutthroats, and savages, but Mr. Mullen was calm and collected.

"Do you have a pistol?" he inquired coolly, and when Mr. Chessman shook his head and gulped, Mullen pulled one from his waistcoat. "I did not think you the kind of man to be armed, but I feel it is now necessary. Take this. It has six shots, so make them count."

"Who could it be—and what do they want?" Hannah asked, struggling to stay upright on the bouncing seat of the coach.

"I'm sure I don't know," Mullen replied in the same cool tone, squinting down the barrel of a lethal-looking Colt .44. There was something about Mullen's face—his calm demeanor and unhurried checking of his weapon—that made Hannah believe differently. It reminded her of Creed suddenly, and how efficient and dangerous he had always looked when cleaning or loading his guns.

"But you *do* know, Mr. Mullen . . ."

He looked up at her, a faint smile curving his mouth. "You have a very active imagination, Miss McGuire."

"Yes, I do, but I'm also rather perceptive at times. This is one of them," she said. Her glance fell on the heavy metal box tucked beneath the seat. "What's in that box, Mr. Mullen?"

"My laundry?" he replied in the same insouciant tone.

"I rather think not. Isn't there a payroll or some gold that's supposed to be delivered?"

"My dear girl, all over the nation there are payrolls being delivered in some shape, form, or fashion. Whatever leads you to believe that I would be doing so in an ordinary coach with no guards posted?"

"Because few robbers would suspect such an innocuous ploy!" Hannah said triumphantly. "The perfect trick—only someone seems to have found out."

"Hey, sounds logical to me, hey!" Chessman puffed. His eyes were bulging, and his face had grown an alarming shade of red. The pistol lay loosely in his slack grasp, and he was staring in fascination at Mullen.

"It may sound logical, but I assure you it is not. Now, may we dispense with such inane frivolities? We have three very desperate-looking outlaws bearing down on us." Mullen snapped. Pointing his pistol out the window, he took careful aim, but his shot went astray. A slender tree limb fell from a jack pine, but the outlaws rode on.

Bouncing about like a ball in a large box, Hannah clung to the leather strap and tried to get a closer view of the outlaws. This seemed incredible to her—too incredible. *Not after everything else, God,* she prayed, *not after everything else!*

But the horror continued. Careening around sharp bends in the road and up steep grades, the coach surged on in its precarious flight. Hannah could hear the coach driver's shouts, the popping shots of the guard's rifle, and the frenzied whinnies of the bolting horses. Behind them—and coming closer and closer—the pursuing outlaws fired at will.

Still clutching tightly to the leather strap with one hand and the back of the seat with the other, Hannah glared at Edward Mullen. "Well—fire at them!"

"I have," was the terse reply.

"But . . ."

"But Mr. Chessman has fired all his bullets and hit nothing but blue sky and trees. At least I have tried," he said tightly. His gaze slid past her to the square of madly passing scenery, a blur of dusty greens and grays. "Sit back and try to pray, Miss McGuire," he said then.

"Thank you for such ill-needed advice!" she snapped. "If you will provide more bullets, I shall use the pistol that Mr. Chessman used. I am thought to be a fair shot at times . . ."

"A ludicrous suggestion!" Mullen disagreed. "A pistol in the hands of a woman is suicide!"

Hannah's lamentable temper flared. "Fiddlesticks! I am quite capable of firing without endangering you, Mr. Mullen! Unless, of course, I happen to be aiming at you . . ."

His eyes narrowed. The metal box on the coach floor begin to slide forward, bumping up with each jolt of the coach. Mullen slid the box back beneath the seat and shook his head. "I am afraid that there is a surfeit of courage aboard this coach. It is running rampant, but should not be extended to such a fair flower of femininity as yourself, Miss McGuire."

For the first time since her last discussion with Creed Bratton, Hannah fought the overwhelming desire to be obnoxiously rude. She bit her tongue to keep from saying the abominable words that lingered there, and instead turned her head to stare out the window again. Mr. Chessman had remained silent and pale during her brief exchange with Mr. Mullen, and now he gathered enough courage to dare a glance out the window also.

"Hey! They're wearing masks over their faces, hey . . ."

But when the outlaws had ridden alongside the coach and forced it to a stop, aiming their rifles at the driver and injured guard, Hannah found something disturbingly familiar about them.

"Reach for the sky, mister!" a hoarse voice cried, words muffled by the scarf across his face. A rifle was thrown down, landing with a dull thud on the dusty road. "Now, throw down your valuables," came the terse command.

Hannah leaned close to the window, daring to peer out at the men. There were three of them, as Mr. Mullen had said, and even with the scarves pulled up over their faces so that only their eyes glittered from between bandana and hat brim, she felt an odd tug of recognition. They wore long duster coats that looked as if they had ridden many miles, and battered felt hats that looked oddly familiar also. Her mind flashed back to that day in Jubile—the last day of what she had begun to think of as her real life.

There was a tight prickle of her scalp and tightening of her throat as she stared at the men, vaguely aware that she was grateful the coach had at last ceased its constant rocking and lurching, and yet fully aware of a cold lump in the pit of her stomach. The driver and guard were forced to step down, hands held high over their heads. Edward Mullen was the first to be dragged from inside the coach. The driver was held at gunpoint and the wounded guard moaned and groaned, holding splayed red fingers over a gaping hole in his chest.

"Get out here!" an outlaw snarled, grasping Mullen by his embroidered vest and yanking him from the coach. He landed in a heap, unharmed but sputtering protests.

"Now, see here! You can't do this!" Mullen cried. He surged upward in a caricature of heroics, but was shoved back down.

"No? Well, we're doing it!" was the rough answer.

Mullen was kicked, and when the driver issued a protest, he received the butt of a rifle across his jaw, knocking him backward and unconscious. He landed beside the guard. "Anything else you wanna say?" the masked outlaw demanded, and no one said anything.

Mr. Chessman was shaking, his quivering, fleshy jowls reminding the terrified Hannah of a bowl of her Aunt Ann's plum pudding at Christmas. He began to babble after a moment of tense silence that was strained still further by the outlaws' distressing decision to rummage through the trunks and luggage.

"I . . . I have money in Canada! Lots of money! I can give it to you if you only let me go . . ."

"Shaddup!" one of the masked men growled, and Chessman subsided to indistinct snuffles and vague whimpers. Hannah wondered if the little man would faint when one of the men snapped an order for him to descend from the coach and stand on the ground. Would she be next?

She watched from inside the coach as they pawed through the luggage, snickering when they reached her small trunk and found her new dainties. Hannah's chin lifted and her cheeks flamed as one of the men held up a lacy undergarment and began to make crude comments. He sounded vulgar, and she bit the inside of her cheek to keep from saying so. There was something about these men that reminded her of another unpleasant event, another confrontation, but she could not bring it to mind. It eluded her, teasing at the fringes of her brain and refusing to show itself. What was it? But it wasn't until one of the outlaws looked up, his pale eyes widening with recognition before darting back to his companions, that she knew. Of course . . .

Though she was half paralyzed with apprehension, a dozen possibilities presented themselves in the space of a few seconds' time. By wearing masks, Stillman and his men obviously didn't want to be identified. Fair enough—neither did she. Some sixth sense warned Hannah that being recognized by Stillman and Roper could be deadly. She flashed Truett a pleading glance. If the others had not yet recognized her, all the better. Fortunately, Hall Truett seemed to share her opinion. His gaze passed over her without a word being uttered, and Hannah sagged back from the open window in relief. She must now concentrate on remaining in the background, if at all possible.

She slumped into the seat and tugged at the brim of her hat, pulling it low over her forehead and wishing she'd had the foresight to wear a veil. Where were those useless feminine decorations when she needed them? Only the silly feather, with its rather tattered fronds, adorned the hat, and it was more likely to attract attention than not. A rush of desperation filled Hannah's throat with fear, and she silently prayed that Roper would not recognize her. She'd not forgotten how he had looked at her, or how he had wanted . . .

"Will you step out, miss?" the voice repeated, and Hannah glanced up in sudden terror. Nate Stillman stood at the door holding it open, his voice carefully polite, but bordering on the edge of impatience.

Ducking her head, she mumbled agreement, gathering her velvet reticule and hiding it in the folds of her skirt as she stepped from the coach. Why hadn't she had the foresight to hide her money before now? *Details, Hannah Elizabeth, details . . .*

Dust puffed up around the small heels of her high-top shoes as she stepped down into the roadway, keeping her chin lowered and her eyes on the ground. Her heart pounded in her throat, and she was trembling from head to toe. Hannah glanced at the two men lying motionless in the dust.

The guard had ceased moaning, and the driver was quiet—too quiet. Was he dead, or unconscious?

"If you don't mind," Stillman was saying, reaching out to relieve Hannah of her purse. His gloved hand tangled in the cords somehow, so that when he went to pull it from her arm it jerked her forward.

Stumbling, Hannah put out a hand to catch herself and Stillman caught her. He frowned, his hard eyes narrowing. "Hey! I know you," he began, but Truett interrupted.

"What about him?" he asked, indicating Mullen. "He's got the metal chest in there, but it's locked."

"Shoot the lock off," Stillman said without bothering to glance around at him. His fingers tightened around Hannah's arm, dragging her even closer. "Look up here, missy!"

Obeying his command because it seemed like the only thing to do, Hannah looked up. Hard gray eyes were fixed on her face, cold and flinty and merciless. The red bandana stretching over his nose and covering his face fluttered slightly when he spoke, and her gaze riveted on it in detached fascination. It puffed out, a small balloon of red formed by his mouth and breath, like a tiny heartbeat, she thought irrationally.

"Do you know me?" he bit out, tightening his grip even more.

"N-n-no," she stammered, her cheeks flushing guiltily. Could he see through her transparent lie? Of course he could. A myopic octogenarian could see through it! Why did she think for one moment that she could carry off any kind of deception? She wasn't good at that sort of thing; in fact, was very bad at it. The truth always stuck out on her like quills on a porcupine.

While all this whirled rapidly through her fear-drugged brain, Nate Stillman was contemplating the quivering girl in his grasp. Huge blue eyes like cornflowers gazed up at him from beneath a thick fringe of sooty lashes—eyes that he remembered. He'd seen this copper-haired girl before, in a small settlement a hundred miles north. She knew him, too—knew him by name. It was evident from the rapid intake of breath, the blank, frightened stare. Stillman released her arms, watching dispassionately as the girl sagged back against the dusty side of the coach.

"The preacher's gal," he said flatly. "I see the Blackfoot didn't get you after all."

The implications of his words didn't sink in for a moment, then Hannah's eyes widened even more. "You . . . you saw what happened?"

"Saw 'em headed that way, yeah."

"Then why didn't you help? Why didn't you warn us?" she asked with agonizing effort.

"And risk our own necks? Not hardly . . ."

There was a loud buzzing in Hannah's ears, a thunderous roar like the rush of a waterfall, filling her world with sound. These men had seen disaster and death riding toward Jubile, yet had not lifted a finger to help. Joshua McGuire had died because of these men's apathy . . .

She watched, not hearing anything but the roaring in her ears as Nate Stillman motioned for Truett to come forward. She was vaguely aware that her wrists were being bound by stout leather strips, that Mr. Chessman had crumpled into a dead faint. Edward Mullen stood tall and firm a few feet away, quietly conversing with Roper, appearing very much at ease, and not at all concerned about the events around him. It did not occur to Hannah then to wonder about his calm detachment.

# Chapter Fourteen

Snatches of conversation drifted to her in wavering fragments—words here and there like fat raindrops on a hot stone, quickly sizzling into oblivion.

"... what'll we do with her? She knows us..."

"It won't work if somebody can identify us..."

"... the plan..."

"... get rid of her..."

"No! She won't talk if we..."

In and out, like waves crashing on a seashore, ebbing, receding, words flowing through her mind in a timeless, meaningless pattern. They'd known, could have saved all those lives, yet had chosen not to do so. How absurd, that so many human lives—precious lives—had hinged upon the cowardly whims of these men.

Hannah gradually became aware of the spokes of the high coach wheel pressing against her back, the firm prod of the hub digging into her tender skin with a vengeance. Leather strips fretted her wrists, chafing the baby softness and leaving them raw. The sharp pain awoke her to her surroundings, to the heated discussion going on between Roper and Truett.

"Dammit! I say we get rid of her! She can talk, I tell ya! She can identify us! This weren't in the plan at all, and I don't like it." Roper, the bandana he wore masking his scars but not the hatred in him, leaned forward belligerently, eyes glowing like heated coals beneath his low hat brim.

Truett, his voice low and urgent, disagreed. "No, she won't talk. I told you already—she's a lady. If she gives her word, Roper . . ."

"Hell! You expect me to be satisfied with some two-bit, preachy female's *word*? I ain't such a damn idiot, Truett, and you shouldn't be neither."

"But she's different," was the quiet rejoinder.

There was a harsh, derisive snort, and Roper jeered, "Underneath them skirts she's the same as all the others, boy!"

Shrinking back still more, feeling the dull pressure of the wheel hub digging into her back, Hannah slid her gaze sideways. She had to get away, flee while they were still arguing over her fate. It would not be easy with her hands tied, but a single glance at the two men sprawled in the dust erased any doubts. A slim chance would be better than none.

But when she would have slipped around the edge of the coach, Truett stopped her with a warning shake of his head. Dare she trust him? Dare she take such a big risk? But what were her alternatives? At least Truett had defended her, and he had not looked at her the same way Roper had—as if she were an insect to be ground beneath his boot heel.

Hannah's hesitation cost her the opportunity, which probably saved her life. Truett stepped forward at the same time Roper did, both men intent on the girl. It was Truett, again, who came to her rescue, stepping in front of Roper.

"I'll take care of her."

"Until this is over with?"

"Until it's over with . . ."

"And then what? Do you take her home like a stray puppy? She'll only slow us down, Truett."

"Give over, Roper," Stillman said at last. "He'll sulk for a week if we don't let him have her. What difference does it make to you if he has to drag her around?"

Roper's fingers strayed to his neck, and Hannah recalled burning him with a spoonful of hot beans. He hadn't forgotten or forgiven, but then, neither had she. Her gaze sharpened when Roper growled, "Just keep her outa my way! That's all . . . just keep her outa my way!"

"Don't worry," Truett said softly, coming to Hannah and taking her by one arm. "I'll watch over you."

In spite of the fact that he was an outlaw and in disreputable company, Hannah had to feel gratitude for his rescue. "It will cause a lot of trouble," she said as he led her to the shade of a tree.

"I know. But I had to help." There was an awkward pause, then he said, "I wanted to come back, you know. They wouldn't let me. We were too close to 'em . . ."

"Come back?" she echoed in momentary confusion, then realized what he was trying to tell her. "Oh—yes. To Jubile. The Blackfoot."

"Yeah. I thought you'd all been killed." Truett hooked one finger in the edge of his bandana and pulled it down so it hung free around his neck. Peach fuzz bristled on his jaw. His eyes were steady and troubled as he gazed down at Hannah's pale face.

She struggled to speak, anger and sadness almost choking her as she cleared her throat. "No, nine of us survived, Mr. Truett—eight children and myself." Her glance fell on Edward Mullen as he still stood loose and relaxed, leaning back against the coach, talking with Stillman and Roper in low tones. Why weren't they worried about Mullen identifying them? Maybe they thought she wouldn't tell him their names, but then remembered that many wanted posters contained good likenesses, but no correct name. Or maybe . . . but that was too ridiculous to contemplate.

"What happened to the driver and guard?" Hannah asked after a moment.

"The guard's dead. The driver's just taking a little nap," Truett replied. He licked his lips in a nervous gesture, managed a brief smile, then suggested that Hannah get into the coach again. "You can sit on the seat while we take care of business. You'll be more comfortable," he said as he led her back to the coach and helped her inside. She settled back against the hard seat and looked at the young outlaw standing just outside.

"What is going to happen to me, Mr. Truett?"

"Nothing. I'll let you go after things have died down a bit. You'll have to ride with me until then."

All things considered, it wasn't as bad as it first sounded. At least she was alive. Mr. Chessman, who had wakened from his faint and was moaning loudly, had been tied to the wagon wheel. Mr. Mullen caught her looking at him once, and shifted from one foot to another, turning his head and crossing his arms over his chest.

"What will you do with Mr. Mullen?" Hannah asked Truett when he brought her a drink of water from his canteen. "Is he to be harmed?"

"Mullen?" Truett seemed amused by her question. "No, he ain't gonna be harmed."

It all fell into place then, the puzzling little pieces that had been nagging at her: Edward Mullen's confidence and lack of fright when the outlaws pursued them; his careless shots that did more harm to pine trees than men; his refusal to allow her to shoot; the mystery of the metal box beneath his seat; and the elaborate theatrics when they had been stopped.

"Is he working with you, Mr. Truett?"

The swift question caught the boyish outlaw by surprise, and he yanked his head up to gaze narrowly at Hannah. "Shhh! Don't let them hear..."

"Hear what?" Stillman asked from behind him. "Hear

that she knows what's goin' on?'' He spat on the ground.
''And when did you figure on tellin' me?''

"She don't know nothing, Nate. She's just guessin' . . ."

"She's too damned close to right for my comfort."

The shadowed coach hid Hannah's face so that Stillman
could not see her fright. They were all in this—it was some
sort of conspiracy that had something to do with the metal
box. But what? Money, of course, or gold. That was usually
the best incentive for robbery and murder. But what did
Edward Mullen have to do with it? And why would he
conspire to steal his own gold? Hannah's head reeled with
confusion. It was too much in one afternoon—too much to
absorb in one day.

"Let me go," she said wearily when Truett turned back
to her, hating the thick edge of tears in her voice, but unable
to stop them. "Please. I won't tell anyone. Who would I
tell?"

"Don't," Truett said softly. "It won't do any good, Miss
McGuire. They won't care. Just keep quiet and be kinda
calm an' I'll take care of you . . ."

Hannah looked at his boyish face—the pale fuzz on his
cheeks and the kindness in his eyes—and she wondered why
he was with these men. Truett somehow didn't seem the
type.

Leaning forward so that she could whisper, Hannah said,
"Have you ever considered leaving such a dangerous life,
Mr. Truett? It will bring you nothing but death and destruction, and I do not think your friends will be able to help
you."

He was shaking his head. "No, Nate and Roper are all
I've got—all I've ever had. I need them."

"No, you don't! You can do anything you like if you will
only try, Mr. Truett! There's a whole world out there, a
decent world, and if you . . ."

"Hey!" Stillman shouted, turning to stare at them with suspicion. "I don't like it when I can't hear what yer sayin'. Speak up!"

A frown knit Truett's brow, and he said quickly, "Don't let Nate hear you sayin' anything like that. Just keep quiet like I told you." Then he was gone, spinning around and leaving Hannah sitting alone in the hot coach.

Several minutes passed while the outlaws conferred. Hannah remained sitting in tense silence. A fly buzzed near and she swatted at it with her bound hands. Tiny rivulets of perspiration trickled down the sides of her face. She sat with damp patches growing on her blue gown and her nose itching, and the silly hat perched lopsided on her head, while a band of desperate outlaws decided her ultimate fate. Was this like having your life flash before your eyes when you were drowning? Perhaps it was. But if so, where were the images of Joshua and Creed? The two most important men in her life should at least rate a moment's memory when she was so close to dying.

Creed—his rugged frame and handsome face, his ebony hair and dark eyes that had glowed with teasing lights at times, making her mad and happy and soft inside all at the same time. How she missed him. How she wished he was here. He could make her angrier and happier than she'd ever been before in her life, and she ached at the thought of never seeing him again—never seeing the way his eyes crinkled at the corners when he laughed, or the way his mouth would tighten when he was mad at her, or the expression on his face when he made love to her. Love— was that what it had been?

Twisting restlessly, Hannah gazed past the outlaws to the distant mountain peaks. Where was Creed? Was he still following Stillman? Perhaps he was close behind, and would rescue her. *Oh, Creed! Please come for me ... please come soon, before something happens ...*

And as she sat there, it occurred to Hannah that instead of praying, as she should be, she was thinking of Creed, silently begging him to find her ...

Creed pulled his bay around and nudged him into a trot down the steep, rocky hillside. It was after noon, and the sun was directly overhead, casting short shadows on the grass. Tall, chest-high grasses waved in the slight breezes wafting across the slope, looking like a benign sea as he pushed through them.

His mind was on Stillman—on the few faint tracks he had run across earlier—so that he was startled by the dim sound of gunfire. Jerking his head up, he reined in his bay in a reflex motion, paused to determine the direction, then drummed his heels against the horse's sides. He galloped through the meadow, then clattered over rocky slopes, small rocks shooting from beneath the shod hooves as he spurred General on. Any gunfire was worth investigating, but when Creed topped a distant rise and saw the racing stagecoach and pursuing riders, he knew he'd hit paydirt.

"Bull's-eye," he said softly, and a grim smile twisted his mouth.

He waited behind an outcropping of shale, watching as the coach was run down and stopped, as the masked men hauled out passengers and a bulky metal trunk. Then his eyes narrowed and his fingers tightened on the leather reins as he saw the woman descend from the coach, saw her wrists bound and the two men arguing. It was Hannah. He'd know her anywhere, with her bright copper hair and slender shape. "Dammit!"

Hannah's attention was distracted from the distant mountain peaks by an argument between the outlaws and Edward

Mullen. She could hear Roper's vituperative words, his harsh, sneering jibes, and Mullen's angry rejoinders.

"Ain't nothin' in here but a bunch of papers, Mullen! Is that what we risked hangin' for?"

"Stocks and bonds! Plummer needs these..."

"Plummer, hell! I'm gittin' damn sick and tired of Henry Plummer and what he thinks he needs!" Reaching down into the heavy metal chest, Roper came up with a fistful of papers. "This ain't spendable, Mullen!"

"It is, if you know how! Sheriff Plummer needs those legal papers, and he hired me to get them to him—which I intend to do, Roper!"

"I can rearrange yer plans for you," Roper said in a deadly quiet voice, his palm brushing carelessly against the butt of his holstered pistol.

Hannah watched with widening eyes as Mullen blanched. His eyes darted to Roper's hand and he stepped back.

Stillman edged closer to the furious outlaw, and his tone was soothing. "Hey, Lane—it don't matter none to us what we get for Plummer. We get paid just the same. And keep your voice down. We've got two witnesses..."

Swirling, Roper snarled, "No, we got *three* witnesses, an' I can take care of that real easy-like!"

Lane Roper, in a calm, biting rage, shot Edward Mullen and the portly Mr. Chessman. Stunned by the swiftness of his actions, Hannah did not even have time to scream, to offer a protest at the sheer waste of human life. Only Hall Truett protested—with his pistol.

When Roper turned toward Hannah with the same deadly calm, Truett put himself between them, his gun lifted and a warning in his eyes. "Don't do it, Roper," was all he said, but it was enough.

Roper slowly cooled, and with Nate Stillman swearing at

him, he walked away. Truett turned to Hannah. "I won't let him hurt you," he promised, seeing her bloodless lips and wide blue eyes smeared with fright. Swallowing the huge lump in her throat, Hannah nodded.

Night fell slowly, purple shadows drifting down and shrouding the landscape. Wavering shadows grew into leering beasts and taunting threats in the hazy dusk, looming over Hannah as she rode behind Hall Truett. He had done his best to make her comfortable, an impossible task when one was seated on the rump of a horse with legs astride bulging saddlebags. Modesty had given way to expedience, it seemed. And apathy had given way to terror.

Roper and Stillman rode ahead of them, the bulky metal box tied on the back of Stillman's horse, bouncing crazily as they rode. Stillman was first, then Roper, then Truett and Hannah, single file down the narrow, rutted tracks that wound through the thick forest.

Lane Roper just waited for Truett to turn his back, to be careless. Then he would shoot her. She read his intentions in his eyes, in the hooded gaze and malevolent smile he would slant in her direction, and it frightened her. It made her bones turn to jelly and her stomach turn over, and she clutched at Hall Truett with both hands, distantly amazed that she would seek shelter from an outlaw, but not knowing what else to do.

The past month had been a stark lesson in humility and patience—in being confronted with grief and seemingly insurmountable obstacles, and forced to overcome them. But she had survived. She had survived the death of her father, the bewildering and frightening flight in the company of a man who made it plain he would rather be elsewhere, then the initiation into love by that same man. *Physical love*, Hannah corrected herself scrupulously. Physical love was obviously at the opposite end of the spectrum from emotional love. It held no lasting ties for some; she had found that out to her bitter sorrow. She would survive everything else, too.

So she hung on, wind whipping through her hair, bouncing and jolting as though she were being dragged behind a Roman chariot. A martyr, Hannah reflected, she was being made a circumstantial martyr. And how could she have ever thought life in Jubile was boring? Idle days now beckoned to her with much sweeter promise than ever before, and she silently vowed never to wish for more excitement in her life again. Joshua had warned her about being careful what she wished for, but she had been too foolish to listen.

Hannah's hands clenched tighter as the horse slipped and slid down the muddy banks of a slope and into the water of an icy creek. Water surged around her ankles, seeping through the thin leather to soak her stockings and chill her feet. Hannah's teeth began to chatter, and she wished she had snatched her warm woolen shawl from the small trunk containing her recent acquisitions.

"Are you all right back there?" Truett half turned to ask.

She managed a nod of her chin against his back because she couldn't speak over the chattering of her teeth, but inside she thought, *No, I am not all right! I am cold and wet and hungry and frightened half to death!* But it would do no good to say those things to Hall Truett, who was, after all, doing the best he could for her under difficult circumstances. She should say a prayer of gratitude for his intervention, but somehow, Hannah could not summon up the words. Her tired brain was confused, and she found it almost impossible to think of a prayer of any sorts. God seemed remote—much more remote and unattainable than He ever had before. She knew, with a detached sort of interest, that her faith was being tested, but in the face of danger, all that seemed irrelevant. What she hadn't known until now was just how much she wanted to live, how fierce the will to survive could be. It lay, an inner steel core enveloped in spongy confusion, beneath her every thought.

Shivering and lost in the gray fog of her thoughts, Hannah was only vaguely aware that they had stopped. She felt rather than heard Truett's comforting words as his warm hands lifted her down from the horse with a gentle, sterile touch, and he pushed her to a sitting position on a large, flat rock inside a shallow depression in the mountainside. Gradually, Hannah focused her eyes and ears and realized he was telling her that they had stopped for the night, that he would give her something to eat and drink and let her lie down in a blanket close to a fire. She nodded.

Her muscles ached. Her flesh was chilled, and she was shaking uncontrollably. When she looked up, she saw Lane Roper's murderous gaze directed at her.

Oddly, instead of sending her further into a mental retreat, it gave her strength. His hatred lent her the courage to stare back at him, her blue, distended eyes matching his narrowed gaze without flinching. The outlaw crouched down beside the fire and finally looked away, and Hannah felt as if she had won a major victory. Truett knelt in front of her, untied and chafed her bruised wrists with his warm hands, rubbing them so the circulation would flow freely again.

Stillman was amused by the entire situation, and while the outlaws made camp and tended their horses, he cut his eyes at Roper and commented, "Whyn't you ask Truett if he'll let his new pet cook us some vittles?" When Roper hunched his shoulders and refused to acknowledge Stillman's gibe, the outlaw leader turned his attention to Truett. "Hey, Hall—see if she's good for somethin' besides decoration and aggravatin' Roper. I'm hongry, and if she wants to eat, she'll have to work."

After a glance at Hannah's pinched face, Truett said quietly, "She can have my share."

"Aw, no, that ain't the way it goes. If'n a body don't work, a body don't eat. Hell, boy, we're all tired. And if you'll jus' recollect, I didn't want that preachy gal comin' along with us in the first place."

Hannah stirred when it looked as if Truett intended to argue more. "No, no. I don't mind," she said, putting out a hand to touch Truett's arm. "He's right. I will work."

Stillman cackled. "See? She's got more horse sense than you do, boy!"

"It still ain't right to make her work when she's so delicate and fragile," Truett muttered. His gaze softened when it shifted from Stillman's amused face to Hannah's. "She's so pretty and sweet—kinda like a flower," he observed softly, flushing when Stillman burst into loud, raucous laughter.

"Like a *flower*? Ain't we gettin' poetic here!"

Roper rose slowly to a stand, his long legs uncurling in a faintly menacing motion. "The woman's got to go," he said flatly. "She's trouble. She's got Truett talkin' like a damned idiot, and I've got one of my feelin's again."

"You sure it ain't a bellyache instead of a feelin', Roper?" Truett snapped. "That's what yer best at, you know. Bellyachin'."

"Yeah? Well, I'm pretty damned good at a few other things, too," Roper snarled. The backs of his fingers brushed against the long duster coat hiding his holster and gun, and Hannah surged to her feet.

"No! Please—no fighting over this! I . . . I'll cook or do whatever it is you want me to do, but please . . . no more fighting!"

"Now, ain't that sweet?" Stillman put in with a gleeful chuckle. "She don't want you two boys fightin'!"

"Maybe she's partial to Truett and don't want him hurt none," Roper observed. He rocked back on his boot heels and watched Truett's eyes dart toward Hannah. "Yeah, and I think he's sweet on her, too. That makes this kinda int'restin', seein' as how she's gonna have to be got rid of soon . . ."

"I told you!" Truett spat fiercely. "I'll see to her!"

Roper's hand appeared from beneath the coat, his pistol gripped in his fingers. "No need. Step away from her, Truett, or I'll shoot you, too," he said with deadly quiet.

A muffled groan passed Truett's lips, but he did not move. The pistol in Roper's hand lifted slightly, its muzzle never wavering from a spot directly above Hannah's left breast. "Lower the gun," Truett said through clenched teeth.

"No. She dies. I'm tired of listening to your foolishness, and I sure as hell don't want to listen to any of that preachy girl's stupid Bible verses." He sneered, and a muscle in his jaw twitched, making the livid scar snaking across his face look as if it was a live serpent. "I heard enough of those that first day we laid eyes on her. If I'd known then this was gonna happen, I'da shot her on sight!"

Transfixed by fear and fascination, Hannah gazed at the posturing figures bathed in the glow of the fire as if they were in a play in a St. Louis theater. It couldn't be real. It could not be happening to her. Her life was being discussed as if she were a chicken for the next Sunday's dinner. At any moment she expected the curtain to be rung down and the uniformed man to come out with the pasteboard placards that announced the next act.

These thoughts cued a remarkable event. A shot rang out, and richocheted from the shallow cave's floor.

Stillman dove for cover behind a flat piece of shale that she hadn't noticed before, and Hall Truett made a running

leap for Hannah. His arms encircled her waist and he
continued with the same forward motion, sending both of
them crashing to the hard floor and jarring the breath from
Hannah's lungs. She was so busy trying to breathe, she did
not notice for several heartbeats that Lane Roper had not
tried to take cover.

He sat abruptly on the cave floor, one hand pressed to his
chest and a strange expression on his face. Stillman shouted
at him to take cover. "For Gawd's sake, Roper! Get down!"

Roper's head turned slowly, as if it cost him a great deal
of effort, and a slight smile curved his scarred mouth in a
grimace. "Too late," he murmured, and it was then that
Hannah saw the blossoming crimson stain on his chest. It
soaked his shirt rapidly, and he gave a faint, deprecating
shrug of his shoulders. "I knew she was trouble . . ."

More shots rang out. Truett pressed her head down behind
the pile of what Hannah now noticed as blankets and saddles
and packs. The metal chest pinged loudly as a bullet
smacked into the side.

"Where in the hell is that coming from?" Stillman
shouted to Truett, and Hannah felt his shrug.

"I don't know, but it's too damned close. Reckon it's a
posse or vigilantes?"

The same thought occurred to all three of them at the
same time: Creed Bratton.

Lane Roper was beyond thinking, beyond caring who had
shot him. He sat upright, his elbows propped on his bent
knees and his eyes staring sightlessly ahead of him like a
grotesque statue of death. Hannah shuddered, turning away.
He would have killed her, but she still hated to see death. It
was never pretty, never a gentle easing out of life, but a
harsh, brutal affair that rent a human being's dignity and left
him naked.

# Chapter Fifteen

"Stillman!" a rough voice shouted in the sudden silence that followed Roper's death. "Stillman, give it up! Roper's dead, and you will be too if you don't throw down your guns!"

"No chance!" Stillman shouted back. "Is that you, Bratton?"

"Yeah, it's me, Stillman."

"Then you know me well enough to know you'll never take me outa here alive. If you want me," he brandished a pistol and rifle in each hand, "you'll have to come and get me!"

"I can do that!" the voice came back.

"And you may die tryin'!"

A brief silence ensued again, and Hannah shivered in Hall Truett's shadow. It was Creed. He had come for her. Or had he just come for the outlaws he had been pursuing? She didn't care at that moment.

"Let the girl go and we'll parley, Stillman," Bratton called out. "No sense in risking her, and it'll go even harder on you if she gets hurt."

Stillman sliced a speculative glance toward Hannah. "I don't think so, Bratton! I've grown kinda partial to her in the past day or so. Maybe we'll just keep her. And maybe, if you don't want to see her get hurt, you'll just ride on outa here."

There was silence; only the crackle of the fire could be heard. Then, "Well, if she gets killed, it'll just go harder on you. Do what you must."

"He's bluffing! Get behind the girl," Stillman was saying to Truett. "Get behind her for cover. He won't shoot her. We'll use her to fight our way out of here."

"No."

There was a brief moment of stunned silence, then another bullet split the tense air, sending a shower of rock splinters over Stillman's head, and he ducked.

"What do you mean—no?" he shouted over the whine of bullets as Creed opened fire again.

"Just what I said. I ain't gonna risk her."

"Don't be stupid, Hall! She's our only chance. Bratton won't take the risk of killing her . . ."

"I don't know that for sure," Truett shouted stubbornly. "I've seen him do some damned hard things a'fore. He ain't gonna get the chance to do so again."

*Hard things?* Hannah was thinking. *What kind of hard things—killing? Would Creed be as brutal and savage as Lane Roper?*

Truett lay over her, his body pressing down on hers and grinding her against the hard cave floor so that Hannah could not see. She could hear him, hear the bullets scream overhead, striking the cave walls and trees nearby, but could see nothing. Yet, she knew Creed had come to her rescue. She had silently prayed for him to come and he had.

Rock dust coated her mouth and filled her nose every time she drew a breath. Hannah pressed her palms against the abrasive floor and waited. Truett's deep, ragged breaths sounded in her ears. She could hear the rattle of her own harsh breathing and the thunder of her racing heart. Shots popped over her head, and she trembled with fear that Creed would somehow be hurt. Hannah tried to pray for his safety, but the words would not come.

When Truett shifted to lie beside Hannah and take aim with his rifle, she put out a hand to stop him. "No, please don't!"

Surprised, he lowered the barrel and asked, "Why not?"

"Because he may be hurt, and I . . . I . . ."

There was a brief pause in which the youth stared at Hannah, and then he nodded. "I saw Bratton leading you and those kids."

"Yes . . ."

"And you fell in love with him."

Hannah opened her mouth to argue, to say that she had *not* fallen in love with Creed Bratton, but it was silly to lie. She had, of course, and anyone could see it.

"Yes," she said simply.

Truett rested his beardless chin on the back of his hand. "I shoulda known," he sighed after a moment. "Only, why'd it have to be Bratton? I don't have much of a choice here, you know. He's after us, and it's us or him." He reached out a gentle finger and touched one of Hannah's mussed curls. "I don't want to hurt you, you know."

"Truett!" a loud voice bawled from behind the nearby rock. "Dammit, what're you doin' over there? Shoot at him!"

Hannah's pleading gaze made Truett flinch slightly, but he shook his head. "I have to," he whispered. "Please understand that."

Closing her eyes, Hannah nodded. "I understand . . . and I want you to know you've helped me and I thank you. It's just that . . ."

"Truett!" Stillman shouted again. Fury thickened his voice to a low roar, and he shifted from behind the rock to peer over it. "Don't you give a good goddamn that Bratton is out there tryin' to shoot our damn heads off? Have you gone plumb loco over that preacher-gal?" There was the scratch of leather on rock, the faint metallic click of a gun barrel, and Stillman rose to his knees, lifting his rifle in a smooth motion and aiming in the direction of their attacker.

"No!" Hannah screamed, and in desperation flung a

handful of dirt at Stillman's head. It worked better than she
had hoped. Though it did not immobilize him, it did blur his
vision and send him diving back behind the rock for cover.
A faint, derisive laugh floated from outside.

"Thanks, lady!"

It was Creed's voice, his rough, mocking, beloved voice,
and she felt a surge of emotion.

"Now you done it!" Truett was saying, shoving Hannah
behind him and glancing toward Stillman. "He'll be meaner
than a gut-shot grizzly! Why'd you go and do that?"

"I didn't want him to shoot Creed . . ."

"For the love of God—don't *do* that! Stillman will kill
you, don't you understand that?"

"Yes." She returned his pale gaze with blazing eyes. "I
do understand that, Mr. Truett."

Sighing, Truett wedged her between the rocks, using his
own body as a barrier. "And then he'll kill Bratton," he ended.

"I don't think so."

The youthful outlaw shoved some cartridges into the
chamber of his rifle, then checked his pistol and looked back
at Hannah. "I always wanted some decent woman to look
about me the way you look about him, you know."

"Did you?" Hannah asked when it looked as if Truett
was not going to say anything else. More bullets whined
overhead, and she could hear Stillman's muttered curses
rising from behind the safety of his rock.

"Yeah, but none of them ever seemed to want to. You're
the only decent woman who was ever nice to me." There
was an awkward pause, then, "I dreamed about you after
we left that day. I didn't want to go. I would have gone back
for you, but the others . . . Roper . . . well, you know how it
is."

"Yes. I do."

"Miss McGuire . . . Hannah . . . you're the first *nice* girl

I've ever known. And the prettiest. I feel lucky just to have known you.''

Hannah shivered. That sounded final, as if he intended to be gone in a few moments. She didn't know what to say. He had helped her when he didn't have to—had asked for nothing from her and had saved her from Roper. How could she repay that?

She looked up at him, at the face shadowed by rock and hat brim, and saw a youthful, lonely boy, not a hardened outlaw and criminal. Hall Truett had helped her with no expectations—just because he knew it was right.

''You've done a good thing by helping me,'' Hannah said at last. ''God must surely be pleased.''

''God?'' Truett ducked another bullet that passed over like an angry bee. ''I don't know about that. He don't ever seem to have been too pleased with me before. I just want you to be pleased.''

Hannah swallowed the sudden lump in her throat. ''I am, Mr. Truett. I am very pleased with you.''

He smiled brightly. ''Are you? Then that's what matters. I don't know what's gonna happen here . . .'' He gestured to the dark shadows outside the cave with his gun. ''. . . but I want you to believe that I would never let no harm come to you.''

Putting a hand on his arm, Hannah said urgently, ''Will you please surrender?''

Truett stared at her in amazement. ''Surrender? You mean to Bratton? Miss Hannah—he'd kill me!''

''No, he won't. Not if you tell him you're surrendering, that you'll go back and give yourself up . . .''

''Then I'll be dead for sure! Look,'' he said, ignoring the flying bullets and taking Hannah's hand between his, ''I can't give myself up. At least this way, I've got a chance. If I go back to Virginia City and Alder Gulch, Plummer will see to it that I don't hang. Bratton knows that, and he'd take us elsewhere. No, I'd rather die by lead than a rope."

"But . . ."

"No, I can't," Hall Truett said, shaking his head. "I'd rather risk Bratton than a hangman."

Stillman chose that moment to surge from his position behind the rock, firing rifle and pistol at the same time, keeping Creed pinned down while he dove for cover. He landed beside Truett.

"Now, we're jus' gonna take this little gal and use her as a shield to get outa here, Truett," he snarled, his lip curling back from his teeth, reminding Hannah of a feral animal. "And I don't wanna hear nothing different from you," he added, pointing his pistol at Truett when he opened his mouth. The muzzle of the Colt nudged Truett's chest.

"Nate . . . Nate, don't do this," Truett said softly. "Don't make me choose . . ."

"Choose? What th' hell d'ya mean, *choose*? Who took care of you when you didn't have nobody else, boy? Who's looked after you for the past four years, since you was jus' a wet-nosed little kid with no mammy or pappy and nothin' to eat? Huh? Who?"

"You, Nate," was the whispered reply.

"Hell, yes, it was me! I took care of you, and I saw to it that you got food, and clothes, and learned how to take care of yourself. Is this th' way yer gonna repay me for all I done, Hall?"

"But Nate, she's a woman, and she ain't done us no harm. I don't want to hurt her."

Stillman's voice grew soft and warm, coaxing, like the spider curled and waiting in the quilted pattern of a web. "No, an' I don't wanna hurt her neither, Hall—really, I don't. Hell, you know me. I ain't like Roper was. I don't kill just for fun. And how many times have you seen me hurt a woman?''

''Just that once, when . . .''

''That was an accident, and you know it. She got in the way of a bullet meant for someone else.'' Stillman's hand fell onto Truett's shoulder in a gesture meant to be comforting. ''We won't hurt her. We just need her to get us out of here. We'll let her go a little ways out, once we've put some miles a'twixt us and Bratton. All right?''

Truett searched Stillman's face during a long moment in which Hannah's heart thumped loudly and her nerve ends screamed. She wanted to say something, to beg Truett not to trust him, but her mouth and tongue refused to cooperate with her brain's sluggish command to function.

''All right,'' Truett said at last, and Hannah's heart sank. She had no faith in Nate Stillman's promises.

''Bratton!'' Stillman shouted, cupping both hands around his mouth. ''Bratton, we're coming out! And we've got the girl with us, so don't go to shootin' unless yer intendin' on seein' her go down . . .''

''Come on,'' Truett said, tugging gently at Hannah's arm and lifting her. ''I won't let you get hurt,'' he promised when she resisted. ''Trust me.''

Hannah wanted to laugh at the absurdity of his words, but it reminded her too much of Creed once saying the same thing and she couldn't. It took a moment before she registered the voice from just outside the cave, heard what Creed Bratton was saying.

''Don't come out without your hands up, Stillman! I don't care who you've got with you—I'll shoot.''

''He's bluffing,'' Stillman said, and stood up. ''Come on, Truett. Bring the gal.''

''I don't know,'' Truett protested uneasily. ''Bratton's likely to shoot her just to make a point.''

Pinpoints of orange fire blurted in the darkness beyond the cave, and a bullet whizzed over their heads, halting Stillman in his tracks and making Truett's hands tighten on Hannah's arm.

A shock went through her, from the tips of her toes up to her head, sufficiently paralyzing her. No, Creed would not shoot her, would not risk doing her harm . . . would he? Was he that intent upon capturing Stillman—that intent upon getting the bounty? Surely not . . .

But it seemed that perhaps he was, because Creed took careful aim and sent Nate Stillman's hat flying from his head. It spun twice and landed in the dust a mere instant before Nate Stillman sprawled on his belly and elbows beside it, cursing loudly.

"Damn that Creed Bratton! The crazy bastard—is he tryin' to kill her? Hey, Bratton!" he shouted then, "if we're dead, you don't get the reward money!"

"Think again, Stillman!" came the answer from the dark. "I bet Plummer pays me for three corpses almost as quick as he pays me for what you've got in those saddlebags!"

Truett and Hannah had once more ducked behind the large rock for cover, and now Hannah wasn't at all certain that Creed would not shoot her if he felt the need. Her fingers dug into the hard rock until they began to ache. *Three* corpses? Was she to be included in that honored number? Or maybe he just meant the three outlaws. Yes, that had to be it. Creed would not intentionally shoot her, but if she turned out to be as unfortunate as the woman Stillman had mentioned earlier who had been slain by a stray bullet—well, then, she'd be just as dead, wouldn't she? Why did Creed persist in shooting at them when she was so close? Didn't he care at all? Creed's next words erased that doubt.

"Hey, Stillman!" he shouted. "Send out the girl, and I'll give you a head start."

Now prone and furiously shoving cartridges into his Henry rifle and Colt .44, Nate Stillman gave a harsh laugh. "Yeah, I bet you will, Bratton!" he shouted over his shoulder.

Creed's voice floated back, "Send her out and see."

"He must think I'm as crazy as he is," Stillman commented disgustedly. Flopping back over onto his belly, he slid the barrel of the Henry over the rock. "Get the girl, Truett, and put her in front of us. I don't trust Bratton for a second. He'll put a bullet in both of us if we don't have her."

Truett turned to Stillman with an agonized expression. "We can't, Nate . . ."

"Dammit! We just went through this a few minutes ago! Get the girl in front of us, Hall!"

Without answering, Truett stood and put Hannah in front of them, his face taut. No rifle fire echoed into the cave for the space of a heartbeat. Then, a bullet slammed into the far wall, showering them with rock splinters before digging a long, shallow furrow into the floor. Hannah flinched as a hot rock shard flew past, skimming over her cheek and leaving a bloody crease.

When she cried out in reaction, Truett took a quick, assessing glance at the damage. "It's all right," he said.

"But . . ."

Truett's fingers dug into her arm and he gave her a quick shove forward. "Run!" was all he said, but Hannah knew it would be her only chance.

Somehow her brain finally got the message to her feet, and she leaped over the pile of saddles and blankets, and the metal trunk, lifting her skirts and running as fast as she could before Nate Stillman stopped her. She heard the outlaw leader's enraged shout and Hall Truett's attempt to grab his gun. The hair on the back of her neck prickled, and her flesh quivered as she waited for a bullet in her back at any moment.

When the shot came, Hannah's heart almost leaped from her chest. She ran into the shadows beyond the near fringe of trees and paused, sucking in huge gulps of sweet night air as she pressed back against a huge oak. After making a quick assessment and realizing that she had not been shot, Hannah could not resist a glance around the tree trunk.

Hall Truett had obviously struggled with Stillman, and the shot meant for Hannah had gotten him instead. The youth slumped against a rock, his pistol falling from his hand to the cave floor. Stillman stood over him, pausing for a moment, his words barely audible to Hannah from where she stood with tears rolling down her cheeks.

"Aw, Hall—what didja hafta go and do that for? You done kilt yerself, boy, and that's a fact."

Stillman backed away a step, his head jerking up when Creed's voice came from somewhere in the shadows. "Lay your guns down, Stillman, and I won't kill you . . ."

But Nate Stillman chose to turn in a half-crouch, his gun hand lifting as he did, orange flame bursting twice from the muzzle. There was an angry shout, a hoarse cry, then an answering shot, and Stillman bucked backward. He sprawled on the ground, tried to lift his head, then collapsed.

It happened so quickly Hannah had no time to think, to do anything but watch. When Stillman fell, Hannah came to life. The cry she'd heard had not come from Nate Stillman, nor had it come from Hall Truett. There was only one other source . . .

Tears mingled with the blood on her cheek and dripped from her chin to the front of her dress as she surged forward. "Creed! Oh, Creed, where are you?" she called, stumbling over rocks and tree limbs in her frantic search.

"Here I am," came the testy reply. "Do you have to be so damned noisy?"

"Where?" she gulped, balancing on one foot and trying to see into the deeper shadows. Something brushed against her leg and she squealed, leaping sideways with the agility and grace of a startled deer.

"Right here. Sorry. Thought you knew where I was."

Kneeling, Hannah saw Creed at last. He was lying in a hazy shaft of dappled moonlight, his long form propped against a fallen tree, one arm cradling his rifle and the other braced against a stout branch. He had a strange expression on his face, and his crooked smile did not quite reach his eyes, a fact Hannah attributed to his being sorry she had survived.

"Why did you shoot when you knew I might get hurt?" she couldn't help asking angrily. Her gaze searched his face in the shadows, saw his teeth flash white in a grin.

Creed held up his black hat and poked a finger through a singed hole in the crown. "He put a hole in my hat," he said, as though that explained it all. "I've had this hat since I was twelve, and I don't cotton to the idea of folks putting holes in it."

Hannah rocked back on her heels and stared at him in angry amazement. "And *that* is the reason you shot him? Because he put a hole in your . . . your hat?"

"You bet."

"But it's just an old hat!"

"No, it's not just an old hat. It's *my* hat. And it was my father's hat. I've worn it since I was so small the brim covered my nose and ears, and it's the only thing—besides General—that I don't like folks taking potshots at." Then, relenting, he added, "Aw, I couldn't let 'em take off with you, Hannah. No telling what would have happened if they had, and at least here I had some kind of control over the situation. I had them at a disadvantage, see, and the next time, it might have been the other way around.''

After a moment of brief silence, Hannah observed tartly that she wasn't convinced her safety had taken precedence over his hat. "But I won't call you a liar," she added.

"Am I supposed to say thanks?"

"If you like. Come on. Let's get out of these woods. It's dark and gloomy in here, and . . . what's wrong?"

Grimacing, Creed tried to sit up, but fell back against the tree trunk again. His breath was coming in strange puffs, and he gave her a wry smile. "I can't come with you, Hannah. I've got a little . . . problem."

"You're hurt!" Hannah gasped, seeing the blood ooze between the fingers he had pressed against his stomach. "Here—let me move this gun out of the way so I can see," she said, tilting back the long barrel of the rifle.

"Rifle, not gun," he muttered through white-rimmed lips that would not cooperate with his effort to keep them from tightening against the pain. "Don't, Hannah. It's no use."

She stared at him blankly when his hand closed over her exploring fingertips. "What do you mean?" Ice formed in her heart.

"I'm gut-shot. You can't do anything for me, Hannah, that's what I mean."

"You're wrong . . ."

"Dammit! I'm lying here wounded and bleeding and you still want to argue . . ." He broke off into a rasping cough that racked his body with pain, and Hannah winced. "I got careless again," he observed when his spasm ended. "Guess I shouldn't have stood up and let him get a good shot at me, but I didn't want to miss this time. Whoa! What're you doin'?" he asked then, catching her by one hand when she lifted the torn edges of his buckskin shirt.

"Looking at your wound."

"I told you there's no need for that . . ."

"Don't try to talk anymore. I said *don't*," she added in a severe tone that effectively silenced Creed's protests. Rising, she looked down at him and said, "I intend to nurse you until you're well, Creed Bratton."

"The hell you will! I'm dying, woman. And besides, I ain't too sure I want some preachy woman quotin' Bible verses at . . ." Creed broke off into another spasm of ragged coughing. Hannah put her hands on her hips.

"Don't think I shall hang black crepe over you, yet, for I refuse," she said tartly. "Now, put one arm around my neck, for I'm not strong enough to lift you by myself."

"Hannah, Hannah—I appreciate your concern, but it's hopeless. A man doesn't live long when he's gut-shot . . ."

Stamping a foot on the leafy ground and feeling the harsh prick of frustrated tears in her eyes, Hannah stormed at him, "You *shall* live! I won't let you die! Not now, not when I've found you again . . ."

Creed gazed up at her through a haze of pain. Her words registered slowly, penetrating the thick fog of pain and self-absorption that attended dying, and he managed a faint smile. "Nag, nag, nag! All right. Have it your way."

"I will, Creed Bratton, I will!"

# Chapter Sixteen

In the end, Hannah literally had to drag Creed back to the cave. He was barely conscious, and each movement caused him such excruciating pain that it tormented them both to move him. Hannah was sweating by the time she had him lying on blankets in the shallow depression. Working with feverish anxiety, she built up the fire, rummaged through the saddlebags and packs strewn about, and dragged the three bodies out of the way to the edge of the cave.

With Hall Truett, Hannah took particular care. She was gentle, and more than a few salty tears fell from her eyes to bathe his lifeless face. He had died for her sake, so she arranged his body with great attention. There wasn't time now, but later, when Creed was resting, she would bury him.

Hannah rounded up all the horses, including Creed's big bay. She unsaddled him and dumped Creed's packs on the cave floor. A single, lacy item caught her attention, and she lifted it curiously. What would a man like Creed be doing with such a thing in his possession? Then she recognized the flowery initial embroidered on one frayed edge. It was a W, which, turned upside down, could be an M—with a giant stretch of the imagination. Hannah's throat tightened. It was the lace handkerchief she had been busily shredding on the last night she'd seen him. He must have picked it up... She glanced over at him. Creed had his eyes closed, and his face was pale beneath the tan. A lump formed in her throat as Hannah realized that the unemotional, unsentimental Creed Bratton had carried with him a remembrance of that night. She crumpled it in her hand and held it to her dry eyes. Was it too late for them?

Struggling for control, Hannah decided that she could not worry about that now. Nothing must deter her from keeping him alive. All else could follow later.

She found and set aside Creed's bottle of whiskey, a knife, and his spare shirt. Then she moved to the bags and packs left by the outlaws. In Hall Truett's saddlebags she found a small medical kit—it was the answer to a prayer.

Though battered and obviously old, the leather-wrapped bundle contained needles and fine thread, a small packet of salve, and a small roll of bandages.

Taking a deep breath, Hannah rose and moved to Creed's side. He was half conscious, and blood had soaked his shirt on the entire right side. She placed Creed's knife in the fire to heat, as she had seen Joshua do. This would take more stamina than anything she had ever done before, and Hannah was not at all certain she could do it. Tending sick children and nursing the grippe and insect bites were one thing, but digging a bullet out of the man she loved was quite another.

Tender explorations with the tips of her fingers revealed a jagged wound in his side. Miraculously, it seemed to have missed most of his vital organs, but it was lodged beneath his bottom rib. The bullet had torn into his body with an impact that had ripped away a huge chunk of flesh, and it looked to Hannah's untrained eyes as if it had also nicked his liver.

Creed opened one eye and looked up at her. "What're you gonna do?" he mumbled.

"Cut the bullet out," she answered promptly.

This served to open both his eyes quite wide. "The hell you say! You ever done that before?"

"No, but I've seen it done. Now, be quiet and drink this," she said, handing him the bottle of whiskey from his pack.

Creed's eyes narrowed. "Now I know I must be dying, for you to be *givin'* me whiskey, instead of pourin' it out . . ."

"Just drink it, please—all of it." Hannah turned the knife blade in the flickering flames of the fire and prayed that the whiskey would not make matters worse. She knew she should not give him anything to drink, even water, but to operate on a fully conscious man would be devastating to her nerves.

Creed's voice floated from behind her, soggy and wry and faintly amused. "Is that the surgical instrument you plan on usin', Hannah?"

She turned to look at him. "Yes, it is."

"Where—if I may be so bold as to ask—did you find it?"

"In your saddlebag."

"I thought so." A reasonable facsimile of a smile twitched his lips. "Sweet, silly Hannah—that's a dining utensil, not a scalpel."

Hannah looked back at the knife in her hands. "It seems sharp enough."

"For butter, maybe. Hey, it's not that I mind you cutting on me, because if anybody has to cut on me I'd just as soon it'd be you, but please—use a sharp knife!"

Hannah sat back on her heels and regarded him with a baleful gaze. "Where do I find one of those?"

"'Member that Shoshoni knife and sheath you admired so much one time? Well, that one's a bit more suited to the job, love."

Hannah had to admit that it was. She turned the long, wicked blade in her hands for a moment, tested the edge with a fingertip, and hissed a sharp exclamation at the instant well of blood. Putting her finger to her mouth, Hannah's eyes dared Creed to say something. He didn't.

The utility knife was returned to the pack for later use buttering bread, and Hannah slid the long blade of Creed's skinning knife into the glowing coals. Just the thought of using such an instrument on him tempted panic, but she firmly thrust it aside. There just wasn't time to yield to panic. Later, maybe, when he was healing.

While Creed tilted back the bottle, Hannah rolled up her

sleeves. She washed her hands with the water from a leather canteen to remove the dirt, then dried them on a clean strip of cloth. Joshua McGuire had studied medicine at one time in his life, and she struggled to recall all his best advice. It had been so long ago, and there was so much . . .

Dragging in a deep gulp of air spiced with wood and ash smoke, as well as the sweat of fear, Hannah pulled the knife from the fire. Creed looked up at her, his mouth slanting in a crooked grin that made her heart lurch.

"This promises to be entertaining and educational," he said with a slur to his words. "Hope I ain't awake to see it . . ."

"So do I," she said with heartfelt sincerity. "So do I!"

Dawn broke over the eastern horizon in a splendid burst of vivid colors, shooting rays of rose and saffron across the milky sky. Hannah sat with her legs pulled up under her and watched the world wake. It was over. Her back ached and her head throbbed, and she wasn't at all certain she hadn't finished killing Creed. He lay tucked in his blankets with yards of linen wrapped around his ribs.

Mercifully, not too long after the first swift slice of the razor-edged knife, he had lost consciousness. Beads of sweat had coated his face, and his lips had thinned. Then, with a harsh groan, he had sagged into welcome oblivion. Now the bullet was out, the blood and infection mopped from the body cavity, and she had taken a few tiny stitches to close the wound. She was no surgeon, and now only time would tell if he would live. Why hadn't she paid more attention to what her father had told her? A sense of amazement filled her when she considered what she had done, and she shuddered lightly. Thank God the bullet had rested so close to the surface . . .

Sighing, Hannah pushed to her feet and went to stand

over him again. He was so pale, his lips were bloodless.
How could she stand it if he died? She knelt at his side for
what must have been the hundredth time, smoothing back
the loose strands of sable hair from his forehead and tucking
the blankets firmly around his body, as if he were a small
child. He looked like a little boy, she thought with a
wrench. Did all men look so vulnerable when they slept? It
was as if the gods of slumber somehow had removed the
harsher planes from Creed's features and replaced them with
softer angles that held traces of the child he had once been.
Only this child had shadows of a half-grown beard on his
cheeks and jaw, and his lips were far too sensuously formed
to belong to an adolescent.

Hannah curled her arms around her body and hugged her
fears to herself, as if attempting to suffocate them. He
wouldn't die—she'd make him live.

But in the next eight hours, Hannah fought a battle that
she ofttimes despaired of winning. Creed's fever soared,
and chills rattled his hot, dry body in racking shivers. She
bathed his forehead with cool water and clean cloths, and
tucked blankets around his long form. At daylight, she set
out in search of a plant to help reduce the fever and lessen
the pain. Not far from the cave she had success. Monkshood, the tall, stalky plant with blue and white hood-shaped
flowers, grew in abundance on a wooded slope. Hannah
gathered a skirtful of the plant and scurried back to camp. It
took a while to extract enough medicine from the roots to do
any good, but finally she filled a tin cup.

She knelt on the blankets and cupped his chin in the curve
of her palm. Her hand shook as she gazed down at his face,
and she steadied it with an effort. At first she tried coaxing
the edge of the cup between his lips, but that did no good.
In his restless coma, he fretted and turned away, almost
spilling the precious brew. In the end she had to force the

brew between Creed's resisting lips, and groaned with frustration when more of it dampened his blankets than was ingested. Finally, she succeeded in getting a fair portion to trickle down his throat.

Sitting back on her heels, Hannah stared at her patient glumly. She felt so helpless, but she didn't know anything else to do. Somewhere in the back of her mind she knew that she should conserve her strength, but if she tried to rest, her mind whirled with so many different possibilities that she would begin to grow agitated. It had become agony just to think. Too many horrors waited, like slack-jawed dragons, beyond the boundaries of her firm resistance. How could she even begin to contemplate a life without Creed? He had tormented her since that first day in Jubile, grated on her nerves like fingernails on a school slate, yet caught up somewhere in that cat-and-mouse relationship was the very real love she held for him.

Love—that elusive, erratic emotion that held such promise in the very word. L-o-v-e. It had a magical sound—like a soft sigh, or the whisper of the wind. Love. A simple arrangement of letters of the alphabet into a single word, yet it remained just out of reach for her. She felt it, oh, yes, but she wanted it lavished upon her—whispered into her ears, her hair; sung to her eyes and lips . . . poured upon her receptive body in a healing balm. She wanted to hear the words, then feel them through the tingling nerve ends of her skin. Closing her eyes against a sudden spasm of pain, she dragged in a deep breath of morning nectar, of decaying humus and sunlit shadows and summer flowers.

Hannah hugged her knees to her chest. Curling waves of copper hair fell forward over her face, smelling of smoke and wind and pine. A gentle breeze wafted the sweet scent of some flower on its currents, carrying it to where Hannah hovered over her sleeping patient. It made her think of St.

Louis, of home and her aunt's highly polished furniture. It had taken a great deal of lemon and beeswax, as well as sumptuous amounts of elbow grease, to keep that furniture glossy, and the reward was a mirror shine and the delicate scent that lingered for hours. Now, here she was, somewhere in the middle of Idaho, with a rock for furniture and an unconscious bounty hunter for company, and she was recalling her aunt's pin-neat parlor and lace doilies. Why not dwell on something more practical? she wondered. Why tease her saturated brain with useless fantasies, instead of possible solutions?

But then she would have to face the very real possibility that Creed Bratton might not survive the rustic surgery she had performed. Why couldn't she have been a proper surgeon, instead of a teacher? Creed *couldn't* die, he just couldn't!

Rising abruptly to her feet, Hannah set the empty tin cup down on a nearby rock and brushed off her skirts. Idle hands prompted idle thoughts . . .

Hannah threw herself into a frenzy of tasks. Her first was to remove the bodies of the three outlaws from the cave. Stillman and Roper she dragged away on blankets and tucked beneath an outcropping of rocks not far from the cave entrance. It was hard work, and once she was positive Stillman was resisting her efforts, as his body caught on a snag. Hannah shuddered. He still looked so . . . so *lifelike*. But he was dead and limp and blood-soaked. And, Hannah told herself fiercely, he had deserved to die. He'd murdered Hall Truett without a single qualm!

Hannah gently pried Truett's pistol from his lifeless fingers and laid it aside. She gazed down at his boyish face and cupped a hand over his eyes, closing them as they stared sightlessly at the shale roof of the cave. The boy outlaw deserved more than just an open grave beneath the stars. Gently, Hannah wrapped Hall in several blankets and scraped a grave from the raw earth, placing him as carefully as she could into the shallow depression beneath a towering pine. She formed a crude cross from two tree limbs and a strip of leather, and wedged it between the rocks she piled atop his grave. Then she sat back on her heels and tried to recall a Bible verse. None would come. They all seemed trite and foolish now—words about eternity and the love of a God who seemed to have turned away . . .

Hannah rocked forward to a kneeling position and folded her hands in a prayerful attitude. Struggling for the words, she whispered, " 'Return O Lord, deliver my soul: oh save me for thy mercies' sake! For in death there is no remembrance of thee: in the grave who shall give thee thanks?' "

The words faded away into the dusk-shadowed forest, mingling with the syrupy chatter of birds and the vague rustlings of leafy branches. The verses were not only for Hall Truett, but for Hannah. She knelt there for a long time, her mind carefully blank as she tried to marshal her courage to go on. It seemed futile. Why go on, when she would only be struck down by another calamity? Why, why, why? echoed over and over in her head, a resounding litany that drowned out the warbling of birds and the whisper of the wind.

But it was not in Hannah's nature to give up, to yield to what seemed the inevitable, without a struggle. And with a final farewell to the young man who had died trying to protect her, she rose from beside the grave and returned to the cave and Creed.

She spent the next hours tending to horses, gathering up food supplies, and sorting out what could be used and what couldn't. Again and again she bathed Creed's face with wet

cloths, poured more of the herbal brew down his throat, and
checked his bandages. The linen strips were red with blood
in spite of her best efforts, and Hannah patiently rebandaged
him. His fevered flesh was scorching to the touch, and the
wound constantly seeped so that at one point, Hannah
wondered if he had any blood left in his veins. Most of it
seemed to have soaked into the linen strips she boiled clean
and hung over bushes to dry.

Wearily brushing the hair from her eyes, Hannah pushed
up from the blankets where she had knelt beside Creed. Her
stomach growled, and she realized that in her efforts to tend
Creed, she had forgotten to eat. It seemed too much of an
effort to cook any of the beans, so she took a strip of hard
beef jerky from one of the packs and chewed on it. As
meals went, it was not the best, but it would keep her
functioning—she hoped. And because she could not sit still
and worry about Creed, she found what her father would
have called busywork to do until the sun rose again. It was
her second night in the cave.

Finally, with nothing left to do but watch and wait,
Hannah went to sit beside Creed. He was sleeping restlessly
now. She wiped his hot brow with a cool cloth. He looked
so . . . vulnerable lying there, his long lashes shadowing his
cheeks and hiding his eyes from view. Reaching out, Hannah
let her fingers touch him in a light caress, and her throat
ached with unshed tears. She wanted to pray, but somehow,
the words wouldn't come. That last comfort evaded her best
efforts, and she bowed her head against the sharp stab of
pain.

Finally, just before dusk, Creed began to rest more easily,
ceasing his endless thrashing and muttered phrases. His
clean bandages showed only a trace of blood. Hannah could
relax her vigil. She placed a hand on his brow and was
relieved to find it much cooler. A tired smile flickered on

her face. Sagging into a curve of relief, she fought the sudden pooling moisture in her throat and behind her eyes. One fine-boned hand pressed over her face, the heel of her palm against her chin, her fingers lacing her eyes. Her fingertips massaged her aching brows and the tiny lines etched between them, smoothing them out. He would live another night—the crisis was over.

Gathering her skirts around her thighs, she removed the lace-edged petticoat beneath and folded it carefully away, then removed her small waistcoat and placed it neatly atop the petticoat. Thus attired in a more comfortable form of nightwear, she smoothed out the folds of blanket at Creed's feet. Curling up in a ball beside the fire, with her head resting on the end of Creed's blankets, Hannah finally slept.

She dreamed of fat, lazy clouds drifting overhead, a bright blue sky, and golden sunbeams that she could ride as if they were horses. For a moment, she heard the distinct clatter of hoofbeats on the clouds. There were rainbows in the dream, fruity slices of heaven making rare appearances on earth—rainbows that promised good fortune to those who saw them. Hannah knew—in that way dreams have—that Creed would live.

# Chapter Seventeen

"Hey."

Fast asleep and dreaming, Hannah wasn't certain she'd heard it at first. Then it came again—a thick voice cozily coasting across the short space between her and Creed.

"Hey . . . Hannah."

Heavy eyelids snapped open and she bolted upright, staring at Creed with delight. He'd been asleep for almost three days. This was the first time he had opened his eyes and recognized that he was still in the world.

"Hey, yourself, sleepyhead," she teased, feeling an unexpected rush of warmth and tenderness. "How do you feel?"

There was a brief pause while Creed reflected, then he said, "Like a boiled grouse." Then he added, "Hungry."

Hannah laughed with pure joy. How utterly normal he sounded! And he was alive, after three days of uncertain agony. "How hungry?" she asked, rising and brushing dust and leaves from her skirts.

"Hungry enough to eat General if he'd stand still long enough." Creed lifted to his elbows, wincing at the pain. "I don't suppose there's any food?"

"Oh, a few things," Hannah replied, fighting the swell of tears that filled her eyes. "I have managed to make do with what I found in the packs."

Creed glanced around at the small cave, his brow puckering in a frown. "What'd you do with the bodies?"

Flinching at his abrupt question, Hannah cleared her throat. "I buried them."

"By yourself?"

"Don't sound so surprised! I'm not exactly helpless, you know."

"Maybe not, but that's how I remember you," was the weak answer.

"Then, it's time for you to change your mind. Do you want beans and bacon, or beans and beef jerky, or beans and beans."

Creed made a face. "Sounds great . . . surprise me."

She did. Cradling a battered tin bowl in the crook of her arm, Hannah fed him a rich broth of wild vegetables and boiled beef. "Tomorrow," she promised, "if you are better, you can have hot corncakes and a bowl of fresh-picked berries. We don't want to feed you too much too soon. Do you like it?"

"Not bad stuff," Creed admitted grudgingly, licking his lips. His side ached with a dull throb, and his head pounded unmercifully, but he was alive. It was still hard for him to believe that Hannah had cut out the bullet and kept him alive this long. How had she done it? She was a constant source of surprise. His gaze flicked over her sweet face in a long, slow inspection. She looked tired. Had she been at his side this entire time? Creed shifted his body on the pallet, and his eyes kindled with a slow fire as Hannah lifted his spoon again. "In fact—that broth is better than anything I've had in a long time, Hannah McGuire," he said softly.

She smiled, and held the spoon to his mouth. When her fingertips brushed across his jaw, her hand began to tremble with reaction. He was staring at her hard, with an odd glow in his eyes that reminded her of . . . of *that night*, and suddenly she began to feel funny inside again. She swallowed, hoping he hadn't noticed how her hand had begun to shake and her mouth to quiver, spooned the last of the broth into his mouth, and set the bowl aside.

"Water?" she asked brightly.

He shook his head. "Whiskey."

"You know how I feel about spirits, Creed Bratton!"

"You didn't think so the other day . . ."

Primly, she said, "I didn't think it mattered then."

Creed said wryly, "You didn't have much confidence in your surgical skills, I see. Hell, Hannah! Even the Bible advocates a little drink every now and then . . ."

Her face tightened. "Don't be absurd!"

A faint smile tugged at the corners of his mouth as he quoted, " 'Give strong drink unto him that is ready to perish, and wine unto those that be of heavy hearts.' "

Interrupting, Hannah flashed back, "If it's quotes you want, I can remember a few, too! 'It is not good neither to eat flesh, nor to drink wine, nor anything whereby thy brother stumbleth, or is offended, or is made weak.' "

"Out of context, dear Hannah: 'Let him drink and forget his poverty, and remember his misery no more . . .' "

Irritation edged her voice as Hannah retorted, " 'Nor thieves, nor covetous, nor drunkards, nor revilers, nor extortioners, shall inherit the kingdom of God.' "

"Multiple choice? Which of the above am I supposed to be? And who said I wanted to inherit anything anyway?" Creed returned. "Maybe my heaven is here on earth, Hannah."

Any quick disclaimers of Heaven being an actual possibility for Creed evaporated as quickly as the morning mist when she met his disquieting gaze, and Hannah's heart did a flip-flop. "What . . . what do you mean?"

"Come here," he said, his voice low and husky as he beckoned to her. When she hesitated, keeping her distance on the blanket pallet, ne crooked his finger at her. "Come here, love."

"Creed, your wound. You're still feverish and should be resting. Don't break open your stitches, or . . ."

"Could you just be quiet for a minute or two? I'm sick, remember? I should be coddled and cosseted, not corrected and cudgeled with strong words . . ." His warm fingers found her wrist and pulled her closer, scooting her forward on the blanket until she lay across his legs.

Her heart thumped so hard she was certain he could hear and see it, and she trembled as if she were the one who had just awakened from a coma. "Creed," she said softly, her hand quivering in his loose clasp, "Creed, I love you . . ."

Appalled by what she had just said, Hannah could not utter another word. She sat with eyes wide, drinking in the morning light, the dark pupils dilated, soaking up gentle rays of sunshine like a sponge and reflecting it back in sharp splinters of blue. He seemed as surprised by her admission as she, and slumped back against his pallet.

Of all possible reactions—and there were many—he had not anticipated this particular one. Creed looked down at the oval curve of her coppery head, bent now so that he could not see her eyes, and it took him a moment to adjust to her proximity. Her soft body lay across his thighs so that he could feel the cushiony pressure of her breasts against them, the rapid pace of her shallow breathing, and the erratic thud of her heart. Clinging tendrils of her hair carpeted his thighs in a silken quilt, and he could see the warm flush of her sloping cheeks bury into the hump of blanket and thigh.

Her bald statement—after a month of fencing with words and anger—caught him completely by surprise.

"Hannah . . . sweetheart—I don't know what to say."

Red-gold curls shimmered in the pale morning light as she shook her head against his blankets. "You don't have to say anything," came the muffled reply, and he could hear tears saturate her voice. "It's just that I was so worried, and when it seemed as if you wouldn't live, I sat and waited and hoped that you wouldn't die . . ."

"No prayers?" he teased gently, and was startled by her vehemence.

"No! No prayers." Hannah's head lifted, and her mouth was a taut line. "Prayers are useless—empty words offered to a being who doesn't exist . . ."

"Hannah!"

"Please. I don't want to talk about it. I've thought and
thought and thought these past few days, and come to the
conclusion that you were right all along, Creed. I've believed in fairy tales—pleasant little stories of spun honey
and sugar plums—and they've brought me nothing but
ridicule and pain. If there was a God, He would never have
let happen what has happened in the past month!" She tried
to stop the flood of words that spilled from her mouth, but it
was impossible. All the hurt, the pain and grief that she had
suffered during the past weeks, poured from her heart and
lips in a torrent. Tears tracked her cheeks as she added
bitterly, "First my father and all the others—did they
deserve what happened to them? Then there was the Carlisle
family—massacred. And then Fletcher, who was just a
child—dying needlessly. And you—you took what I wanted
you to have, but you didn't trade fairly. You gave nothing in
return, Creed—nothing but heartache. After that I could not
have gone unsullied to Joel Allen, even if I'd wanted to do
so. The outlaws, Mr. Mullen and Mr. Chessman dying so
brutally... and then, poor Hall Truett. He took care of me
and asked nothing in return, yet he died trying to protect
me."

Silence fell with her least words—a thick, heavy silence
that lay over them in lingering shrouds. Creed gazed at
Hannah's set face and angry eyes, recognizing the bitterness
he had never wanted her to have. Did life do that to
everyone? Did no one escape the harsher realities? Maybe
not.

"Hannah," he said at last, "don't do this to yourself."

"I haven't. The only thing I did to myself was fall in love
with you, and look what that's gotten me!" she flashed,
jerking away from him and fleeing into the shadows of the

thick woods. Creed could hear her stumbling steps crash through bushes and humps of dead leaves.

Stunned, he sat motionless. Listening to Hannah was like listening to himself not so very long ago, and he wasn't at all certain he liked it. Echoes of the past came to haunt him, and Creed Bratton sat wrapped in his blankets, wondering how to give Hannah back her faith. But how could he accomplish that, when he'd lost his own?

Hannah had sensed his indecision. She paused after her headlong flight from his side, leaning against a stout oak, unable to stand and watch him a moment longer. If there was one thing Creed Bratton knew how to do well, it was protect his innermost thoughts. After blurting out those three words, she had watched the swift metamorphosis of his features, the rearrangement of bone and facial structure from amusement and surprise into polite attention. It was a trick to remove him from the situation, Hannah decided miserably.

Three little words, and they had effectively torn down the last vestige of pride she had. Now she had nothing to hold to, nothing to wedge between them and preserve her dignity. *He knew.* Why had she done it? Why had she revealed her most intimate secret to a man who didn't care? Gloomily, despairingly, Hannah considered the fact that Creed had never even hinted at a similar affection; nor did he seem as if he even remotely loved her. Rather, Creed seemed more disposed toward lust than love, sexual attraction than the more abstract surge of emotion that swelled Hannah's young heart.

Flopping down on a rock at the foot of the spreading oak, Hannah regarded her dirty hands with distaste. No wonder he could not love her. How disheveled she must appear to him, with her hair in untidy straggles around her face, her arms and cheeks scratched and smeared with dirt. Even if that more noble emotion should occur to him—which did not seem at all likely—how could he love a girl whose appearance resembled that of a bedraggled cat? It seemed quite unlikely, under the circumstances.

Hannah rested her chin in the cradle of her palm and sighed. What did she really know about Creed Bratton, anyway? she wondered crossly. The little she did know was not at all comforting: One—he was a bounty hunter who made his living preying upon outlaws and dangerous desperadoes, hunting them down as some men hunted animals. Two—his father had been a preacher (but of what sort, Hannah was not at all certain). And three—he had been left on his own at an early age. There. That was all she had been able to learn about him in the past month—all except, of course, the fact that he was ruggedly handsome and had a devastating, potent smile when he chose to use it. And he could be kind and considerate when he chose, if she took into consideration the fact that he had saved her life and the lives of eight children. Other attributes drifted into her mind then—bravery, perseverance, and a host of others that ranged from tolerance of children to his apparent affection for his horse . . .

Hannah buried her face into the cup of her palms, knowing she had descended into madness. It was the stress. She had been put under such a weight that she had finally cracked under the pressure. She needed a rest. She needed to sit under a tree and think of nothing more taxing than what lace collar to wear on what dress the next Sabbath. It would certainly do her no good to think about Creed Bratton, and whether he could ever love her . . .

Morning shadows had lengthened by the time Hannah returned to camp. She approached silently, almost shyly, and

Creed glanced up before looking back down at the fistful of papers he held.

"These are pretty interestin'," he said after a moment.

"They are?" she asked without much genuine interest.

"You bet. I haven't had such an enlightening hour in a while." He looked up at her and held out a crumpled sheaf of paper. "See this? It says here that Henry Plummer gets a majority of the stock in the Alder Gulch Mining Company. If these papers make it to Sheriff Plummer, he's gonna be one mightly wealthy government official. He'll control every bit of the mine."

"I don't know any Sheriff Plummer. And how can one paper give him that much authority?"

"'Cause it ain't just this one paper. There's a whole bundle of stocks and bonds in here, all neatly tied with a black ribbon and just waitin' on Plummer's greedy little paws..." Creed gazed thoughtfully at the paper. "Plummer is sheriff over at Alder Gulch-Virginia City in Montana. They've hit gold there, and there's a lot of miners pouring into that little town. It's said to be a pretty rich strike, considering. This is worth a lot more than the bags of gold dust I found."

Hannah's stomach lurched. "You're not thinking of...of stealing anything, are you, Creed?"

An amused smile slanted his mouth. "Stealing? Me? I'm shocked and hurt, Hannah..."

"Do be serious!" she snapped back, moving to stand beside his pallet. "And anyway, why would a gold mine in—where did you say...Alder Gulch?—be selling shares of stock in another territory? Edward Mullen, who had the stock, was on his way to Fort Benton from Fort Walla Walla. What would he be doing with the stock?"

"He was obviously the middleman..."

"He's dead now," Hannah put in. "Roper killed him.

Mr. Roper obviously did not see the potential in the stocks that you do.'' She shuddered at the memory. ''So many unnecessary killings, so much bloodshed, and for what—a few stolen horses, a handful of gold dust, and some papers that are probably worthless.''

''Probably.'' Leaning back against a folded blanket that he was using as a pillow, Creed watched her face for a moment, then said softly, ''Don't worry about it, Hannah. I have a feeling Sheriff Plummer won't last long, and neither will the rest of his cutthroats.''

She waved a hand at him. ''Oh, it wasn't just some sheriff I was talking about . . . it's everything.''

''I know. I know, Hannah.''

''Do you?'' Shrugging, Hannah suddenly felt a great urge to sit down. Her knees buckled, and she plopped onto the blanket beside Creed. Raking a hand through the tangled silk of her hair, she added, ''I wonder sometimes if you do see.'' Her mouth drooped. She dropped her head to rest her forehead against her drawn-up knees and closed her eyes. ''There are times I think no one can . . .''

She felt him shift, and glanced up as Creed leaned forward to curl an arm around her shoulders. His fingers tilted back her chin so that she was forced to look at him. Creed smiled into her eyes, his gaze searching, plundering the very depths of her soul, as he murmured, ''I see more than you realize, love.''

Hannah shivered at his familiar use of the word, and, catching her bottom lip between her teeth, struggled for an answer. Nothing came readily to mind. She slid her gaze sideways—anything to escape that scorching gaze burning into her and searing her soul.

''No quick answer? No quotes?'' he asked softly, then added before she could form a reply, ''I'm glad. I don't want to ruin this moment with sarcasm or anger.''

Hannah's heart was thumping loudly in her chest, and she silently warned herself not to expect too much from Creed. He'd never feel the way she wanted . . .

Taking her hand in his, Creed examined her palm, tracing the lines across the baby-pink skin with his fingertip. "I once knew a girl who claimed she could foretell the future by just looking at a man's hand," he murmured after a moment. "She said that this line—" His finger tickled a path from between her thumb and index finger to the heel of her palm and Hannah shivered. "—this line indicates how long you'll live. And these lines—" Again the movement of his fingertip in a gentle whisk. "—these lines are for fortune and love."

"Do you believe in that?"

"Maybe yes. Maybe no. Anyway, your palm, sweet Hannah, tells me that you are going to have a long and full life. Ah, what is this? Do I see fortune in your future? No, that is a husband and three—no, four—children." He held onto her hand when she tried to jerk it away. "Wait. Maybe there is more than one husband . . ."

Hannah removed her hand from his clasp and gave him an indignant stare. Creed smiled lazily and leaned back against his makeshift pillow again. "Sorry. Didn't mean to pry into your future," he said, without a shred of remorse.

"Liar," Hannah sniffed.

"Not always, love. Not always."

Silence stretched for a moment, and Hannah could not take her gaze from Creed. Daylight was a tedious fellow, turning what could be a romantic moment into just another battle of wits. Long shadows lent no mysterious softness to the scene, gave it no alluring quality. Bright light spattering down in wavering patches only examined the common surroundings with a brutal glare.

"And what did she say about your future?" Hannah asked

when the quiet lengthened. She pointed to his palm when he lifted an inquiring brow.

"That I would live a short, dangerous life rendered even more dangerous by my choice of feminine companionship," he answered lightly. "See? She was right."

"I hardly see how you would make that connection," she began, then paused. "Well—maybe she was right, after all. I do seem to have led you into some rather awkward situations once or twice."

"Only once," he corrected gently. "And I may live in spite of her prediction."

"I hope so."

"Do you, Hannah? Sometimes I've wondered. I thought after our last night together that you might not want to see me again."

"Let's not talk about that," she said quickly. "I'm not sure I want to remember."

"Why not? I have. I've thought about it a lot since then, and I wondered just what it was that you wanted to hear me say."

"Nothing that you don't want to say, Creed." Hannah's eyes met his. "Never what you don't mean."

"Maybe there's something you don't understand—or maybe you understand it too well." He paused for a heartbeat, then said, "I find it hard to deal with . . . more intimate emotions. Anger's normal, irritation's normal, but anything else—forget it."

"I know that," she interrupted. "You don't have to tell me. I think I've finally learned that you were right, after all. It's too frightening to be so vulnerable, to love and have that love destroyed by death or indifference."

"No," Creed was saying, shaking his head and leaning forward again, "that's not what I want you to feel, Hannah! I don't want you to be hard, to lose your ability to care for another person. I don't want you to . . . to lose your faith in things.''

Hannah just stared at him. Clouds of pain shadowed his eyes, and thin white lines bracketed his mouth from nose to jaw. Resisting the impulse to reach out and stroke away the pain she saw, Hannah shook her head. ''But I have,'' she whispered softly. ''It's gone, and I can't seem to find it again. Creed—I can't even pray anymore. God has gone from me—turned His back and left me to find my own way in the dark . . .''

# Chapter Eighteen

Time passed in a slow-moving wheel, drifting along for the next three days at a snail's pace. It rained, great gusts of wind spinning glittery droplets into the cave and forcing the occupants to move farther back or get wet. Though Hannah welcomed the respite from the heated days, it soon grew cool enough for her to reach for a blanket.

Creed was able to get around far more easily, though his side still ached unbearably at times. He had moved his pallets to the rear and lit up a cigarette.

''This is the last of it,'' he observed, holding up his limp tobacco pouch.

Hannah slid him a glance of only mild interest. ''Too bad.''

''Why is it you don't sound that sorry for me?'' he wanted to know with a grin.

''Because the tobacco burns my throat and nose and

makes me cough,'' she said. "I think I prefer the smell of
wet horse to your cigarettes."

"Then you should be in ecstasy today," Creed shot back.
"You've got General and three other horses out there to go
and sniff to your heart's content."

"Two other horses. One of them disappeared day before
yesterday."

"Disappeared?"

Shrugging, Hannah said wearily, "I suppose he got tired
of waiting on us to recuperate . . ."

"Hardly my fault!" Creed snapped irritably.

Cuddling beneath the dry cover of a blanket, Hannah
couldn't help the smile that curved her mouth. "Are you
always this cranky when you're healing?"

"Nearly always. It's an inherited tendency, I'm sure."
After a moment of quiet, he observed mildly, "Guess I'll
have to resort to smoking kinnikinnick."

"Smoking what?"

"Kinnikinnick. You know—Indian tobacco. Dried leaves
from bear berries and bark from red dogwood. Do you want
the Latin names?" he asked, seeing her skepticism.

"Do you know them?" she shot back.

"*Uva-ursi*, meaning bear's grape. I don't know the other," he confessed.

"I'm impressed that you know that one," Hannah said
after a moment of stunned silence.

Narrowing his eyes against the thick curl of smoke
sloping backward from the campfire, Creed slanted her a
wary glance. "You've been quiet today."

"Have I?" Hannah looked down at the toes of her shoes
peeking from beneath the dusty hem of her skirts. They
were scuffed and dirty, as was everything she now wore.
Rain fell in waving sheets outside the cave, a misty veil
that shrouded the darker line of trees. It was a friendly

sound, and the sharp scent of wet forest humus was almost comforting. Why did it seem as if she had spent all her life here? The cave had become home. She wasn't certain she wanted to leave, to go back out into a world that had not always been so hospitable. Here, hidden away in the cave, she had time to reflect on the simple things of life, such as sunshine and flowers and birds. She avoided all other thoughts.

Days had become routine—rising at dawn and stirring the fire, cooking breakfast and then tending to the horses, seeing that they had not strayed too far. Wild vegetables grew profusely and berries ripened on heavy vines. Hannah enjoyed searching for them in the dew-wet forest, gathering the plumpest with berry-stained fingers. A great many found their way into her stomach, and she returned with telltale signs of berry juice smeared on her lips and chin. Huckleberries were her favorite—fat, juicy, sweet berries that left her mouth purple with their syrup.

Creed was able to get up for an hour or two now, though his side was still sore and he tired easily. He spent a great deal of his time reworking worn leather straps on bridles and poring over the papers from the metal trunk. The rest of his time he spent watching Hannah. He began to observe the gentle grace of her walk, the sway of her hips and swish of her skirts over her long legs. And he found himself watching sunshine catch in her hair, glinting in the copper silk that she let hang loose and free. There were several dozen mental portraits he now harbored of Hannah: *Hannah Gathering Vegetables*. *Hannah At Rest*. *Hannah At Bath* . . . Ahh. Now, that particular portrait lingered longer than most.

He had surprised her—and himself—one warm afternoon, by walking to the edge of the clear mountain stream that gurgled a winding path not far from the cave. She had been bathing when he had come upon her, and he'd stopped. Maybe he would have turned away and not risked embarrassing her, but she had risen from the shallow waters of the stream like a sea nymph rising from the ocean. Crystal drops of water shimmered over her body, skimming over firm, smooth flesh and breasts formed of the loveliest shades of rose. Wet, dark hair hung in thick ropes down her back, dripping over the alluring curve of her spine and hips. The long slope of her thighs, with water lapping greedily at her satin skin, moved through the current toward shore, and Creed had backed away. Every nerve he possessed had screamed at him to go to her, but he hadn't. It was too soon, and Hannah's recovery could be shattered like a fragile glass icon if he made the wrong decision.

Inside the world of the cave, nothing mattered. Tomorrow or today or yesterday held no meaning. Only the moment mattered—the brief, fleeting space of an instant when one decided whether to look for berries or wild turnips. And in that time, unfettered by any worries beyond a hunger pain or the direction of the wind, Hannah slowly began her own healing process. It was a process very much like Creed's, if not as physical.

She went for long walks in the forest, and let the quiet and peace surround her, wrapping her in a soft blanket of security. When the sun rose she greeted it with a smile, and when it set she felt the prickle of tears behind her eyes at its beauty. At night, when it was dark and her thoughts drifted toward unpleasant memories, Creed seemed to sense it, and would divert her attention.

Like now, when she was staring out at the rain and remembering a time with Joshua, when they had splashed in puddles like children and laughed gleefully.

"Hannah," Creed said softly, "don't you ever feel the urge to walk in the rain?"

Startled by the direction of his thoughts, she turned toward him, her eyes wide. "Yes! How did you know what I was thinking?"

"Instinct." Smoke from the campfire blew in with a gust of wind, stinging his eyes, and he passed his hand over them as if to push it away. After a lingering glance toward the front of the cave, he turned back to her. "How about it?"

"Now? But . . . but the wind's blowing, and my clothes—I don't have any more . . ."

"They're dirty anyway. Wouldn't a good soaking make that dress look a lot cleaner?"

Caught by his suggestion, Hannah was amazed to hear herself say, "I believe it would . . ."

Scrambling up from their dry corner, they ran out into the rain, holding hands and laughing. It fell on them in sheets, quickly soaking them to the skin and leaving Hannah icy and shivering. But when she turned to look at Creed, she began to thaw.

In the past days he had taken to leaving his shirt off during the day, and he wore none now. His broad shoulders were wet with rain, and his skin gleamed in the hazy light, the wide white strip of bandage around his ribs marking a distinct contrast. The rain quickly plastered his dark hair to his skull, and his tanned face was shiny with slippery rivulets, running from brow to cheek. His buckskin trousers grew heavy as the rain soaked them, and began to droop from his lean hips in almost comical fashion.

Hannah would have laughed at any other time, but the glow in Creed's eyes when his gaze met hers prevented her from doing anything other than catching her breath. How had she grown so warm when it was so cool? Her breath came in harsh, painful gasps. The touch of Creed's hand in hers was like a jolt of lightning, shocking her into drawing away.

They had run toward the fringe of woods stretching beyond the cave, so that they now stood awkwardly aware at the edge. Rain pattered down on broad leaves and pine needles, sliding from wet tree branches onto the pair below.

"Do you want to go back?" Creed asked, without making a move toward the cave.

Hannah nodded, yet she did not move either. "Yes."

They stood there while the rain beat down on them. Then Creed was guiding her gently, leading her away from the cave, into the deep woods, where everything smelled fresh and wet and clean. Twigs and small branches snapped beneath their feet, and the rain played a constant melody. Here, where trees grew so thick that sunshine had difficulty penetrating leafy barriers, they barely felt the rain. Hannah was to later reflect that just walking beneath that spreading canopy of branches and rain-wet leaves was the most intimate of experiences. Yet what followed was the most emotionally shattering . . .

With all the delicate mastery of a ballet dancer, Creed turned, his hand subtly altering its pressure on hers, drawing her closer to him. Shivering with reaction, Hannah pressed against him, her rounded palms gliding over curving muscle and slick skin as she instinctively put up her hands.

Creed's hands found and held her slim waist in a loose embrace, his splayed fingers spreading over her hips to cup her closer to him. The hard thrust of his hip bones cut into Hannah like a knife, and she struggled to breathe around the sudden huge lump in her throat. She lifted her arms to hold him at bay, then relinquished her reluctance and curled them around his neck.

Sensing her surrender, the sweet yielding of body and mind, Creed's dark head lowered and his mouth brushed softly over her parted lips. His hands drifted downward again and urged her lightly against him, tucking her curves into the tight angles of his body in a caress. Hannah was searching for the right words to say to express the way she felt when Creed tilted back her head to place tiny, neat kisses on the tip of her nose, her closed eyelids, and the delicate slope of her cheekbones. Her flesh burned beneath the velvet grazing of his mouth. Fragile, blue-veined lids trembled like butterfly wings, and the long sweep of her dark eyelashes fluttered on heated cheeks.

There was no reluctance this time, no resistance. Hannah wanted only this perfect moment, this stolen slice of time, and Creed. The world was a wondrous place of beauty and muted light, of golden haze and vivid greens, of tiny rainbows trapped in swirling light beams, arcing over leaf and bough. He gently lifted her in his arms and placed her in a nest of dry leaves curled within the knobby roots of an oak. Nature's mattress shifted beneath the press of their bodies, and if it was a little damp, neither of them knew it.

Hannah's hair had spilled around her face, framing the heart-touching sweetness with satiny color, and Creed could not resist tangling his fingers in its beckoning wealth. He leaned over her, kissing her, tasting the stinging silk of her hair in the kiss. His tongue gently parted the vulnerable fullness of her lips, sliding between to softly probe the moist honey within—tasting, teasing, until Hannah moaned audibly.

Catching the quick intake of her breath, and feeling the rise and fall of her breasts beneath him, Creed husked, "I love the sounds you make, Hannah, love. I love feeling you hold me, feeling your soft body so close to mine . . .''

Love—but no profession of the same. Hannah closed her eyes against the quick sting of tears. All that should matter now was this . . . this sweet coming together, and Creed's tenderness. His hands were moving over her back, sending shivers along the curve of her spine. It was a brief reminder of the ecstatic heights he had swept her to before, and Hannah clung to him fervently. His fingertips lightly stroked the voluptuous swell of her hip, then shifted to the tiny row of buttons on the front of her dress. With painstaking care, Creed began to unfasten them, pausing between each button to kiss the newly exposed inch of flesh under the cotton.

"Here, love. Let's take this off," he coaxed, smoothing the unbuttoned dress from her shoulders with infinite care. "Let me look at you . . ."

Finally, the soggy material was peeled away like the layers of an onion, revealing damp, fragrant skin beneath. He caught his breath at her beauty, at the full curves and creamy hollows of her body.

"Hiding your light under a bushel, Hannah?" he murmured against the sweet curve of her throat. "I never dreamed a woman could be so beautiful . . ." One hand wooed the tender, hidden arc of flesh beneath the heavy weight of her hair, while the other moved downward through the luxurious copper streamers curling in a scythe over her breast and ribs. His fingers cupped and caressed the round fullness of her breast, teasing the hardening bud into a tight knot with his thumb.

When Creed's mouth replaced the gentle ministrations of his thumb Hannah arced beneath him, her heels digging small mounds into the quilt of leaves. The languorous movement of his lips and tongue from one breast to the other trailed moist heat over her shivering skin. A sweeping rush of fire curled through her veins, and Hannah found it hard to draw in a breath of air. How could she breathe when he was doing that? When his hands and mouth were causing such sweet rapture?

A delicately slow swoop brought Creed's hand across her body to rest on the soft swell of her stomach, his fingers kneading gently, relaxing taut muscles to a supple consistency. Slowly, she let her tense muscles yield to his insistent massage. Everything spun dizzily around her. The entire world reeled in a blur of colors and vague impressions. Blues, greens, golds, prisms of color shot through the moist air in arrows of light as his hands moved over her body in loving explorations.

Creed discovered the sensitivity of that tiny spot just below her ear, the shiver he could evoke when his tongue teased it lightly. His fingertips explored the rich hollows and tempting curves—the pulse beat in the golden cup where her collarbones met, the fine-knit fabric of her flesh and bones, and the delicate sculpture of muscle and tissue that was made even more wondrous by how well structured it was. He discovered that he also liked her tiny imperfections even more, because they were uniquely hers. It couldn't be love, yet—what else could it be? He'd never felt this consuming rush of tenderness before, this desire to hold and protect and cherish.

When Hannah cupped Creed's broad shoulders with her palms and drew him closer, he exhaled softly. His breath stirred a spray of curls over her ear and whispered across her cheek as he nestled between her willing thighs.

"Hold me, Creed," Hannah found herself saying urgently, straining upward, aching for him. "Please . . ."

"Yes, love," he murmured then, shifting his long

body away to quickly strip off his buckskin trousers and boots.

Hannah's body throbbed with desire, and when he returned to her, she accepted him hungrily. Creed's sensual, experienced hands roused her to a fever pitch when he palmed her gentle mound. His mouth smothered her lilting cries as his fingers teased her into a wild, shuddering release. Hot, fiery kisses danced across her parted lips, as he inhaled her essence, sucking her into a whirling vortex of voluptuous sensations. She was drowning in a sea of sensuality, and she loved it.

Echoes of her cries still lingered in the rain-scoured air when Creed once more shifted his lean body across hers. A slow smile curved her mouth as she looked up at him, and her fingers began gentle explorations of their own. Her hands skipped lightly across his band of hard chest muscles, grazing the small curls of hair that caught at her fingertips. The wide, white bandage contrasted sharply with his bronzed skin and dark pelt of chest hair. Hannah's breath caught at his male beauty—the hard ridges and smooth melding of muscles into a superb physical specimen, only slightly marred by the bullet wound in his right side.

"You're beautiful," she whispered with such obvious sincerity and unexpected candor that Creed laughed aloud.

"You say that to all the men you make love to in the rain," he murmured against the tickling spurs of hair that brushed over his jawline. Nuzzling her neck, he nipped lightly at her satin skin.

"No, no," Hannah disagreed playfully, walking her fingers up his belly, gently over the bandage, and to the springy mat of curls on his chest. "I say that only to *wounded* men I make love to in the rain."

"Ah, a fine distinction I overlooked," Creed said huskily,

sucking in a deep breath when her hand dipped lower, over his ribs and stomach.

Nothing was said for several minutes as Hannah became absorbed in satisfying her curiosity with his masculine form. It was only when Creed put his broad hand over her smaller one, holding it still, that she looked up and noticed the fine beads of perspiration dotting his upper lip.

"Keep doing that, love of my life, and you'll rush things . . ."

His hoarse voice was music to her ears—sweeter than any melody she'd ever heard—and Hannah's heart swelled with love for him. *Love of my life* . . . Was she?

Curling into him, putting her arms around him and sliding her body into his welcoming embrace, Hannah whispered back, "I can't wait any longer."

Creed needed no more encouragement. He tucked her soft body beneath his, and the erotic feel of her flesh touching him shivered through his fiery network of nerve ends in a hot sizzle. Their misty gazes met, dark with light. It was a meeting of souls rather than of the senses, a finely tuned sharing of the most intimate secrets they possessed. Creed's brows lowered slightly as if he were in pain, his eyes narrowing with the effort, his mouth stretching into a full, taut line.

It was an expression that Hannah had often dreamed of seeing, a look in his eyes that she would hold in her memory for the rest of her life, and she felt the familiar sting of tears in her eyes. His mouth hovered over her parted lips, and his eyes locked with hers as he felt the quick intake of her breath at his first gentle entry. When he moved forward with a heart-jolting slowness, Hannah's eyes widened and her breath came in harsh, rasping jerks. Her fingers tightened as she gripped his shoulders, and her long legs curled around his back at his murmured suggestion—gently

at first, for fear of hurting his wound. She felt a slow
expectancy build when he began to rock in a slow, primitive
rhythm, and her hips moved in instinctive cadence with
him. There was a wild, fierce urgency in both of them that
took them soaring to heights never before explored, on
rainbows and swan wings that swept them into the clouds
and back.

Hannah was the first to stir opening lazy eyes and gazing
up at sunbeams filtering through the leafy canopy above.
It had stopped raining at some point, and now only
occasional drops fell from crystal pools clustered on the
surface of a leaf. She was curled into Creed's body, her
back pressed to his chest and the hard musculature of his
lean thighs, fitting him like a glove. Contentment rode
her mouth in a smile, and she stretched languorously.
Bruised leaves rustled beneath her uncoiling limbs, and
the drape of the cotton dress Creed had thrown over their
bodies slid lower.

Feeling the tightening of her body next to his, Creed
flexed his arms and brought her closer. "Stay awhile, sweet
Hannah," he murmured against the seashell whorls of her
ear. His palm slid slowly across her body, caressing it
with a tenderness that had nothing to do with sex. And
somehow, that affected Hannah more than his desire
would have done.

A glut of half-formed emotions surged through her, and
she turned in his arms to gaze up at him with eyes jeweled
by tears. Taking his face between her palms, she said
huskily, "I will stay with you as long as you want
me."

Her inference was not lost on Creed, and for a brief
instant, he felt the resurgence of that familiar need to
remain remote—but only for an instant. "Forever?" he

asked lightly, and Hannah pressed her face against his chest.

"Forever," came the muffled reply, delivered through a haze of tears and relief.

Creed's hand swept down her back, the graceful curve of her spine and hips, to cup her even closer to him, until the melding of their bodies was inevitable. There was passion in their embrace, but a passion imbued with such sweet tenderness that it was closer to being an exchange of gifts than mere erotic desire. Each strove to please the other, giving freely of heart and mind and body, until love was indistinguishable from the consuming sweep of arousal.

It was only later, upon their return to the cave and the more revealing light of undiffused sunshine, that Hannah felt a return of her first shyness with Creed. He noted her faint blush, and felt a wash of tenderness tinged with amusement. "What is it, sweet love?" he asked, his voice as light and fragile as a thistle.

A smile trembled on her lips. How could she explain her sudden embarrassment at the memory of her abandonment? In the clear light of the sun all romance was removed, and her wanton caresses were vaguely disquieting in remembrance. He had said he wanted her forever—but how strong was that emotion?

She held out her hands to the warm glow of the fire and shivered against the teasing breath of wind that whisked into the cave. The damp cotton gown clung to her curves in a most appealing fashion, even though it was a bit ragged and leaf-strewn, and wayward sunbeams picked jewel-like at her curling hair. Lifting thick lashes in a shy, steady regard, Hannah found it difficult to meet Creed's interested gaze. "It's nothing that—it's nothing," she whispered in answer to his query.

He came to her then, stepping across the rough stone

space that separated them, and took her into his arms. "Do you need reassurance?" he asked lightly. "I can give you all you need right now."

She tilted back her head. Uncertainty clouded her eyes, and her mouth twisted with frustration. "But, what about later? Can you give me all I need later?"

"Such an inquiring mind you have, love! Why shouldn't I? Oh, I know I haven't exactly brimmed over with loving affection in the past, and while a leopard doesn't change its spots overnight, I think I can meet the muster well enough."

It would have to do, Hannah supposed with a sigh. Although declarations of undying love would have been much more satisfying and rewarding, the fact that Creed Bratton had gone this far was in itself startling and miraculous.

Her smile was sunshine and stardust, a sprinkling of all things magical and wonderful, and Creed found himself enchanted by her. "If you change your spots, how will I know you?" Hannah teased.

"My surly nature will remain the same, I'm sure," he replied. Bending to lift a strip of cloth earlier used as a towel, Creed proceeded to finish drying his upper body with brisk strokes. He slid his arms into the sleeves of a white shirt that was wrinkled from being packed so long in his saddlebags, wincing at the sharp pain it caused along the ridge of his ribs. As the pain subsided and he could catch his breath again, Creed found himself thinking how false his statement had been. He wasn't the same at all.

The past days with Hannah had changed him more than he'd realized until now. For some reason, she gave him a sense of peace that had little to do with the tranquility of this wooded spot. Perhaps it was her air of detachment, that serenity of spirit and faith that she'd captured. For in spite of her denials, she still exhibited deep faith. It seeped through like spring water bubbled from a rock, irrepressible and flowing over all in its path. Faith—would he ever find his again? There were times when he wondered if he'd ever truly had faith in anything or anyone, and other times when he was glad he no longer had to bother with the prick of a bruised conscience. It made too grim a prison at times. When had he become so damned philosophical? Creed wondered irritably. Shaking his head, he turned back to Hannah.

"I don't suppose there's any more stew left?"

The mundane question, after their recent soul-shattering experience and conversation, left her momentarily nonplussed, but—plucky as she was—Hannah recovered nicely.

"I believe there is. And there are still some fresh berries, too. Only a few, though."

"Maybe we can go in the morning and look for more," Creed suggested.

"Yes. Perhaps we shall . . ." Hannah's gaze was dark and mysterious as she faced him; then, shrugging, she turned away and slipped modestly behind an outcropping of rock to change from her wet gown into a dry—but scratchy—blanket. The material slid roughly over her bare skin, and she belted it around her waist so that it hid the most important parts of her body. There was still a barrier between them, a barrier not conquered by physical intimacy. There would have to be more—an intercourse of the minds—before she could achieve the ultimate . . .

Starlight faded and the rising sun quickly burned off the morning mists that shrouded the trees and meadows. It promised to be a warm day, and Hannah reminded Creed of his suggestion from the day before.

"Berry picking?" he echoed with a slow smile. "Yeah, that sounds delicious . . ."

"I said picking, not just eating!"

"It's the easiest way I know to get them back to our little hovel," Creed returned.

"But that particular method makes it more difficult to make a pan cobbler."

"Ahh—is that your plan?"

"It is."

"Then you shall have buckets of berries, love. I'll pull them from the sky if I have to—climb the highest bush and ford the deepest stream . . ."

"I get your point," Hannah said, and handed him a large leather pouch. "Ready?"

Creed rose from his perch near the fire. Scooping up his gun belt and buckling it around his lean hips, he said, "As ready as I'll ever be."

Feeling as lighthearted as a swallow, Hannah ran ahead of Creed, laughing and enjoying the sunshine and fresh wind that tangled in her hair and pinkened her cheeks. The month of June was almost over, by her calculations, and summer had greened the meadows and forest with tender color. It looked like an artist's paint box had been upended and the world had been smeared with the most vibrant of his colors. A collage of reds, pinks, whites, blues, yellows, and shades of purple lavished the hillsides and studded the granite slopes. There was even the glossy black of the odd, olive-shaped coneflower to accent the colorful blur.

Wild roses flowered in delicate, graceful sprays beneath shrubs and on bare hillsides, adding a light, sweet perfume to the sharp mountain air. Hannah waded through tall waves of bear grass spiked with clusters of prickly white blossoms. She looked to Creed very much like a flower herself in her blue dress. The skirt belled out in a circle, and the sun gilded her hair with golden lights. She filled her leather bag with plucked blossoms, instead of berries—clusters of wild roses, creamy white ocean spray, myrtle, mountain ash blossoms, and snowberry. Creed named Indian paintbrush, white yarrow, purple daisies, and horsemint for her as she plucked them, a tolerant smile curving his sensual mouth as he watched Hannah's delight. When she tucked a stalk of baby's breath behind one ear and gave him an impish smile, he couldn't resist pulling her into his arms and kissing her.

Hannah grew still in his embrace, shutting her eyes against the warm press of the sun and Creed's gentle grip. His lips were soft, light as the touch of butterfly wings on her mouth, and as sweet as honey. Bees buzzed in harmony nearby, and overhead, birds soared with lilting songs, providing a sweet serenade for the two lovers. Cloud puffs drifted lazily by, beaming down at them, and from high, high above came the circling cry of a red-tailed hawk. It floated down in drifting waves, mysterious and regal and impressive, and they broke apart to look up.

"Isn't it beautiful?" Hannah said dreamily, shading her eyes with the cup of her hand. "Just floating up there, so graceful and serene . . ."

"Yes," Creed was saying, looking at Hannah instead of the hawk, "very beautiful."

She flushed, still unaccustomed to his compliments rather than his sarcasm. Hannah was far too cognizant of the pleasurable promise of his mouth on hers, and the touch of his hands in a gentle caress, to feel comfortable with him yet.

"I used to make clover chains when I was a little girl," she said in a rush, filling the thick silence. "I'd wind them through my braids, or make necklaces and bracelets and crowns for my head . . ."

"Make one of flowers," Creed suggested practically. A drift of wind caught at his thick hair, which had grown in the past weeks to cover his nape in straight ebony silk. It fluttered against his high cheekbones in a caress, and he pushed at it impatiently, raking a hand through his hair in the old familiar gesture that Hannah recalled so well.

"A crown of flowers," she said gaily, dragging her attention away from his lazy-lidded eyes and the sensual curl of his mouth. "One for both of us . . ."

They strolled leisurely through the high grasses, and entered the tranquil shadows of the deep forest, where moss and lichen cushioned their footfalls and lacy tree branches formed a thick canopy. Hannah's steps slowed as she breathed deeply of horsemint, pine, fir, and nine-bark, a richly aromatic perfume that filled her nostrils with heady scent.

She sat on the curved surface of a fallen tree trunk fringed by delicate fronds of oak fern, feeling its scratchy bulk beneath her thin skirts, and looked up at Creed. He still stood above her, his eyes trained on some distant object, his face in perfect profile. How absolutely handsome he was, she thought with a sudden catch of her heart. Dark-winged brows swooped so gracefully over his deep eyes, and his straight nose was—she searched for the right word—*aristocratic*. Yes, that was it. And his smile was devastatingly potent. She gave herself a mental shake and turned her attention back to the slowly wilting flowers in her lap.

Threading a rose with a white blossom, she worked in the smaller pink snowberry flowers, deftly weaving a fantasy crown fit for a fairy princess. With the abundance of flowery perfume, the warm day, and the soft breeze curling into the

shade of the spreading oak, she began to relax, an unconscious smile on her lips. Creed turned his wandering attention back to her.

"Tell me about yourself," he said unexpectedly.

Startled into shifting her attention from the garland of
flowers to Creed, Hannah paused before answering. Was he
really interested, or was it just idle conversation on a lazy
day? And because she wasn't sure, she gave him a vague
reply.

"I was born in St. Louis, and came to Idaho Territory
with my father three years ago..."

"I already know all that." A lopsided smile courted his
mouth as he sat beside Hannah on the tree trunk. His close
proximity made her flesh prickle nervously, and when he
lifted a dark brow and said, "Well? What else?" she cleared
her throat.

"What do you want to know?"

"More. For instance: What did you like to do when you
were a little girl? Any brothers or sisters, special playmates,
favorite subjects in school?"

"Does this mean you're agreeable to a trade-off of information?" Hannah asked. "After all, I know hardly anything
about you."

"Which is definitely in your favor. But now it's my turn
to ask the questions," he said with a potent, lazy smile that
made her forget every answer that had already half formed
in her sluggish brain.

"Let me see... no brothers or sisters. My mother died
when I was born, and I was brought up by her sister for a
time. No special playmates, and I favored history and
penmanship in class. I liked to play with dolls when I was
small, though I never had very many. I had one favorite—a
porcelain one that had been my mother's. Her name was
Eve. After the first..."

"I know," Creed interrupted with a glance of amusement. "What else did you do, besides sing hymns and
memorize Bible verses, I mean."

"I played the harpsichord," Hannah answered promptly,
"and on hot summer afternoons I would take off my shoes
and socks and go wading in the river and give my aunt a fit
of apoplexy. She claimed I was destined for disaster, and I
suppose she was right, because look where I am."

"Appearances notwithstanding, I've been known to in-
spire confidence in some folks," Creed said dryly.

"Oh. I didn't mean you, exactly," she hastened to
explain. "I just meant, everything that's happened in the
past month or so."

Unwilling to travel that particularly bleak path again,
Creed led her away from the gloomy conjectures confronting
her. "I used to play hooky from school and go fishing," he
said, eliciting a giggle from Hannah. "But once, when I
had caught a particularly *large* trout, the schoolmaster took
me aside—after he had switched me with a hickory limb—
and asked me where I'd caught it."

"Did you tell him?"

"I gave him the location of a nice, wooded spot that just
happened to be the favorite fishing hole of a large, mean
grizzly bear..."

"Oh, Creed!" Mirth danced in her eyes as Hannah tried
to summon a vision of Creed Bratton as a small, rebellious
boy. It was too difficult a task, and she gave it up. "Are you
a native in this territory?" she asked after a moment, and he
shook his head.

"No. Kansas. My parents moved to Oregon when I was
twelve years old."

"Oh." Hannah stretched the silence, waiting for him to
offer more information. When he did not, she asked, "How
did you come to be on your own so young? I mean, you

once mentioned that you had learned at an early age how to survive by yourself.''

Creed's jaw tightened and a muscle leaped, but no other reaction betrayed him as he replied in a level tone, ''My family was massacred by hostiles.''

Instantly recalling the Blackfoot raid and the hideous screams and attending horrors that had struck Jubile, Hannah shuddered. ''Do you think that we can ever live in peace with the Indians?'' she asked after a moment.

Creed gave her a quizzical glance. ''I don't know. But it wasn't Indians who burned my parents and sisters alive in our cabin,'' he said tightly.

''Oh, but you said . . .''

''I said it was *hostiles*, and that was true, but they were white hostiles—greedy men who didn't mind a bit of murder to gain what they wanted.'' Hannah listened as he recited in a flat, emotionless voice how his father had taken in three men, fed them, cared for their horses, and been foolish enough to think he could convert them. They had stayed long enough to discover the location of his strongbox— money saved to build a church—then stolen the gold and murdered the entire family—except for Creed. It was a fatal mistake, as it turned out, for the boy lived only to find them, to hunt them down and kill them.

''It took me four years. I was only twelve when it happened. Some well-meaning friends took me in and insisted I forget all notions of vengeance. 'Vengeance is mine, saith the Lord . . . ' I used to think if I heard that one more time I would kill the next person who said it to me,'' Creed said.

''You . . . you found the murderers?''

''I did. And I killed them—all three of them.'' His jaw tightened again. ''I would have managed it a lot sooner, but like I said, I was delayed. I used to run away, but they'd find me and take me back. I'd stay a while, and then run away again. They finally gave up, and I lived in the woods on my own. I learned a lot during that time. I learned how to survive, and I learned how to kill. It came in handy when I needed it."

Hannah swallowed the sudden lump in her throat. "And that was when you learned your present . . . trade?"

He smiled. "Yeah. I found out that it paid pretty well. And it rid the world of men like . . . like Stillman."

"But to take justice into your own hands, Creed . . ."

"I only kill men in self-defense, Hannah." His tone was gentle and reproving. "Most of them are delivered alive to stand trial and be hung. A bullet would probably be more merciful than a rope, but most don't deserve mercy."

Leaning back against the broad base of the towering oak behind her, Hannah grew quiet. Her tender heart ached for him, and she wished she could erase all his years of pain. He had not told her about his family to garner any sympathy, and instinctively, she knew he would hate it if she evinced any. Creed Bratton was not a man who needed or wanted pity. She folded her legs beneath her, and noticed the forgotten flowers in her skirt.

Nimble fingers wove another garland of blossoms into a crown. "There," she said, holding it up to Creed and gaining his attention. "For you."

A slow smile slanted his mouth. "I think it would look much better on you."

"Which only goes to show how little fashion sense you have," Hannah scolded lightly. "Afraid of endangering your masculinity? Don't worry. There's no one within miles except me."

"I wouldn't be too sure of that," he said, turning his head to gaze out across the meadow again. This time there was a slight frown on his face, and Hannah started.

"What do you mean?"

He turned back to face her. "Are you sure that horse just *wandered* off, Hannah?"

"Horse?" She stared at him blankly, then recalled that the horse that had disappeared from their camp.

"You know," he was saying patiently, "a large animal with four legs and a tail? A horse?"

"Why . . . why, yes. What else could have happened? Oh. Do you think someone stole it?"

"No."

"Then, what . . ."

"Show me where you buried Stillman, Roper, and Truett, will you?"

A sudden chill danced up Hannah's spine. "I can't imagine why you would think—or whatever could have . . . well, really! This is ridiculous!"

"Maybe—and maybe not. I keep hearing something at odd times, like . . . it's a feeling I get, and it's not often wrong."

"Do you mean like prescience?"

"You're the schoolteacher, Hannah, not me. All I know is that I've had this feeling that someone's watching us."

"Oh." She dragged in a deep breath. "But they're all dead, Creed. I buried them."

"Deep?"

She stood up and flowers cascaded, forgotten, from her lap to the mossy ground. "I'll show you . . ."

But when they reached the crevice where Hannah had dragged the blanket-shrouded bodies, two forms still lay in the shadow of the crag. Covering her nose and mouth with one hand, Hannah choked at the sickly sweet stench permeating the thick air. Hall Truett's grave nearby was undisturbed, and she could not hold back a cry of horror as Creed began to shift through the pile of stones.

"No! Oh, dear God, why would you . . . ?"

Pausing, Creed slid a glance toward the blankets and seemed to change his mind. Abandoning the stone-piled grave he strode forward and, ignoring Hannah's shocked exclamation, unwrapped the bodies.

Shuddering, Hannah turned away. This was too horrible to contemplate, too horrible to think about. She wished the beautiful day had not ended so badly.

It was only when she heard Creed's voice right behind her that she could turn around, and when her gaze lifted to his taut face, she knew what he would say.

"He's gone, Hannah. Nate Stillman is gone. There's nothing but a pile of stones in one blanket . . ."

# Chapter Nineteen

Crossing her arms over her chest and cupping her elbows in her palms, Hannah shivered. It wasn't possible. She'd seen him shot, seen him fall, had dragged his lifeless body across sharp stones and through a gully to bring him to this spot . . .

"I don't believe you."

Her flat, colorless voice made absolutely no impression on Creed. "I know. But it doesn't matter. He's gone."

"That's impossible. He was dead. He wasn't breathing. His eyes were closed, and his shirt was all . . . all bloody and singed with gunpowder . . ." She paused to hiccough and Creed put out a hand to her. "Maybe wild animals," she began, but couldn't go on.

Shaking his head, Creed destroyed that idea. "No. The other body has not been disturbed. Wild animals aren't too finicky about that sort of thing."

"Well . . . maybe whatever it was, it was too full to eat both of them!" Hannah snapped, her entire being revulsed by the topic of conversation.

"I think we need to be moving on, Hannah," he said quietly. "Even if it's not Stillman—even if he only made it a short distance away before he dropped dead—*someone* is watching us, and I don't like it."

"But you can't ride yet."

"Why not? I've been walking, haven't I? And I've done a few other things even more strenuous."

His inference was not lost on Hannah, and though she could not prevent the slight flush that stained her cheeks, she was too shocked and worried to be as embarrassed as she would have been otherwise.

"But where will we go?" Hannah asked practically. "It's too far to Coeur d'Alene . . ."

"But not to the Sacred Heart Mission," Creed pointed out. "I can leave you there while . . ."

"Oh, no, you don't!" Hannah flared. Curled hands punched at the slim thrust of her hip bones in an irritated motion as she faced him with a blaze of anger in her hot, bluebell eyes. "I won't be left behind again."

"And I refuse to endanger you any more than you already have been." Creed's expression was closed and his voice flat. Eyes like shiny black agates fixed on her face. "This is not negotiable, Hannah."

"I agree." Her throat tightened with anger and apprehension. To her dismay, her eyes began filling with tears and her voice grew soggy. "You cannot be serious about leaving

me behind again,'' she tried to say calmly, but it came out
more like the petulant whine of a child.

"Dead serious. And we need to pack up now. Now,
Hannah,'' he repeated when she would have argued. "I
don't like this feeling I've got..."

Leaving the cave behind was like leaving behind safety
and security. Hannah could not resist looking over her
shoulder as they rode away, thinking that here she had
known a short time of contentment. Though she consoled
herself with the thought that what had started out so badly
had turned into a peaceful interlude, she ended by acknowledging how badly it was ending. Was her life doomed to
constant strife and danger?

Sighing, Hannah shifted in the uncomfortable leather
saddle. Creed had insisted that she have a rifle and a
pistol—belonging to the dead or not-so-dead outlaws. She
gave a disgruntled glance at the scabbard nudging her knee.
The stock of a Henry rifle protruded from it, within easy
reaching distance, according to Creed. But the mere thought
of firing a rifle owned by Lane Roper made Hannah's flesh
crawl, and she'd told him so.

"Then use Truett's!'' he'd snapped unsympathetically.

That was even more repugnant to her, so she'd taken
Roper's rifle reluctantly. Creed rode ahead of her, and she
was followed by the pack horse, bearing enough supplies to
get them to the mission. Hannah vaguely recalled seeing the
mission in the bend of the Coeur d'Alene River. It had been
built upon a low bank above the rushing waters, and was
visible from the passing road. Surely they could find sanctu-
ary there.

"Damn that Stillman,'' Creed muttered when they paused
on a crest overlooking the river. "He's got more lives than a
cat!''

Turning to see what had caught Creed's attention—and half afraid of seeing Nate Stillman just ahead—Hannah jerked at the borrowed rifle. It resisted. Instead of sliding smoothly from the leather saddle scabbard, it slid from her fingers and crashed to the ground, discharging with a loud report that spooked the horses and made Creed swear at the top of his voice. The bullet passed harmlessly into the air, buzzing past like an angry bee.

Hannah's horse plunged in jerking hops, and the pack horse neighed and reared, forefeet flashing with wicked hooves that barely missed Creed's leg. Cursing and yanking at the pack horse's reins, Creed managed to get him under control an instant before Hannah succeeded in calming her mount. General danced nervously, but being better trained, the bay refrained from reacting—which was a good thing, considering the fact that Creed had all he could handle with the pack horse. As it was, he flashed Hannah a murderous glance.

Shrugging her shoulders in a helpless gesture, she said, "Sorry."

"Sorry!" he exploded wrathfully, impaling her with a glittering dark glare. "Is that all you can say?"

"Terribly sorry?" she offered weakly.

"Not much better. By now Stillman is dug into a safe place and probably laughing himself sick!"

"I was trying to see if . . ." Hannah paused. "Is he near here?"

Putting out a hand to calm the still-quivering pack horse, Creed bit off, "He *was*."

"Did you see him?" At his quick exclamation, she added, "I mean, just a moment ago?"

"Yes, Hannah. I saw him."

The matter-of-fact voice penetrated finally, and she turned to look down the running slope to the flowered valley below.

All that she could see were the waving grasses and bright blossoms of summer. Anxiety made her ask, "Where?"

Creed made a rough, rude comment, and gestured at the ground. "Get the rifle, Hannah. We may need it."

Though she entertained serious doubts that she would use the rifle herself, Hannah dismounted and scooped up the weapon. If Nate Stillman was anywhere near their present location, she fully intended to do the cowardly thing and flee immediately. Having had two unfortunate encounters with the outlaw, a third seemed entirely unnecessary and undesirable. It wasn't that she doubted Creed's ability to protect her, it was just that she did not intend to underestimate Stillman's total disregard for human life. The most pressing problem, however, was how to convince Creed that he should abandon his determined pursuit. Didn't he realize that he was still weak from his recent ordeal?

Clearing her throat and reining her horse close to Creed's long-legged bay, Hannah said brightly, "You know, I hardly think—since you've been following Mr. Stillman for so long already—that another few weeks would make much difference. I mean, you have the gold and papers, haven't you?"

A blistering glance met this thin-clad suggestion, and Creed said tightly, "You seem to have things a little mixed up, Hannah. We are *not* following Nate Stillman. *He* is following us."

Her brow furrowed in alarm. "Oh! Because we . . ."

"Because we have the gold and papers you just mentioned, sweetheart. See the logic in  at? Stillman has killed four men and been wounded for this gold, and he does not intend to give it up easily—especially since he's got the advantage now."

"How is that?"

Flicking his reins against General's thick neck, Creed said, "Simple. I may have the gold, but I've also got you."

"I'm the disadvantage?" she asked swiftly.

He grinned. "Only at certain times, love. Like now, when I would risk anything but your pretty neck."

Only slightly mollified, Hannah said, "But if I'm such a liability, why not forget this?"

"I'd be willing—for a while, at least. But you can bet your last gold dollar that Nate Stillman will be on our trail like fleas on a dog—and just as hard to shake."

Hannah was quiet for a moment, holding onto the saddle horn as her horse skidded down the steep, slippery ridge. Rocks skittered underfoot, bouncing erratically down the slope. "But, why isn't he dead?" she asked when they reached the bottom. "I mean, you shot him, and he looked dead to me. I even buried him."

"Happens that way sometimes. I remember once an old geezer name of Tucker sat up on the mortuary table and demanded his store-bought teeth back. Damn near gave the mortician a heart attack, and they had to send for the doc."

"But he *looked* so dead!"

"So did Tucker. Look, Hannah. Don't worry about Nate Stillman. I intend to get you to Sacred Heart Mission and let the good fathers take care of you. Then I'm going after him."

Fear squeezed Hannah's heart in a merciless grip. "But what if he shoots you?"

"I've been shot before. And what if he doesn't?" Creed added when it looked as if she would still argue. "We could present any number of pleasant and unpleasant possibilities until the cows come home and donkeys fly. It still won't solve anything. Oh, Jeezus! You're not going to cry again, are you? Don't cry, Hannah. I hate it when you cry. It makes your nose red . . ."

Even his least teasing remark did nothing to slow the silvery flow of tears from her eyes, and it did Hannah's poise no good whatsoever to discover that her nose grew red when she wept. She sniffed.

"It still seems to me that you could try to avoid trouble," she said after a moment of silence, when nothing could be heard but the clatter of horse hooves and the creak of saddle leather.

"Why don't we give the subject a rest?" Creed said. "It only gets older with the tellin'."

"How much farther to the mission?" Hannah asked after a stretch of silence.

"Maybe ten miles." He slanted a quizzical glance in her direction. "Anxious to be rid of me?"

"Exceedingly anxious. At least as anxious as you are to go on a wild goose chase."

"And what do you know about wild geese, sweet Hannah?"

"I know you, don't I?" she retorted.

He laughed, a pleasant bass that rolled effortlessly from his lips to spice the air with sound. "Your insults are growing more subtle, and they're a great improvement on your old, tired clichés and quotations."

"I'm happy you're pleased." Hannah's shoulders squared in an effort to stave off the inevitable storm of dismay that threatened like a thundercloud. It hung over her, poised and ready to burst into a torrent of sadness when they reached the mission. Creed would leave, and she would once more be left on her own. There had still been no firm words of commitment, no promises, beyond a vague mention of "forever." And how long was forever to a man like Creed? She was tempted to ask. This could be his way of telling her he had changed his mind, that he wanted to pursue his comfortable, solitary life. Or, she told herself sourly, it could be his way of courting suicide. The latter seemed more likely.

Turning in the saddle as they passed beneath a springy bough of fragrant cedar branches, Hannah opened her mouth to tell Creed that she would much prefer staying with him to lingering within the walls of a dour mission. She never got the opportunity.

A high-pitched scream sounded, and the still-nervous horses plunged in terror. Confused, Hannah lurched forward, her hands gripping tightly to the saddle horn. The world reeled in a blur of greens, blues, and browns, and she was only vaguely aware of Creed's cursing and the horses' frightened snorts.

"Mountain cat..." was one of the few phrases Hannah heard and understood, and her throat closed. A tawny cougar had obviously decided to attack, for some reason. It must have been crouched in the tree, waiting.

Hannah grasped her leather reins with both hands, tugging fiercely on them to halt her horse's excited leaps and bounds over rock and thick underbrush. Loops of dry moss scattered over her from overhead—wispy shreds of lacy parasite that had been dislodged from the tree branches, dusting her head and face and blurring her vision even more. Hannah coughed as the dry fans of moss caught in her eyelashes and nose, inhaling the spores into her lungs with each breath. She was fighting the horse, the moss, and the slippery leather of her saddle, so that it took several minutes for her to realize that she no longer heard Creed.

Wrestling her frantic horse to a panting standstill, Hannah finally managed to look up. Creed had disappeared from sight. The pack horse was loping across the meadow with reins trailing and mane whipping in the wind, but there was no sign of another horse or Creed.

Clearing her throat of smothering alarm, Hannah called out, "Creed! Creed, where are you?"

There was no answer—only the silent wing beats of an eagle, high overhead. Or was that the beat of her heart she heard? Whatever it was, she could almost hear the freezing of the blood in her veins, and the fall of sunlight on the eager earth. Her horse was trembling, and the harsh, rasping breaths tearing the silence were her own. Leaning forward, Hannah gave the horse's neck a comforting pat, wishing she had someone there to pat hers. Where was Creed? And even more important—where was the cougar?

Creed and the cougar had become fast friends. Well, if not friends, at lease *close*. Reflecting that not all his encounters began quite so quickly, Creed stared down at the lifeless cougar. It was a big one, and from the looks of it, half-starved. A mangled paw must have made it slow and desperate for food, hence the startling attack on humans, which it normally avoided. Now the big cat lay crumpled on the ground with Creed's knife in its throat.

Kneeling, he removed the sharp blade and wiped it on the grass, gazing thoughtfully at the big animal. It had all happened so quickly that General—normally a tractable horse—had panicked. Somewhere, in the grass between Hannah on the ridge above him, and where he now stood in a deep ravine, lay his rifle and pistol. Damned if it wasn't the first time he had ever managed to lose all his weapons in one fray! But when General had bolted, bucking like a wild mustang down the slope with the big cat clinging to his rump and snarling, Creed had dropped both rifle and pistol in his efforts to knock the cougar away.

He rose from beside the dead mountain cat and turned to tend his trembling bay. Long scratches marred the smoothly gleaming hide, but none of them appeared to be more than deep lacerations. No tendons had been severed, and with a little ointment and maybe a few stitches, General would be as good as new.

"It's all right, old boy," Creed soothed with a comforting hand and a gentle voice. "You'll be just fine."

"Too bad I can't say the same thing for you, Bratton," came a drawling, familiar voice from the thick bearberry bushes behind him. A tall figure stepped out. "I been here waitin' on you to mosey on down that hill. 'Bout time you got here."

Stiffening, Creed felt the hairs on the back of his neck prickle in warning. Why hadn't he sensed Stillman near him? He should have. Every sense in his body should have warned him, but it hadn't. And now Nate Stillman had the drop on him. Even worse—his guns were an acre away . . .

Creed turned slowly, his movements deliberate, hands held out to his sides. "'Lo, Nate," he said, sizing up the outlaw. "Thought you were dead."

A low chuckle slid through the air. "Well, you tried hard enough, Bratton, I have to admit. But I'm kinda like that old cat there. Only I ain't used up all nine of my lives yet."

"Don't be too sure," Creed began, but the wavering of Stillman's gun barrel cut his comment short. "Okay," he said to the deadly pistol eye, "you can be sure."

"Funny, how humorous a man can be when he's lookin' death in the eye, ain't it?" Stillman observed, gesturing with his free hand for Creed to move away from his horse.

Obliging the man with the pistol, Creed stepped several paces away from the bay and stood with his arms half-raised over his head. The sun beat down on his head as he stood in the open, grassy meadow, watching the outlaw standing just a few feet away at the fringe of a small thicket. Stillman was propped against a broad tree trunk, the pistol steady but his legs shaking. Creed's mind was racing, choosing and discarding several options that included rushing Stillman, throwing his knife, and waiting for Stillman's next move. The last choice seemed the best.

So Creed waited, doing his utmost to appear completely at ease and in control of the situation, and silently praying that Hannah would not stumble across them. Another hostage and potential dead body was not at all desirable. It was inevitable, of course, that she would look for him, but the last he had glimpsed of her before the cougar had dug its claws into General's rump and sent the bay hopscotching down the slope, she had been busily cudgeling her own mount into submission. Maybe it would take her some time to look for him, and during that interval he could figure out a plan.

But it seemed as if Nate Stillman already had a plan, and his did not include ignoring Hannah. "Where's th' li'l preacher-gal, Bratton?" he demanded, slicing a wary glance up the grassy slope. "She was with ya a while ago."

"Well, she's not with me now," Creed answered in a reasonable tone. "Forget her. If I were you, I'd be more interested in that pack horse running loose."

"Yeah, but you ain't me, and I'm int'rested in that stupid Puritan you've been ridin'." He grinned at Creed's darkly narrowed gaze. "Yeah, I seen you out there in th' woods that time. She don't look like a mealy-mouthed little Bible biddy with her clothes off, an' that's a fact." He paused, waiting for a reaction from Creed, but there was none. Motioning for Creed to turn around, Stillman moved up behind him and quickly tied his wrists with a stout length of rope. "Just to ensure that you don't get any ideas a'fore I'm through with you," he said, giving Creed a rough shove that sent him to his knees in the tall grass. "I've an idea that we'll wait on her to look for you. She will. I got faith in that fact."

"And while we wait, that pack horse is halfway to Kansas," Creed said. "Thought you were interested in that gold, Stillman?"

"Oh, I am, sure enough. But it ain't goin' too far, and that little gal might."

"What's your interest in her, Stillman? I've never known you to be partial to any one woman before," Creed said with lightly mocking sarcasm.

Stillman's gun muzzle poked him in the back. "Turn back around here so I can see your face," he barked. "That's better. There's a whole lot about me you don't know, Bratton, an' that's a fact. One of those things," he said, crouching down on his heels so that his face was only inches from Creed's, "is that I was kinda partial to that boy who got hisself killed because of your wench."

"*My* wench?"

Ignoring him, Stillman continued, "I never meant to shoot him, just her. Damned if he didn't get right in the way. I shoulda listened to Roper, but that's over and done with now. I take care of my debts, Bratton. You're one, and that girl's another. I mean to see you both dead before I get my gold and head out."

"What I want to know is," Creed began conversationally, stretching out his long legs and crossing them at the ankles, "why aren't you dead?"

"I could ask you the same thing," Stillman shot back with a grin. He fished in his shirt pocket and pulled out a cheroot. "Now, don't you get to movin' around, 'cause I got a notion that little gal will be here pretty soon. I want her to see you right off, and I don't want her to see me. You're my bait, see."

"And what do you suppose she'll think when she sees me sitting here in broad daylight—that I'm sunbathing? I'm not the type. Let me at least get on my horse, or. . ."

"Ah, no—no tricks, Bratton. I've got that part figured out, too. Here." He stuck the unlit cheroot in Creed's mouth. "You're a man who likes to smoke. I've seen you. When she tops that rise yonder, she'll see you down here enjoying a nice, leisurely smoke." Cackling at his ingenuity, Stillman added, "I could let her think that cat got you, you know, but then she might hesitate 'bout comin' down here to check on you, thinkin' it's loose, you see. When she sees you takin' it easy, she'll come, right enough."

Knowing Hannah, Creed was certain Stillman was right. His hands clenched, testing the strength of the leather strip binding his wrists. It was tight, cutting into his skin and cutting off his circulation. His fingers already felt numb. There was a scratch, a hiss, the sharp smell of sulphur, and Stillman lit the long thin cheroot stuck in Creed's mouth.

"Nothin' to say, Bratton? I'm right appreciative. Now, if you decide not to smoke on it, I can always kill you and go after her myself. No? Thought you might want me to wait. I'm just gonna slide back here into the bushes a bit and wait. It's like settin' a trap for a beaver or cougar. Bait and steel, Bratton, bait and steel."

Sweat beaded Creed's forehead, and he wished he hadn't lost his hat somewhere. It was probably near his lost guns, and he cursed that, too. Of all the rum luck, this day had yet to be beat. His cotton shirt was damp and sticking to his back, and he wondered glumly who had ever decided buckskins were more comfortable than cool cotton trousers. The knee-high moccasins were stifling, and he flexed his toes, narrowing his eyes against the slow curl of tobacco smoke from the cheroot. Any other time he might have appreciated a decent smoke, but not now. His gaze shifted from the empty expanse of the slope back to Stillman, waiting in the shadows.

"So tell me—why aren't you dead?" he asked around the cheroot. "By all rights, you should be. That shot shoulda killed you right off."

"Your aim was off, Bratton. You used to be a dead shot before you hooked up with that loose skirt, ya know. Kinda reminds me of a Bible story I heard when I was a kid. 'Bout a strong man and a woman . . .'"

"Samson and Delilah," Creed said. "You should have paid attention to the moral of the story."

"I did. That's why I ain't never hooked up with no woman steady-like." Stillman rubbed at his right arm, and turned to gaze up the empty slope again. "Puff on that damn cheroot, Bratton. The smoke may bring her."

"How'd you get away?" Creed asked to distract him from his constant observation of the slope.

"Crawled. I'da shot you both then if you hadn't had my guns," Stillman said darkly. His leathery face creased into a deep scowl. "As it was, it was all I could do to get to a horse and ride off. Neither one of you noticed, you tossing and turning in that coma, and yer gal bein' so intent on savin' you." Stillman's mouth curled in a sneer. "If I hadn't been so weak from loss of blood, I'da found another way to kill you. But right then, I couldn't have managed a tussle with even that scrawny li'l preacher-gal. Shot me in my right side, see. An' I still got a bullet in my leg close to my back. Doc said it could shift and paralyze me if he cut it out, so I've got to be careful. Two bullets, Bratton—you done put two bullets in me."

"Not where it counted, obviously," Creed remarked. A

drift of smoke stung his eyes as he watched Stillman's dark complexion grow darker.

"Yeah, well mine is gonna count!" Stillman snarled. "I got me another gun here, and I'll use it! I may have missed the mark with th' last one, but I ain't this time, an' that's a fact!"

"I'm certain you won't mind if I hope you exaggerate?" Creed asked politely.

"Ah, humorous to the end, Bratton!" Stillman shifted position, and the bushes around him shivered. "You know, you was the only man who ever kept on followin' us. All the others, they gave up after a week or two, but not you. No, you kept on our trail day and night, night and day, always back there, hangin' over us like a dark cloud. It used to spook Roper pretty bad. And as fast as Truett was, he never did get used to you behind us. The boy coulda outshot you in a fair fight."

"I don't doubt it. Too bad he hooked up with the wrong bunch." Creed puffed on the cheroot, watching the tip glow red. "What's Plummer's interest in all this? Guess you've figured out what those stocks are for..."

Shrugging, Stillman said, "Yeah. They're counterfeit, of course, not real. Sent all the way to California and had the best forger they got there make 'em up."

"Mullen?"

Stillman nodded. "Mullen. But Plummer said Mullen had gotten greedy, and was insisting on getting a share plus a fee."

"So you had orders to kill him."

"You aren't too stupid, after all. Only we were s'posed to make it look like a reg'lar holdup, see, so's nobody would get suspicious. Then the shares show up, Plummer takes a big bite outa the company, we rob the payroll, and all of us are happy."

"It never would have worked," Creed pointed out.

"But it already has."

"You don't have the shares or the gold, Stillman."

"I will soon. Well, looky there! I think the little she-cat has taken th' bait, Bratton . . . and don't even think about warning her. I won't think twice about shootin' her."

Slowly turning his head, Creed watched in silent agony as Hannah paused on the crest of the grassy ridge. She was looking down the slope and tugging on her mount's reins, obviously deciding whether or not to come and get him. The wind whipped her hair into snarls behind her, brilliant copper tangles that seemed to float like gossamer wings on the air currents. Her blue skirts rode up around her knees in cotton bunches, and her lace petticoat peeked from beneath the hem.

General lifted his head from grazing, spotted Hannah and her horse, and blew a soft whicker of welcome. That seemed to decide her, and she nudged her horse with both heels, starting down the slope at a slow trot. As she drew closer, Creed could see that she sat her horse more easily, one hand holding the reins and the other hanging loose at her side. A smile curved her mouth, and his throat grew tight as he worked frantically at the leather strips cutting into his wrists.

Tall grasses parted like the legendary waves of the Red Sea as her horse moved through, steadily approaching Creed.

"Enjoying your smoke?" Hannah called from a few yards away. "You've grown lazy, Creed Bratton," she added gaily.

Suffocating by slow degrees of fear for her, Creed had almost decided it would be better for her to run and risk a bullet than it would be to wait for a certain one, when things began to happen in slow motion. He saw, as if in a fevered dream, Stillman step from the protective shadows of the

thicket and Hannah look toward him. The outlaw was
grinning, his gun lifting, and there was a loud crack of a
shot. Creed's mind was slow to absorb the implications, a
fact he would later blame on his still-weak state of health.
All he could think was that Hannah had been shot and he
was helpless to do anything about it. He had not saved her;
he had done nothing.

*Oh, God—I know I haven't been much of a moral man,
but if You just won't let her be hurt I'll change. I swear
it!*

Watching, half-rising to his knees with his prayer stuck
in his throat, Creed stumbled forward through the tall,
thick grasses. His eyes were trained on Hannah, on her
sweet face and slender form atop the snorting horse. He
wondered vaguely why she had not cried out or fallen
from the horse, and half formed the hope that Stillman's
shot had missed.

But the bullet had not missed. It had found its mark in a
clean shot, piercing the heart and instantly killing the
outlaw. Nate Stillman, his mouth hanging loosely open in an
incredulous expression, was dead on his feet, his gun still
unfired. When he finally pitched forward on his face, Creed
turned toward Hannah with a puzzled expression.

The long blue skirts were smoking, and as he watched,
Creed saw her lift the hand she'd had hanging loosely by her
side, saw the pistol in her curled fingers and the tiny curl of
smoke drifting from the hot barrel. She had aimed and fired
through her skirt, the bullet striking Stillman without his
ever seeing her gun.

"Hannah! Hannah?" Creed said as he rushed forward.
Her face was chalky white, her lips bloodless, and her eyes
were two large blue smudges in her pale face. "You shot
him!" Creed shouted, a sweeping rush of exhilaration

pounding through his veins. "Here, get down and untie me, and I'll—Hannah?"

Without uttering a single word, Hannah Elizabeth McGuire dropped the pistol and fell from the horse in a peculiarly graceful motion, like a wounded robin dropping from the sky. She landed in the cushioning grasses amidst a cloud of copper hair and blue cotton skirts, her eyes closed in a dead faint.

"Well, I'll be damned!" Creed said in exasperation, kneeling beside her with his hands still tied behind his back.

# Chapter Twenty

"So, how'd you know Stillman was down there with me?" Creed asked, holding out a hot, juicy slice of grouse for Hannah to take. The fire popped and crackled, and the delicious odor of roasting bird filled the night air.

Hannah gingerly lifted the meat from the end of the pointed stick, drawing in a sharp breath at the heat and tossing it from palm to palm. "Easy," she said when the meat had cooled sufficiently and she had bit off a huge chunk. "It was the cigar that gave him away."

Creed stared at her shadowed face. "The cigar?"

"Umm-hmmm. Don't you remember? Ooh, this is good, Creed. Is there any more?"

Automatically holding out another slice of dripping meat, Creed said, "No, I obviously don't have your powers of recollection. What cigar?"

She laughed, a throaty sound that made him want to kiss and strangle her at the same time. "The cigar you didn't have. All right, all right," she added hastily, seeing the expression on his dark face, "I'll explain. Earlier, in the cave, you held up your tobacco bag and said you were out. Now do you remember? And you said something about kennykuk, or something like that."

"Kinnikinnick. Yeah, I remember. And so, when you saw me smoking a cheroot..."

"I knew someone had to be down there with you. And if it had been a *friendly* someone, you wouldn't have been sitting there like a mother hen atop an egg pile. And on the way down the hill, I saw your hat. Now, you might have been smoking kennykoo... kinnikik... something, but you certainly would not have left your hat behind for too long."

Creed sat back on his heels. "And I'm supposed to believe this?"

"I'm telling the truth."

"I bet you are..."

"All right. One more clue, and then you may draw your own conclusions." She took another bite of meat and chewed it leisurely before saying. "Off to the right of where you rode down, the grass had been beaten pretty badly. It looked funny from where I was on top of the hill, and I got to thinking another horse must have gone that way. Well, it wasn't the pack horse, because he headed off to God only knows where, and then I remembered that you'd seen Stillman ahead of us right before the cougar decided to make dinner out of us. Two plus two equals..."

"Five, in your case," Creed finished for her. "Okay. I believe you. Very good, Miss McGuire. Your deductions are remarkably accurate, as is your aim, I might add. I thought you couldn't shoot a gun?"

"I never said that. I said I didn't *like* to shoot a gun."

Contentedly licking grease from her fingers, Hannah missed the expression on Creed's face. It was one of those expressions that she should have seen, because it would certainly have made her feel much better, and cleared up any misconceptions that she might have had about Creed's feelings for her. But she didn't see it, and so it was left to Creed to try and vocalize his emotions, a process that was alien to him by nature and circumstances.

"Have you ever been to the Sacred Heart Mission, Hannah?" he asked casually.

She looked up at him, surprise etching her pristine features. "You know I haven't. Why?"

"I think you'd enjoy visiting it. The old priest there has done a remarkable job of building it, with the help of some friendly Indians."

Shrugging carelessly, Hannah said, "I don't believe I want to visit a mission. Why should I?"

Slanting her a curious glance, Creed came to sit by her, his proximity making Hannah's heart leap. "Because you of all people should appreciate the time, effort, and love that went into building a place of worship," he said softly.

Hannah averted her face, and her reply, when it came, was very soft, almost a whisper. "Another fairy tale palace? A house of cards? A sand castle? Is that what you want me to see, Creed?"

Taking her chin in his palm, Creed gently turned her to face him. "You're a fake, Hannah Elizabeth McGuire—a sweet, lovely fake—and I won't let you continue with this charade you're using as a barrier. Let it go."

"I don't know what you mean," she began defensively, but his fingers tightened on the cup of her chin.

"Let it go, love. You don't have to pretend anymore. I know it's been hard, bu you can't do this     yourself."

Hannah jerked away, unable to meet his   ect gaze. "It shouldn't matter to you what I feel," she began, but he took her into his arms and pulled her body close to his chest.

"Maybe it shouldn't," he murmured against her smoke-scented curls, nesting his chin into the top of her head and drawing a deep breath of the essence that was Hannah, "but it does."

Hannah grew still in his embrace, hardly daring to hope that he might mean more than he was saying. Pressing the tip of her nose into his chest and sucking in a deep, calming breath, she said, "If you're talking about my faith in God, it's not really gone. I can't get rid of it—it won't go away. It nags me, always pricking at the back of my mind, in spite of everything. I thought for a while that I didn't believe anymore, but I found myself talking to Him—shouting at Him that I didn't believe in Him—and then I wondered who I was talking to." She gave a hesitant little laugh. "Joshua McGuire would be pleased to know that. He used to worry that I would fold like wet sponge cake if I evei had to face true trials and tribulations."

"Joshua McGuire would be proud of you, Hannah," Creed said, then paused before adding, "just as I am proud of you."

Not quite daring to move, to look up at him and see only a kind friendliness instead of deeper feelings, Hannah kept her nose against the tight muscles of his chest. It was safer. If she didn't know yet, if she could just hang on to hope a little longer, perhaps . . .

"Hannah. Hannah, look at me," Creed was saying, and his fingers moved to tilt her chin upward. Firelit shadows danced in eerie patterns over the thicket, filling her eyes with glowing light. "Hannah, I . . . I . . ." The words seemed to hang in his throat, and it was only when he saw the shadows chase away the glow in her eyes that he could finish, "I love you."

And, even though she had waited for what seemed like an eternity to hear those very words, Hannah did not know how to react. She said nothing, but only blinked, a slow, lazy flick of her eyelashes that briefly shuttered the wide blue irises filled with firelight. When she opened them again, taking another deep breath to fill her lungs with intoxicating air, she said, "Why?"

It was obviously not the reaction Creed had expected. He released her chin and sat back on his heels, staring at her. "Why?" he repeated finally. "Why. Well . . . well, I don't know exactly *why*, but only that I do."

"That's not good enough," Hannah returned without inflection. "I need to know why you love me."

Having never told any woman he loved her, Creed was momentarily baffled and angry by turns. This titian-haired beauty with the wide eyes and heart-shaped face certainly had a way of wrecking what should have been a tender moment, he decided.

"Oh, for God's sake!" he exploded, pushing upright and towering over her. "I don't know what you want from me!"

Hannah rose, her eyes holding his gaze, her face pale and drawn. "I'm not sure I know either," she blurted unhappily, "only that when I hear it, I'll know it. It's got to be right, or . . . or it'll never work between us."

Spinning on his heels, Creed started to walk away into the deeper shadows of the thicket, then paused, raking one hand through his hair. He turned back around, stalked over to where she waited, and yanked her into his arms.

"Dammit. I love you because you're funny, and foolish,

and brave and tender, and because you take on large responsibilities and expect others to do the same. I love you because you believe good can exist where others say it can't, and I love you . . . dammit, I love you just because you're Hannah and it makes me happy to be with you. And now, if that isn't what you want to hear, it's just too bad, because . . ."

He never got another word past his lips. With a low cry of relief and happiness, Hannah flung herself into his embrace, curling her arms around his neck and smothering him with kisses. Hot tears coursed her cheeks in crystal rivulets, and her voice was thick with them when she said, "It's just what I wanted to hear, Creed Bratton! And I think I love you more at this moment than any woman has ever loved a man . . ."

And then there was no more room for words. For the first time in his entire life, Creed discovered what it was to make *love* to a woman.

Slowly, with irresistible sweetness, Creed lifted her small hand and pressed his lips to the pink palm. The touch of his mouth on her skin tingled in tiny erotic sparks all the way down her spine, and Hannah marveled that it did not start a fire in the dry grass. His lips moved catlike, in little prances, over the heel of her palm to the delicate bones of her wrist, and paused to worship there. The strong pressure of his fingers on her skin as he held her hand did strange things to Hannah. Her breathing accelerated into unsteady pops, and when his tongue flicked lightly against the smooth ivory flesh of her inner arm, she shivered.

"Cold, love?" he whispered, and Hannah felt rather than heard his words.

*No, I'm on fire for you*, she said silently, and oddly enough, he seemed to hear. His sensual mouth curved in the barest of smiles. His dark liquid eyes were backlit with a slow-burning fire that entered Hannah's soul and lingered. Then Creed was cupping her hand within his, his touch gentle and pressureless, with only his eyes indicating his wishes. It was a magic moment. Hannah felt her heart swell with love for him, and knew he could hear the soft emotion, just as she could hear the warble of night birds in the trees overhead.

A soft night breeze licked the air and Hannah's skirts, dancing across Creed's shirt and molding it to his body. It tousled his hair like a lover's fingers, and in the lean-sculpted features there was a subtle altering. It came slowly, a gentle erosion of love and worship into another, more flammable emotion that took away Hannah's breath and left her standing with air-starved lungs and reeling senses.

When he led her wordlessly to the blankets piled close to the stone-ringed fire, Hannah found herself watching his smooth muscles flex beneath the thin fabric of his shirt. The linen bandages had been discarded, and she could see the thrust of his shoulder blades, the curve of his spine, and the tight band of muscles around his waist. Light poured from the flames of the fire, forming a golden haze that glittered over the most ordinary of objects and turned them into enchanted creatures.

A rock—common and gray during the bright light of day—became a wizened gnome perched upon a toadstool. Wood, under ordinary circumstances used for fire, became a knight-errant's lance.

All this registered on Hannah's mind as they paused beside the blankets and Creed turned to face her. She felt his long-boned hand cup her throat, his fingers stroking the soft underside of her jaw with tender motions. His thumb brushed over the fullness of her lower lip in a soft caress, paused to slip coaxingly between top and bottom lip and withdraw to spread moisture-dew over her trembling mouth.

"Honeysuckle," he whispered, "sweet nectar."

Swallowing, Hannah felt a love flush spread over her entire body that seemed to envelop her in a hazy veil of gauze. She ached inside, in every muscle and tissue, deep in the marrow of her bones. There was a violent churning in the region of her lower abdomen that had a far-reaching chain of reaction. It began there, traveled in lightning-quick flashes through her veins, and sparked tiny sunbursts of flames that licked through every organ in her body. It was consuming, a conflagration that a sixteen-bucket brigade could not have doused with the entire Mississippi River.

Cradling her wilting body in his embrace, Creed seemed to understand that she was helpless to move. He swept her against his hard length, lifting her from her feet and laying her gently on the cushiony surface of blankets that had been spread over thick mounds of grass. It was better than a mattress stuffed with a hundred thousand goose feathers.

Long-denied desire rioted in her as Hannah met his burning gaze. The erotic curve of his mouth and the sweet touch of his hands only aided the revolt of her senses, the descent into a world hazed with love. Lifting her hands, she began to unbutton his shirt clumsily, her fingers refusing to heed the love-drugged commands of her brain. In the end he had to help her, his larger hand cupping hers and forcing buttons through their respective buttonholes. Soft cotton tumbled away from his sun-gilded body and pooled beneath them in a puddle of forgotten white. Her hands slid over his skin in light, feathery touches that brought to mind the caress of the wind, touching and exploring with eager anticipation.

As her explorations slowed and became more thorough, Creed sighed heavily. Pausing, Hannah rose to her knees.

He watched through lazy-lidded eyes as she began to undo her own dress, fumbling with tiny pearl buttons and snatching at them impatiently when they balked beneath her clumsy attempts. There were two layers to remove, the waist-coat and blouse, and then she was clad in only her chemise and lace-hemmed petticoat. Returning to him, reveling in the unguarded admiration she saw in his gaze, she let her hands once more begin their studies on the hard planes and ridges of his intricately molded male body.

Enjoying the unfettered press of her full breasts against his skin, Creed pulled her to him until his face was buried in that sweet cleft between the twin mounds. He dragged in a deep breath of wind-brushed skin, and felt the contracting of her muscles that coincided with the erratic thud of his heart. He said her name, a light fluttering of breath against her as she cascaded kisses over the top of his head.

Unconsciously furthering his arousal with the thrust of her body against him, Hannah murmured a response in kind. Her eyes had drifted shut, her arms closing around his head and holding tightly for support. When his hands shifted and replaced the position his mouth had found, cradling the heavy weight of her breast in a cupped palm with his fingers teasing the peak, Hannah shuddered. It was more than she could bear.

Shifting his body, Creed lay with Hannah tucked into his side. He pulled her close, teasing the chemise and petticoat from her curves with gentle fingers, letting his hands smooth over her creamy flesh. She felt good beside him, her sweet body fitting perfectly into the angle of his, her hair tickling his chin in silky filaments.

"Creed," Hannah finally whispered into his chest when he continued to stroke her curves and hollows, "I need you now."

Laughing softly, and acknowledging his own raging need,

Creed shed his trousers and turned back to her, pulling her once more into his embrace. His mouth covered hers in a quick, hard kiss that drew air and moisture from her in a powerful absorption. Nudging between her silken thighs, he slowly entered the warm velvet of her, holding back when he wanted to explode into a thousand tiny starbursts of pleasure. Slowly, he began to rock against her, his breath fanning across her cheek, his mouth seeking and finding the sweet nectar of her lips, tasting and sipping of her until they were both swept along on the swooping wingbeats of release.

Whispering, "I love you, I love you," in her ear, Creed felt the beginning of his own barriers crumble. It was the first time he had allowed such open emotion to enter the dark shadow of his inner soul, and it was as a reviving ray of sunlight, warming and renewing him.

And for Hannah, looking up and seeing the shine in his dark eyes, she knew she had found more than just love. She had faith reborn, and with time, perhaps Creed would regain his.

Scraping the tip of her nose against the stubble of his chin, Hannah whispered, "I love you, Creed Bratton."

His arms tightened. "And I love you, Hannah McGuire."

The sky was a deep, polished blue, stretching in a curve of fleecy clouds and licking breezes. Wild roses climbed log houses and fence posts in fragrant abandon, their sweet, subtle scent mingling with the riper smells of fruit presses and clean, fresh-cut hay. A crusty stone wall ran alongside newly scythed grass and borders of tended flowers surrounding a small house, and children laughed and frolicked in the warm sunshine. Bushes heavy with blackberries and huckleberries nodded in sticky clumps, and several purple-stained urchin faces watched solemnly as the couple paused in front of the six-columned mission.

The Mission of the Sacred Heart of Jesus stood in graceful aplomb atop a high, grassy knoll overlooking the Coeur d'Alene River. Having been moved from its original site because of frequent flooding, the mission had gained more than just a dryer location. Designed by Father Ravalli, an Italian missionary who was an artist, sculptor, and physician, as well as a preacher of the gospel, the tiny mission had been lovingly transformed into an oasis of beauty in the Idaho wilderness.

Father Ravalli apparently strove to duplicate some of the more simple eloquence of the European cathedrals in his design, and he'd been aided by the Coeur d'Alene Indians. Once known as the Schee-chu-umsh, or Skitzu, they had been renamed the Coeur d'Alenes by French trappers who considered them shrewd bargainers. The name was translated to mean "heart of an awl," or as jokingly interpreted, the Indians had accused the French trappers of being less than generous with their offers of trade for furs. It had become a good jest, and the name eventually lingered. These spiritual Indians had invited Black Robes into their midst, and it was due largely to their efforts that the mission had come into being.

Structured from large logs cut near the new site, the mission had been latticed with sturdy saplings, knit together with grass and caulked with mud. This wattle and daub process endured heavy rains, snow, and biting winds. The interior was decorated with hand-painted newspapers the good Father Ravalli had received in the post and cleverly recycled into imposing decorations. Wall cloth purchased from the Hudson Bay Trading Post at Fort Walla Walla adorned the wattle and daub walls. To form classic European chandeliers, the ingenious priest had used tin cans.

Gilded crosses were reproduced in replicas of carved pine, and the wooden altars were cleverly painted and veined to look like expensive slabs of marble.

Not far away from this impressive mission, a self-sufficient village farmed and lived in gentle solitude. It was to this peaceful setting that Hannah and Creed had come to be married.

They exchanged lingering glances, then ascended the few stone steps, their hands entwined. A bridal wreath of baby's breath and wild roses crowned Hannah's bright hair. Creed was dressed in a clean white shirt, dark gray frock coat, and charcoal trousers, his only concession to color the tiny red rosebud tucked into his buttonhole. Hannah had the fleeting thought that he had never looked so handsome.

Stepping into the dusky coolness of the mission, they were met by the waxy scent of candles and lemon polish. Benches shiny from use lined the floor, and the long middle aisle stretched to the cloth-covered altar.

"It's been a long time," Creed muttered, his voice low but sounding loud in the quiet peace of the church. Hannah gave his hand a gentle squeeze of comfort, then released it and laced her fingers together. They paused beneath an archway and waited, listening to the sounds of the church.

Peace waited; tranquility beckoned to them like an old friend, and Creed succumbed to its lure. How could he not? His doubts fell away like old rags and left him arrayed in new garments of trust and love. Maybe he hadn't regained his faith in God yet, but with Hannah at his side, he felt he could confront any obstacle. Time would heal all wounds—time, and the consuming love he felt for this one slender girl with the shining face and beautiful soul. It was hard to put into words, and he didn't know if he'd ever be able to voice what he was feeling inside, but that he had come this far was promising in itself. His dark, melting gaze moved from the gleam of the church appointments to Hannah's soulful face, paused, and lingered. Nothing else mattered.

Hannah felt his gaze and looked up, her smile tremulous as a summer butterfly fluttering over the petals of a flower. Her heart was a thrumming chord inside her chest, and the new gown of lace and rose skimmed her quaking body in a graceful fall. The air vibrated with a surreal quality, and she wondered again if this was what her father had meant when he'd promised she would know when she met the right man. It felt right. It felt as if she was balanced upon the edge of a high crest, and far below her stretched nothing but rose petals and cloud puffs. If she let go and fell, she would land in a downy softness, like a child tumbling into a luxurious feather mattress. She loved Creed. She loved him with all her heart and soul, her mind and body. That was all that mattered. The future could only hold bright promises for them both.

Then the time for conjecture was gone, for the door at the rear was opening softly and a black-robed man was approaching on velvet feet. Turning blindly, Hannah sought and found Creed's warm hand, and this time he did the comforting.

Thirty minutes later Creed and Hannah stepped out into the sunshine, husband and wife, linked in ceremony and blessed by God.

"Do you feel any different?" Hannah asked shyly, and Creed stared at her solemnly.

"No," he said after a moment's grave reflection. "But I do feel hungry."

Hannah gave him an unwinking stare as wide as an infant's, then burst into laughter. Her merry peals drew the attention of passers-by, who looked up and smiled at the handsome couple on the church steps. Sunlight graced

Hannah's hair with fiery radiance, and lent blue-black glints to Creed's glossy mane. She leaned into him, her hand cupping over the hard muscles in his arm, and murmured a desire to be gone.

"Where to, my love?" he asked as they stepped from the church yard to the wide lane passing in front.

"Paradise. The magic kingdom of Wherever. To our castle in the air."

Enchanted by her whimsy and the warm flush of love spreading inside him, Creed smiled gently. His hand brought up her small-boned wrist and he turned her hand palm up, his lips worshipping the baby-softness for a moment. Then he released it with a regretful sigh and said, "Our unicorns have not arrived yet. They are the only ones that know the way to Wherever."

Pleased that he knew how to respond to her lapse into fantasy land, Hannah met his glowing gaze with wide blue eyes and her lips curved into happiness. At that moment she loved him so much she thought her heart might burst with the sheer volume of it. She had a brief mental image of an explosion of love, showering down over them in dainty flower petals, starlight, and honey-drips. It would be a breathtaking sight to behold, she thought.

But pressing matters awaited them, and Hannah gathered her elusive logical thoughts and harnessed them sternly. "I suppose we could take our carriage back to Coeur d'Alene, then. There's a new cabin waiting for us."

"I suppose we could," he agreed equitably. A curious smile touched at the corners of his erotic mouth for a moment as he added, "I don't think General will ever forgive me for harnessing him to such a contraption. It has quite ruined his dignity."

Hannah's gaze moved to the borrowed carriage and the glossy bay harnessed between the rigging. There did seem to be a reproachful gaze in the horse's eyes when he tossed his proud head amid the musical jangle of metal bits. She laughed softly, and said, "He'll have to get used to it."

"I suppose so, now that we're respectable—and not only married, but parents as well. After all—our children await us."

Pausing, she leaned into him, anxiously searching his face. "Creed, you don't mind, do you? I mean, they are so young, and such well-behaved children . . ."

Creed's brows lifted in a skeptical arc. "Well-behaved? I obviously have a much better memory that you do, love. I seem to recall a young lad with a rather lamentable tendency for practical jokes and unmerciful teasing of his sister."

"But Eric loves Ivy. He would never . . ."

"Allow anyone else to hurt her," Creed finished, cupping a hand beneath Hannah's elbow and steering her toward the small carriage across the wide road. "That does not mean he can resist tormenting her himself."

There was a moment of brief silence in which Hannah mulled over their decision to take in Eric and Ivy Ransom, the only two of the orphans left. All the others had been taken in, but no one had had room for the brother and sister. As Creed handed her up into the carriage, she examined his lean features and found no traces of resentment.

"Are you sure?" she couldn't help asking as he scooped his battered black hat from the seat and tugged it over his thick hair.

"Sure of what? Rain? Sunshine? Do I look like an almanac, love?"

"No, Creed. Sure that this is what you want."

Pausing, he put his hands up and took her fingers into his clasp. He held them. His voice was warm and lazy and filled with potent emotion. "I am as sure as I've ever been of anything in my life, Hannah. I'm as sure as there are eagles in the sky and clouds in the heavens. This is our new life, and together we can do anything.''

Drawing in a ragged breath, she offered one last objection, hoping he would wave it away as he had the others. ''But what about the gold? It's...''

''Not that important. I already took care of that. Henry Plummer, by the way, is under public protest because of his illegal intercourse with outlaws. It seems that this last little fiasco has cost him more than shares of stock and a few bags of gold.'' His thumb caressed the small sparrow bones of her hand in a circular motion. ''Does that take care of everything now? Are you fully reassured that life will proceed in an orderly and wonderful fashion?''

She shook her head, and a riot of copper curls danced madly beneath the baby's breath crown. ''No. I need one more reassurance.''

''And that is?''

Leaning forward, Hannah pressed her soft mouth against his lips. The touch was light, pressureless, like the gild of morning light gracing the heavens, the feathery touch of a hummingbird, the soft color of a rose. But bound with the kiss was the rich caress of her hair against his cheek, the sweet-scented promise of tomorrow, and the day after that. The gentle kiss promised forever, and Creed willingly met the promise with his own.

Breaking the contact at last, Hannah drew back and gazed at him with blue-misted eyes. ''Do you know where to take us, my love?''

Smiling, Creed reached out a tender hand to stroke back an errant curl that had the temerity to dangle in front of her eyes. ''Yes, love. I know where. Heaven.''

Dear Reader,

I hope you enjoyed Creed and Hannah's story as much as I enjoyed writing it. My characters are always real to me, but I felt a special kinship with these two, and hope I have succeeded in transferring that feeling to you.

If I have, and you would like to tell me about it, please write. I appreciate hearing from you. Your reading pleasure is always in my mind when I spend long hours alone with my computer and the invisible ghosts of my hero and heroine.

You may write to me in care of WARNER BOOKS, 666 Fifth Avenue, New York, N.Y. 10103.

*Virginia Brown*